The 13th Apostle

RAINA C. SMITH

ISBN - 10: 1463558643
ISBN - 13: 978-1463558642

DEDICATION

This novel is lovingly dedicated to my grandmother Christina Smith.

CONTENTS

ACKNOWLEDGMENTS

Foremost I want to thank my grandmother Christina Smith for her unconditional love, support, inspiration and kindness. Life with her was pure joy. The entire world seemed brighter with her among us. It was she who always encouraged me to write, believed in me and was the very first person to read this novel. I love you grandma.

I also want to thank my parents Mary Ann and Edwin Smith for patiently listening to me read scenes as they were written and always telling me I could accomplish any goal to which I set my mind.

Much appreciation goes out to my cousin Dennis Smith who graciously worked with me to turn my vision for cover art into a reality.

Love and kisses to my dog Buster for sitting on my lap during much of the writing process. Knowing he was there with me is what provided me with the inspiration I needed to see my project to completion.
I love you Buster!

Special thanks goes out to my dear lifelong friend Deborah Barchi who took the time to read several rough drafts, delivering honest and sound advice about what to edit, keep, omit and clarify. Debbie generously helped me make revision after revision.

A warm, heartfelt thanks goes out to Ken and Barbara Iavarone who were eager to read my novel even when I only had a few pages written, always went out of their way to help promote my novel to others and encouraged me to continue writing. They tirelessly helped me review page after page to help me catch any mistakes before this printing. I can't thank you enough for your love, support and friendship.

Additional thanks goes out to my wonderful friend Glenn Laxton and cousins Lorraine Levesque and Darlene Cardin. I have always felt blessed to have you in my life.

CHAPTER 1 -- ANCIENT DOCUMENT

High in the Tibetan mountains a secret monastery alive with the spirit of God hung over the edge of a cliff overlooking creation. Brother David, one of the many monks who called this place home was inside considering the legitimacy and the contents of an ambiguous document which lay before him.

Disturbed he discreetly and cautiously raised his eyes from his reading. He swiveled his head slowly side to side to see what had his sixth sense kicking in. Before this he never knew for sure he had a sixth sense. Somehow he knew now and it was working overtime.

As he scanned the room he saw no one, but could clearly feel the presence of someone or something watching him. Its quiet existence filled the room. Brother David had just intellectualized the most blasphemous material that he had ever laid eyes upon. The human mental consumption of it apparently invited veiled company. What was stranger, the presence didn't feel malevolent. It was strong and powerful but not intimidating. Almost like an ancient guardian of sorts, there to protect the document, but not intervene.

"Where did it come from and what's it doing here in the monastery?" He wondered. Brother David was overwhelmed with physical and emotional stress.

With sweat starting to bead upon his forehead and his heart beginning to race out of control, he stopped what he was doing, hastily rolled up the scroll and rushed down the hall to find the one man he trusted completely, Brother John.

He found his superior on his knees, three rooms down, quietly deep in prayer. Brother David rushed into the room, grabbed his brother's shoulder firmly and waved the dusty, old scroll at him. He did so, while choking out indistinguishable thoughts.

"I... it, it can't... what is?"

What he believed he learned from the document rendered him practically speechless.

"There was no…!" Sheer fright took hold of his facial muscles. He was near collapse. Brother John never before saw such a look of concern and desperation on David's face. Without saying a word, Brother John took the scroll from David's grip.

Both men knelt to the floor with the scroll. As Brother John delicately unrolled the tattered relic, pieces of the documents brittle edges broke off. From its shabby condition, it was clear this item was extremely old. As it unwound, it also released a strange but inoffensive odor. Now, even level headed, John was becoming uneasy.

As John started reviewing the item, now completely laid out before him, Brother David began sobbing uncontrollably. "I can't believe what I'm reading! How can that… be? A thirteenth?… Can? Please tell me… it is not… I can't…" He cried into his hands, to hide his fear.

John had to turn a deaf ear to David's lamenting, as he scanned the scroll. As his eyes fell over the old canvas, David's concern now became understandable. It all suddenly started coming back to Brother John. He had seen this before, about thirty years ago and he had long chosen to forget its controversial contents. He also knew now what had David so confused and frightened.

"David, I understand. Calm down." Brother John gave David a reassuring look. "I've seen this before. Let me explain. I do know a bit about its history." David trusted Brother John. Now finally able to form words, he agreed. "OK."

Brother John rested a comforting hand upon Brother David's shoulder as he started to shed some light upon the mystery.

"Roughly three decades ago, a past leader here at the monastery, made me aware of this." Brother John now placed his hand, palm down, upon the scroll with care.

"He was a dear, dear friend of mine. Brother Michael was his name. Before he died, he made sure to bring this to my attention. When I considered its predictions, I was just as concerned and as disturbed as you are this very minute."

He then looked up at David to admit what he had done immediately after. "I was so concerned about its prophecies in fact that I left the monastery on a quest to seek out the validity behind its claims."

Brother John's memory recalling how confused and distressed he was during that time.

"My pursuit of the truth took me on a trek around the world. However, during this time, I was able to verify only very few details, all of which I knew would be highly controversial if I were to share them with others."

As he spoke he allowed his fingertips to pass over the ancient cloth as though it were a sacred artifact. "I *was* able to confirm the existence of its author, his relationship with Christ and the physical creation of this scroll as well as its whereabouts through time. But, when I came back here to live out the remainder of my years, I decided it best not to share what I had learned. I was terrified of the consequences."

Brother John leaned forward, now placing both palms along the borders of the breakable fabric. He stared down at it, hard.

"I hid it, apparently not very well, and decided to put it out of my mind for the rest of my life." A tear rolled down his right cheek as he confided in Brother David. "I always knew in my heart, I was making a mistake, but I didn't know what to do. Now, here it is before me once again. I must answer to God and to myself for stalling its message."

Brother David's eyes grew large as he listened.

"This was meant to come forth in the world. I cannot stop it. It has a message for all of this world to hear." Brother John said with newfound certainty.

He looked at David with relief. "The time has come. You have been hand selected by God to pick up where I left off, my friend. I will share with you, what I know, and then it will be up to you to do with it what you think is right."

He smiled when he realized this tremendous responsibility had finally passed from him. "Perhaps my role was merely to gather information for the one who would carry out God's wishes."

Brother John warmly reassured David with a wink. "I'd like to think I had a small role in helping God's plan. Now let me share with you all that I know."

Brother David braced himself mentally, as though he were about to receive communion from Christ himself.

Brother John closed his eyes, preparing to expound upon what he promised himself he would never tell another living soul.

He began, speaking slowly and carefully. "I can tell you for a fact, this document was written by a man who met the Messiah in Jerusalem and followed him and his apostles two thousand years ago. Evidence of his existence was recorded within ancient artwork found in caves and upon stone tablets in the Holy Land. All works depict Christ, followed by thirteen men. They are believed to be the apostles themselves accompanied by the author of this unique creation. In each representation he is shown as an extremely large man with a long wiry beard and holding a box of some sort. What's interesting about his image in each work is that he is seen standing slightly apart from the other twelve. He is represented as being just as important as the apostles, but different in some way. It is this person, who took copious mental notes of everything he discussed with Jesus during their time together. The most important of which, are highlighted here as a warning for mankind about his uncertain future. In the twilight of his years, he placed this scroll inside a box and buried it somewhere deep beneath Middle Eastern soil, where it was later discovered, over a thousand years ago. Shortly thereafter, it became the property of the Vatican. That's the abbreviated version. But in brief, I was able to verify this much."

Brother David nodded his head, astounded.

"My research suggests Christ's own disciples had no idea what this man's purpose was and didn't question it, either. As the apostles were sent forth by Jesus to preach the Gospel to the world, this man was sent forth with a purpose all his own." Brother John explained, so sure his research supported his theory.

David sat speechless, hanging on every word.

Brother John made sure to look his friend directly in the eye before he relinquished the next piece of horrifying news. "His purpose David was to predict what would happen to the world if man didn't live according to the word of God. In other words, he was sent forth to predict the end of the world."

Barely taking another breath, he elaborated. "The twelve apostles were chosen by Christ to teach the world how to live their lives according to God. But this man was sent forth to reveal when man's actions were in direct conflict with God's commandments."

The young monk couldn't believe what he was hearing. "What did our Lord impart unto him?" David shyly asked his superior.

Turning his eyes downward, toward the item at hand, Brother John answered. "That man was born with free will and if that *will* collectively favored hatred and destruction, he would be wiped off the face of the Earth. This record, which lies before us, promises specific occurrences in time, denoting man has selected such a pathway. A pathway, which, man cannot reverse."

A deep breath. "The end of this world David. The end of time for us… for mankind."

"Have we?!" Brother David was so intrigued by the information he didn't realize he was interrupting, again. "Selected such a pathway, I mean?"

John resumed where he left off, before David's outburst. "Before his death, like I said, he took care to permanently record, what Christ's direct warnings were. He locked it away inside a box Christ made for him with his own two hands. He then took that box and buried it far down in the earth for safekeeping, until time deemed it necessary for it to be revealed to the world."

Brother John used his hands to illustrate what he was saying. "Over the centuries, time and weather eroded the surface of the earth, bringing the box closer to man's grasp. It was around this time, in Galilee, when a blind six-year-old child digging in the sand discovered the small, locked, wooden box. The little girl, a child of poverty and neglect, was thrilled with her discovery. She held the box up to her face to smell what kind of wood it was made out of and ran her fingertips over its rough, dry surface. Eager to learn what mystery may lie inside for her, she tugged at the tiny lock but was unable to break its hold on its hidden contents. Her neighbor, an opportunist, by the name of Hector, noticed the girl becoming increasingly frustrated with her find. As he sauntered over to see what had the child riled, he realized she'd found something quite old and possibly valuable."

David knew this had to be where the scroll fell into enemy hands.

"With *his* own best interest in mind Hector offered to take the box into his home, where he had tools, to remove the lock for her. The girl unwittingly entrusted her neighbor with her treasure and it was never returned to the child."

Brother John sighed, before telling the rest of the story.

"Hector had heard rumors of a sacred box. Its discovery carrying with it, great fame and wealth. He knew its great historical and monetary value were beyond his wildest dreams and he acted upon his greed."

David shook his head in disgust as John spoke.

"He eventually sold the box, unopened, to the highest bidder, the Vatican. That's where the scroll remained shrouded in secrecy for centuries."

Brother David looked confused now.

Brother John clarified. "This is, until two crude copies of it were made and stolen from the church. One of the copies, I don't know how, fell into Brother Michael's hands and now lives here in the monastery. I cannot confirm the whereabouts of the other."

Brother John was finished but Brother David knew there were volumes more to this story. Both men, still kneeling, sat there looking seriously at each other. Neither one spoke a single word.

The silence felt safe, right now.

CHAPTER 2 -- PAPAL UNCERTAINTY

Meanwhile, thousands of miles away at the Vatican, several priests congregate outside the ailing pontiff's private quarters. Some sit, several pace, while others conference with clergy. All, concerned with what's going on behind the giant, hand carved, cherry wood door.

That's where the Pope was, being tended to by private doctors and nurses who rushed in and out of his chambers with fury. Whatever was going on in there was serious. No one, absolutely no one, was granted admittance.

Anyone coming to check in on the pontiff's condition was told, "He's stable right now and being made comfortable as possible in his bed." The sterile, blanket statement memorized by all members of the medical staff and delivered randomly with detachment, made no one feel better. It really just made things seem worse for anyone who cared.

"He's not doing well at all." Father Joseph whispered under his breath, to his longtime friend of forty years and fellow priest, Father Matthew. "In fact, I don't think he'll make it much longer. He may have only days left." He added.

A small group of clergymen overhearing the pessimistic remarks shot discerning looks at the two.

"It's terrible and like the death of the church in some ways." Father Matthew replied. "No one will ever be able to uphold the integrity of the church and help lead the world to spiritual righteousness, the way he did." He added.

Father Joseph felt the same way. "I agree."

Holding that thought fresh in his mind, Father Matthew dashed off. "Follow me!" He waved, walking briskly down the hall.

With Joseph at his heels, he made his way to a room at the very end of the hall.

The last door on the right let out the softest of creaks, as Father Matthew made his way inside. As he did, he motioned for Father Joseph to stay close to him. "Come in, hurry. Don't let anyone see you come in here."

He led his confidant into the poorly lit room. Dark wood lined all four walls, which exhibited many old, religious paintings. Across the way, Father Joseph could see a dusty, antique desk. Father Matthew went to it, blew the dust off the top and took a seat behind it.

"Lock the door behind you Joseph." Matthew said, panicked.

Joseph did as he requested.

"What's this about?" Father Joseph asked.

Father Matthew lit a tall, vanilla colored candle and started to stroke his long, gray beard. He pondered what he was about to reveal to his friend. Drawing in a long, deep breath, he then told Father Joseph why he brought him there.

"I have something that I want to show you, but I must have your word you won't tell a soul." Father Joseph reluctantly agreed. "Uh… O.K." not quite sure what he was getting himself into.

Father Matthew then reached behind his cassock, cautiously removing a key from his breast pocket. He sheepishly unlocked the desk's top drawer.

As he slowly pulled the drawer open, Father Joseph could see a long, rolled up, tattered looking piece of cloth, lying at the bottom. He stretched his neck to get a better look. He knew it must be what Father Matthew wanted to show him. "But why the secrecy?"

The cloth made its way out of the drawer, in Father Matthew's careful grasp. With great care, he placed the item on top of the desk and unrolled it, at a snail's pace. Joseph knew it was all the brittle cloth could handle.

Once entirely unwound, Father Joseph leaned in, trying to read the writing on it, but it was in a foreign, unfamiliar script. All he could make out was what looked to be a drawing of a world map in the center, with much exotic writing around it.

"What language is this in?" He questioned.

"It's in Aramaic." Father Matthew answered.

"I can't read Aramaic. I can't read this."

Father Matthew's shifty behavior was making Joseph nervous. He wanted answers and he wanted them now. With even more perspiration beading on his forehead, Father Matthew unbuttoned his collar and took off his jacket. He was ready to address his friend's concern. "I'll read it to you. But first let me explain what this is and again you must keep it to yourself." He insisted.

"You have my word." Father Joseph swore.

Father Matthew took a minute to collect his thoughts before he entrusted what he knew to be highly sensitive and classified information to his fellow clergy. He looked down at the item, mumbled a prayer under his breath and began speaking slowly.

"This ancient document, my friend, is the direct word of Christ." Father Matthew said circumspectly, while closely gauging Father Joseph's reaction.

Joseph, taken aback, stood there, with a vacant look on his face. What he was hearing wasn't making any sense. As far as he was concerned, the direct word of God could only be found in the gospels within the Bible and this was no Bible. Father Joseph peered at the document with intense scrutiny as Father Matthew continued. He trusted Father Matthew and wanted to keep an open mind even though nothing he was hearing was making sense.

"When Christ walked the Earth, it is recorded that he befriended a man by the name of Yashmiel. His place of origin, still unknown. Yashmiel, as history records it, walked alongside the apostles as one, yet apart, of them." Father Matthew went on, Father Joseph listening intently. "I know that sounds like a paradox, but you'll understand soon enough."

"Christ secretly prophesied to Yashmiel, as he did the apostles but Christ's message to him was starkly different. Yashmiel was to serve a purpose all his own and quite opposite of the blessing the apostles bore."

Joseph struggled to keep an open mind as the information he was hearing flew right in the face of everything he was taught and believes in.

Father Matthew continued explaining. "As the apostles were sent forth to spend the rest of their lives preaching the word of the gospel to save man, Yashmiel was charged with spending his years recording the hidden secrets of man's soul and his potentially imminent demise, which would be revealed in due time. Christ apparently assigned Yashmiel to detail definitive signs all creation was coming to an end, if man did not mend his sinful ways and live according to his word."

Father Joseph wanted questions answered before he let his friend finish. "There were only twelve apostles who Christ ministered to, we know who they were and their role, there is no account of another present at this time?"

"None that the Vatican will allow the world to find out about." Father Matthew answered prudently.

Father Joseph couldn't believe what he was hearing. Matthew, the unwitting bearer of bad news growing increasingly more agitated and nervous as he continued to explain the importance of what lie before them. The priest, standing from his chair, paced back and forth as he spoke to Father Joseph.

"The words on that scroll are a direct warning from Christ that man's choices here on Earth have condemned us, my friend!" He bent over the desk and positioned the dilapidated antique so Father Joseph could see it better.

"See the map here, at the center." He pointed furiously.

In a numbed state, Father Joseph looked to the map. "Yes."

"Yashmiel drew this crude map long before the oceans and the continents of the world were charted." Father Matthew started to speak louder and faster as if he couldn't get the information out fast enough. "There was no way for Yashmiel to know the positions of land masses and large bodies of water back then, yet he was able to accurately draft a map of the world!"

"How! How!" Father Matthew begged of a speechless Father Joseph.

"Because Christ revealed it to him, that's how!" Father Matthew pointed out. "And he did so to prove that Yashmiel walked with greatness."

Pounding his fists on the desk before Father Joseph, he screamed, holding up the scroll. "Current carbon-dating technology has proven this document to be over two thousand years old! The scientific accuracy of this map proves that something magnificent and holy such as Christ, ministered to Yashmiel and deciphered great mysteries unto him to validate their acquaintanceship and embolden man to heed his warnings."

Father Joseph fixed his eyes on him, not sure what to make of all this.

"This is Yashmiel's work, Father Joseph, and it contains a prophetic description of the end of the world!" Father Matthew exclaimed, collapsing in his chair from emotional exhaustion.

"Are we talking about an apocalyptic event?" Father Joseph asked, his eyes widening with great fear.

Father Matthew had just enough energy left to answer. "Yes, and great devastation is looming as man marches himself into hell."

"Read it to me." Father Joseph demanded, unsure whether he believed what his friend was telling him.

With regret, Father Matthew read word for word what Yashmiel wrote so many years ago. "See how there is a column of writing going down the left side of the map and then there's a column going down the right side of the map?" Father Matthew asked.

"Yes." Father Joseph saw that.

"The column on the right describes the state of the world just before its complete self-destruction due to man's own will."

"Read what it says!" Father Joseph demanded again, beginning to lose his patience half out of anxiety and half out of irritation.

With some trepidation and appearing to fear the written words themselves, Father Matthew translated the Aramaic language for Father Joseph. He used a candle to further illuminate the decaying cloth for his confidant and used his index finger to carefully follow each powerful word.

Speaking firmly, he read aloud, "When man has emptied his soul of his own free will and the world cries amidst tremendous domestic and international conflict, a seraph will be summoned by God to walk the Earth."

He continued with a seriousness Father Joseph had never seen before.

"This visitor among men will search the world over, with his nemesis by his side, for the last pure soul on Earth who is blessed with a holy bloodline. It is within this sacred person among men, where hope for mankind lives in its purest form. This natural "monarch" of man has the potential to triumphantly rise up against sin in the name of the Father and is why they are sought equally by the angel and the Archfiend."

Father Joseph wasn't sure he bought into what he was hearing, but the next part Father Matthew read, caught his attention.

"This time on Earth will be recognized when an exalted holy spiritual leader dies in the West and is replaced with a fork-tongued rogue."

Both men looked toward the door, questioning if their Holy Father who lay near death could be that leader. They held their glance there for a long pause.

Not sure he followed, Father Joseph interrupted. "When man has emptied his soul of his own free will? What does that mean and how could that be possible?" He looked puzzled.

"And, how could a mere mortal here on earth be blessed with a holy bloodline? What is Yashmiel implying?" The more questions Joseph had, the more confused he became. "He mentions a monarch, is he referring to a king or a queen of some sort or maybe a sitting president?"

He looked to Father Matthew who was unsure himself, for guidance. "For centuries, only a handful of privileged men have been granted access to this hallowed document and for centuries still, its content is debated and interpreted a variety of ways. Our interpretation is as good as anyone's. But it is indisputably, talking about the time we are living in, Joseph!"

The man Father Joseph knew to be well versed in ancient religious literature clearly wasn't sure of all the meanings in the work. But, he seemed convinced the time it suggested was now.

Much of what Father Joseph had been taught by the Church was now possibly being negated by this one sketchy, yet undeniably authentic, ancient piece of textile. He rubbed his forehead back and forth hard, he was extremely uneasy about it. "I… I… I have trouble believing there was this man that Christ…the apostles… and… Wh… Wh... Why was his existence kept so secret and by whom or what agency?" Joseph was beginning to break down, mentally.

"Please, let me continue." Father Matthew insisted. "This next part is critically important."

"As the jewel of heaven and his vixenish shadow lay their feet upon blackened soil, scourged from waste and natural disaster, they will see desperation in the eyes of man." He carried on. "When the last spirit turns foul, so will the Earth turn foul and furious with rage. Unless, the chosen one recognizes their destiny, man's imminent damnation will be set into motion and it will be the beginning of the end of the world."

Father Matthew looked up from his reading to see Father Joseph's expression. There was none, just a blank stare.

It took everything Father Matthew had to painfully read the last sentence. "Until then, the sun will continue to warm the Earth and hope will live until the last spirit knows not God." With that last word, Father Matthew and Father Joseph looked at each other and then again at the map and trembled.

Feeling somewhat betrayed, Father Joseph questioned. "Why have you not shown this to me before, my friend?"

In defeat, Matthew responded just above a whisper. "I didn't want you to know it was the Vatican... The Catholic Church... Which you faithfully devoted your life to, that is responsible for suppressing evidence of one of the most important men in history. Yashmiel is the best, kept secret of all time." With the truth, came confidence for Matthew. He could now again look his friend in the eye. "I was afraid."

In disbelief, Joseph pressed further. "Then, let me get this straight. Yashmiel is… …was a living, breathing person who… walked beside Christ, was brother with the apostles, wrote a docket of man's potential plunge to damnation under Christ's direction and this is his work? Can you promise me that all this can be proven, Matthew? This changes organized religion, as we know it. Don't you realize?"

Ashamed of the deception Father Joseph would feel in light of his response, Father Matthew couldn't help but look away, "There was conclusive proof, Joseph, but not anymore." Father Joseph knew exactly what, "…there *was* proof" meant.

"You have to trust me on this, Joseph. I guess our predecessors felt the idea of a "fortune teller" or "psychic" if you will, no matter the application or context, was too explosive for their religious followers. The very idea of it had the potential to crumble the Catholic Church to its foundation. Yashmiel was as real as Christ and the apostles themselves. A small, select assemblage of clergy, were sent, in secret, to destroy all evidence of him and his work. Paintings, writings, his home and even his fam… I am sickened by the thought." He couldn't continue.

Father Matthew combed his coarse, thick, wiry hair with his fingers psychotically; he needed to collect himself before uttering another syllable.

"All were permanently, well, "lost" in the interest of the saving this… this… I don't know what."

He looked around the room, but beyond its walls and ceilings. He wrapped his mind around this entire universe known as *the Vatican*. For him, everything here was now a farce. "Righteousness, built on the stench of sin in the interest of selfishness and greed, that's what!"

"They wanted to single-handedly customize Christianity?" A further disillusioned Father Joseph guessed. "My next questions would be, who on earth is blessed with a holy bloodline? How is that possible? And, do we have company yet?" A chill ran up his back.

Father Matthew had no more answers than Father Joseph did. "I'm glad I finally told you."

"I'm glad you did too." Father Joseph said, sincerely thankful.

"Now what does Yashmiel write on the left side of the map?" He asked.

Looking at him straight in the eye, Father Matthew said. "It no longer matters, the wheels of our fate have already been set into motion by our own handiwork, there's nothing we can do now."

"Tell me!" Father Joseph wasn't asking, he was telling.

The sound of men's voices charged up the hall. A distracted Father Matthew quickly rolled up the decrepit scroll and slammed it to the bottom of the desk drawer and locked it. He feverishly buttoned his collar back up and grabbed his jacket. Father Joseph wiped the sweat from his robust, cherub face and composed himself before they left the room.

As they walked up the hall, returning to the Pope's private quarters, Father Joseph whispered under his breath to Father Matthew. "It says, until that moment, the sun will continue to warm the Earth and hope will live. There's still hope, Father Matthew."

Looking at Father Joseph as though he were as naïve as a child, Father Matthew placed a comforting hand on his shoulder and replied, "Joseph, my dear friend, the wheels of fate are turning. Man's egoistic heart has doomed the human race." With one last shake of his head, he confided. "There's no stopping it now. I'm telling you."

Whispering back, in a respectfully defiant tone, Father Joseph refuted. "If a holy bloodline walks this earth, there is still hope among men." Joseph locked eyes with Matthew as he said it, smiling, confidently.

Matthew returned the grin. "My heart can only hope."

CHAPTER 3 -- THE VISIT

The sky this August morning in Eastern Nebraska was a sparkling crystal blue. Miles of corn stalks blew in the summer wind as far as the eye could see in every direction.

Just then a solitary cloud passed over the fields. As the cloud suspended itself overhead, casting a shadow below, something unearthly happened. A man appeared out of nowhere right smack dab in the middle of the cornfield. Dressed neatly in a tailored cream-colored linen suit, he stood proudly at about five foot eleven inches tall with a medium build and golden brown hair. As a warm summer breeze passed over his face he opened his eyes and looked about the majesty of this place. He was pleased.

Without hesitation he walked out of the field to a dusty, dirt road. Never stopping, he followed it for three hours, until he came to the center of town.

Here he found this small town's social Mecca, a local eatery named "Harry's Lunch Spot." Through clean spots in the grime-caked glass window, he could see some customers inside. He walked in and sat at a booth. His suit was still meticulously pressed and his shoes hadn't a spec of dirt on them.

Harry's Lunch Spot was dated and run down, but you could never tell the locals that. It looked like something out of an old fifties movie. Silver metal stools with round, red leather seats bordered a dining counter on the other side of the restaurant. This must have been where kids congregated, years ago, ordering their root beer floats on Sundays, after church. The coffee pots behind the counter were old fashioned too. Giant metal dinosaurs churned out pot after pot of thick, strong coffee. It was amazing they still worked after all these years. On the floor, a black and white checkered pattern drew one's eye downward. This is where the locals gathered, gossiped and ate. This was their comfort zone.

A waitress with an eighties hairdo approached him to take his order. "What can I get you handsome?"

With a gentle smile he responded politely. "Nothing."

Finding his response awkward, she stood there for a second and then walked away confused. As she did, she couldn't help but look curiously back over her shoulder at him. She thought to herself that he had a kind and peaceful air about him, even though he was strange.

Others sitting nearby, overheard and stared. They had never seen this person in town before and didn't know what to make of him. Locals here were wary of strangers. They wondered to themselves who he was and what he was doing here.

A local farmer extended his arm across a neighboring booth to the newcomer. "Chuck Jones at your service sir, welcome to Kismet, Nebraska. Never seen you around here before, what brings you to these parts?"

Accepting the invitation of a friendly handshake, the man everyone was so curious about spoke.

"Thank you, Mr. Jones. I'm Glenn. I've come to your lovely town on business."

Looking shocked there was any business in town other than farming, Mr. Jones didn't know how to respond. "Business?"

The stranger nodded his head yes.

Chuck was left speechless. He did what any good, decent, stumped person would do. He pressed his lips tightly together in a semi-smile, nodded his head welcomingly and turned back around to his wife.

The waitress, wearing a "Terri" name tag on her uniform, returned to her quirky customer with the daily paper. "How are you doing sir, you look like you've traveled a long way. Thought you might want to catch up on your current events." Clutching the newspaper in her hand, she stretched her arm forward toward him. "Here, when you're ready let me know what I can get you. We make great omelets here at Harry's!" She proudly boasted about the restaurants quality egg dish.

Glenn grabbed the end of the newspaper with one hand and holding his grip, he looked Terri square in the eye compassionately. "How *are you doing*, Terri?" He asked.

Staring into his eyes, her heart filled with sadness at his question. Fighting back tears, she hastily responded, "I'm fine, let me know when you're ready to order." Then, like a tornado she flew across the restaurant and through the stainless-steel double doors, which led to the kitchen in the back.

Everyone in the entire restaurant could hear a coffee pot smash to the floor and Marty the cook yelling. "Terri, watch out! What the hell are you doing!?"

Every customer was so quiet, they could have heard a pin drop anywhere in the place. The regulars had their ears pitched to the kitchen in the event there was more interesting dialogue to consume. They had never seen Terri so flustered before. It made them uneasy and concerned. Did the unfamiliar man sitting at Table 8 distress her? They all wondered to themselves. Chuck Jones turned around again to size up Glenn, asking himself whom he had just met.

After about fifteen minutes, the hoopla in this tiny eatery died down. Terri had pulled herself together and returned to her peculiar customer at Table 8 with her order pad and pencil in hand. But when she looked up, she saw he was gone. Her mysterious friend had vanished, taking the newspaper with him.

She looked around to some of the other customers for an explanation.

Three customers, including Mr. Jones, spontaneously and in synchronization, shrugged their shoulders and pointed toward the door.

Before she could look for him, something caught her attention. She noticed a strange object sitting in the very center of the table. A small, circular, smooth, blue colored rock sat there. It was unusual. She had never seen such a beautiful, sparkly stone before. It was deep, dark blue with green and white trails running through it. "Looks like a mini-replica of the world." She said, rolling it around in the palm of her hand. "Yeah, it's like a little globe made out of stone." She said, smiling.

But, there were also some ugly black spots living on its surface. She didn't know why, but this "thing" gave her a sense of urgency. She figured the man with the kind face left it behind. When she turned the rock over, she discovered what she believed to be Arabic writing. She had no idea what it might say. "How strange." She whispered to herself.

Terri went to the door to see if she could catch her customer, but he was walking briskly up the road and had already put much distance between them.

"There he is." She mumbled to herself. She recognized him by his neat suit. "He's not driving a car, he's walking!" Terri called out to the patrons, knowing they too would find it odd. No one bothered to get up to see for himself. "Where the heck does he think he can make it on foot?" She shook her head with disbelief. Looking again at the stone, she considered calling out to him, but he was too far away to ever hear her, even if she did. Even though she didn't think she'd ever see him again, she slipped the strange looking rock into her pocket for safekeeping.

It was about three o'clock in the afternoon now and the sun was high in the sky and the wind was starting to kick up. Blankets of dust and dirt lifted off the road and whipped against a wooden fence like it was being punished. Glenn had been walking for hours.

Behind him, a faded red 1957 Thunderbird convertible lazily made its way up Route 137. A very ambitious Glenn marched remarkably unaffected in the stifling heat, carrying his newspaper tucked tightly under his left arm. He could hear the car's engine, which sounded like it needed a tune-up.

As the vintage car slowly drove-up, coming parallel with him, the playful driver called out. "I have an offer for you, you can't refuse."

Glenn didn't so much as offer a return glance. He felt uneasy about her.

With a smile, she called out to get his attention once again. "How 'bout a lift, to get out of this sun?" Her voice was strong and her words articulate.

Glenn now finally decided to turn toward the voice. He saw an attractive woman in her thirties, with a nice figure sitting behind the steering wheel. She had a fair complexion, reddish colored hair with blonde highlights and bluish-green eyes. She looked a combination of English and Irish and was fairly fashionable. She wasn't about to leave until she engaged him and he knew it.

The roar of her motor was starting to drown out the beautiful expression of the songbirds he had been listening to in the area. Their gift of music to the world was virtually silenced upon her arrival.

As he continued looking at the driver, a combination of heat and fuel rising off the car came between them, creating a hot, wavy barrier through which to see each other. Her image through the gaseous combo appeared to distort and move, but Glenn could see that she was still smiling at him. He smiled back and reluctantly gave in to her offer. "Sure, why not."

As the Thunderbird rolled to a stop, Glenn eagerly climbed into the passenger seat. "Thanks for the lift Miss, I really do appreciate it." He was cautious of but thankful for her generous offer.

"Don't mention it." She said, looking away and over her drivers' door to avoid eye contact with him.

"So, where are you headed?" He asked.

"You tell me." She turned to look at him for a response he didn't have.

With Glenn now securely in her care, she hit the gas. With no headrest, Glenn's head snapped back from the acceleration. When he gained control of his head and neck muscles, he massaged the sides of his neck, wondering if he had whiplash. He wasn't sure what was going on. The skin between his eyebrows crinkled as he tried to regain his bearings.

He looked once again to the driver who seemed too preoccupied to care.

The car raced up the road, its engine screaming all the while. The car was going so fast over the bumps it tossed the two like rag dolls on top of their bucket seats. Glenn now turned to get a better look at his driver. She turned to inspect him as well. They locked eyes, wanting now just to observe each other.

"I see you got the daily rag there." She said, anxiously looking down at the newspaper, Glenn had placed on the seat next to him. He wedged it tighter under his left thigh, knowing she had a suspicious interest in it.

"Yes, as a matter of fact I do." He confirmed, looking straight ahead through the windshield.

"So, what's happening around the world these days?" She prodded. "I've been out of the loop for a while." She let out a hearty laugh like it was bottled up for a decade. It was kind of crazy.

"Well, I haven't had a chance to look at the paper yet." Glenn knew now to be more cautious of her. He didn't feel she had good intentions at all.

She wasn't laughing anymore. "Well, I'm interested in today's news, so why don't you read me what's above the fold as I drive." She demanded. She again looked at him directly and smiled.

Glenn refused to return the gesture and was not engaging.

The woman's demeanor was steadily morphing from generous and decent to rude and crass. He looked at her distrustfully. "What's your name?" Glenn asked, redirecting her.

Her eyes rolled to the sky with impatience. "Uh, how 'bout Falene." She growled in a quiet voice, her smile turning sarcastic.

"Beautiful name for a beautiful woman." He confirmed with an equally sarcastic smile.

"Yeah, I thought you'd like it."

Glenn searched his mind for a moment.

"It also has an interesting meaning. Do you know what it means in many languages?" He asked, turning his gaze to his passenger window, to view the great outdoors.

Without any interest, she played along. "You tell me?"

Carefully watching her expression, he told her. "It means Queen."

The two returned eyes to one another, staring each other down.

"In Old German it means, wise guardian." He verified.

"Wonderful." She called into his face. "Queen. Wise Guardian. It fits. I rather fancy that."

"Now what's in the paper?!" She snapped.

Glenn could sense things between them growing increasingly tense.

Irritated, she lit a cigarette. As she exhaled, she carelessly blew the smoke in Glenn's direction. From where he was seated, he could see the needle on her speedometer continuing to climb higher and higher. She waited for Glenn to do as she'd asked as she stared at his paper.

He decided to play along.

Glenn delicately unfolded the newspaper, scouring each page followed by each section, not saying a word. His eyes scanned every line of every column on every page, like a speed-reader. He only paused at the photographs. The images themselves appeared to have a greater affect on him than the actual detail-laden news stories. He said nothing, but continued staring at the photographs. He was squinting at certain ones, trying to get a better perspective of what was going on in the picture.

"Soooooooo, I'll ask again, what's happening in our world!" Falene pressured him for an answer.

Glenn answered dejectedly. "Many bad things, that's what's happening." He wore no expression and kept his eyes lowered. Glenn then hastily closed the section of the paper he was reading and organized the newspaper back together in perfect order by section. It found its home again tucked tightly under his upper left thigh for safekeeping, but it wouldn't stay there for long.

Using her left hand to drive, Falene used her free hand to rip the paper out from under Glenn's leg. He didn't fight her. She tore the paper wide open. Some of the pages were sucked out of the open car by intense wind and went tumbling down the road behind them. She scoured the paper's headlines herself, like an addict desperate for a "word fix." Now, she was bent to infect Glenn with her disease.

She screamed the headlines over the roar of the engine, so Glenn wouldn't miss a syllable. "Mother Drowns Twins in Maryland River!"

No response from Glenn.

"Prison Guard Found Guilty of Raping Thirty-two Female Inmates in Alabama Penitentiary!"

Nothing from him, still.

"Detroit Man Stabs 3 month-old Daughter to Death!"

He winced.

"Tsunami kills thirty-thousand in Southeast Asia!"

Glenn's mouth pulled to the right.

"CEO of computer-company nabbed on Child Porn charges!" That did it. Glenn squeezed his eyes shut for a moment, his lips pressing tightly together.

Falene liked that. She waited until he opened his eyes again. "Did you see some of this stuff in here?" She held the paper inches away from his face, smiling contemptuously, awaiting his take on such matters.

Glenn turned again to the beauty just outside his passenger window for some relief. For comfort, he fixated on the scenery rushing by, as she continued.

"Kindergartners Witness Teacher Suicide!" Falene announced yet another tragic headline from the newspaper. The sicker Glenn became, the more spirited her personality.

"F.B.I. Blames Texas School Bus Bombing on Terrorism!" Another line shot out of her mouth. "Pope Near Death; Who Will His Successor Be!" She was now shouting the words directly into Glenn's face.

He had nothing to say. No response at all. He wasn't even able to commit to subtle facial movements, communicating his thoughts. Nothing. For five long minutes, he stared out the window saying nothing as she tormented him. Then he carefully chose his words.

"Boy it's pretty in this part of the world."

Falene sat back in her driver's seat. She made a half angry, half confused face. She was pissed Glenn was removing himself from the anguish of the situation.

She thought for a minute about how to bring him around.

Tilting her head backward over the top of her seat, and then turning it sideways to face Glenn, she spoke to him above a whisper. "There's nothing or no one pretty out there, my friend. In fact, it looks like we've got a whole world full of sinners out there. This whole place is going straight to hell." She glared at him.

He blinked twice out of nervousness.

"What do you truly see when you look out there?" She asked him, really wanting to know.

He thought about it for a second. "I'm not sure yet."

"I know what I see." Falene turned her head back around to look out her driver's side window. She couldn't wait to share her perspective with someone who clearly didn't want to hear it.

"I see evidence of man's true spirit. It's polluted with all sorts of good stuff, like greed, sloth, wrath, pride, envy, gluttony and lust." Her head bobbed back and forth like she was trying to make him laugh.

He didn't.

She unsympathetically waited for Glenn to say something. Anything. Yet again, Glenn remained quiet. Although this time, he appeared to be contemplating the truth in what she said.

"Would you agree!" She yelled, verbally swiping at Glenn.

Startled by her yelling, Glenn blinked a couple of times.

His silence incited her. "What are you, blind or stupid or something? Look, at this paper, you dumb ass!" Spittle was flying out of her mouth along with her condemning words. "It's filled with people killing one another and others taking advantage of whatever they can!" Her words came out faster and faster. She was working herself into such a lather she was having a hard time catching her breath between sentences. "You don't know, you say?!"

She wagged her finger outside the car. "You don't know what you see when you look out there?" Falene was disgusted with how ignorant she thought Glenn was.

The only thing he did know for sure. She was nuts!

Glenn closed his eyes and drew in a deep breath. He would give this woman an honest answer, but only when he had one.

He turned his focus from her to man as a whole, his accomplishments and his failures. He remembered what he'd seen so far in Kismet as well as what was making news around the world. He let himself go with it.

During this trancelike state, it wasn't long before his spirit separated from the imprisonment of his body and moved away from him. He let it drift off as far as it needed to in order to gain a better perspective on the current state of man and the world. Before he knew it, his spirit had traveled out into the universe where he could take a peaceful, impartial look at things.

Glenn was now sitting high above everyone and everything, concentrating even harder. His view, the same God must have when he looks down at creation.

From here, he could clearly see radiant swirls of ocean and atmosphere mingling together in harmony. Landmasses served as an imposing and conspicuous backdrop. The land cared for men and beasts, the seas for all marine life. It was all so inspiring and magnificent to Glenn. The world, he thought, was the most beautiful creation of all time, designed with a perfectly balanced ecological system, supporting all life and promoting natural development. Like a good mother the planet took care of herself and her own. The cycle of life kept in a state of continuum by a food chain hierarchy and a cycle of life for all living things.

Glenn felt the powerful life force emanating from this massive planet, like a constant surge of energy washing over him. It was the life force of *all* living creatures, not just man. He could feel the presence, the soul, of every single living thing in his blood and his bones all at once. It was an overwhelming feeling, which took over his spirit.

Life is sacred. Whether it was the microbes contained within ocean spray, a single-celled organism, a human being or field mouse, the unique life-energy of each merged together to create one collective life force. All, equally significant to the planet and possessing a voice poised to speak unequivocal truth to Glenn should he ask.

With patience, collectively, that voice would reveal to Glenn what the state of the world is and why.

But something struck him. The hum of this immense surge was distinctly diminishing with each passing second. Glenn wondered what was causing it to slowly ebb. Just then he felt an aching feeling take over his entire body. It felt like the flu. But it was some sort of communication.

He fixated even more intently on Earth to receive the communication properly. Glenn further opened his mind and spirit to allow the resolve of everything here, including man and beast to envelope him totally.

Within moments, Glenn's mind and body became charged with enlightenment. But with that enlightenment came the feeling of dread.

Staring at what was once a proud planet, teaming with life and potential, a long, deep sadness overcame him. He lowered his head. Glenn let out a cough, then another. He put his hands over his eyes and rubbed, fighting back the urge to cough more. But he couldn't control it. He kept coughing until he almost threw up. He moved his hands from his eyes to his ears and began rocking back and forth. "Oh dear God, Oh dear God…" Glenn kept repeating the same line over and over to himself.

There was but a single thought reaching him and it was devastating.

"We're dying." It was a clear, matter of fact, undeniable and repetitive message. Mother Earth was dying and as a side effect was taking everyone and everything with her. In an attempt to save herself and at least some of her children, she was purging as many of her offspring as possible. "But why?" Glenn reached for more information.

She and everyone and everything on Earth, writhing in intolerable pain, could be seen and heard by Glenn. Every voice of every living thing, infected by man's touch, screamed out.

The enormity of it all almost killed Glenn. He continued coughing, grabbing at his chest. It hurt. But no relief came, as there was no relief for her. He listened further.

A malignant cancer was growing here, he realized. A cancer man had been unconsciously engineering since the beginning of time and it had now become untreatable. In a domino effect, was categorically killing everything in its path, all the way down the food chain. Man's perpetual disrespect for himself, each other and for his home, came at a lofty price. That price, his life and that of every living thing ever created, including the planet. Even though man created this mess, he still had no idea he was inadvertently killing himself in the process. Glenn understood this.

In the late stages of disease, however, Glenn could see Mother Earth still trying to save her family. With hope always a refuge from despair, she did her best to alert man to her plight.

Sudden climate changes, freak weather patterns, sickness and an increase in violent crime, all red flags.

But still, little to no, response or help from man. "Is man in denial?" Glenn wondered. "Or, does he just not care anymore? Has he given up?" He quickly ran threw a few explanations in his head.

Glenn watched as she continued to suffocate. It was almost unbearable. Mother Earth's children selfishly focused on the pain of their own infected tissues, which caused them to perpetuate further hatred upon each other. It was an unyielding, ugly and painful demise for all.

Glenn, feeling the onset of a burning fever was able to decipher more from the communication as he continued concentrating. He could hear the wheezing of greed, the sniffling of envy, the itch of lust, the unattractiveness of obesity and the lack of self-esteem due to sloth circulate through his bloodstream. He too was becoming sicker and sicker, just from watching.

Wanting to gain yet a better understanding, he zeroed in on various hot spots around the world.

As he focused in on the United States he witnessed immeasurable immorality. He watched as mothers, early in the morning, rushed out of their homes to head to work. They had time to check their mirror for confidence about their appearance, but forgot to kiss their children goodbye. As they dashed to their cars, they were intent on beating the morning traffic. As they did, they forgot the whole reason they went to work in the first place. That was, to make a better life for their families. Those families now a forgotten factor within the equation.

Glenn's now even slower beating heart fell to his stomach as he watched one mother leave without remembering to tell her son and daughter she loved them. What was at the top of her agenda that morning? Remembering to take her file with her to the office.

He witnessed husbands straying from their wives. Adulterers discreetly meeting at clandestine hotels for an afternoon rendezvous on their lunch breaks. He knew the anguish the men's wives would suffer if and when they found out about their husband's selfish and callous behavior.

Glenn also observed children talking back to their parents, using cuss words, disrespecting and disobeying their family members. Their parents were too lazy to incorporate punishments or lessons to teach their children right from wrong. The children now left to decide the difference on their own.

Another glance at society in one of the world superpowers made him recoil as a priest in a Catholic church took a young boy behind closed doors to commit the unspeakable. Glenn then put himself inside the boy's mind, offering love, hope and faith. But, the only emotions he could feel come from within the deepest part of the child's soul were despair, shame, hopelessness and fear. It all happened in a house of worship, built in God's name.

Glenn grew sicker by the moment.

Each glimpse at the United States brought continued sadness to Glenn.

Race relations were strained between blacks and whites and religious differences between Christians and Jews fueled further contempt for each other. Each group struggled to keep the other down financially, politically, socially and academically.

Children with social and/or behavioral problems here in the U.S. became the target of multimillion dollar pharmaceutical companies. Any kid with a sniffle could get a prescription for antidepressants, uppers or downers. Doctors who were "in bed" with the billion dollar industry went out of their way to persuade parents to keep their kids hooked on the stuff. Their reward for doing so, the "appreciation" of the pharmaceutical companies, usually displayed as gifts or cash. The parents' reward, a country full of children, dependent on chemicals.

Violent crime was also on the rise here. The local and national media fed upon it like starving vultures. For every twisted detail within a story, the media found ways to capitalize on it. If it bleeds it leads, the mantra in every newsroom nationwide.

This is also where homophobes committed heinous crimes against gays on a daily basis. Glenn could see the hate in some men's hearts for a population they could not understand.

As Glenn peered even closer, to see just how intolerant things had become, he watched an atrocity unfold.

On a dark, poorly lit street in the city of Boston, a gay couple holding hands, walked toward their car. Both men were completely unaware of the misfortune about to come their way. A group of "tough guys" from a club down the street saw the two men leave a well-known homosexual club and quietly trailed them to their vehicle. Before the couple ever had a chance to get into their car, five straight men jumped them from behind with a vengeance. They beat them senseless, while calling them names like "faggot" and "homo." With each damming blow, the gay men knew why they were the victims of such violence. They were born different from the majority of the population and some people hated them for it. It was that simple.

Glenn chose to endure the onslaught along with the victims, as God would. Glenn winced and his brow bloodied with each strike. A steady stream of blood trickled down his forehead, nose and cheek. He could feel other parts of his body tear apart as the angry men continued pounding his flesh. All of it, nothing, compared to the anguish inside of the men's minds. They were both battered and humiliated, their will broken.

God always accepted the pain a human being felt when they were victimized. Glenn now afforded that same privilege. He put himself inside the bodies of the men. He wanted to see what they were seeing, feel what they were feeling. Know what they knew. That's how God was able to fairly judge sinners and their victims, come Judgment Day.

Having seen and felt exactly what was happening in this part of the world, Glenn moved his view East to the African continent where the AIDS epidemic was devouring entire countries. Poverty and lack of education had spread the deadly disease throughout this once great land. People cried out through prayer, asking God why he allowed them and their families to die such a torturous and lengthy death.

In Northern Africa, Glenn saw war and genocide. Rulers, kings, entire governmental bodies were exterminating their own people for pure greed. Here as well, it was about man hating man.

With this knowledge, Glenn grew ever saddened about the destiny of the human race.

He bowed his head, murmuring to himself. "How could this be?" And another profound thought. "How could this ever get better?"

Glenn knew the descendants of Adam and Eve had chosen their own fate. The evidence was undeniably all around him. "Is the answer as obvious as it seems?" He contemplated if what he was seeing was the essence of man's soul speaking. "Is this what they've become?" His disappointment was crushing him.

In spite of it, he couldn't stop taking it all in. Information was power.

Still focused on Northern Africa, he converged on the Middle East. He saw the Arabs and the Jews abandoning their instincts of right and wrong and forgiveness and holding on to ancient old angst. Proprietary rights over the Gaza Strip, a piece of land the size of a small American city, caused continental neighbors to declare war against one another. Suicide bombers were the heroes of this society. Their sole mission, to kill as many of their enemy's men, women and children as possible. Doing so, they believed, would provide a rewarding eternal life in heaven for accomplishing their God's work.

Religious differences between Israel and Palestine helped fuel vicious attacks on one another. Its people, citing religion of all things, as their motive.

Terrorists from Arab nations blamed the United States for its problems. Historically, the United States politically supported Israel and not Arab nations. In response, the Arabs were now expressing their displeasure on American soil. Their success measured as the nation's most symbolic structures crumbled to the ground.

The situation in the Middle East was no better than in the United States. Man's love of warfare was evident here as well as in the West.

Glenn wondered if things weren't better elsewhere.

Over in one volatile nation, he saw they were working hard to secure nuclear capability.

Glenn, with his infinite wisdom, knew why. That country was looking to secure its place as a world superpower.

If the United Nations knew they possessed the components for a nuclear bomb, especially weapons-grade Plutonium, it would make the rest of the world take them seriously. If they had the muscle to take over less influential countries, it would strengthen their army and thus, their empire.

Wherever Glenn turned his eye on the world, man's actions stung.

Upon every continent, singers, musicians, writers and artists wasted their God given talents, meant to inspire others, making the world a bigger and better place. The reason, success took work. It was easier to take the less complicated road and settle for doing something else. The nagging feeling people felt, when they were not living to their potential, still not enough to jumpstart a yearning for living a meaningful life. These people walked around every day, never truly feeling they were fulfilled the way they needed to be. Everyone knew someone like this. Wasted lives, was one of the saddest things on the planet.

The sadness didn't stop there.

Spouses worldwide opted for divorce rather than trying to find it within themselves to reconcile. Consequently, families were destroyed. In today's world, many opted for the reward of employment status and financial gain over self-sacrificing to properly raise a family. In the end, it was the children who suffered. They were left to find their own way in the world with an immature and confused mind. Often, these misguided children growing up to become misguided adults.

And the cycle continues.

Over time, priorities worldwide had changed, and not for the better.

Not only had people lost sight of what was important, so did the organizations designed to lead them.

Glenn was sad to see that hardly anyone had faith in the Catholic Church anymore, as it too had become corrupt. Parishioner attendance dropped with each day as reports of priest abuse hit the airwaves. The drop in participation and donations were forcing the church into financial ruin.

That, coupled with pricey lawsuits filed by sex abuse victims, was also forcing the Church to sell off its properties to settle its legal woes. For decades, the Church had turned its eye from the horrors being committed under its roof. In many cases, even covering it up at the expense of the victims. Now, payment was imminent. The Church's reputation was tarnished so badly many questioned how long it would remain in existence.

This was the sad reality of what the world was now and Glenn knew it.

After carefully assessing the state of affairs in today's world, Glenn sadly cried to himself and ruminated. "It seems as though man has followed a reckless path and has brought all the world to its knees."

Everything he saw brought great physical pain upon his body. He sat there, doubled-over, tortured and crippled with hurt.

That's when he suddenly felt the wind, again. It whipped through his hair as if trying to wake him from his distant thoughts. He remembered now. He was still riding alongside Falene in her car.

She didn't miss a beat.

Catching his last thought, she sharply snapped Glenn's attention back to the present.

She spoke to him with a tired, throaty, hoarse voice. "Any thoughts?" He still appeared groggy from his little trip. He shook his head as if trying to shake it off.

"Would it be fair to say that man, which The Almighty created in his own image follows a path of wickedness? From your perspective, do you see it that way?" She waited for a response, her hair now whipping across her face in the intense wind.

Glenn knew now, whom, he was in the company of.

He was the jewel of heaven, sent by God. That made her, his vixenish shadow, sent by God's chief enemy. They both here for the same reason, to scour the earth for the last pure soul, if he or she even exists at all.

Falene knew Glenn had figured it out.

"If you look at modern man, as you just were, it seems that evil itself has become the role model for man's intentions." She said in a confident tone.

Then posing a question to him. "Even though man has always had a choice between right and wrong?" She hesitated for a second so Glenn could digest this. "Wow! How 'bout that?!" She made a goofy face as she said it.

Falene's chest expanded as she drew in the deepest possible breath she could through her nose. She smiled as she spoke to Glenn. "Mmmnnnnhhhhh, smell that?" She looked up from her driver's seat, her eyes scanning the vast sky above her.

Glenn wouldn't acknowledge what she was doing.

"I can smell the indecent air swirling about the world." She confirmed, trying again to provoke him. "Can you?"

Turning unenthusiastically toward his driver, Glenn bit. "No I can't."

Again, another deep breath accompanied by a sickly exuberant grin. She turned back toward Glenn, exhaling a foul stench at him. "Smell it!" Her face grew ugly, along with her intentions. "Smell it!" She yelled again at him.

Not the slightest of reactions from her disgusted passenger. This annoyed her.

To greater define man's plunge to the dark side, Falene took Glenn's mind back to a special time in the world's history, about two thousand years ago.

"I want to tell you a little story and you tell me if you can guess who it is." She facetiously acted as though it was going to be a fun game. Glenn knew it would be nothing of the sort.

"There was once a great man sent to walk the earth. He did so to save man." She said, her eyes growing wide. Falene watched Glenn closely as she spoke. She was looking for any indication he knew whom she meant.

He said nothing, but his skin immediately began to glow as he reflected upon that time, when Jesus Christ was sent to spread the word of God. That was enough to let her know he was aware.

Glenn remembered how Christ's brief stay inspired the world and future generations to come. He remembered how Jesus gave sight to the blind, healed the lepers and made the lame walk again. But most impressive of all, he demonstrated love in the face of hatred and forgiveness during persecution. He changed the world and showed man how to make the world a better place for himself.

Aware of all of his thoughts, Falene started to feel sick herself.

It wasn't long before Glenn was moved to speak. "Christ's message of love, tolerance, forgiveness and kindness did heal man. But, it disrupted the philosophy of his time and he was crucified. Jesus held steadfast to his convictions, even as he was nailed to a cross and left to die. In a loving proclamation he told man he would perish as a sacrifice for man's sins, so man could be forgiven. Long after his death, his message lives on. Man eventually creating Christianity in his honor, which is still one of the most pervasive religions of the world."

A grin appeared on Glenn's face as he thought about this chapter in the world's history.

He remembered how life in the beginning was simple but good.

Families for centuries would attend church, abide by the teachings of the Old Testament and try their best to be kind and fair to each other.

Neighbors would help each other and look out for each other's children.

Women respected their families and themselves.

Family members made time for one another.

People had deference for the planet.

Business owners did things by the book and were honest with their taxes.

People were afraid of the law and were respectful members of society.

And on and on and on.

Remembering man during this time brought Glenn great hope.

While he sat proudly by Falene's side, she decided it was time to drag him back into reality. She rudely shifted his focus back to the present-day and to the dismal reality of where man has traveled, spiritually, since those times.

"But that's not how it is today, is it Glenn?!" She sniped cruelly to her passenger. Glenn just sat there, saying nothing. He had developed a natural disdain for her by now.

As Glenn pondered just how careless man had become with his soul, he couldn't help but feel frightened. He still however believed man to be inherently good and he had to hold on to this idea if he were to be successful in finding the person he was sent to find.

Falene asked Glenn smugly, "Do you really think man's heart lives according to the word of God? Most don't even remember who the hell Christ was!"

Her voice grew deeper and began to wane. "What you're watching now is the long, drawn out and painful process of man self-destructing. In fact, everything Christ did here was in vain and a waste of his time. Most people even today, find it hard to accept this person was the Son of God. Forget believing in his promises of eternal salvation."

She put her finger crosswise to her lips. “Look, man’s fate is sealed, this world is at the end of its run.”

She was baiting him.

As the car she was driving continued careening down the roadway, her tresses appeared more like little tiny garden snakes whipping around her head, rather than the twisted pieces of hair they were.

Glenn now knew Falene knew exactly who he was. She seemed to know the precise moment he arrived on Earth. She had been stalking him since his arrival.

Unwilling to be snagged by her haste and deceit, Glenn replied with optimism. “Man’s fate is not yet sealed. In fact, his best day is yet to come.”

Now, he was baiting her.

Glenn’s love and hope for man caused his driver to lose her temper in a fit of impatience and insolence. She sat as erect as she could behind the steering wheel and cocked her head toward Glenn. She screamed her words with blood curdling force so they echoed across the universe.

“You sure about that! Man has paved his way, straight to hell, hasn’t he! It’s only a matter of time before all of mankind and the Earth is destroyed because of man’s lust for power!”

She threw his newspaper at him, opening page after page, exposing negative headline after negative headline and pushing them in his face.

“What are you waiting for?!” She yelled. With intensified violence her words grew ever more demanding and insulting. “You have to admit that mankind has a hypocritical affection for hatred and war, even though he’ll say he’s a proponent of peace!” Falene now felt compelled to convince Glenn of man’s true identity soon as possible. “Man is a devil in disguise!” She snarled. “Tell the truth! You’ve seen it for yourself! It’s all around you!” As Falene’s heart pounded with excitement, Glenn tried to keep a level head. He wasn’t going to get caught up in a debate, when he still wasn’t sure he knew man’s whole story.

Just then, Falene put a question to Glenn that she thought would paralyze him. She was looking to use his good sense of honesty against him and bring herself one step closer to helping bring mankind to his knees.

"True or False?" Falene now calmly prodded as she clutched her steering wheel with both hands at ten and two. "Mankind as a whole has consciously chosen to destroy one another, thus himself, and the Earth." She knew he couldn't deny the facts. Each end of her mouth curled upward as though she awaited a tasty treat.

Without missing a beat, Glenn rendered his answer. "False." With increased confidence, he supported his answer with an irrefutable explanation. "The state of man's heart today is the result of perhaps many hearts. But not all. Therefore, it is not the will of mankind as a whole."

The ends of his mouth now started an upward decent as hers began to fall.

Unwilling to back down from this clash, Falene propositioned Glenn. "Since you're so confident in man's inherent goodness, you wouldn't have a problem proving it to me, would you?"

Wondering what this manipulative and cynical witch could possibly be getting at, Glenn replied. "Why would what truthfully exists in the world need to be proven?"

"Oh it's very simple." Falene said. "If you could, prove to me what you say is true. That would be a big help. Because, during my travels here and I've been traveling quite a while, I have seen no evidence of a single human being not displaying at least some form of malice, jealousy or greed toward another."

"In fact." She included. "The true spirit of evil has succeeded in causing man's demise. Men and women have overwhelmingly been tempted with the vices God unwittingly made available to them in the natural world such as sex and power and they caved… Oh, they've caved for decades and centuries and millenniums. Yes, they have!"

Glenn thought about that.

"Prove to me what you say is true. That man as a whole is not purely evil. Because, I am positive there is no soul left on Earth that is pure." She was serious. "I'd just love it if you could prove me wrong. By proving me wrong, you'll show man and me what he is made of. That will preserve his place here on earth." Falene convinced. "Or, if you can't prove me wrong… well, there might be another outcome." She smiled wickedly.

With an increasingly louder voice, the she-devil placed a wager with Glenn. "Tell you what. Select any person on Earth, man or woman, that you feel possesses mankind's best qualities and let me enjoy the privilege of meeting them." She said. "That's all, I just want to meet this amazing person, spend a little time with them, get to know them and get to the bottom of who they are. The real core of who they are." Her phony concern bleeding through her statements.

"This fictional person you've created in your mind. Do they really exist? And if they do, spending time with me could never break their will. Right?" She hesitated before putting the offer formally on the table.

"What do you say?"

Falene's right eyebrow arched with anticipation as she waited for her answer. "I'm always interested in meeting new people!" She rudely laughed out loud.

Glenn thought about the offer as Falene tried a little more convincing.

"I'm curious to see if I can help this person reveal what truly lies within their heart. Let me meet them Glenn and it will help make me a better person. Maybe at the same time I can help them be the best person they can be." She looked at Glenn with yet another deceptive grin accompanied by a dead stare.

"If you're so sure this person has a pure heart, you won't have a problem letting me spend a little time with them." She repeated. "Right? I'm interested to meet anyone who I can potentially help bring to full maturity."

Then, she offered a promise. "If this person is truly an example of the pure virtue that still lives and breathes within man."

She muttered. "I'll have no choice but to just get out of here, let things be as they are and go about my business. A whole new start, let's say, for everyone."

Glenn thought carefully about this.

"We'll call it a rebirth for man!" She added. "Something like that."

He knew that for sure she could not be trusted, but her bet could actually benefit him. He did need to find such a person anyway. If such a person exists, he knew there was no better test than to allow them to meet Falene. If they could beat her at her own game, they *were* the one.

He had to get this right.

If there was no such person left on earth, the world was being turned over to hell anyway. Heck, it was already on its way from what he could see. He was sure a savior was out there somewhere and he needed to find them fast as possible. It meant a whole new beginning for mankind.

Glenn turned his whole body sideways on the seat, to confront his foe face-to-face. "I will need thirty days to scour the Earth." He said. "Then, you'll see a soul that cannot be broken. Then you will see, beyond the shadow of a doubt, that good still prevails among all the treachery that seems to surround us." He twirled his finger in the air as he said it. Now he was smiling sarcastically.

Falene returned the smile and readily agreed. "Great, Glenn. So sorry you'll be spending thirty days…" She leaned in toward him. "…wasting your time!"

Falene extended her hand, which Glenn shook to seal the deal.

With that, the passenger door to Falene's car swung open and she shoved Glenn out onto the road with a tremendous push.

Glenn flew out off the seat and landed on the dirt-covered roadway. Before he knew what had happened, Falene slammed on the gas and spun her wheels until her tires grabbed the road, leaving Glenn behind.

As her car sped off up the road, Glenn looked up through the dust cloud she created. He could hear her muffled voice blazing through.

"See you in exactly thirty days!"

CHAPTER 4 -- THE SEARCH

A bit dazed Glenn slowly got up onto his feet and brushed himself off as he watched Falene's car speed toward the West.

"Nice girl." He said, as her car made it up over a hill and eventually over the horizon and out of sight.

When Falene's car disappeared, Glenn thought about what had just happened and felt the weight of his burden suddenly bearing down on him.

He knew focusing on their run-in was only a waste of precious time. The wager had been placed. Now, he had work to do and he would devote every second he had to finding one very special individual.

"Where to begin?" The wheels in Glenn's brain began to turn.

He was back in the hot, sweaty summer sun, walking along the same long dirt road he'd been walking earlier. Cornfields, again, stretching as far as the eye could see. It seemed to lead to nowhere for hours. Yet he knew he was on the right path… figuratively.

Glenn then suddenly had the urge to walk off the roadway and directly back into a cornfield. There he stood, comfortable as ever, in the middle of it. Corn stalks swayed and bent all around him, the rustling of the brittle leaves music to his ears. Looking to the tops of the dry, crinkly, paper-like cornhusks, Glenn could see tiny insects buzzing about.

"Everyone's got a job to do." He said, smiling.

Glenn then closed his eyes and felt the warmth of the sun soak into his face. "Oh that feels good." He said, feeling the burn.

He stood silently for a while until he felt calm and centered. When he did, he stretched his arms out to his sides, turning his palms upward. A few seconds passed. Then he tilted his head far back. So far back, his face gladly met the sky. He let a few more seconds pass and opened his eyes.

The atmosphere above him was so peaceful and beautiful. Glenn could see what a captivatingly, vast and expansive place this was. So awe-inspiring for human beings, yet unattainable. One could only admire its allure, but never covet it. That's what made the sky so romantic for people. It's why men and women looked here when they prayed, sending their requests straight to heaven and why they turned here at nighttime, wishing for their heart's desire.

Glenn knew it held another secret. It was where the energy from all of man's history, his hopes, his dreams, triumphs and tragedies was indefinitely captured forever. The sky possessed the energy and the knowledge of all of time. It had seen everything below it there was ever to see and it kept a perfect record.

Glenn tapped its energy, absorbing all the information it held for him.

As he slowly closed his eyes again, he drew in a deep breath and called upon only the positive energy of the current world. He knew that's what would lead him to what he was looking for.

Millions of images, sights, sounds and happenings flashed through Glenn's mind.

Then it stopped. He was tuned in to something. Something good.

Just then, a fierce, turbulent wind of tornado proportions blew from the East. Glenn turned his head toward the gusts to take in all the tidings the wind carried with it. In it, he could feel the distinct presence of each soul it passed over and the quality of their hearts. He had just ruled out a hundred thousand people as a possible savior for this world. The wind kicked up harder with violent consequences, which seemed to only be assisting Glenn.

Nearby houses and barns were smashed to smithereens and tractors could be seen hurling across a nearby highway. Farm animals sought shelter as well, anywhere they could. The windstorm so unexpected, a local television station was flooded with calls about the damage the weather system caused across the county.

Glenn's hair whipped around, pulling on his scalp as he tried to keep steady footing upon the ground. He held tight to the buttons on the front of his shirt so they didn't tear open from the gale-force winds.

Information from across the entire globe was pummeling Glenn. Through it all, he was still smiling. He could feel how much good and decency was still left in the world, as corrupt and immoral as it had become.

Then, from the sky as if out of nowhere, a freakishly large and powerful bolt of lightning struck down in the exact spot Glenn was standing.

BOOM!

Glenn stood there in silence, not moving a muscle. The lightning had gone right through him and into the ground beneath his feet. He felt a strong charge of electricity living within his body now and it lingered there.

He slowly lowered his arms to his sides and tilted his head back up facing forward. "Wow!" He cried out, shaking his head.

The wind instantly began to die down and conditions in the cornfield became normal once again. The storm had done its job and was gone.

Glenn took a breath and regained his composure. He straightened up, fixed his hair and rearranged his clothing, which was all twisted around his body.

Now he suddenly began to see someone in his mind. Not sure whom... but someone he knew he needed to focus on. He concentrated harder, squinting.

Still no clear vision, just a vague outline of a robust man stuck in his mind. Although there were no vivid images of this man's physical characteristics to identify him, there were feelings about him Glenn could pick up on. He knew he may not recognize him right away, but his gut instinct would tell him when he found the right man.

He felt deeply in his heart, there was true hope, after all. "Maybe this person has something to do with it?" He thought. "Or maybe there's someone else?" Glenn wasn't sure and was keeping his mind open to all possibilities.

As polluted with perverse souls as the Earth was, there were also many people here who tried in various ways to do the right thing. He knew should he attempt to pinpoint the exact location of this specific person, he could accidentally be diverted to others making passive attempts at moral uprightness. This was a world of billions. He would have to consider each and every soul carefully, before arriving at his particular man.

And he had to find him or someone else by the end of thirty days.

As these thoughts passed through Glenn's mind, he was not the only one to hear them. Another was listening with ears pitched to his inner voice.

Glenn knew his every thought and move was being monitored by Falene. She would be there to pounce the second he decided on someone, so he had to be sure of what he was doing. Knowing she was keeping a close eye on him couldn't distract him.

"Could one person save all of mankind?" They would have to be a near faultless human being. He thought about that, starting to get a little apprehensive.

"Is that possible?" Glenn questioned. "This person would have to be Christlike in all ways, including within the very pit of their soul where darkness often hides." He emphasized to himself.

"That darkness often reveals itself when a person is pushed to the end of their limits either physically, emotionally, spiritually, intellectually and so on."

He knew many could keep up the façade of being a good person, a good person to the core for years and years. That is, until they were put to a true test. A test, where they had to decide whether to figuratively or literally slay someone either emotionally or even physically to selfishly preserve something about their existence on this earth plane. That's when a person is most dangerous. That's when they'll sacrifice another for themselves. That's where true evil exists within mankind.

"Hmmmnnhhhhh." Glenn mumbled, thinking harder about that.

Glenn knew Falene must have people he[illegible]ping her and that they would have big plans for whomever h[illegible]ted. "I'll just have to keep my eyes and ears open for them." [illegible]d, suspiciously looking around.

What he was convinced of was that if [illegible]rson did exist, it would be impossible for them to fall victi[illegible]g Falene and her crew could bring on. He just had to find t[illegible] and they would take it from there. That comforted Glenn a[illegible]wed him to continue his arduous journey.

Just then, Glenn sharply jolted his head to the West. There was something there. He felt that living energy again within his body start to rumble. It was ramping up quickly.

"Whoah!" Glenn extended his arms, almost losing his balance. He was feeling a great electrical charge overcome his body. He held his breath because it hurt and he thought that would alleviate the pain.

It didn't.

"Whoaaaahhhhhh!" It almost took him off his feet this time.

"Whoooooaaaaaaahhhhhhhhhh!" He was unable to hold his breath any longer, but closed his eyes instead to avoid any further sensory overload.

Then without notice, he disappeared from the cornfield as if he'd never been there.

When Glenn opened his eyes moments later, he was doubled over in a hospital. He looked around, trying to make heads or tails out of it. "Where am I?"

After a few minutes the pain subsided and he was able to straighten up.

A sign on the wall read Jefferson Hospital – Los Angeles, California. So he knew he had been transported across the country.

A man here, named Norm Wilcox anxiously awaited the results of a paternity test inside the local healthcare facility. He had been with his longtime girlfriend for 15 years and shared a seven-year-old son, Jared.

During a recent argument, his girlfriend told him that Jared might not be his son. She revealed that eight years ago when they had broken up for a week, she slept with another man, but never breathed a word of it to a soul. She said that when she learned she had become pregnant, the two had reconciled and she lacked the courage to confess her indiscretion. This secret she kept until now. In minutes, a test would tell Norm whether he was Jared's father or not.

Glenn was brought here to Norm by a highly selfless and compassionate thought the man had. As Norm paced the hallway of the hospital he thought to himself. "I've loved and cared for this child as if he were my biological child, for seven years. If I find out I'm not his father I will continue to love and support him for the rest of his life. I am his father, the only one he knows and I love him."

Glenn knew the results, but waited for the nurse to reveal them to Norm. He wanted to witness Norm's reaction. Man, after all, had free will. Sometimes even when man knows what the right decision is, the choice is still difficult.

Just then a nurse holding a small pink piece of paper with some writing on it, walked up to Norm and his girlfriend Sarah. She told them she had the results and asked them if they were prepared to hear the news.

"Yes, we've waited this long and we both want to know the truth, conclusively." Sarah said.

With a firm voice, the nurse read the results aloud. "The results show that it is 99.93% probable that Norm Wilcox is *NOT* the father of Jared Wilcox."

With that one sentence life changed for Norm, Sarah and Jared. But how it would change depended on if Norm could find it within himself to forgive Sarah and love Jared, despite knowing he was not the boy's father.

As Norm pondered the outcome, he paced back and forth across the hospital floor and then exploded with a vicious verbal attack on Sarah.

"You filthy whore!" He screamed from the top of his lungs. "I loved Jared as if he were my very own son his entire life, now I've no place in his life!" Yelled Norm.

"I can't believe you did this to me!!! To us!!! To him!!! I hate you! I never want to see you again!" Norm assaulted, stalking the hospital hallway.

The nurse whispered to Sarah. "Do you want me to call security?"

Sarah was frozen in place and didn't answer. She felt she deserved this.

"That's it! It's over! I'm done! I'm not taking care of your bastard child! You do it! You and your bastards father, whoever the hell he is!!!" Norm had reached his top vocal range.

With that, Glenn knew that Norm meant every word he said and that he would no longer care for Jared. The intent in his voice was clear. Norm's sense of betrayal clouded his love for Jared. Out of spite and hatred for Sarah, Norm would punish her by walking out of Jared's life permanently, regardless of the bond they had and how much it would devastate the boy.

At that very moment, Glenn knew there was no reason to stay a second longer.

Again, an electrical charge overcame his body and he vanished. He was interested in yet another.

Glenn moved across the world as if he compressed planes of space to get there.

He was now in an alleyway in Tokyo.

"Hmmnnhhh. No longer in the United States." He thought out loud.

Glenn stood in place, looking around at the streets, which were flooded with people.

He saw an elderly man walking past; completely unaware, his wallet fell right out of his back pocket and onto the sidewalk. He kept walking.

A professionally dressed woman walking a short distance behind him noticed it, picked it up and examined it.

The streets were bustling with foot traffic and the woman had no idea who dropped their identification and cash.

"Did someone lose their wallet?!" She yelled out to the pedestrians standing all crammed together on the sidewalk.

No response.

"Did anyone.....?!" The woman held the wallet over her head so everyone could see. "... lose their wallet?!"

Still, no one responded.

The police station was just across the street and she could see the sign from where she was standing.

"Tokyo Police Department." She read.

She thought briefly to herself. "Let me take an extra minute out of my schedule to run over there and hand it to an officer so it can be delivered to its rightful owner."

Her instincts were right on, but a nagging voice inside of her told her to just drop it into her purse and keep moving, a couple of bucks richer.

After peering inside the wallet, she was shocked. She knew if she kept the wallet, what was inside could pay off her credit card bill.

That's all it took. The well-dressed lady, whose income was greater than seventy-five percent of the population, cupped the wallet in her fist and kept it for herself.

Her decision left her feeling badly, but not badly enough.

As she approached the next crosswalk, Glenn was there, staring at her. She felt uncomfortable, knowing she had just done something wrong and tried to redirect him.

He kept staring at her.

"Can I help you sir?" She asked, trying to get him to look away.

"Nope, just contemplating the state of the human race." He said.

"Okaayyyyyy..." She said, confused.

She took off on foot across the city, shrugging him off as if he were just another street kook, never again considering bringing the wallet to the police so it could be returned to its rightful owner.

Glenn kept watching her as she hustled to her meeting.

"If only people would listen to their gut instincts more, this world would be a better place." Glenn said under his breath.

"No need to stay here any longer, either."

He started walking away when he began feeling funny. There were those beginning-feelings of that electrical charge again. He put his hand to his head. "Uhhhhh-no." Glenn whimpered.

A sudden jolt to his stomach sent Glenn hurling backward onto a dirt road before he had time to think about it.

He was in Mexico and had just been hit by a car. There he lay, on the ground, severely injured.

The driver of the late model Jeep slammed on the brakes, swung open his drivers-side door, leapt from his seat to the dirt road and knelt down to see if Glenn was O.K.

"Oh my God, sir, I'm so sorry! I didn't even see you in the street, you appeared out of nowhere! Are you all right, can you speak?!" The man was frantic.

Glenn was in so much pain he was unable to answer. He was bleeding profusely from the gut and was starting to lose consciousness.

The petrified man put his hands on Glenn's stomach, trying to stop the bleeding. "Sir, sir, can you hear me! Are you OK!" He lifted Glenn up by his back, trying to prop him up.

Glenn's head hung back as if he'd passed out.

"Jose get him out of the street! If someone sees this, you will go to jail!" Shouted a passenger from the Jeep.

"This man is going to die if I don't get him to a medical clinic!!!" Jose shouted back, hysterically.

"We can't take him to a doctor, Jose, you don't have a driver's license! Roll him over the ditch, let's get out of here!" The fearful voice instructed.

"He will die, Renaldo, I'm telling you!"

Glenn's lifeless body lay limp in Jose's arms.

"You will die in prison, if you get caught for this, Jose! Roll him down the hill, do it now!!!" Renaldo shouted, trying to convince Jose this was the right thing to do.

Against his better judgment, Jose's fear got the best of him. He ran to the back of the Jeep and pulled out some old rope stored there for emergencies. He ran back to Glenn, tied his limbs together and heaved his lifeless body down the hill, into some dense brush alongside the embankment.

As Glenn lied there on the cold ground, he opened his eyes slightly to see what Jose was doing. He saw the driver walking away, wiping tears from his eyes and climb back into the Jeep. Glenn could hear Jose's final thought before he started the engine and sped off.

"I'm so sorry Mister, I'm so sorry, but I can't get into trouble for this." Jose said to himself.

It was apparent that Jose's selfish desire to save himself allowed him to leave another to die.

Glenn's heart grew heavy.

As Glenn watched the Jeep flee down the road, he felt sorry for Jose. He knew somewhere deep down within his heart Jose was a good person who lost sight of what was important in life, to help others, to tell the truth and to listen to his instincts.

As the sun began to set behind the mountains, Glenn could feel a chill set into his core. He was traveling rapidly through space, drawn to benignant people, in search of *the one*.

Glenn now found himself in the biting cold which seemed to deaden the skin on his hands. He rubbed them together in circles to keep the blood circulating. There was someone here with great moral character and his humanitarianism brought Glenn to this barren place.

As he walked toward what looked to be a makeshift building, snow and sleet rained down hard on Glenn's face.

He was in the Antarctic at an international research laboratory. He quietly walked inside and hid to go undetected.

Here, he observed Dr. James Levesque in a white overcoat squirting some liquid into test tubes.

Dr. Levesque had been working on a potential cure for multiple sclerosis in the isolated laboratory for nine months. It had been his life's quest since his mother died of M.S. at the age of thirty-eight when he was only thirteen.

The good doctor was dedicated, ethical and driven to save others like his mother. There was nothing he wouldn't do to scientifically preserve the human race.

Glenn stood in a corner, carefully watching Dr. Levesque. The physician never suspected a thing.

Doctors from all across the world were working at this facility. The reason for their icy headquarters, a newly discovered bacteria that lived at subzero temperatures, had been found in the ocean near the North Pole.

A bacteria discovered by Dr. Levesque. Dr. Levesque was the only doctor in the world to prove the bacteria, if injected into the bloodstream, severely diminished the progression of multiple sclerosis.

However, an absolute cure still eluded the team. That's what they were here working on.

Hailed a genius by his colleagues in the medical community, Dr. Levesque didn't stop with his Nobel Laureate winning discovery. He continued to work tirelessly to find a cure for the degenerative disease, which stole the dignity of those it afflicted.

Glenn felt proud to watch the doctor and his heart lifted. He could see the greatness mankind could achieve if he could learn to love himself and one another.

Dr. Levesque was just one of twelve doctors that shared the laboratory. All of them were ivy-league educated and had a wealth of medical experience as well as personal and professional triumphs to their credit.

Dr. Levesque sometimes felt a little guilty for getting jealous over the accomplishments of one of the other doctors there, Dr. Vladimir Yeltsin of Russia.

Dr. Yeltsin was well liked at the compound and making great strides with his experiments, greater strides than *he* was currently enjoying. Dr. Levesque didn't like that even though he was the one with the household name. Although he knew his own resume far out shined Dr. Yeltsin's it still galled him.

As Dr. Levesque started thinking, then obsessing about how his elevated position in the medical community would ebb if Dr.

Yeltsin ultimately discovered a cure for Multiple Sclerosis, he started to panic.

As Glenn watched from a dark corner of the room, Dr. Levesque walked over to Dr. Yeltsin's workspace and changed an entry in his experiment log.

Glenn lowered his eyes to the floor.

This would taint all of Dr. Yeltsin's future results.

Even though he knew it was wrong, Dr. Levesque stared at the log modifications and delighted in it. He closed the book and walked away, never once thinking about correcting his malicious deed.

Glenn knew without doubt it was time for him to leave, but first wondered to himself. "How could a man who had received so many gifts from God be so greedy as to begrudge another his moment of glory?"

The answer didn't matter and off Glenn went.

Glenn now found himself standing before a wall of televisions inside a mainstream retail store. Every "boob tube" was blaring, set to a different network.

Mothers with their children riding in carriages rushed in front of and behind Glenn as he stood staring at the maze of electronics. As Glenn's eyes scanned each screen, one by one he caught news programs from across the country.

Before him he saw glamorous news anchors reporting the usual tragedies of the day. Shootings, stabbings, child molestation, robbery, terrorism and the like, headlined each show. Each story was accompanied by graphic images of blood and gore, to create urgency and affect.

As he continued watching he began to sweat and his heart started pounding.

Turning sideways on his heels and looking down about two feet to his right, he saw a five-year-old boy also standing before the barricade of bad news. The child was licking a lollipop and watching the same shows as Glenn. The only difference between Glenn and the boy was that the boy was expressionless and unfazed by what he saw. This was normal to the boy and part of his world.

It broke Glenn's heart. He felt his chest grow warm from stress.

Suddenly, the volume from one television set seemed to increase and stand out from the others. Ironically, an anchor had just tossed to a field reporter who started out her live shot saying, "A new report says children see over twelve thousand acts of violence on television each year and are likely to either mimic it, encourage it or allow themselves to become a victim of violence."

With that, Glenn looked again at the child with pity.

To save this child and so many others like him, Glenn needed to move on. Time was of the essence.

For days more, he traveled the world from shore to shore and pole to pole. He roamed continent to continent, within the blink of an eye, lured by the initial intention of good deeds by millions and let down often by man's inevitable weaknesses.

Day twenty-eight was now bearing down on Glenn who had investigated nearly ninety-eight percent of the world's population for purity of heart, without finding whom it was he was looking for.

He found that most he observed opted for whatever was in their best interest, regardless of the consequences.

At this moment, he now found himself somewhere in the woods. Where, he wasn't sure.

Seeming to match his mood, Glenn's once gleaming, cream-colored suit was growing wrinkled and stained for the first time. Glenn was visibly unshaven and starting to get tired.

He was drawn less and less to the prospect of people doing good deeds. That's because those deeds were becoming fewer and fewer in the world by the day. He couldn't understand why it was taking him so long to find the one person on earth who could make a difference. He knew they existed, he felt them that day in the field when he began his quest.

"Why can't I find them?" He asked himself, remembering that feeling as best he could.

Nighttime had come, he noticed, and it was time for a well-deserved rest.

Glenn sat down wearily, in the middle of this wooded stretch, on a big boulder contemplating what to do.

For a few minutes, he allowed himself to be still, listening to the cry of this planet, which had become overrun with selfishness. Its voice was composed of every thought from each spiritually and physically dying creature on the planet. Its sound was grief stricken and desperate in the night air. With all that was going on, it was as if people were living a hell on earth of sorts. A hell they created all by themselves.

He put his head in his hands and rocked back and forth as if being tortured. He knew he had yet to find "the one" and time was running out. As he sat there alone, something broke his concentration.

A small dog, a Boston Terrier scampered his way. A black and white male with a look of worry made his way over to Glenn, hopped up on the boulder and sat shivering by his side. The feeling Glenn got was that the dog had run away from home.

Glenn patted the dog on the head, offering him friendship and safety.

Having been abused by his owner for far too long, the dog left to find a better home elsewhere, even if it meant never finding food or water or shelter. It was worth the risk.

Glenn looked down at him. "Hey there, little guy." With one glance directly into the dog's trusting brown eyes, he watched the animal's torturous story unfold in his mind's eye. In one instance, he saw the dog cowering underneath a kitchen table while his sadistic owner tried to beat him with a belt for not coming when he was called.

That was all Glenn could take. He didn't want to see anymore.

Glenn stroked the dog on the head and back and propped him up on his hind legs so the two were eye to eye. Looking into his eyes deeply, Glenn said. "It's over, you are going to be saved, just like everyone else on this planet."

As the dog's little snip of a tail started to whip back and forth, Glenn knew he understood. "I'm going to call you, Lucky."

Glenn said smiling at his new best friend. "And you can stick with me. I could use a friend right about now."

Even though Lucky couldn't answer, Glenn knew he agreed.

Just as the two started to get to know each other better, Glenn looked up through the fog and saw an apparition moving toward them. "A female... it's a woman." Glenn squinted, trying to make out who it was.

The woman's image became more defined as she cut through the field, coming closer. He could hear twigs snap beneath her feet. He recognized her. It was Falene.

"How's it going!" She yelled, smugly, from fifty yards away.

Glenn felt sick to his stomach.

As if things couldn't get worse. His nemesis was approaching swiftly on foot through the darkness. She was dressed in a long white sheer dress, with ropes crisscrossed around her chest and waist. She was smiling and appeared angelic to Glenn, although he knew better.

As she grew closer, he could see her hair was long and curled and blowing gently in the wind. She effortlessly climbed the boulder he was sitting on and crouched down beside him.

"See you've got a new friend to keep you company." She said craning her neck to get a better look, but never attempting to pet the dog.

Lucky shifted closer to Glenn and turned his head away.

"So, how's my favorite guy?" She asked sarcastically, taking in the cool, damp smell of the wilderness. The look on her face was of victory.

He looked into her eyes with just a smile. "I'm your favorite guy?"

"Of course you're my favorite guy." She confirmed, flirtatiously. "Any girl could fall in love with a man who wants to give her the world." Falene continued to smile at him as she spoke with such bold arrogance.

"Don't count your chickens, sweetheart."

"Anyone you want to introduce me to?" She prodded, knowing there was no one.

"I have two days left, my dear." Not being able to bear being near her one-second longer and not wanting to waste his time as she was undoubtedly trying to do, he stood from his stoop and jumped down to the ground. Lucky loyally following.

Glenn took a few steps away, turned back, and looked up at her. "That's when you can come, meet my new friend, not a second sooner."

She stood, staring down at him with contempt. "I don't think you're going to like who that person turns out to be!" She snapped back.

Glenn knew to turn away and walk off with his faithful companion, leaving Falene in the dark, behind him. He couldn't let her get into his head, which is exactly what she was trying to do.

He just kept walking as she tormented him.

"See you then, sweetheart!!! See you then!!! Not a second later!" She screamed, her voice echoing deep into the woods.

As Glenn continued to make off into the forest, through the heavy fog, he suddenly stopped and closed his eyes.

Lucky looked up at him and cocked his head as if he knew something were about to happen. In the peaceful quiet of the wilderness he thought about what it truly was he was searching for.

Glenn knew that when man was created, it was promised to him that God would always listen to his heart. When someone desperately called to the Lord, asking for whatever it was they needed, often their prayers were answered if it fit into God's plan for them.

Glenn would use that basic law to help himself in his time of need. That time was now.

In his heart and mind, he held a vision of a human being who loved himself wholly and completely and who knew how to love others and, a person who knew how to accept love, sincerely. He saw clearly how that person could remember forgiveness at times when it was easier to condemn and punish. Glenn also saw this person give when they had little and put others before themselves. He pictured how this morally elevated individual did not know prejudice or malice.

Glenn's melancholic heart started to beat with health, growing strong and steady with each thought.

These were the same qualities God imagined on the day he proudly created man with love in his heart. Glenn held that sacred image within himself and let it envelope him completely. He called upon all the forces of earth to carry him to the one place where this may still exist in its purest form.

Before he knew it, he and Lucky vanished.

CHAPTER 5 -- MEETING WEI-XING

Glenn looked around yet again at his new unexpected surroundings. He realized that he was somewhere on the Asian continent. Exactly where he wasn't sure. He didn't care because this was clearly where he needed to be.

The beginning of perspiration began to bead along his forehead as the afternoon sun climbed higher and the temperature broke the one hundred degree mark.

"Boy, it's not like this where I come from." He said, half laughing. He removed his suit jacket and rolled up his sleeves and the bottoms of his trousers for relief. It wasn't much help. He was smack dab, deep in a formidable jungle. He was now in a race against the clock to find out why.

Everywhere Glenn looked was lush and thick with vegetation. Overhead, monkeys and several different species of tree inhabitants watched from their perch as their awkward visitor struggled to forge a path for himself amidst the plants grasp. As he did, precariously, monkeys chattering to one another sounded more like laughter than common primate vocalizations.

At one point Glenn stopped and with a sense of humor, looked up. "Oh yeah, you think it's so funny? How would you like your testicles to grow to the size of coconuts?" He continued on his trek, "giggle-free."

"Smart monkeys." He smirked. "That's what I thought."

The plant varieties and brush because of their size, appeared to be from prehistoric times. The searing climate, high humidity accompanied by frequent precipitation in this region made for ideal growing conditions.

And it was the last place on the planet present-day man had never set foot. It was still pristine and completely in its natural state as evolution left it; free from pollution, corruption and commercialization.

Glenn took a moment to recognize what a sacred place this was. If there was still a "heaven on earth" left, this was it. Straight ahead of him, further into the jungle, he could hear people and the sounds of work being done. He wasn't sure what it was but he was sure it had something to do with why he was there. He let the faint sounds in the distant reaches guide him to where the activity was coming from.

As Glenn broke through the last bit of vines and greenery he came upon a clearing. From his location he could see a remote village, nestled ever so quietly among nature.

Unsophisticated and simple, Glenn observed a tremendous feeling of peace here.

Glenn drew nearer to gain a better perspective. His eyes scanned the tiny settlement for any information he could gather about its people.

He could see that the village sat inside of a clearing in the shape of a circle. The cleared land served as both a boundary for the colony and offered a hardened dirt floor, which supplied a foundation for the entire community.

The village was also dotted with shabby teepee style tents and large iron cooking pots, which were overflowing with steam.

Glenn saw villagers bustling about, hard at work on their daily chores. Despite the amount of work being done, it was relatively quiet here. There was barely any conversation between the villagers and when they did speak to one another, it was with the softest of voices.

Even though Glenn had only observed the group for a few moments, he understood these people had a mutual respect for one another, their community at large and their environment.

Some of the women walked around, balancing large bowls on their heads. Inside each basin was something different. One woman carried water, others food. The women would stop to distribute their goods into smaller bowls that were placed throughout the village. Other females congregated in small groups before their shabby tents, focusing their energies on sewing projects.

And as the women tended to things at home, Glenn noticed the men were nowhere to be found.

Only the elder members of the village, the women and children were here right now, taking care of the usual business of the day. All had their designated responsibilities within the hierarchy. It was the epitome of socialism.

As Glenn thought about how well this unassuming society managed itself, flora at the village's parameter moved in an unnatural way.

Lucky let out a slow, deep growl. "Grrrrrrrrrrrrr." His little body gave the warning of a dog much larger than he.

Glenn's eyes met the movement at the opposite end of the village.

An adult male tiger was adjusting his seat in the thicket. Unconcealed the whole time, the beast had been watching Glenn's every move. When it was evident that Glenn was aware of his presence, the animal tried to use his naturally intimidating demeanor to try to shake Glenn's confidence. He stood his large muscular lean body tall on all fours and began walking toward Glenn, suspiciously careful not to touch down inside the village border. His head hanging low, his giant paws carried him closer. Glenn knew this was no ordinary tiger. He took it as a sign. He was getting closer to something genuine.

The ferocious creature was nothing to worry about, although Lucky thought differently. "GRRRRRrrrrrrrrrrrrrrrrrr!!!!!!!!!!!"

"Take it easy, boy. It's o.k." Glenn tried to reassure him.

Glenn ignored the brute, turning himself and an ear away from the tiger.

Something else, more important, caught his attention.

He heard the sound of rushing water and turned to face it. It was about a quarter of a mile in the offing. Not only could its tremendous force be heard but it seemed to be summoning Glenn.

This is where the world's treasure in human form, which he was looking for, would surely be found or so he thought. For no other reason would it so intensely be guarded.

The village was intentionally situated in proximity to a massive, roaring river for practical purposes. Its water supply, vital to the tribe's survival, was within walking distance. It also served as a place to bathe and wash clothing and cooking supplies.

Glenn closed his eyes, letting the sound of the rushing water envelope his entire being. He was allowing the river to pull him closer. It did.

Once he opened his eyes he found himself standing along the bank of this thundering waterway. White-capped water crashed itself violently on top of humungous boulders set in the riverbed. The magnificent images it produced was a reminder of the powerful forces, which naturally exist in the universe.

Just across this raging entity and in between the splashes he caught glimpse of the matriarch of this village. She was the eldest member of the tribe, about eighty-eight years old. Years of experience were etched deep into her thick facial skin.

From where he was standing, Glenn could see her long silvery strands of hair gathered neatly in a ponytail and that her body was tanned like leather from the hot sun. This old woman was hard at work, slumped over, humbly washing clothing in the river water. She took articles of clothing from an endless mound, one by one, scrubbing them against a rock to remove the soil. From the smile on her face, it seemed as though she took great pride in her labor. Considering the pile she had next to her, she may have been doing laundry for the entire clan.

As Glenn stood quietly watching her from his rest, the old woman felt his overwhelming aura surround her. She stopped what she was doing and raised her head instinctively in Glenn's direction. Caught off guard by the outsider's unexpected visit, she froze in place, holding her stare at him.

"Who is he and what does he want with *me*?" Was her first thought.

Glenn could hear her thoughts. Understanding her fear, he gently held his gaze, accompanied by a reassuring smile.

All at once she could feel the entire jungle fill with an unearthly sense of peace and inspiration.

She and Glenn continued to lock eyes for a few moments before she was able to regain her composure. The truth of who he really was could never be masked for a woman this wise. It was all becoming clear for her now. Her day had finally come.

Once Glenn knew the old woman understood that he was not there to do her harm, he felt confident to move closer.

Before she could think about it, he was standing by her side.

He towered over her tiny frame. Yet, his presence did not intimidate her. It calmed her in a way she had never known before. Now that he was before her, they continued looking at each other. Her eyes traced his entire body from head to toe.

"Beautiful." She said softly, gazing up at him. Perfection radiated from every part of his body. She had no doubts who he was. Glenn could feel her allow herself to slip into a permanent sense of calm.

Only then did he bend himself at the middle, offering his hand gently. "Glenn." He said in a hushed tone, introducing himself.

Accepting his graciousness, the old woman bowed and introduced herself as well. "Wei-Xing Wang." Her voice was restrained but clear with perfect diction.

"It's nice to finally meet you Wei-Xing." Glenn said, almost in a whisper.

"You as well." She smiled. She knew Glenn had been called to her and that their encounter was meant to be. Now, the question that puzzled her was. "Why did Glenn need her?" Ironically, it was something she felt she had been preparing for her whole life.

The two stood with each other there in the vast, wild jungle seemingly relaxed that fate had finally taken them to this moment. But, as relaxed as they both were, they knew something "big" was ahead of them. Not even God himself had any idea of what the eventual outcome would be.

Wei-Xing then picked up a load of clean laundry and with her head, motioned for Glenn to follow her. She turned and walked over to a large, dead log, which had fallen across the river, serving as a bridge. She scampered across the slippery surface effortlessly.

Glenn was amused by the confidence in her petite body as she quickly traveled across the tree's trunk.

Afraid she would totally disappear into the thick wilderness, Glenn next made his way across the log to catch up with her.

When both were on the other side, Glenn followed Wei-Xing closely on a worn footpath, back to her home.

Both reserved conversation as they traced a foot trail through the complicated jungle. As they walked, Wei-Xing was mentally hard at work, processing experiences from the past and the present, trying to figure out how they played a part in what was happening right now.

As Glenn concentrated on Wei-Xing's quick yet physically perfect movements directly in front of him, the sound of a faint voice called his attention away.

"One day left." He heard in a low female voice, which sounded familiar.

As he turned to where the voice was coming from, he was confused. No one was there.

All he saw was the ferocious tiger, which had previously been eyeing him at the camp. The beast kept pace with them, walking parallel with Glenn and Wei-Xing, with only a ten-foot buffer of vegetation between them. His huge face cocked straight at Glenn as they advanced through the jungle. His body was lean and strong and his fur coat healthy and thick, painted a magnificent bright orange. Each one of his large, penetrating gorgeous eyes contained all the colors of a South Pacific sunset and didn't move an inch off of Glenn's form. He was the most regal member of the jungle's kingdom.

There was no further explanation as to where the voice came from.

As Glenn watched, the tiger now seemed to lose interest in him, and took a path deeper into the jungle, fading out of sight.

Interestingly, Wei-Xing never murmured a sound during the brief but fearsome encounter. She clearly knew the tiger was there but he was of no interest to her. She ignored him the whole time.

Glenn picked up on what unusual discipline Wei-Xing displayed. He saw how she demonstrated tremendous respect for all beings, including for the beast that probably didn't have her best interest at heart. She simply observed and processed the exchange as she maneuvered her way back to her village, never asking a single question, about whom they had met in the jungle or what they wanted.

"How are we doing Wei-Xing?" Glenn asked his guide who was intently focused on her footsteps.

Without missing a beat, Wei-Xing turned and smiled back at Glenn. She'd answered his question without saying a word.

CHAPTER 6 -- RELIGIOUS TURMOIL

As Father Matthew and Father Joseph hastily made their way up the narrow corridor, hoping no one would notice where they were coming from, some other clergymen walking in the opposite direction dodged past them as though they weren't even there.

All, unintentionally, displaying a look of worry and distress on their faces.

"What the..." Father Matthew whipped his head around as one priest trotted by.

He recognized the man as a typically reserved, Father Anthony. The priest was visibly emotional and trying to avoid making eye contact. He was so distraught he was talking out loud to himself.

"Oh my God I can't believe this..." Father Matthew heard him say in a low, slurred, detached voice.

This characteristically composed man of the cloth was at the brink of tears, holding his mouth with one hand, while inaudible murmurs of fear and sadness lifted off his tongue.

"Father Anthony, what's wrong?" Father Matthew shouted at him with great concern.

No response.

Father Anthony carried on down the hall, stumbling, his cries echoing along the walls and the ceiling of the passage, but trailing off as he made distance between them.

"What's wrong with...?" Father Joseph couldn't even finish his sentence before both heard screams coming from the Pope's private quarters.

"God no, please have mercy upon us!!!" Father Matthew and Father Joseph heard one of the pope's nurses yell from the top of her lungs. Both men charged up the hallway to see what was going so wrong in their normally sedate world.

Just as the two made it to the source of the pandemonium, the doors to the Pope's chamber unexpectedly smashed open. The sound of it and the chaos, which followed, rumbled like thunder through the building.

A gurney, carrying the Pope's lifeless body shot out of the room like a cannon. "Oh my dear Jesus!" Exclaimed Father Joseph. He instantly jumped back so as not to be run over.

Emergency personnel were on either side of the bed, running alongside it, as they wheeled the apparatus at top speed down the hallway, toward the Vatican's private hospital. The small, plastic, black wheels at the bottom of the rickety cot were shaking uncontrollably and turning revolutions faster than the speed of light. A trail of the Pope's nurses and doctors stampeded behind. The whole scene unfolded as if in slow motion before Father Joseph's eyes. Even the ambient sound of what was happening distorted to a slowed, tempo. It seemed too coincidental, considering what he had just learned from Father Matthew.

"He's white as a lamb's fleece." Father Joseph murmured.

"He's dead." Father Matthew said plainly.

"We don't know that yet!" Father Joseph snapped at his friend.

"Oh yes we do, Joseph!" Insisted Father Matthew. "And we know what is to follow, as well!" He frowned.

Losing his temper with Father Matthew, Father Joseph clenched his fist and raised it toward his fellow priest, roaring, "This world was a perfect creation and beauty exists in every one of us!" He barked. "If your scroll is true and this denotes the beginning of the end, then there is much work to be done. I am certain that God's work, in its holiest form is being done somewhere on this earth and as God is my witness, I will not let this world go to hell without a fight!" Father Joseph stormed off, leaving his pessimistic friend behind.

At this point, Father Joseph knew he'd bought into the prophecies of the scroll. He wasn't sure he did until now. Now that the Pope was dead, or at least he thought he was, the predictions in the scroll seemed a little too coincidental.

A frightened and desperate Father Joseph walked a distance away, so as not to come in contact with anyone else. He wanted space to wrap his mind around the magnanimous possibility that Father Matthew was right, that this could signify the beginning of the end of man's existence. It was almost too much to take.

As he stood there, contemplating what this all meant, he tilted his head upward, toward the heavens, looking for guidance from his king.

"Please help me serve you, Lord. I don't know where to begin. I don't know what to do." He wasn't even sure at this moment, what was happening was connected to what Father Matthew showed him. Rubbing his head, "Oh my God, I am so confused."

Just then Father Joseph rested his head backward against the wall.

An endless angelic scene, spanning the entirety of the ceiling, lay high above. In all the colors of the spectrum, the story within the artwork depicted a peaceful and abundant earth, lovingly caring for its children. The earth's children, in return, loving and caring for each other and Mother Earth.

As he engrossed himself in the scene, Father Joseph's bushy, black and gray eyebrows wrinkled together and tears fell from his mature brown eyes. He must have studied this impressive creation at least a thousand times before, but never did its message touch him so deeply. It was as if he were truly seeing it for the very first time. As he turned round and round with his head cocked back, straining his neck muscles, he scrutinized each detail of the painting and realized. "That was what could have been, but what was lost."

More thoughts flooded his mind as he continued to scan the work. "Can we ever find our way back to this place?" He asked himself aloud.

Softly he pleaded with his savior. "Oh my dear Jesus in heaven, let all of mankind see the beauty of his own strength, once more." With increasing sadness in his voice he offered himself up to the Lord. "I am but one man, but I will give an army's worth of heart to stop what is about to befall this world."

Putting his hands together in prayer, he held his hands upward, toward the ceiling and begged God, “Please let me help you do your will!”

He knew it was time to be silent now, he knew God heard him as he hears all the souls of the world. Father Joseph also knew he would now need to keep his eyes, ears and heart open, to allow God to speak to him. It was his personal belief that God communicated with his flock in a multitude of complex and profound ways, through people, coincidences and circumstances. Hearing God’s messages would now be crucial, there wasn’t much time left, he reminded himself.

“All I need to do is trust my instincts and follow my heart and I will be doing God’s work.” He said, trying to convince himself he was sensitive enough to interpret the will of the Lord. “I promise you, Oh Lord, no matter the degree of difficulty or at what cost, I will give all that I am for you and this glorious world you have shared with us.”

Father Joseph’s face started to spasm as he loudly and unapologetically began sobbing, like a child. “Please Lord, please, show me the way, let me help!” His eyes still fixed to the masterpiece above.

Father Joseph was now satisfied he had offered himself as completely and generously as he could to his savior. He knew the good Lord understood his heart and would ultimately decide whether he would be used in his plan. He felt whole inside.

Exhausted from this emotional torture, Father Joseph allowed himself to finally relax his focal grasp of the painting. He slowly lowered his eyes from the ceiling, down the side of one of the walls. Something else now caught his attention.

A huge portrait of the current Pontiff, created in unusually brightly colored oils, hung there.

Father Joseph had long revered his Pope as one of the greatest religious leaders of modern times and felt he was one of the most personally inspiring human beings he had ever known. He walked over to the painting to get a better look.

The man in the painting held a world title but was really just a mere mortal, like anyone else. What set him apart was that he held himself and his personal calling to a higher standard than most. It was a discipline Father Joseph and people around the globe admired. Christianity had been revolutionized under this man's influence. During his reign, he was known to be heavy on forgiveness and understanding and light on condemnation.

It was an attitude the devout and religious critics alike gravitated toward and the church saw parishioner participation rise because of it. The common man felt he had a shot at heaven under this new, loving philosophy. It gave the masses a sense of hope.

Prior generations had only learned to fear an angry, punishing God under past leaders. They were sick of feeling scared.

As Father Joseph continued to gaze at the painting, he was pleased to see it captured the essence of the Pope's naturally peace-loving disposition.

He remembered how much he loved this man as he fixated even more intently on the religious leader's well-drawn face.

"Are you still with us?" He begged in a now raspy voice.

The Pope's silent eyes seemed to have a life of their own and they stared back at him desperately. It was as if the Pope had something to say, but was sentenced to silence within the artwork.

Father Joseph was shocked when, continuing to stare at the painting, he received an answer.

"No, he's not." He heard a female voice say bluntly.

He lowered his eyes further, just below the lowest edge of the ornate, gold frame, which housed the Pope's picture.

Standing there, an attractive, svelte nurse in uniform. She was smoking a cigarette. A cloud of smoke hung around her head like a protective fog, slightly disguising her facial features.

He adjusted his vision to see who it was. Upon closer inspection, he didn't recognize her. He couldn't remember ever seeing her at the Vatican before. After all, he knew every member of the Pope's personal medical staff. She wasn't one of them.

Again, she spoke with callousness. "He's dead. So no, he's no longer with us."

She watched as the shockingly sad information gripped him, as she knew it would.

Father Joseph's expression faded to a blank stare after hearing such devastating news. He felt like he was losing his balance.

The woman gave him the once-over, hoping he would fall.

"How did he die?" He questioned emotionally, just above a whisper.

She waited until he composed himself.

"Let's just say, it was just his time to go." She replied coldly, wearing an insensitive grin.

Without missing a beat, the nurse dropped her cigarette to the floor and snuffed it out with her designer high heel shoe. She stepped out of the smoggy mass containing her and proceeded closer to Father Joseph.

"The Pope's successor has already been named." She said harassingly, waiting to see if he'd snap and maybe even ask her who it was.

Joseph blinked uncontrollably, trying to process all of this.

"That's impossible." He said totally confused.

"There has to be a whole…" He was unable to continue explaining protocol to her. He was too devastated.

"Want to know who it is?" She leaned in with a smile, egging him on.

Father Joseph had to look away from this taunting bitch to prevent himself from reacting. "Why would she act like this, is she crazy?" He thought to himself.

He didn't answer her.

"Who are you, anyway?" He asked.

Joseph again raised his eyes up to the Pope's picture. He was looking for guidance, if not from the Pope himself, then from his spirit. Memories of the years they spent together flooded his thoughts. His mind started reeling with information overload and questions he wanted answers to. The Pope was dead and another was already poised to take his place? How could this be? Does this have anything to do with what Father Matthew told him?

It was too much for the priest to take in, in such a short a period of time.

"Could this really be happening?" He asked himself. He struggled to reconcile this latest development and what he had recently learned from that alleged secret scroll Father Matthew showed him.

Bringing her face even closer into Father Joseph's personal space, the nurse delivered what couldn't be worse news.

"Cardinal Victor will head the Vatican now." She said in a victorious tone. "Just thought you'd be interested to know." She added, sardonically.

Father Joseph's eyes immediately crashed to the floor. Suddenly feeling a little nauseous, he put his hand to his stomach.

Father Joseph knew of a Cardinal Victor. Last year, on June the 7th, the now deceased Holy Father formally created eight new Cardinals and inducted them into the College of Cardinals. The new Cardinals were from 5 different countries. Cardinal Victor was one of them. He was former Archbishop of Rhemenia, a newly formed kingdom in the Middle East most knew little about. Originally part of Dabhadia, rebel forces helped it's people split from the country and become a nation with it's own menacing government.

Rhemenia was a fledging regime infamous for terrorism, dictatorial rule and genocide. This is where Victor was from. Joseph had met him only a handful of times and never truly felt comfortable around him.

Having managed to finally truly disturb Father Joseph the nurse appeared appeased. In an instant, she pivoted on one stiletto and started walking away, humming an unfamiliar melody. She was satisfied for now.

"What's your name?" Joseph called out to her before she vanished.

She hummed a few more bars to her tune.

"Falene!" She yelled back to him, still in transit. "Falene!"

As she made distance between the two, the sound of her high heels smashed along the hard marble floor as she made her way up the hall to the Vatican hospital. Just as she turned the corner to its entrance, she looked back at Father Joseph and smiled fiendishly, before disappearing.

"Why that son of a b…," He stopped short of finishing his sentence.

"Who was that?" Asked Father Matthew, who was quickly approaching.

"I don't believe I know." He answered, still staring up the hall where the stranger took cover.

"Do you know a Falene?" Father Joseph asked his brother.

"Falene? No, I don't know anyone around here by that name." Father Matthew said, looking in the direction she went.

"Come on, let's go!" Father Matthew was tugging at Father Joseph's sleeve, pulling him in the direction of the Vatican hospital. "Let's find out what's going on."

Father Joseph dug his heels in, changing the subject. "Listen. Matthew. I want to go back and take a look at that scroll again." He debated, pulling in the opposite direction.

"It's too risky, Joseph, I won't do it!" Father Matthew refused, continuing a tug-of-war with Father Joseph's apparel.

Wearing a determined face and in a serious voice, Father Joseph spoke to Father Matthew in a manner not to be disregarded. "Oh yes you will." Father Joseph gave one last yank and broke free of Father Matthew's grasp and started walking toward the room at the far end of the hall.

Father Matthew chased after his headstrong confidant. "What do you think you're doing Joseph?!"

"Whatever I can." Father Joseph said, keeping a sharp eye on his target, his feet now pounding forward with even more determination. His robust frame was like a locomotive hauling its way down the hall.

With all the power in his arms, Father Joseph burst back into the secret room with Father Matthew in hot pursuit. The door swung open and smashed against the wall, creating a loud crash, which echoed down the hallway. A fearful Father Matthew kept pace with his persistent friend in order to try to keep a lid on things in this room.

"I want you to read to me what was on the left side of that map!" Father Joseph yelled at Father Matthew, waving his index finger impatiently at the desk.

The paranoid priest hurriedly shut the door behind them and got between Father Joseph and the desk, serving as a blockade. He held his finger to his lips as he looked up at this erupting volcano of a man, "Shhhhhhhh!!!!!" He admonished. "Others may hear you and wonder what you're talking about!" He chastised.

Father Joseph crossed his left arm in front of his chest and with one long sweep, shoved Father Matthew's slight frame out of his way. "It doesn't matter who hears what, anymore." He quipped.

Father Joseph extended his hand outward, palm up to the priest. "Hand over the key."

Wearing a look of defeat on his face, Father Matthew again, pulled the key from his inner pocket and dropped it into Father Joseph's hand.

"Thank you."

Father Joseph couldn't get into the drawer fast enough. His hands were shaking as he pulled the scroll from the bottom of the drawer and unrolled it on top of the desk. A cloud of dust exploded into the air as the document unraveled across the desktop. Father Matthew carefully placed a candle by the side of the cloth, to provide some light for Father Joseph's aging eyes. Father Joseph stood there in silence for a few moments. He was studying the scroll for himself, hoping to make sense of it. But, the foreign scrawl was still beyond his comprehension. He left the translating to Father Matthew.

"Read to me what it says on the left hand side of this document." He charged.

Against his better judgment, Father Matthew came around to the other side of the desk, where his concerned friend stood. He dragged the drippy, vanilla candle closer. Running his finger down the left hand side of the map, he kept track of each word as he nervously read aloud. He drew in a long, deep breath, before he began carefully converting ancient Aramaic into English. His eyes scanned the words, before he recited them back to Father Joseph.

"The true depth of man's soul will remain secret until it faces its ultimate challenge." He said. He looked at Father Joseph as if he were frightened to read further.

"Continue." Ordered Father Joseph. Father Matthew returned his eyes to the document.

"The human spirit is capable of great suffering and great triumph and the time will come for it to rise or fall amidst the shadow of its creator." He read on. "There will be great affliction before the earth may know world peace." His voice starting to crack. "When the victorious one stands alone, it will signal the end or the rebirth of the world."

"Stop!" demanded Father Joseph. "Read that last part again."

Obligingly, Father Matthew repeated the statement. "When the victorious one stands alone, it will signal the end or the rebirth of the world."

He looked at Father Joseph for a clue.

"Hmmmmm…"

"What is it?" Asked Father Matthew.

"I'm not sure if…"

"What!" Father Matthew begged.

"That nurse you saw me talking to." He paused shaking his head free from his thoughts. "I got a bad feeling about her. I wonder if she's somehow… Oh, never mind. I'm probably reaching."

"What is it." Father Matthew moved closer with his words.

"She said that Cardinal Victor of Rhemenia has been selected to take over, now that the Holy Father has passed on. I mean I'd not heard he would be our leaders successor, but… Do you think that "victor-ious" could imply the name Victor, in that statement?"

Not even considering it a possibility, Father Matthew brushed off Father Joseph's idea. "I think you're reaching Joseph. They mean victor, as in a victorious one. It's not used as a proper name here."

Shrugging off his own paranoia, Father Joseph redirected the unconvinced priest.

"OK then, forget it. What else does it say?"

"OK, this is the last line." Father Matthew read slowly and emphasized each word, so as not to miss anything.

"I'm ready." Father Joseph braced himself.

"The fate of the world lies with the purest of heart."

"What does that mean?!" Father Joseph lost his composure. His eyes immediately darted from place to place as he scanned his brain for every possibility of what this could mean. The baffled priest appeared to be at the brink of a nervous breakdown as Father Matthew just stared at him, unable to be of assistance.

"Do *you* have any idea of what it means?" He now locked eyes with Father Matthew. "Does the purest of heart lie with a human being or could we be overlooking maybe an animal on this earth, a dog say, which is among the loyalist of all God's beasts?"

They both cracked-up, realizing they were over thinking it.

Father Joseph started his trademark pace back and forth across the floor, scratching the top of his head and talking to himself.

"We know it means something, but what, is the mystery!"

Father Matthew watched helplessly as his longtime friend wracked his brain for answers. Then another idea flew out of Joseph's head.

"Was it our dearly departed Pope that possessed the purest of heart? He changed the world for the better before he died, he helped man to know God!"

Father Matthew just shrugged his shoulders. "I have no idea about anything anymore. I don't know what's real, what's in my imagination or anything else. I'm tired. We're never going to be able to figure this out and why even try at this point?"

He was now beginning to become frightened, himself. Father Joseph clearly considered it a personal mission to see to it that the world was saved. Matthew, on the other hand, didn't feel they could be effective at this late date. What he didn't realize was that half way around the world another had the same idea.

Father Joseph walked back over to the table and looked over the foreign writing, again. Although he couldn't read the writing, the words Father Matthew spoke to him were now permanently emblazoned in his mind. He lowered his head and allowed his fingers to caress the crudely drawn map on the cloth.

"There is hope." He said. Then lifting his face toward Father Matthew, he exclaimed. "I don't know how I know, but I know there is hope! There is!"

Suddenly, the newly familiar sound of high heels obnoxiously smashing against hard marble reached their eardrums.

Father Joseph rolled up the scroll feverishly and shoved it into his pants waist. He wasn't about to leave this precious document behind, ever again.

Two voices could be heard in the hallway, a female's, accompanied by a male's. Father Matthew pressed his ear against the door as he heard the footsteps stop just outside the door.

"That's Cardinal Victor I hear." He whispered to Joseph so they couldn't hear him.

"What are they saying?" Father Joseph tiptoed over to the door to eavesdrop.

Both men could hear the woman give a subservient Cardinal Victor instruction. "You're going to go here." Victor's feet could be heard shuffling across the floor to get closer to her to see what she was referring to.

"See here on the map?" Both men could hear the woman tap the map she was holding with one of her long fingernails. "This place here at this longitude and this latitude. Do you see it?"

Cardinal Victor barely answered her. "Mmnhh-Hmmnh."

"That's that nurse Falene that was talking to me earlier, I recognize her voice." Father Joseph whispered back to Father Matthew.

A terrified Father Matthew's eyes grew big enough to say, "Shut up!"

The slightly muffled dialogue continued. "Search the area, find what we're looking for, destroy it and… whoever has it!" They heard her dictate.

Behind the massive wooden door, the men's brows furrowed with concern as they listened to the confidential and diabolical conversation.

"It'll be my pleasure." Victor answered, accepting his assignment.

Father Joseph and Father Matthew could hear papers rustle between the two before one pair of footsteps ambitiously made their way up the hall. By the sound of their weight, they belonged to Victor.

Both priests turned to each other in disbelief. "What's going on?" Father Matthew said audibly.

Then they remembered there was a second pair of footsteps, belonging to a woman, possibly Falene, that hadn't yet left. They turned their heads forward, as if trying to feel what was behind the door.

"Is she still there?" Father Joseph mouthed the words to Matthew.

Father Matthew shrugged his shoulders.

On the other side, a set of bluish-green eyes accentuated with thick black mascara, stared hard at the door.

CHAPTER 7 -- RECOGNIZING DESTINY

Brother David back at the monastery stood tall and confidently after prayer. He always felt better about the world, his place in it and life after he devoted a good amount of time to prayer. It gave him a fresh, renewed sense of purpose. He genuinely liked it.

David had a slight but strong frame, a shaved head and piercing blue eyes. He wore what everyone else here wore, a modest brown hooded robe tied with a rope at the waist and brown, well-worn sandals. Through his robe, you could see his sinewy body.

For weeks now, he contemplated what he had recently learned from the scroll and what had frightened him and Brother John so deeply. Being a patient and obedient man of God, he knew to take time to properly digest and understand what he'd learned. He wouldn't rush to judgment or force an explanation upon himself to satisfy his intellect and emotions.

He also considered that the scroll must have fatefully come into his hands for a reason. He accepted and welcomed that. Now the challenge was to figure out what to do about it and what the proper path was. He spent weeks looking for the answer to come from God. What was his mission? What should he do first?

That's when he realized his mistake.

"*I'm* supposed to decide what to do." He said, pointing to himself, the corner of his mouth curling upward at one end. It finally dawned on him.

"The reason this responsibility fell to me, is because I know what to do, even though I don't know what to do yet." He realized, how blind he'd been this whole time. "The answer was there before me the whole time, I just didn't see it. Now, I know what to do."

David realized although God sends us signs and signals to help us find our path, the true answer to our destiny lies deep inside our souls.

"The answer is always there, so why do we find it so hard to find at times?" He wondered why the obvious often eluded us.

The young but sensible monk focused himself before his philosophical thoughts lured him into unproductive confusion. It was easy to do. He knew better.

Brother David reminded himself that the road to fate is always present but is often paved with temptation and obstacles, which can throw a man off his intended course. As long as he made conscious decisions to "do the right thing" when various situations presented themselves, he would be guaranteed to expediently navigate his way to his life's fortune. Everyone had the same shot, a shot at a uniquely glorious life. That was just the way this magnificent world was. Each person was equally loved and given the opportunity for greatness by God.

David understood God was always present in man's life, but man had to decide how to help himself before he could receive the gift of his true destiny.

Man's challenge while on earth, to navigate the mysterious maze of his life. He did this by selecting good choices for himself during his life. Within those good choices were hidden clues to help lead man to experience and understand certain things about the world and about his life, which ultimately would help man understand what his role is on earth. Once that was revealed, it was man's job to see his unique mission through. By doing so, man would fulfill his destiny.

Once Brother David reviewed in his mind what he knew to be the universal laws of his worldly home, he was mentally and spiritually prepared to begin his mission. Brother David knew there wasn't much time left and needed to start his quest immediately.

"So, what is it I need to do first?" He quietly asked himself. "What's the first step in this journey I am about to begin?" Now speaking out loud, looking up to the ceiling. "I am ready to be your servant, God!"

Just then the wind, ever so lightly, blew the scroll, which was lying on the floor, toward him. The breeze was just strong enough to brush the scroll up against his ankle. He looked down at it, and then it dawned on him. He whisked the fragile document up off the floor and held it up to his face. He smiled as if he'd just been given a little gift from up above.

"Thank you." He whispered to it.

He dashed out of the room and charged down a long, imposing hallway with the scroll still in hand.

Brother John, who was walking in the opposite direction, fearing he could be body-slammed by Brother David, put both hands up along with one knee to brace himself from a collision.

"Where are you going in such a hurry, Brother David?" He said with both eyes half closed, hands still up in a self-defense position.

Without breaking his stride, he shouted the great news to his friend. "Italy!"

"Wait! Italy?" Brother John hollered, as he chased after his frantic friend.

"I haven't time, Brother John, I'm on a mission!"

Brother David was already in his room "speed packing" what few possessions he had in this world. He stuffed a robe, second pair of sandals, a cross and some food in a sack and cinched it closed. He tightly wrapped the drawstring around two fingers and flung the sack over his shoulder. He was ready.

He made a dash for the door but was blockaded by a confused Brother John.

"Wait! Wait! Wait!" Brother John insisted, wheezing from his sprint. He forced Brother David back into his room to answer a few questions before letting him leave.

"What do you mean you're going to Italy?" He had to take a deep breath in between every other word to catch his breath. "And why?"

With a look of satisfaction on his face, Brother David delivered the obvious answer. "Isn't that where this came from?" He held up the scroll.

"Well, yes. But so what? Why must you go there?" Brother John asked.

"To return it to its rightful home, that's why. It's the right thing to do." He replied with conviction. "That's got to be the first step here. Return this!"

"What do you expect to find when you get there, my dear friend?"

"The next step!" Brother David informed as if it were a no-brainer.

He clarified a bit. "I'm not sure *what* I'll find there, but I do know whatever it is will take me one step closer to my destiny. I will answer this calling."

Brother John smiled with understanding. He knew what he meant and he wasn't going to stand in his way. David would take things further than he ever did and he was grateful the burden had fallen to someone so capable.

"OK then, David." The two smiled at each other. There was a sense of mystery, of relief and of excitement all at once for them.

Getting that out of the way, Brother David walked over to his trusted confidant and sincerely thanked him for the years of inspiration, guidance and friendship he'd given him.

"I want you to know that I've studied you all the years I've been here." He told Brother John. "I chose to study you because of how you effortlessly allow God to reveal himself through you."

Brother John's face gleamed with pride.

"Everything from the way you live your life, to how you treat others and how generously you give of yourself has all been inspiring to my heart." He elaborated. "It has provided me with insight into what it is to truly live a fulfilling life. Because of you, I know how to better understand my role in this world and how to make it a better place. Thank you for that, please know that you have changed my life for the better." David said, as he touched Brother John's arm.

Then he looked into his teacher's eyes. "I've taken a part of you into my heart John and now I'm ready to go into the world and use what I've learned from you to help find my destiny. *You* did that for *me*."

He made Brother John understand what he had done for him. Brother John knew from David's words, he meant what he said. Brother David's words made John feel as though he had triggered a domino effect of goodness in the world. There was no better calling.

Brother John then looked down as Brother David let go of his arm. John knew the time had come for he and this man's paths to part.

John placed his right hand on David's shoulder. "It's one thing to try to live a good life, but when you've inspired another to do the same based on your example and the world becomes a better place because of it, it is the highest compliment one can ever receive." He told David. "I believe in you David. I truly believe in you."

"I want you to take my bible with you on your journey." He put his well-read bible in David's hands, but the shy monk felt embarrassed to take it.

"No John I can't."

"Take it!" He forced the good book back into David's grasp, wrapping his rigid fingers around the hard cover. "I want you to remember me always David and that I believe in you. Now go!" He pointed toward the door. "Go I said. Go!"

David took the bible, squashed it into his sack with the rest of his things and began his exit out of the monastery. John was sure he would never to see the young monk again.

Looking out from the open-air balcony, which overlooked a majestic landscape, Brother John quietly watched as his friend made a treacherous trek down the mountain's steep slope. It seemed only seconds before he was out of view, marching courageously toward his destiny.

"Good luck, my friend." Brother John said compassionately as his eyes followed his trail. He wished good luck for his friend even though he knew he didn't need it.

Brother David had everything he needed now to fulfill his destiny and do God's work.

CHAPTER 8 -- WORLD CHAOS

Unbeknown to Vatican officials as well as Father Joseph and Father Matthew the fact of the Pope's death was no longer a secret. Someone had leaked it to the press.

Now media outlets from around the world were salivating like vultures just beyond the Vatican walls.

Priests peering out of windows from their protected fortress could see that hundreds of live trucks equipped with satellite capability had descended upon Rome. An army of journalists, photographers and field producers from news bureaus across the globe were surrounding the Vatican, like they were about to storm it.

The press could be an intimidating beast when it wanted information, especially on a story this big. They wanted answers yesterday.

Aggressive broadcasters perched themselves outside the Vatican's limit, besieging anyone entering or exiting the compound with questions about the details of the Pope's death. Even maintenance crews were interrogated about what they knew, microphones and tape recorders shoved in their faces.

These reporters were assigned to a story that could make or break their careers and they knew it. This story had all the sex appeal anyone could ask for. A dead Pope, an apparent attempt by Vatican officials to delay that information reaching a world full of followers and a newly named Pope no one knew much about. For a reporter, that's a story straight from broadcasting-heaven.

Reporters with any information confirmed by church officials, would hit the air, mere minutes or seconds later in a live shot. The idea was to make air before the other networks and for a journalist this could mean the difference between winning and not winning an Emmy that year. The competition was fierce.

The sensational news of the Pope's death splashed across television sets, on every continent. Live pictures from the Vatican were broadcast worldwide with a graphic crawl along the bottom of the screen reading, “Pope dies. Successor named.”

It was major news and an “event” in the business. Networks worldwide carried round-the-clock team coverage of the story most dubbed, “History in the making.” The networks could get away with it, because they had their audience hooked. Lay people, especially devout Catholics, in every corner of the world remained glued to their sets, to find out the, who, what, where, when, why’s and how’s. Those who weren’t home crammed into local café’s and pubs to catch the latest updates on television. No matter where one looked, not a single daily paper could be found. There was a buzz in Rome that reverberated across continents.

That’s when things became even more chaotic in Rome as curiosity-seekers and religious fanatics alike flocked to be near where history was unfolding. Everyone knew it wasn’t long before they found out the name of the Pope’s successor. That’s what everyone was waiting for, because it could mean big changes, worldwide.

People could be heard in the streets asking one another. “Any idea who will replace the Pope? Do we know who the Pope’s replacement is, yet?” And of course the obligatory question. “What’s the latest update from the Vatican?” That’s the line news organizations lived for.

Strangers suddenly found something in common to converse about.

Who would it be? That was the question of the day. Everyone wanted to be there for the big announcement. It was like being a part of something larger.

While reporters lay siege to the Vatican, things elsewhere seemed to be falling apart as well.

Globally, weather seemed to take on a life of its own. Freakish weather systems with an apparently evil objective developed around the world. There was an inordinate amount of natural disasters occurring, touching every race and every religion.

Tragedy was becoming a common ground for people around the planet.

A collision of four storms in the Atlantic Ocean created a hurricane off the Northeast coast of the United States. The weather pattern developed so quickly, there was little time to warn those at sea. Even those lucky enough to receive advanced warning couldn't make it back in time to avoid getting caught in the mega-storm's path.

Eighteen fishing boats in service in the New Bedford, Massachusetts area at the time of the storm went down. Entire crews on each presumed to have gone down with their vessels.

The storm wiped out dozens of fishing boats in the surrounding areas, which had a considerable impact on the local fishing industry as a result.

Just about half of the seaworthy vessels between Maryland and Maine were destroyed from the violent surf and wind. This meant the owners of those boats were unable to work to support and feed themselves and their families.

In the Northeast, harvesting the ocean was a major contributor to the local economy. Now, that economy was compromised. The unemployment rate began to skyrocket in these areas. With the heightened unemployment rate and tremendous property damage in the area came another problem. An increase in domestic violence calls to police. Out of work fishermen were taking their frustrations out on their wives and children. The disaster was snowballing into more complex problems.

Thousands of miles away on the opposite coast, California was dealing with a mess of its own.

Beneath the Pacific Ocean, in depths only recently chartered by marine biologists, nineteen active volcanoes forming a circular shape had been discovered. The discovery had scientists baffled. No movement or activity had previously been detected from the formations and they were so deep in the ocean no one ever knew something so potentially dangerous was there.

Fresh studies proved there had been no substantial activity from the volcanoes for millions of years.

That is until now.

Pressure from inside two of the volcanoes had blown holes through its sides, superheating the salt water for eighty-five miles in each direction and killing off all marine life in its wake.

The World Geological Society was turned on its ear.

Not an inch of the nearby California coastline was spared from sea carnage. The sight of dead fish, whales, sharks, dolphins and octopuses bobbing lifelessly on the water's surface and washing ashore were making people sick to their stomachs. It was like an unfair mass murder of these helpless creatures.

At the same time, the ocean was churning up important information with its dead. Among the corpses, to the bittersweet fascination of biological experts, the remains of species never before discovered or long believed extinct. It was truly a smorgasbord of sea life. As sad as this situation was scientists saw it as a tremendous learning opportunity. Large bulldozers and medical equipment were hauled to the shore to harvest any viable remains. Whole or parts of sea creatures were brought to medical storage facilities for experimentation.

The stench of the rotting fish wafted inland for about five miles. Residents could be seen walking around their own property wearing surgical masks to cut the odor, which was strong enough to take one's breath away. No one could get away from it.

Nothing like this had ever happened in the United States, or anywhere else. It was truly bizarre.

As usual the insatiable media was present.

The sky was dotted with News Choppers gathering all the gory and sensational images. Enterprising photojournalists hung themselves on the outside of the helicopters by harnesses to get the most creative shots from the air. Anything this graphic and disturbing was a guaranteed ratings booster and they wanted to be the ones to bring home the money shots.

News stations all over the world would exploit the hell out of this story.

The best video would be run and rerun in show after show after show. The most disturbed by these pictures, of course, those in the United States.

News gathering and broadcasting was big business here. Millions of dollars could be made upon a single image, as long as it was sensational enough, people would keep tuning in to see it over and over and over. Censoring was not in the storyline here.

The American fishing industry was taking yet another financial and emotional beating from Mother Nature. The media figuratively fed upon the dead carcasses washing up on shore to add insult to injury.

In yet another part of the world the people of Jordan, although compassionate toward the situations on both American coasts, had their own big problems.

An earthquake registering an 8.0 on the Richter scale rocked the capitol city of Amman.

Large craters opened up in the streets, swallowing cars and even buildings. People dove into humungous caverns immediately after it happened in search of their relatives and friends. It was pandemonium.

Over two hundred people were missing and emergency crews were overwhelmed with calls. Anguished personnel were out conducting recovery missions all across the capitol city. The injured and maimed sent to local hospitals where they awaited news of the fate of their loved ones.

These unpredictable storms and natural disasters worldwide not only destroyed property and killed innocent people. It fragmented families, crushed communities and took the will of the people along with it.

It hurt survivors beyond comprehension.

A remote camera mounted to the top of one of the buildings still standing in Amman, caught a glimpse of a little girl who had walked into the camera's frame. She was about six years old with long, dark, curly hair and a pudgy belly protruding from the bottom of her shirt.

She walked alone, dragging a blanket and dirty teddy bear in her left hand. Crying, she stammered aimlessly along the cracked and crumbly street, with no one to comfort or shelter her from the nearing rainstorm. As quickly as she entered the frame, she left.

This was just one of many children left parentless by the quake. This camera would record and show many more to the world as time passed.

Each child told a heartbreaking story with his or her scruffy appearance and distraught behavior.

Another child, a boy looking to be about ten years old, ran naked with a dog into the arch of a doorway to get out of the rain. The boy crouched down on the bare cement, to keep warm. His dutiful pup, doing his best to cuddle up against him. The dog appeared to be trying to position himself to serve as a blanket against the boy's cold, wet body. They waited out the storm together, as friends.

The camera a good distance away, managed to capture a great big smile on the boy's face, as he patted his dog on the head for being a good boy. Perhaps he didn't understand how dire his circumstances were and if he did he still had room in his heart to love a loyal friend. As the dog sat, facing the camera's angle a dog tag sparkled in the sunlight.

The boy wrapped his fingers around the tag. As he did, the dog's name reflected toward the camera's lens. "Pal" it read in Arabic. The boy's mouth could be seen mouthing the word. He smiled again at his new buddy. They both knew they were indeed lucky.

It was a tender moment that lasted several minutes. For those who saw, it represented true spiritual triumph over tragedy.

What no one expected was for this beautiful moment to be cut dramatically short by a pitiless woman who suddenly turned up in the frame with the boy.

Although the camera never captured her face it was quite obvious from the shape beneath her hooded robe that it was a woman. She walked to and fro the doorway, watching the boy. As she did, the boy continued his open display of affection for his small dog.

Her movements suggested she wasn't happy. The boy's dog then instinctually stood on all fours, bearing teeth and hackles raised. There was no audio, but it didn't take a rocket scientist to see the dog was now growling, in an effort to warn their visitor that he was a formidable opponent.

The child's faithful companion stood guard until the woman finally left them alone.

"Who was she? What did she want? And, why would she be so agitated by what she saw?" Those were the questions floating around in the minds of all who saw the video.

One could only imagine who and where the parents of these helpless children were. Were they were alive or dead? And without them, what chance did the little ones have of survival.

People around the world were awe struck as these cataclysmic events unfolded before their eyes via television. One breaking news story followed another, each one more unbelievable than the next. It seemed surreal to the masses. What would be next, an asteroid hitting the Sphinx?

Although many around the world bonded because of the tragedies and out of earnest compassion for their fellow citizen, the devastating events still weren't enough to move world leaders toward peace.

To them these events were mere unfortunate coincidences. Not enough to prevent the major superpowers of the world from declaring war on one another.

Aggressions continued to escalate between the United States and the Middle East and between other nations at odds with each other religiously, politically, culturally and in every other fathomable way.

The question on everyone's mind was simply, "Why was all this happening at once?"

CHAPTER 9

FORCING ANGELS FROM THE RUINS

Why could only be answered by one person and he was now following Wei-Xing back to her home.

Her slight frame made its way through the thick brush effortlessly. She moved like a phantom in broad daylight. As Glenn trained his eyes intently on his guide, he squinted. For how quickly she was making time, she made little to no noise. As she tore through the surrounding plants and vines, not even the snapping of leaves could be heard. It was unbalanced.

"God this little creature's fast!" He said, gasping for breath. His legs were still straining to keep up. "And I get a body like this to do the job?"

"Glad to see someone has a sense of humor!" He hollered skyward. He would have laughed if he had time.

As Glenn continued his harried hike back with Wei-Xing, he could feel himself being called to the larger picture.

Dizzy, he held his head with both hands as he moved through the jungle. Millions of images came flooding into his mind. He did the only thing he could do.

"Stop!" He called out to Wei-Xing.

Her feet fell still upon his command.

Then he stopped, shut his eyes and gave in to it.

His head remaining in both hands, his eyes closed, he looked into his mind's eye, surveying the world. The heart of man, beast, land and sea was heavy.

His eyes darted back and forth, following the many images and sounds in his head. Awful and endless, they swirled about like psychotic fireflies. Scenes of destruction, cries for help. So many needed so much.

Unlike before, things were different.

All the sights and scenes were the same, all the cries familiar. But now, wherever Glenn turned his attention, individuals stood out from the crowd. They were set apart from the ruins and from others. They were seen in a solid state, everyone else was transparent.

"What's so different about them?" Glenn asked. He wasn't sure he was seeing correctly.

Granted, he saw only but a few, but they were special in some way.

As quickly as the flash came, it went. Glenn was back to the present.

He stood there for a few seconds to regain his balance and collect his thoughts. It was critical at this point to remember everything he experienced. There was a reason for it.

"It's O.K. Wei-Xing, sorry about that. Go ahead." He rubbed his head.

She did as he requested and the two continued on with their journey.

As he followed closer behind Wei-Xing he did his best to relax his body.

He kept his thoughts focused on his mission as they walked. "O.K. now that meant something. I just don't know what yet." Glenn shook his head.

It wasn't long before the two arrived at Wei-Xing's home and what a magnificent home it was. A little slice of heaven, right here in the middle of nowhere. Green, lush and quiet. Quiet despite the number of people here. What looked like hundreds of four-hundred-year old trees formed a border around this modest colony. The prehistoric-looking trees stood there, disproportionately larger than everything else in view. They looked to be the guardians of this secret place. Wei-Xing's refuge nestled safely below.

With all the confidence in the world, Wei-Xing walked right into the center of camp with her new friend close in toe. She offered smiles to many and a tickle or two to some of the small children passing by. Glenn smiled politely as well.

Surprisingly, no one in the camp seemed to be alarmed or even very interested in the newcomer. Nor did they seem concerned with what he wanted with their village matriarch. As the two walked past, Glenn wondered why.

"Do I really look *that* harmless?" He asked himself, swinging his head around in all directions to see if he roused anyone's interest.

He made a scary face at one. Nothing.

"Hmmnnhhhhh." Glenn was surprised.

"Maybe it's my approach?"

He cautiously nodded "hello" to a couple of women walking in his direction. They kindly returned the gesture and nodded. But again, he was of no serious concern to them and they went on about their business.

"OK then. Well, I guess I'm not that interesting after all." His ego bruised a tad but still with a good attitude he straightened up, and tugged at his shirt, neatening up a bit.

"This place is interesting, already. I like it." He said, proud he'd found it.

Just steps away from the direction they were heading, stood a hut. It took both of Wei-Xing's small hands to pull aside a huge tarp, which served as a front door. As she disappeared inside, she waved Glenn in.

As Glenn scanned the room with his eyes he realized this must be her home. There were some animal skins on the floor, which looked like they must be her blankets. A water jug, which had been carved out of wood sat up on a small makeshift table crafted out of logs. Holes sliced in the sides of the hut walls served as windows to let light inside. It appeared she was living with the mere basics, not much else stood out. Her modest dwelling a testament to the simple life she led.

"May I?" He asked, pointing to a spot on the floor. Wei-Xing quickly ran over to straighten up the area before her guest sat. Then, like any hospitable host, with arm extended and palm up, she offered him his seat.

"Thanks." He sat.

"It's nice in here." He complemented, as he looked all around the space.

Lucky poked his nose from under the bottom of the tarp. At first all they could see were two wet nostrils opening and closing, trying to smell who or what was in the room.

Then, "Nnnnnnhhhhhhh!!!" In one long, never ending breath, he sucked in all the air he possibly could. After a long pause, he exhaled.

Glenn rolled his eyes.

"Man's best friend right there." He acknowledged, pointing to the nose. "Not too bright sometimes but as loyal as any beast on earth and man's best friend, nonetheless." Glenn beamed.

Then as fast as it had appeared, the nose disappeared. The bottom of the tarp had wrapped to the shape of Lucky's nose and now in its absence, a patch of sunshine came blazing through in that exact shape.

"Cute! Very cute!" Glenn said, loud enough so Lucky could hear.

Amused, Wei-Xing took her seat across from but close to Glenn. She sat legs crossed, face to face with her guest.

With her ever kind face, she looked into his eyes and calmly asked, "Do I now get to find out what you want with me?"

"Of course you do." He answered, adjusting his position. He liked her.

Glenn used his hands when he spoke. He liked to communicate by using his whole body.

"There's an ancient saying." He revealed. "When the student is ready, the teacher will appear."

Wei-Xing smiled with her gentle face.

"I believe, you may be my teacher." Glenn told her.

They looked at each other as if in agreement with that.

"I am looking for someone." He confessed to her. "I've been unsuccessful so far in finding them and I've begged God for help in finding them. Now, here you are." He returned her smile.

"I'm certain you are not the person I am searching for, for some reason. Something tells me that very definitively. However, something does tell me you can help me locate where this person may be."

Everything about Wei-Xing was peaceful. Glenn could feel it sitting across from her. He felt he was in the right hands.

"I asked for help from the Lord and help came. That help, is you. Now, I don't know where to begin with you, but, let's just see where this goes."

Wei-Xing sat patiently, waiting to hear what he needed from her.

Glenn adjusted his seat once again, out of nerves. "Let's see, can you tell me about this place, where you live? And, maybe even something about yourself?" He asked.

"What do you want to know first?" She was more than happy to oblige.

"Well, what about you? How did you get here, why do you live here and what's this place about? It's absolutely beautiful. There's peace here, but what I'm most interested in is finding out why there is so much peace here when it's sorely lacking in the rest of the world?"

Sitting angelically alongside him on the floor with her legs crossed, she laughed. "I know."

"So?" He inquired.

"I think I know what you want." Her voice fading as she bowed her head toward the ground. "I think I can help you find whom you're looking for."

Wei-Xing reached for Glenn's hand. She placed hers over his as she spoke to him. She, like he, communicated beyond words. When they spoke, they spoke from their hearts.

There was something comforting about Glenn's presence, she thought. She could feel that from the warmth emanating from his hand. He was kind, friendly, even loving and special in some way. Wei-Xing knew to trust him and help him in any way she could.

She was also aware that somehow fate was playing a role in what was happening this day. He was here for a reason. True to form, she would do her best to understand what messages he brought to her.

Wei-Xing had learned through experience this was part of the excitement and the beauty of life. Life always finds a way to carry you where you needed to be. But, depending on the choices you make once you get there, it is you who will determine your ultimate fate. Everyone has an equal shot at finding his or her true destiny. Life could certainly be an adventure when you mix free will with destiny.

Now, life had brought her and Glenn together.

In an effort to answer all of his questions, she started from the beginning.

"I was born in this lovely village. So were the others, but it wasn't always so peaceful here." She briefly reflected upon a time that brought tremendous sadness to her village. Her memories were a painful but necessary reminder that it was these very memories, which helped make her the woman she is today. She knew that and appreciated the bad along with the good.

"Anyway…" She continued, trying not to go off on a mental tangent. "What's important is we all understand our role here." She waved her hand in the air, indicating the world around them. "And I believe we do here."

"Here, we live by simple philosophies." Wei-Xing put her index finger up to Glenn's chest. "One of them is, we do unto others what we would have them do unto us."

"I'm listening." He said.

Now, placing her hand to her heart and looking deeply into his eyes, she said. "The greatest joy is living a good, honest life to help bring our destiny to light. In finding and living our intended destiny, we can live our lives to the fullest and make our world a better place. In doing so, we decide how great this world becomes."

Then, looking down, she paused. "Or… we move away from that." A deep sigh followed.

"I'm listening." He said again.

She held out her hand, palm up and used a finger from her opposing hand to illustrate her words.

"Life, or the world we live in is like a big puzzle and every living person is in a constant state of trying to solve it, sometimes without even knowing it. The pieces that solve this puzzle are right here in front of us. They are all of us here on earth right now." She said pointing to each of them.

"We are the players *and* we are the pieces that solve this puzzle, all at the same time."

Glenn tried to grasp what she meant.

"But there's a twist." She said. "To solve this puzzle, all the pieces need to make a proper fit."

Glenn scratched the top of his head. "Well, Wei-Xing, if we're…" He wagged his finger in between the two of them. "… All the pieces of the puzzle and all the pieces are present, then why aren't the pieces falling into place? If all the pieces are present, then why isn't this puzzle, solved?"

"Here's the twist!" She informed, growing increasingly pensive with each word. "Because being a *piece* of the puzzle isn't enough."

Glenn looked away, trying to figure out what she meant by this.

"Each of us needs to form into our intended "puzzle shape" to make the proper fit." She added.

"I'm really confused now. How can we do this?" Glenn sat there patiently, as Wei-Xing explained herself.

Wei-Xing slowed her tempo.

"When each of us are born we are essentially blessed with our rough shape. It's up to us, during our lifetime, to nurture it into the biggest and the best shape it can be. With the proper attention and care we can turn our ordinary shape into a marvelous creation, brightly colored with definitive edges, or we can starve it out of existence."

Glenn looked even more confused, but paid close attention.

"As we mature and live our lives, experiencing the triumphs and tragedies and everything else that goes along with living, we all get an equal opportunity in life to mold ourselves into our mature shape, whatever we decide that will be. We mold ourselves by the deliberate choices we make and the paths we pave for ourselves. That's free will. Free will has historically been a problem for mankind."

Glenn rolled his eyes. "Yeah, you can say that." He nodded in complete agreement.

She became increasingly passionate about what she was speaking about as she continued on.

"Here's how it works." She said.

"When we make choices, whether they are good for us, or bad for us, we are all completely aware of what the probable outcome will be. Good is born of good intent, and bad the opposite. We know what these probable outcomes will be because inside each of us, we know the right choices to make. We know when we're making a mistake and sometimes we do it anyway. But when we're doing the right thing, watch out! There's no stopping us. We also have instincts that guide us along our way. They're the voices of little angels in our heads. The goal for each of us is to select our paths wisely. If we do, we move toward our intended destiny. In doing so, we change our piece from its original state into the shape it's supposed to be and move closer to helping solve the puzzle."

Glenn looked like he was starting to catch on. "O.K.... I think."

"In other words, we need to become what God sent us here to become. We were all sent here with an instinct trained toward our destiny. In following that we become what we were meant to become. Everyone knows in their heart what that means, for them." Wei-Xing loved talking about this.

Glenn asked for clarity. "But... I still don't get how we're supposed to know what shape we're supposed to be?"

"That's the challenge." Wei-Xing pointed out. "When we're born each of us are provided with the tools we need to become the person we are meant to be. If we follow our God given instincts and pursue our deepest desires, to become the person we were meant to be, we change. We change for the better, into the person we're meant to become and the shape we're meant to become to help solve the puzzle. It's also important to remember how important all of us are to this process and how we all need to work together to solve this puzzle for all mankind. That's why each and every one of us is equally important for the divine evolution of this planet."

Wei-Xing knew what she was talking about. "This is how we can change our shape and become the shape we're supposed to be. When we're the shape we're supposed to be, we fit into the puzzle, helping solve it. Get it?"

Glenn thought about it.

"The only way to solve the puzzle is if everyone does it at the same time. We all have to arrive at human life's pinnacle. Time has provided us with the opportunity over and over through the generations to try to get this right." Wei-Xing looked into Glenn's eyes to see if he was catching on.

"You see, the challenge is for all of us to arrive at the same place of enlightenment at the same time." She smiled brightly.

"It's the only way all the puzzle pieces will be in their proper shapes to fit together to solve the puzzle. Each member of mankind has to see their true destiny, their potential and realize it... live it, to change this world and set it in the right direction."

Another strong, "Nnnnnnnhhhhhhhh!!!!" rumbled from the bottom of the tarp.

"OK Lucky..." Glenn turned toward the sound.

He stared, frozen in place. The nose peeking from beneath the canvas wasn't Lucky's.

The hair at the back of Glenn's neck stood on end and goose bumps rose off his forearm.

"Nnnnnhhhhhhhhhh!"

Wei-Xing turned to see what had Glenn spellbound. She saw the nose. It was eight times larger than Lucky's cute little button.

The intruder didn't surprise Glenn. It did, however, remind him how sensitive time was.

He wouldn't let it distract them from their productiveness.

As the tick of time echoed in his ears, he began to test Wei-Xing.

"People die every day without ever achieving this idyllic ambition."

"And they keep sending new ones..." She said bobbing her head up and down. "We've been given chance after chance."

He laughed nervously and then shut up.

"Maybe the master plan is to keep going, keep sending new pieces throughout time, until there is the ultimate result. Eventually, we will either bring the world to its glorious state or we destroy it. The end." He suggested.

Glenn pondered his new idea. "And... we've run out of time. So, that's why I'm here." His assignment suddenly held more meaning to him.

Adjusting her seat, she continued on her rant. "So, again, here's how we begin to change our shape. We start by trying to live a good and honest life. That's first." She spoke with authority.

"Making choices we know are right and good in our hearts is essential. Helping others, being a friend, striving to make the most of your God given talents all helps put us on the right path, toward our fate.

Allowing ourselves parsimonious pleasures only stunts our growth and opportunity for positive change."

They both nodded with understanding.

Wei-Xing tried using another example to help paint her picture in his head. "Think of life like a big, giant footpath map. With each correct turn you make the closer you get to your destination. With each incorrect turn you step farther away. It's much like good decisions and bad decisions. Good deeds and smart decisions bring you your life. The opposite applies when you allow yourself the pleasure of sin. With each proper turn in life you get one step closer to becoming the best *you,* you can become and the world is better for it."

"Oh My!" He couldn't stop laughing. It was as if he'd found what he was looking for. "You!" He said pointing at her. "Are a breath of fresh air!!!"

Wei-Xing smiled her gentle smile wider.

Now Glenn was ranting. "I am the student! I was ready, asked for help and presto my teacher appeared. That's you!" Then he thought. "I still haven't found the person I'm looking for but I know you've helped me get closer to them, somehow, someway."

"Come on, I'm listening! What next!" Glenn begged for more.

Wei-Xing was pleased he was pleased.

She gave him more to go on. "Again, the only way the puzzle can be solved is if each piece in the puzzle discovers and morphs into the piece it was meant to be. It's collective. It has to be the collective heart of man, whatever that is." She reiterated.

The whole time she spoke, her smile never left her face.

"The greatest gift, my friend, is to help yourself and others become the best we can be. We start by setting a proper example no matter the cost to us. Help others and you're helping yourself. It is the key to unlocking heaven on earth."

Her words came from the truest part of her soul. She was clothed in dignity and courage. She was the most beautiful woman Glenn had ever seen.

"And that is what we've established here. That's why you see so much peace here when it's sorely lacking in the rest of the world. In our tiny community, we've created a true heaven on earth." The village elder explained. "It's here for everyone, everywhere… we just know how to tap into it better than the rest of the world."

Wei-Xing wanted to help Glenn understand completely. She continued to speak slowly and clearly.

"We all must understand, our choices are married to fate. Whatever comes our way comes our way for a reason. That reason, like all reasons, to put your soul to the test. What are you made of? We must be willing to sacrifice ourselves for this world, for each other. This is how we speak to the universe."

She nodded to see if Glenn understood her. He did.

A tear welled up in his left eye. He knew what she was talking about. He loved her. She was good. No. She was great.

Glenn could suddenly feel energy fusing into his bones, his body. Something was happening to him physically, spiritually. He could feel greatness.

"Go on." He motioned her to continue on with her thoughts.

"We do not question it or fear it." She stopped, staring deeply into his eyes. She believed what she preached.

"We simply accept it. It is one of the only guarantees in life. No matter what, no matter what! One is to confront evil, understand it, stand up to it and be willing to die to eradicate it from our world. There are no choices there. It is the only thing in life to aspire to."

She looked about the room, thinking about what was beyond the walls.

"There are no other choices for us here, but the right ones, the good ones. We also believe what goes around comes around. Therefore it's in your best interest to commit to good or positive works to produce good energy in your life. Negative or evil doings only brings misfortune, chaos and jeopardy or bad energy into one's world. We've seen that first hand here. No one here cares whether they are king or conquered. Each destiny is beautiful in its own right and equally essential to the balance of the universe. Each knows they have an important role to fulfill."

Here, more than anywhere else in the world did they do their best to reach this ultimate goal. Glenn could feel this all around him.

It explained the uniquely pure, spiritual peace that existed among the people. Since his visit he'd never before seen a place absent of jealousy, greed, malice or hatred. It was all amazingly and delightfully absent here.

Just when Glenn thought Wei-Xing said all she could say, there was more. She seemed to go on and on, but Glenn loved everything she had to say, it was beautiful, smart and exciting.

"From the moment of conception, the spirit is foreordained to be a neutral being. In other words, babies are born completely innocent, not knowing love or hate. They will learn the value of such concepts and about the world around them, firsthand, as fate guides them on their earthly journey throughout life. The culmination of genetics, family dynamics, society, education, choices coupled with free will, life experiences and heaven's desire, will mature this soul into a human being, for better or for worse. It is the inherent challenge for every soul during their lifetime to uncover what God's master plan for them is. Getting there can be the greatest and most rewarding journey of all." She explained.

"The beauty in the design of this master plan is that although not everyone is born with the same lot in life, all have the same opportunity to reach their destiny and in doing so may become an angel here on earth."

Glenn's ears perked up.

Wei-Xing was spewing information like an erupting volcano.

"It's sort of like climbing a ladder. Each good decision allows one to take a step up on the rung of life. Each bad choice either holds a person in place or forces them downward to repeat the step. One may even go sideways, but never up toward where they're supposed to be, wherever their destiny lies. It is important for people to understand this idea as early as possible, as life is inevitably filled with choices. Even though there is the potential for a person to make millions and millions of decisions over the course of a lifetime, it is often crystal clear what the correct decisions are."

Both Glenn and Wei-Xing could hear the wind begin to kick up outside.

"At birth, people are also given a sixth sense or gut instinct for right and wrong, although they don't always listen to their inner-voice. Those inner voices are really the voices of God's attendants, whispering help into the ears of the confused and frustrated."

Wei-Xing was on a roll, Glenn wasn't going to interrupt.

"God always finds it peculiar, when someone knows what the right decision is, yet continues to choose the opposite, even as they witness it taking them further away from happiness. However, he has compassion for why. Fear and lack of faith in God paralyzes people into ruining their own potentially magnificent lives. Why wouldn't men and women be living in such darkness? After all, look at what the world has become. It is difficult for people to feel they have the potential to succeed when everything around them is failing. They think to themselves, why would I have what it takes to be successful when no one else does? They don't realize their own individual power to change the world. All it takes is one."

Wei-Xing was almost in a trancelike state, trying to get all this important information out to Glenn fast as possible as if she knew he was in a rush.

"The key is to have inner strength and blind faith in God. Faith, that when trying to do the right thing and making often, difficult decisions, that God will carry them through to greener pastures. The insightful among those on earth know when they make a positive decision, leaving negativity behind, God will send something better in its place. There's no way of knowing what that will be, but they know it will be great and it will make their journey here on earth all the more pleasant." She added.

"Life can figuratively be described as a gigantic maze, paved with lush green paths, but within these tempting paths, God has placed invisible doors. This is so he can test man's resolve and make sure human beings earn and appreciate their destiny. As man navigates his way through life, making common and life-altering decisions, he can work his way forward or backward through the maze. For each positive choice he makes for himself and the world around him, a door opens for him and he progresses forward. For each negative decision, he unproductively veers off course and doors or opportunities never seem to open for him. As man forges a path of goodness for himself, there are guaranteed gifts along the way. Along this path, he achieves personal and professional goals, he makes long-lasting friendships, he is revered and admired by his peers, he raises mature and responsible children who adore and respect him. Thus, leaving him feeling immense self-fulfillment. This is how man earns his earthly wings, if you will, and becomes a "common angel."

"Hmmnnnhhhh." Glenn considered this.

Wei-Xing still wasn't done. "On the contrary, as men and woman alike spend a lifetime, focusing their energies on selfish gratifications, there are guarantees here as well. Guarantees such as wasted time and unrealized dreams, unfulfilled goals, the resentment of his or her own children and failed relationships. These people will go to their graves with an empty heart, with no one to miss them, for they left nothing but pain behind for those unfortunate enough to have known them. These people can live an entire lifetime, never positively touching the lives of anyone. They are often criticized by others and looked upon by society with scorn.

Everything they touch turns as foul as they are inside. These are the people that have the potential to manifest into "earthly devils." They will provoke others for as long as they live to join them in their misery."

"How'd you get so smart, living out here in the wild?" Glenn asked facetiously with a grin.

Wei-Xing smiled wider than ever.

Glenn leaned toward her. They embraced, as if getting ready to prepare for battle. They sat there holding each other for some time, thinking about the complicated world they were in.

With an understanding expression Glenn said, "Thank you teacher, I understand much better now."

Wei-Xing pulled away from him ever so slowly and gently. There were tears streaming down her face.

"Why are you crying?" He asked.

"I always knew this time was coming, I just didn't think it would be this soon."

Glenn got the idea she might know who he was. He squinted as he looked at her.

A loud "Phhhhffffffttttttttttt!" broke their concentration. As they both turned to see where the noise came from they laughed.

There sat Lucky, happy as could be after a good hearty sneeze, his tail wagging a mile a minute from the attention.

"Doesn't it look like he smiles?" Glenn asked Wei-Xing.

"All dogs smile." She said astutely.

CHAPTER 10

ANATOLI VANKOV

Media were still present outside the walls of the Vatican and reporters were growing increasingly agitated as they waited to confirm information about their stories. Journalists were beginning to snap at their photographers and vice versa. There's only so long two broadcasting coworkers can coexist in the same mobile newsroom until they get fresh with each other.

Everyone was exhausted and frustrated. They wanted to get their story, get it on the air and go home. Things were growing tense everywhere.

Just when they thought things were tough, they got tougher.

A man named Anatoli Vankov was now handling all media inquiries. Vankov, a man no one had ever heard of before had just been named the Vatican's Director of Communications.

Everything was going through him. He was letting little information out.

Those who had a natural endowment for foreign languages knew the name had a Russian sound to it. Those who had the chance to speak with him confirmed the accent was Russian.

"Have you ever heard of this guy?" One reporter asked another holding up a press release.

"No, and I've been covering the Vatican for a decade. I've never heard of… Ana…tol…i Va…n..kov." The woman replied, using her finger to trace each syllable, sounding it out. "I did get the press release too."

Both women laughed. This was their life, trying to figure out proper pronunciations and spellings of names and places.

"Oh well. I guess we'll get to know him soon enough. Poor guy, he's probably never stared down the throat of a beast like the media before. We'll break him in!"

They heartily chuckled together, releasing some of the stress of the day.

"Doubt it!"

"Let me know if you hear anything?" One said to the other.

"Will do."

The pretty but punchy news reporters walked off to their respective live trucks, press releases in hand, to do more research and to wait for Anatoli to return their calls.

In another part of the city a lone live truck sat idle, parked well outside the congested parking area reserved for media vehicles only. Inside, crews working nonstop to write, cut, edit and get their pieces on the air by deadline. Through the windshield, they looked like busy worker bees, confined to a small cell, toiling toward a common goal.

Without catching the attention of anyone inside, one of the large side doors to the live truck cracked open slightly. Inside a number of television sets tuned to various stations blared, the audio from each competing with one another. As a hand pushed the door open even wider, one of the sets caught the eye of the person inconspicuously peering inside.

It was a news station covering a massacre at a Tibetan monastery.

He stopped dead in his tracks. "Huuhhhhhh." He gasped, drawing in a deep breath.

The television news anchor delivered the gory details of the story matter-of-factly. The pictures that followed were even worse.

"Tibetan officials confirm this was the work of a single person. We do want to warn you the images you are about to see may be too graphic for some viewers. Authorities believe someone with a machete found his or her way high up into these mountains, to the monastery and viciously attacked everyone inside. The bodies of the monks who lived here were left exactly where they were struck down."

The man watching the story from outside the truck became ill as he saw the tragic story unfold.

"You can see from this video, the intensity of the struggle between the monks and the assailant. Investigators point to the blood spatters on the floors, the walls, everywhere. The place was completely ransacked. Let's listen as officials tell us what they found."

Then there was a sound bite with a member of law enforcement. "I've never seen anything like this before in my life. Who would want to hurt these people? They lived here in peace and in harmony with nature. I can't imagine who would do such a thing or why? Whoever was here was looking for something. We don't know what or if they found what they were looking for. But we are now looking for *them!*"

Then it switched back to the news anchor.

"There are no survivors we are told. As police mentioned there, they say they are now looking for suspects."

The last image of the news package was that of Brother John lying face down in a pool of blood.

"Uuuuhhhhhhhhhh." The stranger, suddenly dizzy and short of breath fell against the truck, dropping what he'd been clutching in his hand his entire journey.

A photographer hard at work inside the truck heard a thud and turned, noticing the door to the live truck was ajar. He walked over and stuck his head outside the door to see if anything was there.

"Oh my God! Are you all right?" The photojournalist leapt out of the truck to assist him.

The man on the ground couldn't get any air.

"Breathe! Breathe!" He pleaded. "Help! Someone, we need help!"

That's when one of the reporters inside answered his calls for help. She whipped open the door, looking down at the man in her coworkers arms.

She hesitated for a second, not believing her eyes.

"Gil! He's one of them! He's one of the monks, he must have escaped or something. How the hell did he get here? Get out your camera! Start rolling!" The female reporter shouted.

Gil laid the man back down on the ground gently and ran into the truck as fast as humanly possible. He got his camera out and stuck it in the man's face immediately.

"Uuuuhhhhhhhh." The man moaned, unsure of what happened to him. He rubbed his head.

Next, came a blinding light and a microphone and a barrage of questions from the insensitive reporter bent on serving her career.

The stranger put his hands up to protect himself from the penetrating beam, which hurt his eyes.

The reporter grabbed his arms and pulled them down to his sides.

"Sir. Keep your arms down! Can you tell us how you got here? Are you one of the monks who lived in that monastery, the monastery where the massacre happened?" She shot her questions out one after the other.

He didn't even have time to process the first one and she was on to several more.

The man was speechless.

"Sir. Can you tell us your name? Sir, your name, please!" She was relentless until she got something out of him. Anything.

"D…ddd…ddddd…avid." It was almost impossible for him to speak. He stuttered. A look of anguish was well defined on his crinkled up face. Grief began to overcome every one of his senses.

"Gil. Call the desk, see if they can find out if there was a Brother David that lived at that monastery or not!"

Gil secured his camera to his tripod and ran back into the truck, leaving his reporter to look after the man.

Just then, a priest cloaked in a hooded, dark robe approached as if sent by angels.

"Excuse me, are you a news reporter?" He asked the woman.

"Well, of course." She answered, looking at the huge live truck she was standing near.

"Anatoli Vankov has just called a press conference for all members of the media. It's in exactly five minutes and at the front gates of the Vatican." He informed her.

She didn't know what to do. She had two stories on her hands. Which was the bigger one, she weighed. She let go of David and ran back into the live truck to give her photographer instructions.

The big door slammed in their faces. Behind it, the sound of verbal jousting between the reporter and Gil were heard clear as a bell.

"You're free. Come with me." The priest said. He grabbed the man's arm and pulled him up to his feet. "Let's go! This way!" He said pointing off in the distance.

Before David took off with him, he bent down to pick up what he had dropped before he was accosted.

The sight of it froze the priest in place. "Is that…" His eyes fixed on it and then he looked directly at the monk.

"Never mind. Let's go."

The two took off down a dark, wet alleyway, under the cover of fog. In no time they had vanished from sight.

While the two sought refuge from the vultures calling themselves journalists, members of the media gathered at the front gates of the Vatican for their press conference.

They all waited impatiently for about forty minutes in a light misty rain before they were graced with the presence of this mysterious man named, Anatoli Vankov.

As he walked toward the army before him, it was evident he reveled in the limelight. He marveled at the cameras and the lights taking his picture and posed as he made his way through the crowd to the microphone stand.

His appearance didn't match his confidence. He wasn't very tall, maybe about 5'4" or so, bald and pudgy. The one thing he did have going for him were his beautiful blue eyes. They were large and sparkling.

"He's a little vain for a priest, isn't he?" Someone insinuated.

As he walked closer he stretched his neck out of his collar a bit and smiled as he moved closer to the messy assemblage of audio equipment in front of him. He couldn't wait to get to the microphones. Playing coy was not his strong suit. Being crudely obvious was.

"Well, this is different." Someone said, getting a laugh from the people around her.

"Yeah. He likes himself more than we like ourselves." Another joked.

"That's almost impossible! We're as conceited as you can get!" Someone else replied.

Everyone within earshot erupted with laughter. They knew it was true.

"Who is this guy?" One reporter questioned her producer who just shrugged her shoulders as she text-messaged someone.

Then, he finally planted his feet firmly at the makeshift podium.

"I am Anatoli Vankov." He said, charmingly. "I am here to answer all of your questions." He spoke in broken English, but clearly and with a good vocabulary.

"Can you tell us why it took the Vatican so long to confirm the death of the Pope?" One reporter shot out immediately. "And what did he die of?"

"Why was Cardinal Victor selected?" Another followed up. "Why him above the others? Especially considering the fact he comes from a place of such oppression and suffering like Rhemenia. How was it done so fast?"

The surefooted spokesperson had all his answers planned beforehand as any Communications Director worth his salt would.

"We wanted to make sure we had all the information anyone would want available before we confirmed anything." He paused so the cameras could adjust if they needed a better angle.

"As far as the Holy Father passing away and why we didn't rush to call news bureaus around the world. There's a lot of protocol that goes on here when something like this happens and that takes time." He announced with a phony sincerity.

"As for the how? Well, something natural and of this world took his life. It seems it was just his time to go. He was in the twilight of his years and had accomplished everything he set out to do in the church. He lived a full life and was thankfully taken quietly from us in his sleep." Anatoli added.

Members of the Press Corps looked strangely at each other. "Thankfully taken quietly from us in his sleep?" They mouthed to each other as they put pen to paper.

Some started to question Anatoli Vankov's credentials to hold his position. He didn't seem very polished.

He continued. "As for Cardinal Victor. As many of you familiar with the protocol of the church already know, it is the Cardinals from around the globe who decide whom will be the new leader."

This, the media and most of the public already knew.

"They have been present here for days and have come to an unanimous decision that Cardinal Victor should become the next successor of St. Peter. We expect the Cardinals to remain with us here at the Vatican for an extended period, during this time of transition."

One reporter, semi-familiar with Vatican protocol demanded an answer to what everyone else there was thinking. "First of all, Ana-toli Van..ov…"

"Vankov!" He corrected her.

"Vankov. Sorry. Vankov. The media is always immediately notified of the death of a sitting Pope. We, the media, are the vessel to disseminate such world news to the public. But we weren't told. Why?"

Anatoli Vankov glared at her from the microphone stand. He didn't like his authority being questioned and being put on the spot this way.

"Furthermore, it takes time for the Cardinals from around the world to gather, discuss and vote for whom they feel is the best choice to succeed. We didn't know about that either. How did it all happen so fast and under cover like this?" She pointedly asked him.

"Then, like in the movies, smoke is released from the rooftop, or something like that, signaling a new Pope has been named. What about all that? What happened to that tradition?"

"Yeah! Yeah!" Jeers rang out from the crowd. They knew Anatoli was trying to dupe them in some way, but they weren't sure how.

He had an answer for everything. "Well, the Pope's death was of course so sudden and unexpected, there wasn't time to do all of that. We, here at the Vatican had to get down to the business of, well, business. With the new regime here, things are being done a bit differently. Just because things used to be done a certain way doesn't mean it's going to stay that way." Vankov smirked arrogantly.

Reporters looked at each other with expressions of disbelief on their faces.

"What are his credentials? What makes him the best candidate to be the Bishop of Rome? What are his positions on gay marriage, abortion, war! How are his views different from the late Pope's?" A determined newspaper writer questioned from the back of the pack.

With an unshaken attitude, Vankov replied. "I assure you he has the best interest of mankind at heart. He is especially outstanding for his doctrine, morals, piety to his religion, and prudence in his actions. He is committed to ruling with fortitude, even if it means spilling his own blood to guide St. Peter's boat to his true intended destiny. That's all you need to know right now."

That was it. He was done. He shut them out.

"That's all we need to know!" A reporter angrily hollered at him.

"What?!!!" Yelled someone else.

"Are you…? What? You've got to be kidding!"

Everyone was shouting over each other to get his attention.

Soon as he appeared, he disappeared. One quick turn on his heel and he was heading back toward those impermeable walls of the Vatican.

A swell of media crowded him, incensed at his flagrant disregard for how important their work was.

"Well, I must be on my way. I have church business inside that can't wait. Thank you for joining me for this press conference.

We'll be doing it again soon, I promise." Vankov walked and talked as he ended the briefing, making his way past the pissed-off reporters and back to the front entrance.

"Wait, where are you going, we're not done! We have more questions!" Anatoli hadn't even begun to satisfy their appetite for information.

"We'll do this again, I promise!" He declared, waving back at the angry mob.

"That's all we get!" One credentialed member of the group exclaimed. "Why did you even gather us for this? This was nothing but a waste of our time!"

An untrustworthy smirk never left Anatoli's face as he made his way past the Vatican's main entrance and inside the fortress.

The group disbanded, more irritated then when they came. They took off in every which different direction like a sea of ants.

As the pack continued to dissipate, only two stood stationary, never moving from their place on the street.

Neither Father Joseph nor his new best friend Brother David could find the energy within himself to move a single inch.

"I think I might know what brought me here." David said stone-faced, staring straight ahead.

"I think I might too." Admitted a frightened Father Joseph, looking down at the scroll in David's hand.

They looked to each other for answers, but feeling more vulnerable than they ever had in their entire lives.

"Do you believe in God, I mean really believe in God?" David asked Father Joseph. "I know that's a stupid question to ask a priest. But, do you? Do you believe he can work miracles through you if you completely turn yourself over to him for the good of man no matter what the cost to you?" He grilled. "Because, doubt is starting to creep in to my…"

A long pause came as Joseph thought about how to best assure him.

"As sure as I am the sun will rise and set every day!" Father Joseph's answer so proud and confident, spit flew out of his mouth. His beard and unkempt hairdo covered in tiny droplets of rain.

That was all David needed to hear. He paused for a moment, looking at his new mentor with renewed vigor.

"Let's go then!" Brother David said with a cocky attitude, uncharacteristic of a modest monk.

The two put up their hoods and took off running toward a side street. That's where they found a locked door, which looked like a public portal, but really served as a secret private entrance into the Vatican.

"This way!" Pointed Father Joseph, pulling out a key from his pocket.

Neither realized they were being watched.

High above the street and almost out of view, the newly appointed Pope, Victor stood in a tower window several stories up, watching everything.

"You need to get a hold of those two." An agitated female voice ordered behind him. "Before things get more out of control."

Although his temper was rising, Victor didn't respond.

"Looks like one got away, didn't *HE*?!" She ridiculed. "I thought you said you took care of everyone in Tibet? I sent you there for a reason. You know that reason."

"He was not there when I got there." Victor snarled, never taking his attention away from the window. "He apparently had left prior to my arriving. I didn't know anyone was missing from the group."

Falene infuriatingly walked closer, speaking directly into his ear from behind.

"I really don't care how or why you didn't get him. Just get what he has and get rid of him as well." She demanded, clenching her eyes shut with exasperation.

Pope Victor turned away from the window and around to face her. Their eyes locked. She wasn't backing down. He didn't expect her to.

Intentionally devoid of emotion, he nodded in agreement with her instruction and headed out the door.

Just about at the end of her patience Falene walked over to the window herself. "Can't even get that right. Should have gone myself." She snipped.

Here, all of Rome could be seen. A vast city filled with art, culture, magnificent architecture, and great food and wine lie before her. It was the perfect setting for romance to bloom.

Just below on the street she could see a couple walking in the rain, holding hands. The man stopped to kiss his lover passionately on the lips. Her excitement exploded as she threw her arms around his neck.

The sight of it made Falene sick.

Anatoli was frantically jogging up the hall as the new Pontiff exited his meeting with Falene.

"Sir, I have a bit of bad news!" He called to him.

"And what's that?!" Victor bellowed. He had enough on his plate to worry about.

Anatoli struggled to catch his breath.

"The media is requesting interviews with the Cardinals about your appointment!" Anatoli shrieked. "What should I do?"

"Just hold them off a while." Victor kept walking down the hall not at all concerned about the media's demands. He had other, more important, things on his mind.

"But… they're… they won't back off, sir!" Anatoli tried to warn, chasing after him for better direction.

As Victor continued walking, in the distance, he could hear the footsteps of two clumsy people nervously making their way through the building.

He stopped and listened carefully, sensing they were intruders of some sort.

"Male." He was sure.

Victor, in his mind, could practically track exactly where they were in the Vatican by the sound of their footsteps.

Anatoli stopped in his tracks as well.

"The other one's male as well." He confirmed by the strut.

He closed his eyes and focused on the footsteps more intently. His eyes moved back and forth behind his eyelids at a rapid pace.

Then his eyes popped back open.

"Anatoli… Anatoli." He whispered.

"Anatoli!" He said a little bit louder this time, waving him closer.

Anatoli came scampering to his side. "Yes, sir."

"They're making their way to the Sistine Chapel." Victor suspected.

Anatoli immediately knew what to do and took off, while Victor stood there contemplating.

It wasn't long before Father Joseph and Brother David arrived at what they were looking for. They were standing right outside an immense, and intimidating carved wooden door, adorned with gold leaf. A sign hanging on the wall next to it read, *Cardinals' Private Quarters* in Italian.

"This is the Cardinals' Private Quarters." Father Joseph read the sign to Brother David.

"The Princes of the Church should still be inside I would imagine." He said optimistically, as if he could see through the door. "So let's go in there and get to the bottom of what's going on."

Father Joseph listed their agenda. "When were they informed of the Holy Father's passing? When did they get here? Why did they select Cardinal Victor who comes from a place of terror and pain… as Pope so quickly and secretly?" Joseph urged that those should be the initial questions.

Brother David shook his head up and down in concordance.

"I also want to know who organized this whole thing. Who was the contact person?" Joseph speculated. "That could be a big clue here."

Taking the initiative, Brother David ambitiously walked over to the entryway, turned the doorknob and pushed the right side of the commanding door open. It was heavy. He pushed harder, using both hands. It wasn't locked as it should be.

He stuck his head inside to take a peek before entering.

What he saw made the hair on his back stand on end. It was horrifying beyond his wildest imagination. David pulled his head back out quickly and let out a cough as he stumbled to the floor. He couldn't look at Joseph.

"What's wrong?" Shocked at his reaction, Father Joseph leaned over to check him out to make sure he didn't have a seizure or something.

He helped David stand upright. "What's wrong?!"

Joseph looked back at the door, afraid of what might be inside.

"It's just like what happened at the monastery." Brother David whimpered, clutching at his chest.

"What?!" Joseph looked at him confused. "What do you mean?"

Joseph sternly walked over and pushed the door open himself and stuck his head inside.

"Oh my good…!" He exclaimed, jumping back.

"Oh my…! Oh my God!" He repeated himself several times, covering his eyes. Although, it was too late, he'd seen the gruesome images inside.

"David, there was a massacre here!" Sheepishly walking into the Cardinals' Private Quarters in the Sistine Chapel, Father Joseph led Brother David inside. Both weren't sure what could happen next.

What they saw incapacitated them.

All the Cardinals from around the world, the former reigning Pontiff's closest advisors, were still sitting in their assigned seats, which formed a large circle around the great room. They'd traveled here, summoned, upon the Holy Father's death, to exercise their right and obligation to choose among them, a successor to the Apostle Peter. Here, behind the closed doors of the Sistine Chapel, the Cardinals were left in conclave, to cast votes.

The entire College of over one hundred-fifty of them was present. Behind their heads, great works of art hung on the walls, above them the finest crystal chandeliers dangled. At first glance it was a truly glorious sight, until reality sunk in.

"Their throats and their wrists have been slashed!" Joseph yelled inaudibly. "The Senate of the Church has been eliminated!"

He and David were in complete and utter shock.

"All but one..." Joseph quickly realized, beginning to put the pieces together. "One... apparently made it out O.K."

David wasn't making the connection yet.

"There's so many of them! How could this happen?! Why didn't somebody stop this?! There's so many of them!" Joseph, afraid to get closer to the bodies was in a frantic state of mind. He didn't know what to do first.

"There's blood everywhere!" David pointed out, looking in all directions around the room. "This reminds me of what happened at my monastery. It's the same type of killing!"

Father Joseph finally mustered up the courage to stiffly walk over to one of the deceased members.

He examined the grisly condition they were left in and then investigated the workspace before them for any clues left behind.

"Before each of them there's a white sheet of paper on the table!" He noticed, alerting David to it.

"What do the papers say?!" David called over from another part of the room, trying to help figure this out.

Joseph used his fingers to gently spin one of the papers around on the table, so he could read it.

"What does it say?!!!" David pressed, knowing their time was limited.

Joseph couldn't believe what he saw.

"On each slip of paper, the name Victor is handwritten in what appears to be their own blood! There's one in front of each Cardinal!" He described.

David came trotting over, to see for himself.

Joseph suddenly stopped talking, interrupted by a strange sound.

"What's that?" He asked his friend who knew about as much as he did.

The eerie noise caused more adrenaline to pump through his veins.

"Listen! What is that?" He urged David to give a hard listen as well.

Joseph's eyes scanned the room, from floor to ceiling and from wall to wall for any indication where it was coming from.

"There it is again! It's coming from down there!" Joseph pointed to the other end of the humungous room, which was the size of an airplane hangar.

It was the gurgling sound of death, wrapping its clutches around one last remaining victim.

"I think someone's still alive!" Father Joseph howled, desperately hoping.

Joseph and David ran as fast as they could to get to the dying man.

By time they got there, both their chests were heaving.

"It's Cardinal Shanley from Ireland!" A shocked Father Joseph discovered. He knew him well.

"Hold his head up! His neck is pretty bad, I don't know if he can speak!" Joseph insisted.

David did as Joseph said. "I think he might be able to tell us what happened!" He suggested, propping him up.

"Cardinal Shanley can you hear me?" Father Joseph grasped the sides of the Cardinal's face and softly spoke directly to him. "Look at me Cardinal Shanley. Can you hear me? Who did this to all of you?"

Cardinal Shanley could barely focus. He'd lost too much blood.

"I think we're losing him Joseph."

"Hold his head up!" Joseph charged. "Hold it up!"

"Cardinal Shanley! Who did this to you? Please, you have to help us find who did this!" Father Joseph pleaded with the dying man.

"He's trying to speak Joseph. Let him speak!"

"Cardinal Shanley. Who?" Joseph begged.

With the last bit of energy within his expiring body rapidly slipping away, Cardinal Shanley opened his eyes and looked directly at his old friend Father Joseph and smiled warmly.

He even tried to raise his right hand to his contemporary, as blood continued discharging from his carotid artery and his wrists, but failed. He was almost gone now.

Father Joseph nodded his head with understanding and encouraged him to tell him whatever he could.

"Please… Please Cardinal Shanley."

Cardinal Shanley was only able to eek out a few words. They were slow and stammered, but the words he did choose were significant.

"Hell……. hath… nooooo……" His eyes rolled back into his head as he let out his last breath.

That's when a faint golden light shone over his face.

Father Joseph's face lost all expression. He knew.

"He's gone Joseph. That's it." David confirmed, patting Joseph on the back. "I'm so sorry."

As gently as he could, Joseph laid his old friend back into his chair and closed his eyes for him to preserve his dignity.

It caused the normally self-controlled priest to surrender to his emotions. He couldn't hold it in any longer. Not after all this. It was too much for him. Too much for anyone.

"Oh God, why? Please help me to understand this. I don't know if I can do this work for you! Please help me to understand." He pleaded with the Lord to show him the way during this, the darkest of times.

David didn't know what to do for Joseph.

"I know how that is supposed to go. Hell hath no fury like a woman scorned, but that doesn't make any sense." The monk offered, trying to distract Joseph.

"Oh, my naïve friend. Yes, it does. Yes, it does." Father Joseph hinted he had an idea of why it *did* make sense. Perfect sense.

"Gentlemen!"

Joseph and David jumped.

Vankov had been standing right there the whole time. They'd never seen him.

"What happened here! What happened here!" Joseph instinctively ran at him in a murderous rage. David chased after him, not sure what the priest was capable of after seeing this.

"Tell me what happened here! I know you know!" Joseph accused unapologetically, up in his face.

"You can see why I tried to keep the media at bay. We need to get to the bottom of this." Vankov ignored Joseph's accusation and tried to redirect him, addressing the grave situation here in the Cardinals' Private Quarters instead.

"Get to the bottom of this?! Get to the bottom of this?!" Joseph spun around, his arms outstretched at the carnage surrounding them.

"This didn't happen by accident! You have to know something! Who did this?! Who did this!!!! You tell me right now, or so help me!!!..." Joseph waved his fist in the air.

"So help you what?!!!" Vankov taunted.

"So help you whaaaaaaaaaaaaat!!!!!!!!" Vankov tried to incite Joseph to attack him. He was baiting him.

Now Joseph knew for sure Anatoli Vankov knew who was responsible for this. That made him a very dangerous man.

The two fixed eyes.

Joseph decided to back down for now, not taking the bait. He didn't want to reveal his cards too quickly.

That's when the sound of high heels entering the room conveniently broke their concentration.

"What's happening here?" The cocky woman interrupted, sauntering in.

It was the nurse Father Joseph had an earlier encounter with.

"You're the..." He stammered.

"You're that nurse, Falene."

Joseph then looked back at David who knew about as much as he did at this point.

"Good memory!" She kept a lit cigarette at the end of her painted fingertips as she spoke.

There was something about her that made Joseph feel uneasy. He couldn't quite put his finger on it but he knew there was something wrong about her.

The guarded priest didn't move a muscle, didn't utter a sound. He just stood there, staring at her.

The hair on the back of Joseph's neck stood on end. "So what in the hell are you doing here? What are you here for? What's your part in this?" He demanded answers from her as Brother David drew closer.

She stared back, but much less affected. He was more of a nuisance to her than a true rival. As she looked around the room, a contented smile appeared on her face.

"Getting the job done, brother. That's what I'm doing here." She answered sarcastically.

Not even the slightest hint of emotion was in her voice as she stood in a room full of dead men, dead men who were revered religious leaders from around the globe.

She unsympathetically took a drag from her cigarette.

"You or someone you know is responsible for this, isn't that right?" Joseph extended his chubby arms, referencing the butchery before them.

He didn't need her to answer, he already knew.

Falene smiled in an admitting way. "Mayyyyybeeeeee."

Joseph was incensed by her indifference.

"I can feel your presence, but I cannot feel life inside of you." He told her. Joseph's eyes shifted between her and Anatoli Vankov. "I can't feel it from either of you." As Joseph spoke, he could feel his blood pressure steadily rising and his face flush with stress and anger.

Neither offended, they still didn't offer up what they knew about the situation.

"You both bear the mark of the Beast." He insulted.

Falene and Anatoli stood there, neither confirming nor denying.

That's when Pope Victor entered the room slowly. He took his time as he made his way into the vast meeting hall, looking to and fro. He proudly wore a sweeping, bright red robe held together by a golden rope tied around his waist, which accentuated his stocky frame. He walked with certain majesty.

When Victor made his way to them, he scrutinized the room, which was beginning to smell of blood, decomposing flesh and death.

"Gentlemen!" He said loudly, inhaling the stench through his nostrils.

"Falene, Anatoli why don't you give us some time alone." He said bowing his head toward them.

Anatoli and Falene vacated upon request.

Victor walked over to near where one of the Cardinals lay slain, the back of his chair spattered with blood. On the desk before him, a white sheet of paper. With three fingers on his right hand, Victor turned the paper in his direction to read it. A limited smile stretched across his face.

"You fiend! You murderer!" Brother David held Joseph in place by his sleeve as he tried to get to Victor.

"It's Your Excellency, to you Joseph." Victor sneered.

"You evil sadists organized this mass-killing, didn't you?! Why would you do something like this?! You'll be found out, you know!!! You won't get away with this!" Tears filled Joseph's eyes and began rolling down his cheeks, his words exploding with emotion. "I will give my life to stop you! You won't get away with this!" Joseph's fists waved furiously at Victor.

Holding his head up and walking with great confidence Victor came closer to the two.

"What do you two think you're doing here?" He asked, leaning in toward them both. "You're getting in the way and I'm really starting to get annoyed." Victor threatened.

"I just have one question for you." Joseph said, unthreatened by him. "Now that the Sacred College has been eliminated… who have *you* put in place to replace them?"

"Exterminated you mean to say." Victor corrected. "They were exterminated like the cockroaches they were." He explained contemptuously.

Before Joseph had a chance to slug Victor in the mouth a news reporter who'd lost her way in the Vatican stumbled into the room with her photographer.

"Hey!..." She called to them.

Then she noticed a strong, foul smell. A smell her olfactory senses had never experienced before. It was overpowering and driving her out of the room.

"What's... that sm...?" She took a step back, covering her nose. Her face dropping as she looked around. The young woman began to scream in terror once the images she received reached her brain and she knew what she was looking at was real. "Oh my....... God!!!!!"

Victor lunged at her, leaping forward with huge strides, waving his arms menacingly.

"Get out! Get out of here!" The new Pontiff shockingly transformed into a lunatic, before the unsuspecting news team, screaming his head off. He sprinted towards the journalists, his robe whipping in the air.

"Get the hell out of here, you bloody idiots!" He blasted. "Get out!!!!"

The news crew was totally taken aback, not expecting to see the new Pope act like this. It disoriented them.

"Oh! Oh! Oh! Oh my God!" The news reporter shrieked, assessing the crime scene. She put her hand up to her mouth. "Oh my God, I'm going to be sick!"

Without wasting a single second and unfazed by Victor's wrath, her photographer threw his camera up on his shoulder and started shooting.

"Got it. It's in focus." He said, panning the room.

The camera rolled for about four-seconds before Victor came upon him, knocking the camera off his upper arm. Thankfully, the cameraman was wearing his shoulder strap, which caught the camera and prevented it from smashing to the ground.

"Too late!" The cameraman boasted.

With one huge shove, Pope Victor was thrown to the ground by the quick thinking, younger and athletic photojournalist.

This gave the news crew a chance to make a run for it, but not before the reporter did her job and grabbed a white sheet of paper off one of the conference tables.

"Come on, let's go!" She shouted to her coworker. She grabbed him by the shirt and both took off running.

Before Victor could get back up on his feet, they were gone. Too far gone to catch. The sound of their footsteps running down the hall echoed against the marble walls.

As Victor looked behind him, to take care of prior business, he noticed Father Joseph and Brother David had disappeared as well.

CHAPTER 11

UNCOVERING A COVER-UP

At the pace they were traveling on foot it didn't take Father Joseph and Brother David very long to reach a private room where they were sure they could remain in hiding for a short period. After all they were in the Vatican, an enormous city within a city. It was easy for one to get lost if they wanted to.

"This way!" Father Joseph waved. He'd found the door unlocked.

They ducked into the small, cramped room on the top floor. Joseph hurriedly slammed the door shut behind them and locked it. They felt they were safe, at least temporarily.

Both were out of breath, out of patience and scared to death.

"Catch your breath my brother and then we'll come up with a plan of some sort." Father Joseph hospitably assigned himself David's caretaker, being that the monk wasn't from around here and that they had taken up the same cause.

David nodded with relief and fell to the floor as Joseph found a chair to collapse into.

Both men vacantly stared into space for at least fifteen minutes, reliving the horror of what they had just seen and trying desperately to understand the motives of the new regime here at the Vatican. It wasn't easy on either of them.

Father Joseph sighed deeply as tears streamed, glistening down his face. He didn't care if David saw. David however, had no tears left. He was spent emotionally and physically.

When he was able to collect himself, Joseph still sitting in his chair pulled out the scroll he'd been hiding from the waist of his pants. A ray of sunshine blazing through a window shined down upon it perfectly as it lay in his hands.

"Well, this makes it easier to read." He said, half laughing. "One of God's little surprise gifts which sometimes are the best ones."

Joseph unraveled it and began to examine the document once again. He still wasn't able to read Aramaic, but he memorized each word Father Matthew shared with him. He turned it several different ways to try to get a better understanding of what its messages might mean, beyond Father Matthew's interpretations.

"I still can't read a darn thing on here." He was totally dumbfounded. "What good does this do me if I can't read it for myself?" He looked to David.

That's when David pulled his own scroll from beneath his robe and handed it to Joseph. "Here. Take mine."

Joseph's eyes grew wide. When he'd first seen David outside the Vatican his curiosity was peeked when he thought David was carrying with him something that looked identical to the ancient scroll Father Matthew made him privy to, but he wasn't sure.

"I never in a million years thought I'd see another one of these things." He was astonished.

He took it from David's hands, got down on the floor and unraveled it slowly next to his.

"Yup, this is the same exact document all right. It's identical." He threw his hands up in frustration. "Great! Now we've got two very important pieces of history and they're both in Aramaic and I can't read either one!"

Joseph continued comparing the two side by side out of sheer disbelief. "Yup. They're definitely identical, a lot of good that does us." Joseph got up off the floor. Disappointed, he handed David back his copy.

"Maybe you can read that one then?" David said mysteriously pointing to a huge old map hanging on the wall. Columns written in English ran vertically down either side of it.

Both Joseph and David looked up slowly as if in the presence of a great blessing.

They stared at it in amazement. It had been there the whole time, staring them right in the face and they hadn't seen it.

"It's the same as…." David spoke hesitantly.

"Oh my great goodness!" Joseph exclaimed. The two men gradually made their way to the wall. There, hung an enlarged replica of their scrolls.

Joseph's mouth fell agape.

"It has all the same language, but in English." Joseph said to David, pointing to the work. "I remember what Father Matthew read to me, word for word. It's all here! It has all the same words, but in English, thank heavens." He pressed his hands together in prayer.

"The map in the center there…" David pointed out, making his own observations. "…Is exactly the same as in our scrolls. It's the same hand-drawn picture. Land masses are depicted in the same way and so is everything else in the drawing."

The monk started figuring out more.

"This must be the third and final copy of the original." He told Joseph, referencing the scroll on the wall. "You Joseph. You must have the original because it's in ancient Semitic script and was found here at the Vatican. I must have a copy of yours. Because mine, the map on it, is not as well defined as yours. Mine must be the one smuggled from the Vatican and somehow wound up at the monastery I am from."

"This one here." David pointed back up to the other copy on the wall.

"This one must be another copy of yours and it must have been written in English many years after the discovery of the original and kept here at the Vatican the whole time, guarded by your superiors." David guessed. "I bet it was translated to English so it could easily be read and studied by modern-day theologians who were sworn to secrecy by the Catholic Church."

Joseph thought he might be right.

"Is that a number written in the lower right hand corner?" Joseph squinted.

Brother David moved in closer to take a look-see. "Nineteen-twelve." He read.

"What do you think that means?" Joseph asked him.

"Maybe the year it was translated to English?" David rendered his best guess.

As the two looked elsewhere around the room they found other very intriguing pieces of art and literature that Joseph had never seen before.

"What is all this stuff?" The priest asked himself aloud, walking around randomly picking things up. He couldn't figure it out.

"This stuff belonged to someone, but who?" Joseph wanted David to consider this question as he too poked around.

Joseph next picked up a timeworn, beaten-up, old broken-down wooden box to investigate its design.

"This looks very old." He said twisting and turning the box every which way to get a better perspective on it. Then he smelled it. "It's definitely old."

David was looking around for evidence of anything, which could bring answers as well. He read a silver plaque nailed to the bottom of the frame of one of the large oil paintings leaning up against a wall. "The word of Yashmiel." He recited.

"What's that again?" Joseph asked, turning away from the box in his hand.

"The word of Yashmiel." David reiterated louder.

Father Joseph stood at attention.

There, as plain as day, lay a painting of the infamous Yashmiel. The man both of them had learned the historical importance of recently.

David blew off the dust and wiped the rest off with his hand as Joseph came closer.

"That's him! That's him!" Joseph shouted. He closed in on the painting.

David looked again at the man in the painting. "Who?"

"That's what he's described to look like. He's an extremely large man with a long wiry beard. See, David. Just like that." Joseph traced the portrait of the man with his fingers. Joseph's thoughts ran faster than his mouth could.

"In this portrait he's holding a wooden box." He stood farther back to get a better look at his face.

"Oh my! It's this box, right here in my hand! This was his!" Joseph shouted again out of sheer disbelief.

"There…" His eyes fixed to the painting. "…Is the greatest kept secret of all time." Joseph realized, stunned by his own words.

David looked a little lost, not sure he understood what had Joseph so awestruck.

"It's Yashmiel, David."

Brother David didn't know that name. "Who?" He asked again.

"Yashmiel! The thirteenth apostle! David, this man right here is the thirteenth apostle."

A light bulb started to go on for David. He listened closely to what Joseph had to say as he remembered what Brother John had secretly revealed to him back at the monastery the day he found the scroll.

"This man right here…" Joseph pointed to the man in the painting. "… His name is Yashmiel. He walked alongside Christ and the apostles as one yet apart from them. As history records it, Christ ministered to him as he did to the apostles. Only, Yashmiel was to serve a purpose all his own and quite opposite of the blessing the apostles bore."

They couldn't take their eyes off of his image in the painting. The sight of his face was glorious to them.

Joseph continued on. "As the apostles were sent forth to spend the rest of their lives preaching the word of the gospel to save man, Yashmiel was charged with spending his years recording the hidden secrets of man's soul and his potentially imminent demise, which is said to be revealed in due time. Perhaps now, David."

David listened to the details Joseph knew so well.

"Christ apparently assigned Yashmiel to detail definitive signs all creation would end, if man did not mend his sinful ways and live according to his word."

That's when David had to interrupt. "I too know of this man, only I didn't know his name. I too was told of his existence and the purpose he served here on earth." He turned to face the painting.

"So this is him? My elder and my teacher, Brother John, explained the significance of this great person to me." David confided in his new confidant, the priest.

"Look, there's other things here as well." Joseph scanned the room full of ancient artifacts. As they inspected the private stash, they found other relics. There were bowls, apparently from that period, more artwork and writings.

"Look at all these belongings! This is all from his time, or it was his I'm assuming?" Joseph began scavenging through all the antiquities in the overcrowded space.

"Look! Another painting! In this one, Yashmiel is pictured with twelve other men and what looks to be Jesus leading the group." Both Joseph and David deliberated over the images in the work, trying to establish authenticity to confirm what they'd recently learned.

"I thought they destroyed all record of this man? I guess they stored here what they wanted to save for their own study. This must be all of what's left and it's been hidden here for centuries, literally centuries!"

The determined clergyman had accidentally or maybe through divine intervention stumbled into something that could possibly help them.

David crouched down, by Yashmiel's portrait once again and began running his fingers over Yashmiel's face. "The thirteenth apostle. Who would believe this?" He started to pray as Joseph continued mining the room.

Joseph eventually made his way back over to the large map hanging on the wall.

"We have to take this with us." Joseph recklessly decided. "Help me lift this off the wall!" He summoned David to his side.

Reaching up and lifting it off its secure hook, the work came down effortlessly.

"Help me break the back off." Joseph exacted, requiring David's help.

With one huge pry, the men broke the back off the frame. The sound of wood cracking and splintering reverberated off the walls.

In a sweaty haste, Joseph ripped the work from out of its frame and used a little elbow grease to fold the large, stiff canvas to manageable size. He stuffed it into the back of his pants for safekeeping.

"Let's get out of here! This is not the place to be." Joseph clamored, getting his things together.

With lightning speed, the men got their possessions and what they wanted to take with them from the room and headed for the door.

As the door whipped open, a stranger confronted Joseph and David.

"Oh!" Startled, Joseph leapt back.

It was Glenn. He was smiling warmly, waiting for them on the other side.

"Hello gentlemen." He greeted kindly.

David wasn't sure what to do and looked to Joseph for a signal.

Joseph and Glenn locked eyes and Glenn placed his hand upon Joseph's shoulder to reassure him.

"It's O.K. Joseph." He said. "I've been looking everywhere for you. If you would, I'd like you to come with me."

Although Joseph had never met Glenn, he inexplicably felt comfortable with him. He trusted him, and somehow knew something big was about to happen for him.

Joseph accepted Glenn's invitation and he and David followed Glenn out of the Vatican.

CHAPTER 12 -- TIME'S UP

In carefully measured steps a pair of sexy, black, high-heeled expensive designer shoes boldly made their way by the Hassler Roma Hotel along the Piazza Della Trinita' Dei Monti. Wearing them, a woman whose confidence was palpable.

With every striking step men's heads turned.

As the slit up the front of her dress flew open, onlookers could see the shape of her well-toned, muscular upper thighs. Below the hem sculpted, athletic calves which tapered, ending with pretty petite feet jammed in those pricey stilettos.

A loud whistle bounced off one of the buildings. "Whhhheeeeeee! Whhhhheeeeeeeewwwwwwwww!"

Falene nodded approvingly to her admirer. That was enough to let the man know, she acknowledged his interest in her.

"Ciao Bella!" He called out, waving his arm. "Andiamo!" The man wanted her to come over to him, so they could go off somewhere.

"Andiamo! Andiamo!" The suitor called to her again, egged on by his buddies. "Let's go! Let's go!" Their laughter, provoking her.

"Va faire in culo!" In his native Italian tongue, Falene told him to go fuck himself in the ass.

When the Italians cursed, they came up with the most creative insults they could manufacture in their imaginations.

Her wooer couldn't believe she embarrassed him like that in front of his friends.

"Va fangul, Ragazza!" He shouted back, flipping his hand from under his chin, telling her in Italian, to go fuck herself as well.

Falene rolled her eyes and kept walking.

"Va fangul!" He yelled, shamefully belittled by her.

She sauntered past the nearby restaurants, the cafes and the shops without interest. Her stride, quick and precise. She knew exactly where she was going.

Behind her, the pitter-patter of four tiny feet, racing to keep up.

As she looked back, to see who was tracking her, she smiled. "Well, hello there, Lucky." She greeted with phony pleasantry, turning back around with a grimace.

"He must not be far from here." Falene surmised, referring to Glenn.

As she held her hand out, palm facing the sky, she could feel a light rain beginning to fall.

Another roll of the eyes was in order. Falene didn't like getting her hair or her clothes wet.

She conveniently ducked into an historic church for cover. The large, heavy, ornate wooden door was almost too much for her to conquer. She sloppily managed and entered.

Lucky also snuck into the church by weaving himself between her legs as she made her way inside.

"Don't mind if you do..." She said contemptuously, regaining her balance.

Once inside, she began shaking the tiny beads of rain off her dress. They fell in a random pattern as wet dots on the dusty dry floor by her feet.

She'd walked a good distance and it took a moment for her to dry off, and get her breathing back under control.

The church she found herself in was more of a cathedral than an ordinary house of worship.

"This is it." Her feelings told her she'd found the right place.

She looked all around at the architecture and the history. It was quiet and peaceful here, which made her feel uncomfortable.

"Hmmnhhh." She grumbled.

She was incapable of appreciating all it truly had to offer.

Somewhere nearby, the sound of men's voices carried to her.

She walked a few steps, beyond a large column, which obstructed her view and craned her neck.

That's when she saw the voices were coming from one of the front pews near the altar. There, one man sat alone, talking with two other men who were standing in the aisle, by his side.

Falene was still near the front door, and still some distance away, out of immediate view. From where she was standing she couldn't quite make out who they were or what they were saying. The man sitting had his back to her. He was the one doing all the speaking and he looked somewhat familiar.

Quickly, those four little feet that followed her here hustled to make their way to the man. Her eyes suspiciously followed each one of his hurried steps until he hopped up on the pew, taking his seat by his master.

Lucky was greeted with a smile and a fond squeeze.

"She's here." Glenn said to his guests.

That she could hear.

That's when the two men standing in the aisle walked off behind the altar and disappeared into a back room.

"I knew he wasn't far." Falene validated herself.

When Falene was ready she strolled down the center of the long, grand aisle alone. Her black high-heels bore a sharp contrast to the ruby red rug running the length of the aisle, beneath her feet.

Stopping at the pew just before Glenn's, she took a seat directly behind him.

She stared at the back of his head for a while before any words were exchanged.

"I do believe I feel a hole burning in the back of my head." Glenn said, reaching behind, running his fingers through the back of his hair.

"Maybe." She replied, her posture stiffening with each word.

Glenn chuckled dismissively.

"Guess what time it is, asshole?!" She cursed, inclining forward. Spittle from her mouth landed on the back of Glenn's hair. Her voice so filled with rage, it reached the second level of the church, where the choir sits.

Glenn thought for a second. Looked at his watch.

"Howdy Doody time?" He went into a fit of laughter, hysterically giggling and snorting. His body was convulsing and contorting in his seat.

Not so much as a smile out of her. "No, it's not Howdy Doody time." She scowled.

"Oh come on, have a sense of humor!" He turned to look at her. "No? Not even a little?" He measured the diminutive amount of her humor with his thumb and index finger.

"I'm really not laughing." She said scathingly.

The smile on Glenn's face faded. He turned back around and began to pat Lucky on the head, speaking in baby talk. "It's O.K. buddy. The mean lady will be gone in a little while."

"Time is, time is up is what time it is!" Falene screeched, reminding Glenn of his deadline.

Lucky, lowering his head, pinned his ears back to drown her out.

"Oh, I'm completely aware of what time it is." He acknowledged sedately, feeling sorry his dog had to listen to this.

"You're awfully smug for a guy who doesn't really look like he has anything for me. Or do you?" She asked.

"Falene." He said turning his head to the side. "Would I let a beautiful woman like you down?" He answered with his eyes meeting hers.

Leaning forward, with a caustic reply. "Oh, I think guys like you are a constant let down." She was now wearing the smile as she looked down at her watch. Her foot bobbed up and down at the end of her well-shaped leg, which was crossed over the other.

"I'm here then to make sure I don't disappoint you sweetheart." Glenn replied disingenuously, looking deep into her eyes before they were interrupted.

"No. *I'm* here to make sure that doesn't happen. It's me you want." Father Joseph said. He and Brother David emerged from behind the dimly lit altar.

Falene's eyes grew wide upon seeing him.

"Sorry to interrupt, sir." Joseph apologized to Glenn, taking a few steps closer.

Falene now knew, for sure, whom Glenn had been conversing with.

"Hello Falene. I believe we've met before." Joseph approached, never taking his eyes off her.

She glared back in silence, wondering if he was who she thought he was.

"Because I know whom and what you are that I know it's *me* you want and no one else. I won't have it any other way." Joseph took a firm stand. David stood quietly behind.

"You're a dead man. Do you know that?!" She shot back.

Joseph never hesitated a second at the thought. "I do." His voice exultant.

The faith Joseph had in himself caused Falene to pause. He wasn't challenging her in any way and he seemed unequivocally committed to his decision.

She sat still, allowing the energy Joseph's body emitted, to reach her. Falene allowed it to communicate information about Joseph to her. She could feel a strong, powerful, impenetrable force around him. That told her he would hand over his body, mind and soul to achieve his goal, no matter the cost.

Glenn sat forward in his pew, putting his head down and grew quiet. He listened to the exchange with his eyes closed.

Falene remained in position, her demeanor stone cold. She was thinking of what to say next. Her stare turned into a series of rapid blinks as her leg continued bouncing nervously on her knee. She looked between Glenn, Joseph and David over and over again. They were a team that was clear.

Her lungs filled. "What did you think of the redecorating in the Cardinals' quarters?" She provoked Father Joseph. Her head cocking to the side, as if to better hear.

"I did see it indeed." He admitted sadly, making sure not to give away too much about what he did and didn't know.

Her left shoe slipped off the back of her foot and was caught by her big toe. It hung there as her leg continued jerking up and down.

"Any idea who helped us with that project?" She said, her voice winding down to a whisper.

"No idea. I can't imagine who would."

"Well, I just thought the room needed more red!" She exclaimed, throwing her arms to the side.

"We hired the best man in town for the job. You'd love him. He is so good at what he does. It just makes you want to put more effort behind your own work. He was a real inspiration." Falene cackled. "I oversaw the entire project. He let me help a little too."

"I'm sure." Joseph verified, remembering the gruesome sight.

Knowing his job for now was done and that he was no longer needed, Glenn got up out of his seat and lifted Lucky into his arms. Then, he looked down seriously at Falene.

"He is the one who is blessed with a holy bloodline." Glenn said, nodding in Joseph's direction. "He is who I've selected. It's him. He is the one with the purest heart in the world. He is the perfect example of the best of mankind. If he doesn't embody the collective heart of man, no one does."

"Him?" She mocked, giving the man before her the once-over.

Joseph stood before her resiliently.

She thought. Then corrected Glenn.

"There is no direct bloodline linking him to Christ in any way or to anyone from his inner circle for that matter." Falene knew she was right on this. She had her history down. The real history, not the history the establishment wrote to influence the masses. "Therefore, he cannot be blessed with a *holy bloodline*."

She looked puzzled at why Glenn chose Joseph.

Glenn snickered at her ignorance.

"He is truly descended from holy ancestors, my dear." He said, leaning down to whisper in her ear. Glenn knew Falene would have missed this.

Falene thought some more. "OK? Tell me how!" She insisted.

"He is a descendent of a long important holy bloodline here on earth. However, they are not related by pedigree. They are connected by the most basic and crucial building blocks of mankind. That's not blood. It's the purity of the human spirit and it's a bond that transcends space and time and yes, even science and chemistry. It is a link more authentic than anything else in the world."

Falene looked baffled.

"On Joseph's mother's side, there is a recorded and proven lineage of men and women who have demonstrated absolute love and compassion under impossible circumstances. All of who, never surrendering to that which goes against their natural grain, to be selfless always. None are or were biologically related to Jesus or the apostles in any way but they did follow Christ's teachings to the letter. In doing so, they *are* holy." Glenn confirmed.

"Therefore, he is blessed with a *holy bloodline*." He corrected Falene's previous take on things. "However, it's not the type of *bloodline* you were thinking of."

She smirked, realizing she'd missed the potential interpretation and had been embarrassingly duped by Glenn.

"I see." She quietly accepted.

With that one-up on Falene, Glenn turned to the *chosen one*.

"Joseph, remember. I am never far away. I have every faith in you." Glenn offered one last warm smile to his two friends Joseph and David.

"As for you..." Glenn turned, pointing to Falene. "I'll be back to collect my guy and get *this place*..." He referred to the world and everyone in it. "...back in order, when you're done. I bet you won't be smiling then."

Glenn then shifted Lucky's weight on his hip and unpretentiously exited the cathedral.

Falene waited for the sound of Glenn's footsteps to fade out of earshot before she spoke.

"How'd he find you? When?!" She demanded an answer. "I've been shadowing him for thirty days and I wasn't aware of him meeting you."

Joseph and David looked at each other.

"You don't need to know how or where he found me. All you need to know is it's me he's presented to you." Joseph stated matter-of-factly.

Falene didn't like that answer. "Fine! You don't have to answer me. Have it your way. I'll be tending to you later." She forewarned, straightening up in the pew.

As Glenn made his way out of and down the front stairs of the Cathedral, he heard sirens from emergency vehicles racing away from the Vatican and in his direction. They were close, very close.

"Get out of the way!" He cautioned one woman crossing the street too slowly. "You're going to get run over by these guys if you don't watch out!" The daydreaming pedestrian, was thankful for his warning and quickly made her way safely to the sidewalk.

"Thanks, mister!" She waved appreciatively as an ambulance flew by where she'd just been walking.

The alarms and horns were so loud, Lucky had to bury his little head in Glenn's jacket to escape it. There were dozens of ambulances in the streets, some parked, some speeding off.

"This is complete pandemonium." Glenn thought, watching the scene unfold before him.

As Glenn stepped down to street level, one ambulance was forced to drive slowly by him because of congested traffic. He could clearly see inside one of the windows. There, he saw a black body bag. It was filled, but the emblem on the top of the body bag is what caught his attention.

"Oh my…" He put his hand up to his mouth.

On top of the body bag, a large red, embroidered cross was sewn into the fabric of the bag. "Those are body bags for Cardinals only." He uttered.

Inside that bag, he knew, lay a deceased member of the College of Cardinals.

Then another and another and another ambulance sped by, all with the same body bags inside and they were all filled.

"These are all the dead Cardinals being removed from the Vatican." He realized, turning his head slowly toward the papal government, towering in the distance.

That's when his train of thought was broken by the sound of heavy footsteps. Anatoli Vankov and Pope Victor were sprinting down the street, heading in Glenn's direction.

Their heads down, they were gaining ground fast, making their way quickly toward the church. Glenn knew he had to leave immediately.

Glenn turned his face away from them so as not to be recognized and pulled his jacket over Lucky's head and took off.

Quasi-jogging, Glenn made it through the narrow streets and put distance between he and them in no time flat. When he felt it was safe to stop, he did and set Lucky back upon his feet.

His faithful companion had waited a long time to relieve himself and decided to do just that on a fancy restaurant's large ornamental outdoor pot.

As Glenn dashed to grab Lucky to put him in a better spot for this kind of thing, he heard a media report blaring from inside.

"We want to tell our audience, this video is very short but shocking. A camera crew, who were inside the Vatican earlier, discovered a crime scene in one of the great rooms. They were only able to get a few shots of what they saw, but the video is telling. I warn you, the clip you are about to see is graphic and disturbing. Children should not be in the room for what we are about to show you." The news anchor reported.

As Glenn let go of Lucky and looked up, he saw a four-second clip of the most distressing scene he could ever lay eyes upon. God's devout flock put to death in a violent, inhumane manner.

The anchor spoke over the blood-soaked pictures.

"It appears there has been a massacre inside the Cardinals' Private Quarters at the Vatican. At this hour, officials are still looking for whoever did this. From the few details we have, we understand that most or all the Cardinals of the Catholic Church have been brutally murdered." The voice-over explained.

One restaurant patron left her seat at the bar saying that she was going to be sick by what she saw on television.

The images were quick; off-center and some partially out of focus, but Glenn knew what he saw. It was just as reported. The pictures didn't lie. Glenn turned his head from the screen. He didn't need to see anymore and he mentally tuned out the broadcast.

Glenn thought about the fact that the entire world would soon begin to wake up to the reality of what was going on.

CHAPTER 13

A NEW MYSTERY FOR THE PRESS

It was as if someone hit *Rewind.* The scene was exactly the same outside the Vatican as it had been when the Pope died.

News vehicles, reporters, photographers and producers besieged the Vatican yet again. Just like before, masts on live trucks reached high into the sky, tuning in their shots to broadcast live to their respective networks.

Most of the big networks planted their crews here until further notice. This is where the heart of the story lived and where official sound would come from.

Well-groomed male and female reporters, fitting their earpieces in tightly, gave audio checks into their microphones.

"Test, two, three, four. This is… Can you guys hear me back at the station?" One asked peering into a glass camera lens.

Others took different story angles this time. Some formed barricades outside the local Coroner's Office and Police Headquarters. No one made it in or out the front doors without answering to a swarm of journalists. Any new information about *how* the Cardinals were assassinated or by whom would come from here.

This story was just as big as the Pope's death if not bigger. It definitely had more sex appeal.

There was mass murder, a suspect on the loose and no apparent motive. Of all places, it happened at the Vatican. What more could a storyteller ask for? There was great sound and great pictures and that's all TV really is. Just throw a pretty face at the front and the end of the piece and you've got yourself a news segment.

Seasoned journalists knew this sort of story could continue to unfold with twists and turns for months. Most importantly, it would generate ratings, which translates into dollars for top executives.

The networks began renting hotel rooms and apartments by the month for their crews. Everyone was going to be here a while. By housing news teams here they had a better chance to mingle with the locals and dig for more information. There was that off chance that one reporter would make friends with the right person and get the story behind the story, sending their network to the top.

The story now had legs, because of the investigative skills of an ambitious news team who'd snuck behind the guarded walls of the Vatican to find out if there was more to the story than met the eye and as the world now knew, there was. Thanks to them, all the national networks had bought the sensational video or bootlegged it and the gruesome images splashed across televisions everywhere.

The story was out.

One of the basic principles of good journalism is to root out the truth of any story and bring it to the surface, exposing any type of corruption or wrongdoing if there is any. Most people who pursue this field are naturals at this sort of thing. They were the ones who were on the debate team in high school, thought about becoming trial lawyers or politicians and/or who chaired advocacy groups.

There was a mass murder in what many believed to be the most sacred place on earth. It begged the question of who was responsible and why.

Details were scarce so reporters stretched all they had to work with.

"I'm Alexandra Hart, live here at the Coroner's Office in Rome. Information is limited at this hour, but here is what we know. Inside, dozens of Cardinals from nations around the globe have been transported here from the Vatican where we've learned each was murdered in a similar manner. Exactly what that manner is, we are unclear at this point. But the graphic video you see here on your screen verifies the brutal manner in which they were slain. Other video we can show you here, was shot earlier today by a freelance photographer and it shows the bodies of the deceased taken from the ambulances and brought into the Coroner's Office to be autopsied."

The reporter got distracted as another news crew began setting up right alongside her live shot.

"There has been little activity here all day as the Coroner works on wrapping things up here within the next few days. The news media has been promised a press conference later today to update everyone on the progress that's being made. We'll have more for you as this story develops. For now, I'm live in Rome at the Coroner's Office, Alexandra Hart – News Channel 12."

The scene at Police Headquarters was similar.

"Juan Veliz here at Police Headquarters in Rome. Not much to report at this hour, but I can tell you investigators are piecing together clues to help them figure out what happened inside the Vatican, leading to the deaths of over one-hundred fifty Cardinals. Police do say they have some leads, but are keeping tight lipped about what those leads are and if, in fact, they have any suspects."

Just as Juan was finishing up his hit, the Chief of Police, followed by several subordinate officers, burst through the front doors of Police Headquarters and outside where a host of journalists awaited them.

The Chief's large, stocky frame forced people in his path back. He was in official police regalia, hat and all.

He was hot, so he had his sleeves rolled up and the black curly hair on his forearms puffed up above his skin. He was the Chief of Police but he looked more like the criminals he arrests than the head of the department.

Juan jumped out of the way, pulling his microphone cord with him to clear a path for the Chief.

"Chief Morgera. Can I…" Juan stuck his microphone in the Chief's face but was ignored.

The Chief and his officers claimed a spot at the top of the stairs and spoke over Juan before he could finish his sentence.

"Ladies and gentlemen of the media, if I can have your attention please…" He first waited for everyone to quiet down before he began.

"I will give a brief and I repeat brief press conference to explain to you what the latest developments are in this case."

Before he could begin, the mob of reporters started shouting questions at him. They all spoke at the same time, their voices colliding, making anything anyone said completely inaudible.

"Do you know who did it?" Shouted one.

"How were they killed?" Shouted another.

"How many people are believed to be involved in the murders?" Yelled, yet another.

"Is anyone under arrest?" Another question heard coming from the back.

"What was the murder weapon and have police recovered it?"

"Yeah!" The rest of the lot demanded.

Everyone panicked to get his or her questions in.

"Hold on! Just hold on everyone!" Chief Morgera motioned for the salivating vultures disguised as reporters to simmer down. He was growing greatly displeased by the level of disrespect.

He raised his hands before the crowd.

"Just hold on!" He yelled again from the pit of his belly.

"This is not amateur hour, I am not about to be bullied by a bunch of over zealous reporters." He looked the crowd over with a scowl.

"Keep it up and I'll answer nothing and you'll have nothing new to go on the air with! How does that work for 'ya?"

He stared out over the group. Suddenly those who thought they were in control of this story realized they needed to make nice-nice with the right people in this city to get what they wanted and needed.

Silence. Not a peep came out of anyone's mouths. They got it. He was calling the shots, not them.

"Much better. Thank you." The Chief seemed to calm in response to compliance.

"Now! On to the business of the day." He announced while his subordinates surveyed the assemblage.

"We have over a hundred dead Cardinals, victims of a mass homicide. Each had their throats and their wrists slashed. At the request of the Swiss Guards, the Vatican's security force, my top officers have been called in to assist with the investigation."

Gasps came from the legion of journalists. Even seasoned reporters' stomachs turned at the thought of the Cardinals' final moments.

"Before each of the Cardinals my investigators found a white piece of paper with a name written on it in their blood. Don't even ask what that name is because we're not revealing that yet."

As the Chief looked up briefly, he saw the crew responsible for getting the footage from inside the Vatican. They were standing at the back of the crowd watching the press conference.

He acknowledged them both with a wink.

"We have collected evidence from the scene and are now taking statements from witnesses about what happened. Thankfully, the cameraman responsible for getting the footage we've seen broadcast around the woooorrrrld... " He hollered, waiving his arm around in a circle in the air. "... is a true professional and able to think quickly on his feet." He commended.

A gratuitous nod and smile came from the back of the crowd.

"Thanks to that quick-thinking news team, we have evidence that may lead us to an arrest. But unfortunately, the fact that the video has been seen by so many may hamper the investigation and set the suspect on the run. I will brief you when we have more to share."

With that, the Chief made a one hundred and eighty degree turn and as fast as he came out, he walked back in to the building, his entourage close in toe providing a buffer between he and the throngs of hungry broadcasters.

No one wanted to be the first to shout out a question, after his initial admonishing. So everyone just stood there, quietly as he retreated back into Police Headquarters.

"Well, at least we have something new to run with in the six o'clock newscast." One reporter said to her photographer.

The crowd dispersed and everyone went back to his or her news vehicles to write their pieces.

At least all but one.

A lone woman wearing dark sunglasses and a scarf over her head, tied neatly beneath her chin stood there in silence in her sexy, black, high-heeled expensive designer shoes, after everyone else walked away.

The slit up the front of her dress blew in the wind as she absorbed everything she saw and heard.

CHAPTER 14 -- A TEST OF WILLS

Flanked by Anatoli and Pope Victor, Father Joseph found himself at Rome International Airport.

"Passport, sir." An airport security officer requested from Joseph.

"Here you go. Was never too big on the picture though." Joseph joked, nervously offering his passport.

The airport security officer, wearing a very serious expression, looked at the picture, then again at Joseph, then back again at the picture on Joseph's passport. Then he approvingly handed Joseph back his passport and allowed him to pass through the security checkpoint.

"Let's go." Victor ordered.

He led Joseph and Anatoli through the busy airport and to their terminal.

Although Victor was the new Pope, he traveled relatively unnoticed. He disguised himself in traditional priest attire and because the general public wasn't familiar with his face yet, no one noticed.

When they arrived at their terminal, everyone took a seat and Victor immediately produced a book, beginning to read. Never bothering to tell Joseph anything about where they were going or why.

Joseph got down to the business of trying to figure this out.

He looked up at the assemblage of screens before him. One grouping read Departures, another grouping read Arrivals. He looked down at his boarding passes and found his flight number, Italian Airlines flight #5321.

Joseph matched the flight number up against the Departures and froze.

"We are bound for Boston, Massachusetts?!" He squawked. "We're going to the United States?! But why?" He questioned emphatically.

Joseph looked to his travel companions for answers. Anything he could get out of them would be helpful at this point.

Victor never even looked up once from his book to acknowledge Joseph's concerns.

Joseph then tried to get Anatoli's attention. "Why the United States?" He quizzed.

Anatoli was too busy scoping out a young boy sitting with his mother. Fortunately for him, she was too distracted talking on her cell phone to notice Anatoli take an interest in her son.

Anatoli gaped at the child, offering a smile.

"Hello, son." He said, wiggling his fingers at him.

The boy, not sure what to do, remained stone-faced.

"He might be young, but he sees what you're about." Joseph chastised.

"You can be felt. You're uncomfortable to be around. He senses that." Joseph seethed, making sure nothing progressed.

Anatoli's sight never left the boy. He wanted to see what he could get away with.

Afraid, the child turned away from Anatoli and buried his head in his mother's breast.

"There's many of us like him, you know." Joseph educated Anatoli.

"We know right from wrong just by the mere feel or sight of it. We can see it a mile away and we'll do anything to eliminate it from our world."

"The last thing I need from you is a lecture." Anatoli retorted.

Victor interrupted them both.

"We'll see how smart you really are soon enough, Joseph. I think you're just hot air and when the going gets tough, I'm willing to bet you get going." Victor's eyes never left the pages of his book as he spoke condescendingly to Joseph.

Realizing any conversation with these people was a waste of his time Joseph tilted his head back, for a rest, while he awaited his plane to board.

It seemed like minutes later, Italian Airlines flight # 5321 was called.

Joseph's eyes popped open. "That's us!" He announced sleepily, trying to regain his composure.

Still half-asleep, Joseph struggled to get his chubby frame out of his chair and look for his belongings at the same time.

Victor and Anatoli were already standing with their bags in hand, looking at him.

"Come on. Let's go!" Victor barked, waiting for Joseph to get it together.

Further instructions came over the airport's Public Address System.

"Passengers for Italian Airlines flight #5321 we are ready to board. Rows A through C, please come forward to get checked in, please. Rows A through C, please come forward to get ready to board."

"That's us." Victor told Anatoli and Joseph. "Let's go."

Joseph hesitated to fall in line with everyone else.

"I said, let's go." Victor commanded in a low, firm tone.

Joseph followed orders this time.

All three men walked to the check-in point where their boarding passes were checked, stamped and they were given permission to board.

"First Class... Hmmnnhh." Joseph noticed on his ticket. He wasn't impressed with his accommodations.

As Joseph walked down the aisle, locating his row in First Class, he slid in and took his seat by the window. Victor left one seat vacant between him and Joseph and took the next seat available, while Anatoli sat across the aisle in the same row.

That's when Victor's cell phone rang.

"Yup." He answered simply.

"Mmmnn Hmmnnhh. Mmmnnhh Hmmnnnhhh. Yes. We should be arriving by eleven o'clock tonight. Pick us up at the airport and we'll drive. Mmmnnhh Hmmnnhhh. Mmmnnhhhh Hmmmnnhhh. Yes. That's right. OK. Thanks, Bye."

Father Joseph listened as hard as he could but he could only hear one end of the conversation. It obviously had something to do with their travel plans but he had no idea what. He had no idea who was at the other end of the phone. He said nothing.

Then Joseph thought hard to himself.

He knew he would be right to be scared of being with these two treacherous men. He knew his life was at risk. His sixth sense told him he was returning to a place where he somehow would be faced with the greatest test of his life. Yet, he *wasn't* scared. He was glad to know such a heavy burden fell to him because all he ever wanted in life was to make a difference while he was here, no matter the price.

Joseph didn't know what the future held, but he was sure how he would handle whatever came his way.

The right corner of his mouth arched upward as he rested his head back, confident in himself.

Hours passed as their airplane flew over the Atlantic Ocean. Joseph slept most of the way, while the Pontiff continued reading. Anatoli just sat there staring into space, thinking about their plans for Joseph.

Then, Anatoli's cellphone rang, snapping him and everyone else back into the present.

Joseph woke up abruptly with a snort. "Wha… Who…. Ha…?"

Anatoli reached into his pocket and flipped his cellphone open to answer.

"Anatoli Vankov here. How can I help you?" He seemed perturbed by the caller. He listened to the person at the other end intently for about three minutes before interrupting.

Victor and Joseph, whose interests were piqued, eavesdropped to try to find out whom Anatoli was talking to.

"Really!?" Anatoli was surprised by something.

He tensely tried to end the call. "Well, we are aboard a plane at this hour, making our way to America for official Church business and 'uh, I can't find that out for you right now because he is resting and requested not to be disturbed." Anatoli looked at Victor who was wide-awake as he said it.

"I can take your information and get back to you with an answer but it may be a while. OK then, thank you. God Bless." He rolled his eyes into his head as he hung up with the caller.

Waiting a beat. He anxiously turned to Victor across the aisle.

"You were captured in the video. You're seen in that video the news cameraman shot in the Cardinals' Private Quarters. It's all over the news."

He finished. "That was a reporter from one of the networks. He wants a statement from you or me about why you were there and what you know." Anatoli was visibly shaken.

"How do you want me to handle this?"

Victor thought before he answered.

Then Anatoli's phone rang a second time.

"Anatoli Vankov here. How can I help you?" He tried to sound upbeat as he answered. But his face fell shortly thereafter.

"Chief Morgera, sir. How are you? What can I do for you? Mmmnnnh Hmmnnhh. Mnnhhhh Hmmmm. Yes, right. I do understand the importance of the matter. Right now, we're aboard an Italian Airlines flight bound for the United States and he is asleep in his seat. I will get this message to him as soon as possible and have him get back to you immediately. Thank you sir. God Bless. Yes, I do have your number. Again, thank you sir." Anatoli shut his phone, more neurotic than after the first phone call.

"Well, you know who that was. Now police want answers. That was the Chief of Police in Rome. What do you want to do?" Anatoli pleaded with Victor for direction.

A flight attendant passing by with a cart stopped to offer the men a beverage.

"Juice, soda, coffee?"

"No!" Victor swiped at her. "We're talking!"

The flight attendant just stood there like a deer caught in the headlights. She couldn't believe she was just yelled at by a priest.

Hurt, the young, attractive woman made-up like a doll shrugged him off as just another cranky passenger and continued down along the aisle.

"Don't worry about a thing." Victor calmed Anatoli.

"Just stick to the plan. Everything is in place. Nothing is going to go wrong." Victor reassured his Director of Communications that their plan was foolproof.

The voice of the pilot came over the plane's public address system.

"Good evening ladies and gentlemen. The time is 10:48 p.m. Eastern Standard Time. We are about fifteen minutes away from landing at our destination, Logan International Airport in Boston, Massachusetts. The temperature is currently seventy-six degrees with winds out of the Northeast. Skies are partly cloudy but it's a beautiful night nonetheless to be in New England. I hope you enjoyed your flight. Please remain seated with your seatbelt fastened as we prepare for landing. Again, thank you for flying with Italian Airlines."

Just as the pilot promised, about fifteen minutes later, the plane came to a safe landing and everyone aboard disembarked. Victor, Anatoli and Joseph who were in First Class were among the first to be let out of the plane.

"Where are we going boys? You might as well tell me because it really doesn't make a difference anymore." Joseph questioned straightening out his clothes.

"You'll see soon enough my son." Victor warned coldly.

Anatoli still seemed startled by the two phone calls he received on the plane. He intentionally kept his head low as he walked through the airport and said little.

As the three men rode an escalator down to the first floor they were greeted by a familiar face when they arrived at the bottom.

"Welcome to Boston boys." Falene saluted them smugly.

"How'd she..." Joseph began to say.

"Never mind. It really doesn't matter." He concluded and kept walking.

Joseph, Victor and Anatoli followed Falene's lead. She walked through the terminal to an exit where a shiny, black, rented private car awaited them out front. She slid in to the driver's seat.

"Get in guys!" She dictated, slamming her door shut.

"We've got a long ride ahead of us, so buckle up!" Falene requested.

All three took a seat in the rear. First Anatoli got in, and then Joseph who sat in the middle with Victor climbing in last.

Everyone put their seat belts on as she'd asked.

Falene, who was carrying the newspaper with her, laid it down on the passenger seat beside her. It made a dull crumpling sound as it hit the taut leather. The pages were well read and crinkled all over as if they had been left out in the rain, left out to dry, and then put back together again.

"Anyone want to read today's paper?" She giggled mischievously.

No one answered. Joseph just shook his head no, seeing what a mess she made of the paper. He already knew what type of stories must be in there, if she wanted him to see it.

"Have it your way." She dismissed, combing her now longer red hair with her fingers.

"There's great news for us in there though. Joseph, I thought you especially would be interested to know what's going on lately?" She peered at him through her rear view mirror.

Joseph glanced back at her, not giving her an inch.

As everyone settled in Falene started the engine, hit the gas and off they were.

Joseph kept his eyes fixed on his driver. She spent half her time watching the road, and the other half checking her make-up in the rear view mirror. She knew he was watching but didn't let on.

As Joseph sat in the backseat, crunched between two men he despised, he watched for any roads signs that would tell him where they might be heading. The signs were hard to read because it was dark outside, but he did his best. After about ten minutes he finally saw what he'd been waiting for, a federal highway sign reading 95 South. Joseph kept his eyes fixed on the sign until it passed them by.

His face now wore a pained expression.

"Oh my gosh, I think I know where she's headed." Joseph kept his thoughts quiet in his head.

"This is really going to be tough." He contemplated.

Victor perked up.

That's when Joseph couldn't help but let out a long sigh. "Ahhhhhaahhh."

"You know where we're headed." Victor guessed intuitively.

Joseph was shocked he knew.

"You can't hide it. Don't even pretend. We knew you'd catch on pretty quickly." Victor admitted, turning to face Joseph.

Joseph engaged.

The two stared at each other for what seemed an eternity trying to read each other's minds. Everyone else in the car kept quiet.

Joseph knew Victor was trying to get the better of him.

As he looked intently into Victor's eyes, a testament of defiance against everything Joseph felt Victor stood for, he noticed something odd.

Victor's brown eyes had life in them. The available light from oncoming traffic and the streetlights provided just enough illumination to see it. It was infinitesimal, but it was there.

Inside of the slight green flecks scattered throughout Victor's brown eyes there was life. It was the same life that breathed inside of Joseph and everyone else on the planet.

"Did this mean Victor was part-human?" Joseph struggled to figure it out in his mind.

With this unexpected and unsettling feeling, Joseph's heart began to beat faster. He didn't understand why or what he saw, but his body reacted to something unknown to him. As soon as Joseph recognized it, he saw the green flecks in Victor's brown eyes grow larger as if they were receiving life saving oxygen. His heart began to really beat out of his chest now.

Victor, who now was also breathing heavier, immediately took his eyes from Joseph, looking out again from his rear seat window. He did his best to prevent Joseph from seeing his labored breathing.

A feeling of both potential hope and dread washed over Joseph all at the same time. Although he was still unsure of what he'd seen and what it did or didn't mean.

"What are you?" Joseph asked, leaning over to see Victor's face more clearly.

"Who are you?" He prodded again.

No answer as Victor worked to bring his breathing back to normal.

"What in the world are you?" Joseph repeated with deeper conviction, yanking on his sleeve.

Victor pulled his arm away violently.

"God damned potholes! Why don't they fix these shitty roads!?!" Falene yelled from behind the steering wheel, pounding it once with her right hand.

Joseph knew it was time to drop it. But he wouldn't forget what he'd seen.

Joseph and Victor disengaged and returned their attention forward.

Before everyone knew it, they were crossing the Massachusetts/Rhode Island border and Joseph's heart sunk even further.

"Welcome to Rhode Island!" Falene shouted with open arms, welcoming her passengers to the Ocean State.

"Make a wish! We're crossing the border!" She cackled, clenching her eyes shut, making hers.

"This is the smallest state in the union! But it's home to one of the greatest minds in the world!" She rejoiced to everyone in the car.

Joseph had no idea who she was talking about.

"What did you wish for?" Joseph asked Falene.

"That you die." She said in a cutesy voice, looking at him in the back seat, in the rearview mirror.

Joseph had never been around anyone who spoke like this. He was always shocked at the things she came out with.

"Oh!" He thought about that. "Well, it's not going to come true now, because you told me." He needled her in the back of her shoulder with his index finger.

Falene thrust her right shoulder forward, out of his reach.

Joseph pulled his hand back.

"We'll see. I'm used to getting what I wish for." She bragged.

As he looked around at his surroundings from the rear window of the car, Joseph noticed everything pretty much looked the same since the last time he was here. Yes, he knew this place. But he'd intentionally left it behind years ago, never planning to return.

Again, another sorrowful sigh escaped his lips. "Aaaaahhhhhhhhhhhh."

His distress alerted the others that their plan had already begun to work.

Falene glanced at Victor in the rearview mirror to make sure he caught that. He did.

The car swerved and swayed down Route 95 South as Falene incessantly checked her make-up and her hair in the rearview mirror as she drove. She was obsessed with her appearance.

Joseph noticed that even though she looked great, she was always trying to fix something. She was never satisfied. It was like a sickness.

Time flew by. He was so tired from the plane ride, the car trip; it was all now starting to become a blur for Joseph.

He passed out for the rest of the ride and remained asleep even as Falene periodically crashed into potholes and cursed about it.

About thirty minutes later Joseph awoke to the sound of a blaring horn.

"Beeeep! Beeeeeeeeeep!! Beeeep!!!! Beeeeeeeeeeeeeeeeeep!!!!!!!!"

Falene had her hand firmly pressed down on the horn, announcing their arrival.

"We're here!" She cried out. "We're finally here!!!"

Anatoli and Victor, who'd also both fell asleep from exhaustion were straightening themselves up in their seats, getting ready to get out of the car.

At about sixty miles an hour, Falene veered hard, pulling the car up a long, impressive driveway. Inside the car, Anatoli, Joseph and Victor squished together like sardines from the force, leaned stiffly and unwillingly as a group to the left, and bounced atop their seats. Falene was driving so fast and erratically, gravel shot out from beneath the cars tires like bullets.

Without warning, Falene took an unexpected sharp turn to the right, around the grand circular driveway, to park in front of a magnificent estate more beautiful than words could describe.

They were finally here. This was apparently their destination.

As Falene parked the car, Joseph stared out the window at the mammoth German-style mansion with elaborate gable trim before them. The entire property was lit up like a military base, heralding their arrival.

"Oh my….." He gasped.

Before them, an imposing dwelling sat regally atop a hill, overlooking the Atlantic Ocean. Tall, red brick chimneys, more than Joseph could count, sprang up from the pitched rooftops. From what Joseph could gather, the mansion was about four stories. By the number of windows he could see from his vantage point there had to be dozens of rooms inside.

"Holy… Goodness, gracious." His eyes couldn't take in enough.

A colossal copper fountain, which lived in the center of the circular driveway they pulled into, shot water high into the air. Some of its' mist landing on their car.

Joseph looked in awe at the place.

"Newport. Why Newport? Why Rhode Island?" Joseph asked, not taking his eyes away from the house.

"This is where we're staying for now." Falene answered sleepily, stumbling out of her driver's seat.

"Get out. Get your things and settle in." She said tiredly.

"Who lives here?" He questioned her, before he did what she wanted.

"Get out, Joseph! Get your things!" She hollered, pointing to the car.

Joseph looked at her with detest.

"What a witch…" He whispered under his breath as he reached in the car for his bag.

Everyone exited the cramped vehicle and gathered their belongings to stay the night.

Victor took some quiet time to collect his thoughts.

He walked to the side of the mansion, toward the vast lawn stretching out toward the ocean. Being nighttime, it looked like the lawn simply faded into blackness.

There was something out there. Something Victor was drawn to.

In the distance the commanding sound of the ocean overcame all other senses. You couldn't see it but it was there. It was so loud. The churning of the water, the crashing of the waves, the spray shooting up, forming a mist in the air, its presence dominated everything around.

Victor continued steadily walking into the darkness. As he did, he too began fading into it. The only way Joseph could see he was still there was because of the wind. It kept flipping the bottom of Victor's robe in random directions. The ambient light was just enough so Joseph could see the colored lining of Victor's robe. But soon he couldn't even see that as Victor completely faded away.

Joseph watched carefully.

"Let's go, man!" Falene called out to Joseph.

She was holding up one of his bags he'd left behind in the car. She was heading toward the front entrance of the mansion where dozens of servants awaited them.

As Joseph caught up to and made his way with Falene and Anatoli to the top of the front stairs, he was greeted warmly.

"Hello Joseph. I'm so glad you could join us." A woman with an intoxicating voice said, taking his bags.

"Thank you... Who are you?" He said to the attractive, fifty-something year-old woman, dressed in a maid's uniform.

"I'm Jean." She replied.

"Pleasure to meet you Jean. Great house you've got here." Joseph said looking all around at the house, now from the inside.

"It's not mine." She said, smiling sarcastically.

Joseph returned the smile. "Yeah, I guess I knew that."

"Boy someone must have made a real lot of money to have built this years ago." His eyes were full with the expansive rooms, ornate furnishings and artwork in the home.

Jean laughed. "Follow me, to your room." She coaxed Joseph to follow her.

As Joseph followed Jean, Falene and Anatoli took off, going their own separate ways in the house. Falene went up a long flight of stairs to the upper level of the mansion. Anatoli walked down a long corridor to what looked like the West Wing of the manor.

Jean led Joseph to the East Wing.

"Who lives here, Jean?" Joseph asked her along their walk.

"You do." She said with a smile, continuing down the hall.

Joseph looked confused and frightened by her reply.

When they got to Joseph's room, Jean unlocked and opened the door. A gorgeous suite awaited him.

One of the windows in the room was opened halfway and the sound of the ocean outside exploded into the room. It was thundering. He knew his room must overlook the ocean, which he still couldn't see because of the darkness, but knew it was there. Its presence was too great to be concealed by a few walls and some glass. The smell of salt water permeated the room.

A long, white shear curtain secured to the top of the opened window blew freely in the breeze while the other curtains hung unmoved.

Goose bumps raised on Joseph's arms as he walked into the room. It was chilly.

"Holy smokes, this is beautiful." Joseph gushed, looking at the room from floor to ceiling and all around.

"I can smell the ocean, I love it." He said, just as Jean began closing the window on him.

"I'm glad you like it." She said, as the window hit the sill.

A large, luxurious looking bed sat against the right-hand wall. On the opposite wall, windows lined its entirety. Joseph knew it was going to be a spectacular view in the morning. On the other two walls, old, original works of art hung. Interesting, antique furnishings filled the room's interior. Having studied art history, Joseph walked up to one of the paintings, inspecting it closely.

"This looks to be by the German artist…" Before he could finish, Jean interrupted.

"Again. Glad you like the room sir."

Jean placed his bags at the foot of the bed for him and offered him her services.

"If you need anything sir, simply ring me. The phone is there…" She pointed to the phone on the bureau next to his bed. "…The operator will put you in touch with me at any time of day or night."

She paused.

"If you need anything else of me, sir." She spoke softer now.

"I am sure I can accommodate you in any way you need." She stared at him with a strong sexual tension.

Joseph felt strange about the change in her voice and gave himself a minute to process.

As Joseph looked back into her eyes, he suddenly began to envision himself having sex with her. He liked it. He began wanting her, like he never wanted a woman before.

Her brown eyes were clear and sharp, seeing right through him. Her dark brown hair cascaded down her shoulders in long layers. It was healthy and full like her breasts. Her fair complexion looked soft and unblemished. She was older, mature with experience and could handle a man like him. He knew it. She was a complete turn-on for Joseph. She had his undivided attention.

In his mind, he saw her naked, wanting and satisfying him. Joseph kept his eyes fixed on hers longer than he knew was best because he liked how it felt. He wanted to imagine longer how they would be together, intimately.

Torrid sexual images flashed through his mind, evoking feelings of lust he'd suppressed for what seemed to be a lifetime. He never wanted a woman so strongly. He started to breathe heavier and heavier now.

As he allowed himself to become overcome with his desire, he started walking toward her. Her draw was so strong it intimidated him.

She too, began breathing heavily. He could hear it. It turned him on even more, his pants beginning to tighten around his crotch.

Joseph knew once he made it across the room to her, it was all over. He would succumb to his lust for her and he would break every vow he made to God and every promise he made to himself. Right now, he didn't care.

Then, in a very deliberate act Joseph broke his stare with her and looked at the floor, ashamed of what he'd been thinking.

Disappointed, Jean stood there still gazing longingly at him.

"I'd like you to leave now, Jean." Joseph strongly requested.

Hoping he would return his eyes to her, she waited.

"I'd like you to leave now." He said again, unyielding.

With that, Jean scowled, understanding she wouldn't have her way with him tonight.

"O.K. Joseph. Whatever you want."

She marched out the door, leaving Joseph alone with his thoughts.

"See you in the morning." She said thwarted, her voice trailing off behind the closed door.

Joseph stood in place where Jean left him. He was trembling and feeling insecure about himself after coming so close to losing self-control.

He rubbed his arms to get some feeling back into them and he rolled his head around to get the blood flowing back into his brain.

"Guess I should get some rest. I'm really tired." He rubbed his head as he walked over to the window to reopen it for some fresh air.

As he lifted the window up and open, a rush of air almost knocked him off his feet. Again, the thunderous sound of the ocean exploded into the room. As he struggled to catch his balance, the document he had stashed in the back of his pants fell out. It had been there since he and David found it in that secret room at the Vatican.

"I almost forgot I had this." He said in amazement as though he was looking at it for the first time.

The ancient work he'd cut out of its frame was really in bad shape now. It was completely flattened and wrinkled from all the traveling he'd done while trying to hide it at the same time.

Joseph cautiously picked it up and gently placed it on the bed. He delicately unfolded it so it had a chance to breathe.

"Ahhhhh. English. You've got to love English." He said admiring the work translated into a language he could finally read and understand.

He scanned it over quickly before moving on to other business.

As Joseph began to unpack, he noticed a television set across the room.

"Hmmnnhh. There's got to be a remote control around here somewhere."

Joseph went into the drawer of the bureau beside his bed to look for a remote. Inside, he found a book covered in filth. It was the same size as the Bible and assumed it was just that.

Joseph picked the book up to examine it closer in the dim light. He tilted the book toward the bed lamp. That's when he could see a bold swastika on the cover.

"Oh my dear Jesus in heaven." In disbelief, he took a closer look.

It had been in the drawer a while and had a thin layer of dust caked on the top of it. Joseph began wiping it clean with his hand

and blew the residual off with one great big blow. Sheets of dust fell flew off and on to the bureau, which Joseph wiped off with his hand.

As Joseph began thumbing through the content of the book, which was written entirely in German, he realized it was a Nazi guide or handbook of some kind.

"What in the world is something like this doing here?" He wondered.

He began looking around the room differently now. The German paintings he remembered seeing when he came into the house began to make sense, the mansion's architecture made sense, the European furnishings and the literature. It was all coming together.

As Joseph thought to himself, he remembered years ago learning of a man by the name of Jan Reichmann. During World War II, Reichmann was appointed by Adolph Hitler to head a secret German extermination camp, which was a sub camp of Treblinka.

Because of its distasteful nature, the purpose of this camp was carefully concealed from the rest of the world, including anyone outside of Hitler's immediate circle. It was a little known subdivision where select Jewish children who were separated from their parents were taken. Without the protection of their parents or guardians, the children were totally vulnerable, riddled with fear and could easily be mentally broken down and used by the Nazis.

There, Reichmann committed some of the most heinous crimes against children ever known to the world, including torture, mutilation, forced labor and murder. It was a place more horrific than even the most well publicized concentration camps where adults were subjected to sheer barbarity.

Reichmann's rule and revolting legacy during World War II was well documented but where he fled afterward is not. He managed to escape capture when the Allies liberated the camps in 1945. Historians believe he was able to alter his identity so convincingly he managed to secure his money and assets and sneak himself and his family out of Germany and into the United States, where he set up an underground Nazi headquarters.

The authorities were never able to hunt him down. Some speculate Reichmann bought police protection to evade capture.

Joseph once remembered it being reported that there was a rumor Reichmann set up residence somewhere in New England where he continued to propagate anti-Semitism. Many suspect him to be the secret founder of the skinhead culture here on U.S. soil, where today his devout followers number in the hundreds of thousands.

He was allegedly hunted the rest of his life for crimes against humanity but never brought to justice. Many historians and law enforcement officials still have no idea whether he is dead or alive.

As Joseph looked around the room again, he was sure he knew where he was.

"This is his place." He deduced, acknowledging without a doubt what he knew to be the truth.

"I just know it is." Joseph began to get nauseous just thinking about it. He continued speaking to himself in a whisper so no one could hear.

"Reichmann built this place as a testament to the Nazi party, where he figured no one would search for him. He hid out in the open. He built this house off the blood of the Jews." Joseph couldn't believe the gall.

He glanced back down at the book he was still holding in his hand and threw it onto the bed as though it were a highly contagious, deadly disease.

Then, he knelt down on his knees on the floor as though he were about to be sick and placed his hand over his mouth. He dry heaved a few times before slowly getting back to his feet.

"I am in the midst of total evil here." He said softly, wiping his mouth.

As Joseph began to try to get back to normalcy a little yellow butterfly flew into his room from the opened window.

"Well, would you look at that."

It flew right to his shoulder where it took a seat. Even though it was so small, Joseph could see its tiny, fragile body vigorously expanding and contracting as it struggled to breathe. Its petite wings looked heavy and tired.

"Hey little visitor. Where did you come from?" Joseph bent his finger at it, gesturing hello.

The insect, finding a safe-haven upon Joseph's shoulder, adjusted its knobbed feelers.

"That's a nocturnal butterfly, Joseph." Falene answered, suddenly standing in his room.

Her popping in and out of places was becoming the norm for Joseph so he went with it.

"What's a nocturnal butterfly?" He wanted to know.

Walking closer to see the tiny creature, Falene tilted her head to get a better look.

"Believe it or not, nocturnal butterflies have microscopic ears on their wings. They developed them over millions and millions of years ago." She answered patting it delicately on its left wing.

"Butterflies and moths used to be deaf, but over time they developed these microscopic ears to hear a bats echo-location signal. This way, these little guys can hear their predators coming ahead of time and it helps them escape the hungry, predacious jaws of bats. Unlike their daytime cousins, they remain creatures of the night." She wore a toothy grin.

Shortly after she finished her sentence, sure enough, a bat flew in through the same window, taking a seat on *her* shoulder.

"Well, look who we have here!" She looked to Joseph for a reaction.

Falene leisurely moved closer to Joseph and positioned herself so they were now shoulder to shoulder. As she did so, the creepy flying mammal with a mouse like body, stretched its neck out as far as it would go. Its fierce looking mouth with long, sharp teeth plucked the willing butterfly from Joseph's shoulder and began to feast upon it.

Joseph was astounded the butterfly didn't try to fly away or fight in some way to save itself.

"That butterfly gave up." Falene proudly pointed out. "Had nothing left to even put up a fight." Falene scanned Joseph's eyes for any reaction at all, to see what he was thinking.

"She's been chasing him for miles." She told Joseph. "When the butterfly didn't think it had the energy left to try to survive, it turned itself over to a power greater than itself. It knew not to try to fight the inevitable. Why bother?"

Joseph got sicker to his stomach as he watched the sweet, delicate butterfly be dismembered and devoured by the vile beast, sitting on top of her shoulder.

Joseph understood why. "That's because the butterfly didn't know enough to rely on its faith to survive."

Falene was pissed off Joseph wouldn't see it her way.

"Whatever! I just came to tell you to be ready by the morning. We're taking a little trip and you need to be ready on time. I'll see you downstairs around seven o'clock tomorrow at sunup. Have a nice rest Joseph, you'll need it."

As quickly as she'd come, she'd gone. She shut the door behind her, giving Joseph his privacy once again.

Knowing it couldn't keep her out, he locked the door behind her anyway.

"Good-bye and good riddance." He said, gladly saluting her departure.

As he would for a member of his own family or a stranger, he heavy-heartedly began dusting some yellow powder off his shoulder and said a prayer, wishing the butterfly eternal peace.

CHAPTER 15 -- UNEXPECTED BLESSINGS

Back in Nebraska, Terri who'd left work early at Harry's Lunch Spot was picking her child up from chemotherapy at St. Joseph's Hospital in Kismet.

As the two headed out the front entrance of the hospital she asked her son, "How do you feel Tommy?"

He first made sure to adjust his Boston Red Sox baseball cap properly so no one in the parking lot would notice he was bald.

"I'm so sick of this, mom! I don't want to do it anymore!" He begged, looking up at his mother.

"Please, I can't take it! It's awful and I'm sick all the time!" He continued pleading, hoping she might bend and not make him go anymore.

"You have to." She said sternly, looking down at her brave little soldier.

Tommy always did this after treatment. Always begged never to come back but Terri knew how to take his mind off things and try to make him happy, even if it was just temporarily.

"Now, let's go get some ice cream!" She whooped.

A great big smile appeared on Tommy's face.

"Yeah, I'm getting strawberry this time!" He jumped up to yell to the world.

"I'll beat you to the Chevy!" He screamed, taking off as fast as his little feet would carry him.

As Terri watched her weak young son race toward the car, she began bawling. Long, wet tears streamed down her face. She went to pull a tissue from her purse to wipe her face so Tommy wouldn't see she was crying. As usual, there were none.

"Damn it! I never have any when I need one!" Terri fumbled through her massive sack she called a purse.

Before she knew it, someone was waving a tissue right in front of her face.

"Here you go." The man said.

The stranger shocked her. "You should really watch your language, especially with an impressionable young man around." He advised warmly.

"Why… thank you?" She couldn't believe who it was.

It was that odd customer she'd waited on who ordered nothing and then vanished up the road, leaving a small rock behind on the table.

She took the tissue from him and began wiping her face dry.

Then she remembered.

"I didn't think I'd see you again. What are you… You forgot…" She stammered, trying quickly to get something out of her pocket.

"Look, I saved it for you." She beamed, so proud of herself, holding the rock she'd held for him.

"And, it's changing color." Pointing out where with her finger.

"It used to be deep, dark blue with green and white trails running through it. But, to be honest, there were some ugly black spots on it, but…" She spoke so fast, she tripped over her own words. "I kind of thought it looks like a tiny replica of the world, if 'ya ask me."

She held up the rock so Glenn could see it better in the sunlight.

"Ummnnhhh, see, but now it has many more black, ugly spots and they're bigger now." She looked to him for an answer.

"There's some writing here on the bottom…" She showed him, pointing to where. "What does that say? It looks Arabic? Or maybe…"

"Aramaic." Glenn corrected her.

"Ara…." Terri had trouble with the pronunciation.

"Aramaic." Glenn repeated.

Terri felt embarrassed she couldn't pronounce it and didn't attempt it again in front of him. She'd always felt intimidated by others because of her lack of education.

"Can you tell me what it means?" She asked instead.

"Ara." Glenn answered.

"Ara...ma...." She tried again.

"No, Terri." He laughed.

"The word is Ara and it's *in* Aramaic."

"Oh!" She laughed, covering her mouth, embarrassed once again.

"What does it mean?" She looked to him kindly.

"It's an ancient name. Ara. It means King." He answered as kindly as she'd asked.

"Oh. That's it?"

"That's it." He said.

Terri wasn't sure what to ask or to do next. She felt, intellectually, over-her-head, so she didn't feel comfortable asking any more questions. "Anyway, you forgot this." She nervously tried handing it back to Glenn who was graciously standing before her.

"Here." Terri held the rock out for him to take.

Totally composed, Glenn acknowledged intentionally leaving it with her. "I didn't forget it Terri. I left it for you."

He smiled, looking at her, knowing she would be confused.

"Why? What is it?" She questioned, rolling it around in her hand, hoping to gain a better understanding of what it was and why he wanted her to have it.

"Come on mom! Let's go! I want to get ice cream before it gets too late! Come on!" Tommy was hanging out of the passenger window of Terri's car, waving his arms from side to side to get his mother's attention.

She had to holler for him to hear her from such a far distance. "Just a minute! I'm talking to a friend! I'll be right there!" She waved for him to lower himself back into the car and get back in his seat.

"Come oooonnnnnnnnnn!" Tommy flipped himself back into his seat and folded his arms to wait for her. He knew not to press the issue.

"So, what is this?" She asked Glenn again.

"It's a glimpse into the future." He answered mysteriously.

"What!?!" Terri laughed awkwardly. "Are you some kind of weirdo or something?!" She continued rolling it around in her hand.

"Well, I'm sure some people think I'm weird, but no, I'm no one to be afraid of." Glenn responded by crossing his eyes and rolling his head around in random directions.

Terri began laughing wildly. She threw her head back and coughed she was laughing so hard.

"Wow! You've got a great sense of humor!" She hadn't laughed this hard in a long time.

Glenn also began laughing at himself.

"Terri." He said more seriously, grasping her hand, which clutched the rock.

"Hold on to this. I promise you, it's a very special gift."

"But how... why?" She wanted to know, scrutinizing it at all angles more intently as if it contained magic.

"Just trust me." Glenn insisted in a well-meaning way.

Terri knew to trust him. There was no reason not to. She really liked him.

As she looked toward the parking lot, she saw a patient young man sitting in his seat, wearing his seat belt. He periodically glanced her way to see if she was coming and remained quiet as she finished her conversation with her friend.

"He's a really good kid you know." She told Glenn, tears beginning again to well up in her eyes.

"Oh, I know he is. I also know he has a really wonderful mother, too."

Terri used the tissue Glenn gave her to wipe more tears away from her eyes.

"OK then, I will hold on to this. I'm still not sure why or what is so unique about a stone, but I will take your word for it that it is." Terri pledged.

"Thank you." She expressed her gratitude with what little emotional energy she had left.

In typical Glenn style, he smiled knowingly and said little.

"Thank you." She repeated, reaching out to hold Glenn's hand.

He nodded with appreciation for her genuine sincerity.

"OK Tommy!!! Here I come!" She called out to her son. "But, I'm getting Strawberry this time! You got it last time!"

The smile on Tommy's face was so bright it could be seen from where the two were standing.

"He's happy." Glenn told her knowingly.

"Yes he is and I plan to keep him that way." Terri promised herself, trotting off toward her car.

As she did, she turned back once to hold her gift up in the air. "I'm going to hold on to this! See you later! Take care!" Her voice faded as she made her way closer to her car.

Glenn watched until she took her seat behind the wheel and strapped in.

"Who was that mommy?" Tommy asked.

"He's a friend of mine." Terri could see Glenn still standing at the entrance of the hospital. He was watching them.

"Look what he gave me." She handed the rock to Tommy.

"What is this?" He asked, making a face.

"It's a special rock, Tommy." She rolled it around in his hand with her index finger. "See, all the colors."

"It is? It's kind of ugly. What makes it so special?" He wanted to know.

"Well, I'm not sure yet why it's so special. I just know that it is. I want you to hold on to it for me, OK?" Terri entrusted her gift with her son. "Don't let anything happen to it, it's for us, OK?"

Tommy seemed pleased she wanted him to safeguard it.

"Ummnnhhhhh, OK I'll keep it." He smiled, putting it in his pocket for safekeeping.

Now that was taken care of, he had something else more pressing on his agenda.

"Now, let's go get some ice cream, pleeeeeeeease!!!!!" He begged with his hands in the prayer position.

Terri laughed at her son's impatience.

As she put the car into drive and began to press the accelerator, she waved in Glenn's direction to say good-bye.

"He's gone, mom." Tommy said, adjusting his baseball cap.

"Did you see him walk off?" Terri asked.

"No. I just know he's gone."

Terri looked around to see if she could find him. But he was nowhere to be found.

"Ah, the 'ol disappearing act, again." She muttered.

CHAPTER 16

SCANDAL AT THE VATICAN

Rome International Airport was now the scene of complete pandemonium. So many camera flashes went off at the same time that it completely illuminated Terminal C in a light purple cast. Camera crews and journalists who were contained behind barriers shoved each other out of the way and fought for position as the new Pope made his way off his long flight from the United States.

"Holy Father! What do you know about the Cardinal murders at the Vatican?!" They called out.

Unlike the casual way he left the airport, he was now dressed in full papal regalia. His assigned security details were uncharacteristically and suspiciously absent. He walked around like a commoner.

"Are you assisting police with their investigation?!" Microphones from television and radio networks from around the world reached his way.

Behind those microphones, zealous reporters, being paid to get the story and the pictures.

As Pope Victor, wearing an expression of superiority, continued making his way through the terminal, one reporter caught his attention with very accusatory and pointed questions.

"Why were you in the video?!!!! How can you remain quiet, when we all know you were there?!? You have to know something you're not telling!!!" The man charged with his uniquely quirky voice.

The others all turned to look at him. They weren't sure how the Pontiff would react to such allegations.

Victor slowed his pace to a halt. He looked directly at the reporter buried deeply in the crowd and moved closer.

"Pope Victor, son." Victor introduced himself calmly. "What can I help you with?" Victor extended his hand in the man's direction.

"Nice to meet you sir. Fred Grogan from Mississippi's leading news talk station." He advertised, pushing his way forcefully through the mob to the front. He accepted the Pope's hand and then knelt to kiss his ring.

The other reporters were silenced by the fact that this young, relatively inexperienced reporter from a little known radio station got the Pope to stop and talk. They wanted to hear how Victor would respond to such aggressive questions.

The reporter nervously reiterated his questions; unsure Pope Victor caught them the first time.

"I… I… I'm wondering what you were doing in the video, seen around the world, placing you at the scene of the Cardinal murders at the Vatican?" He asked as bravely as he could.

The whispers of the media behind him sounded like white noise.

"What are you talking about son?" Victor asked, beginning to look a little worn.

"You're in the video, sir." Fred looked at him wondering if he'd just given the Pope information he wasn't aware of.

"You were at the scene of the murders, sir. Why? What do you know?" Fred held his ground.

Taking a deep breath, Victor thought before he spoke.

"You can be sure my son that there is a perfectly good explanation for what you and everyone else saw." He teased behind his phony smile.

With bated breath, most all the reporters and photographers leaned in to hear what he might reveal next.

"Because there is an ongoing investigation with the local authorities as well as Vatican officials, I am limited to what I can say to the media."

Fred looked disgusted.

The mob leaned back with disappointment. They knew where he was going with this.

"I can assure you, I am assisting the police in any and every way I possibly can with their investigation into the horrific crimes which took place at the Vatican."

The reporter wasn't finished with him yet.

"Sir. That's all well and fine. But, how can you explain being in the room so close to the time the Cardinals were murdered. I mean, you either saw who did it or..." Fred smiled awkwardly.

Everyone there wondered if he'd go for it and say what everyone there was thinking.

"... Or... or... or, *you* did it." He joked.

The media broke up. Fred wore a great big smile, laughing at himself for having the nerve to say such a silly thing to a sitting Pope.

All of Victor's teeth were gleaming from behind his broad, calculating smile. He rolled his eyes, patronizing him as he waited for the group to simmer down.

"You never know." He said with a wink.

Fred could hear everyone behind him snickering. But those who were devout practicing Catholics looked at their colleague with disdain.

"Well, at least we know he has a sense of humor!" Fred shucked off Victor's remark as flippant.

As Fred put his pen to his pad, he had nothing to write. The tip of his pen sat on the blank sheet of paper briefly before flipping it shut.

"OK then! Everyone have a good laugh at my expense!!!" Defeated, he looked around at everyone surrounding him who was giggling.

The media crush disbanded as Pope Victor walked off, unwilling to take any other questions from the media.

"You idiot!" Someone yelled.

Fred was humiliated but he was still glad he asked. He had to.

"No one else had the nerve to ask that question!" He shouted to the horde, but no one paid any attention.

Fred put his notepad away and joined the others to follow Pope Victor to his car.

At police headquarters, Chief Morgera awaited arrival of the Holy Father for questioning.

As he did, he poured over a mountain of evidence sitting atop his desk. Among it, a video tape. He held it up on its edge with two fingers, inspecting each side of it carefully. He knew its contents well.

"Hmmnnhh." He said, replaying the images over and over in his head as he stared at the case.

"Let's see what you have to say about this, 'eh?" He tapped his fingers circumspectly on his desktop.

"Let's see…." He began again before being cut off.

His door abruptly swung open with one of his officers making an excitable announcement. "He's moments away, sir."

Completely unaffected, he acknowledged the event. "OK then. Let me know the moment he arrives."

"Yes, sir." His door swung shut as instantaneously as it had opened.

The Chief placed the videotape in his drawer for safekeeping and straightened up in his chair. He started clearing his desk in anticipation of the Pope's arrival, but left one piece of evidence in clear view.

Now, suddenly hearing the sound of a car coming to a screeching halt outside, the Chief spun around in his swivel chair, pulling the curtains aside.

"Yup. There he is all right." He said, preparing himself.

Pope Victor was getting out of his car with the media closing in by the second. A crowd of reporters chased the Pontiff to the front door before he was able to slip inside, safe from any further questioning. He looked taller and younger in person than the Chief remembered him looking on television.

"You ain't seen nothin' yet, folks." The Chief knew, turning back around to his desk.

Before Chief Morgera could form another thought, someone was banging on his office door.

"Come in!"

It was the same officer who had burst in previously. "The Pope is here to see you sir." He announced.

"Please. Show him to my office."

Again, the door shut furiously.

Mere seconds later, the next knock was quieter, more controlled.

Chief Morgera knew who it was by the sound of that knock.

"Come in!"

The door opened and sure enough, it was Pope Victor. He wore what one would expect him to wear publicly. He was still adorned in full papal regalia, minus the headpiece. He and the wardrobe commanded the respect of a King. But, before he entered the office he motioned with one hand for his bodyguard to remain outside the door.

Chief Morgera stood.

"Welcome Father. We have never met, but I am the Chief of Police here in Rome. I am Chief Morgera. It is a pleasure to meet you sir." Smartly, he showed the appropriate amount of respect to the Holy Father before kneeling to kiss his ring.

"Why thank you my son. It's my pleasure to be here. I thank you for working so hard, along with your police officers to keep this beautiful city free of criminals and sinners. Now, please tell me how I may be of service to you?" Victor asked compassionately with his hands folded in the prayer position, pointing downward.

Offering his elder a seat in front of his desk, Morgera pulled out a chair. "Please, of course, take a seat and make yourself comfortable."

"Yes, I will. Thank you." Victor began gathering his robe close to his body to take his seat when he noticed a paper on the Chief's desk. He recognized it and took an extra second to confirm it was what he thought it was. None of it going unnoticed by Morgera.

"I'm pressed for time. I left a very important conference in the United States to be here to help with your investigation into the horrific murders at the Vatican, but I do need to get back soon as possible. So, if you don't mind I'd like to get down to business and get back to the U.S." Victor was polite but strict about his timeline.

"Of course. There's nothing I would like more than to get this out of the way." Morgera agreed.

Victor appeared satisfied with the Chief's apparently down-to-business attitude.

Pulling out a witness sign-in sheet, the Chief asked Victor to confirm his presence that day at Police Headquarters with his signature followed by the date. "If you don't mind." He said putting it in front of his guest.

"Not at all." Taking a pen from Morgera, Victor began signing his name. "Not at all." He repeated in perfect compliance.

Morgera watched as Victor wrote his name out.

"A lefty." That's interesting, Morgera remarked. "I swear I've seen that handwriting before… Victor… written just like that." He said, squinting at Victor's unique penmanship.

Victor hesitated, looking back to the paper left sitting atop the Chief's desk. "Yes, well, you know what they say. We're the only ones in our right minds." He validated Morgera's keen information gathering techniques with an affirming nod.

As he waited for his signature to dry, Victor sat back in his chair ready for what he came there for.

"Thank you." Morgera removed the sign-in sheet from his desk and placed it securely in his top desk drawer and began the next portion of the investigation.

"So…" Chief Morgera tapped his fingers on his desktop again. "You know about what happened to the Cardinals. You know they were killed, and by now, *how* they were killed, but what we want to know is *who* killed them. That's where we're at in the investigation."

Victor just looked at him, offering no additional information of his own accord.

A pregnant pause.

"Any idea who's responsible for this?" Morgera asked frustratedly, as though Victor should naturally be of more help. "Any idea who would want all of these men dead, so badly?!"

"No." Victor answered swiftly and matter-of-factly.

The Chief knew Victor wasn't going to give him anything useful unless he had to.

"Well, we know you were in the room, at least immediately following the murders if not sooner. Who else was there?" He snipped.

Another well thought out answer.

Victor spoke slowly as though he were replaying the scene in his mind for the Chief. "When I heard a commotion coming from the Cardinals' Private Quarters I ran to see what was going on… I remember that's when I found a news crew, who'd discovered the slain Cardinals inside."

Victor gripped his upper torso like he had chest pains, as he elaborated. "I was horrified at the carnage in the room! They… the Cardinals were all slaughtered like… like animals. The news crew was just about to set up their camera to film, when I intervened, trying to preserve the crime scene for Vatican officials and the authorities."

The Pontiff wiped his brow, as he recalled the images burned into his mind's eye.

Victor thought to himself for a few moments. He wanted the Chief to think he was searching his memory for more.

"And, Father Joseph was there as well! That's right, I saw Joseph there!" He conveniently recollected.

"…With a friend I'd never seen before in my life. I don't know who it was, but he… he looked like a monk or something." He stuck his index finger in the air alerting the Chief to the critical nature of the information.

"A friend?" Morgera asked.

"Yes, some man… a monk possibly… with a slight but strong frame, a shaved head and bright blue eyes." Victor pulled out more tidbits from his memory bank.

"He wore a brown, hooded robe tied at the waist with a rope and he also had on… old sandals. Brown! They were brown as I recall. He was carrying a sack of some sort. I've no idea who he was or what he was doing there, I just know he didn't belong there." Victor added to his statements.

"You may want to seek out Father Joseph Maggiacomo." Victor urged the Chief.

"He was there before I got there and may have some real solid answers about what happened and who that man was." He directed, now casting suspicion upon Father Joseph and Brother David. "I tried to ask them if they knew what had happened, but they strangely took off running before I could stop them. Don't know why..."

The Pontiff looked at the Chief to see if he was buying any of it.

"If you like *I* may be able to locate Joseph for you and bring him to you for questioning." Victor proposed.

Chief Morgera jotted down everything Victor said on a notepad. Victor's eyes scanning every word he scribbled.

"You know. Now that I think back, I did see Joseph with Cardinal Shanley from Ireland. The moment I walked in... I did in fact see Joseph holding Cardinal Shanley's head in his hands."

Chief Morgera looked up from his notes, his eyes met Victor's.

"His friend, that monk, was looking on as I think back." Victor described.

"And?" The Chief pressed.

"Cardinal Shanley was bleeding profusely from his neck and both he and Joseph were having words before Shanley passed away in his arms. Father Joseph was enraged, at the time. Oh, he was irate about something, all right! That, I remember well, because his demeanor shocked me."

Morgera sat there, taking it all in.

"I don't know what dialogue was exchanged, but poor Shanley was in desperate condition with Joseph hovering over him in a highly agitated state. I just stood back. I wasn't sure what was going on."

The Chief pressured for more facts on the case. "And then?!!!"

"There's something there, I don't want to accuse anyone of anything if they didn't do it, but…"

Before Victor could finish his thought the Chief interrupted.

"Go back… Back to the beginning, when you claim you entered the Cardinals' Private Quarters. Why did you knock the camera off the photographer's shoulder if it was recording evidence?" He interrogated. "That evidence could have helped this investigation." Morgera said, peering at Victor suspiciously.

"I didn't." He insisted. "It slipped off when the cameraman jerked back."

"It slipped? He dropped it in such a fashion that it swung around his upper arm and almost crashed to the floor?!" Morgera countered. "That doesn't make any sense! When things fall, they hit the ground and that's it."

"That's right." Victor retorted, stone-faced. "It slipped off…"

"We're all done here!" Disgusted, the Chief abruptly adjourned their meeting. He got up from his chair, extending his hand for an obligatory handshake.

"Done?" Victor double-checked.

"Done." Chief Morgera closed his notepad, confirming it.

Victor also rose from his seat, accepting Morgera's handshake. "Well, I do hope I've been of assistance to you and your fine organization. Should you have any further questions or need me to help you find Father Joseph, you have my number and you have Anatoli Vankov's number as well. You know how to reach us. Again, we'll be away in the United States for that conference."

"Where in the United States are you headed?" The Chief wanted to know. "What's the conference all about?"

"To the Northeast. For a conference about religious tolerance." Victor shared.

"Yeah? Maybe I'll attend the conference next year." Chief Morgera wisecracked. "I could use a little religious tolerance right about now."

"I'll put you on my list."

Victor's bodyguard was still waiting for him as he opened the door. He exited Morgera's office with more arrogance than he'd entered with.

Chief Morgera sat back in his chair and opened his desk's top drawer. He looked again at the sign-in sheet and smirked, proud of his days work.

CHAPTER 17 -- A TRIP FOR JOSEPH

This morning the sun was coming up over the Atlantic Ocean with great pride. The huge, fiery ball reached over the Newport skyline into a perfectly clear sky.

As Joseph launched his bedroom window upward he was forced to block the sun's stinging rays from his eyes with his hands. "Oh, great glory you're a beautiful one today!" Joseph knew to always be sincerely appreciative of the good which existed in his life.

He could feel the comfort of a warm breeze rushing over his face and he could smell the fresh salt air again. He drew in a deep breath and exhaled. "Mmnnhhhh. It's great to be alive. Thank you for this new day. Thank you for another glorious opportunity to do your work."

Before he had a chance to fully complete his thought, there was a knock at his door. He turned toward the sound; sure he'd not be happy to see whoever was on the other side of the door.

"Be right there!" He called out.

Joseph crossed the room to his bed where he claimed his robe, wrapping it tightly around his pudgy body. That's when he noticed the scroll, still unfolded on top of the bed.

Another knock came. This time, the knocks were quicker and harder.

Joseph yelled to his impatient visitor. "I'm coming!"

Before answering the door, he made sure to roll up the scroll and hide it away in his sack for safekeeping. "In you go, we'll take a better look at 'ya later."

His groggy, lumbering self made it over to the door. "I'm coming!!!" He announced again.

As he heaved the heavy door open, there she was.

"Morning sunshine!" Falene greeted with a great big smile, fully outlined with lipstick.

"Uuuggggghhhhhh." Joseph groaned.

"It's a beautiful new day to accomplish a great deal!" She exclaimed zealously.

The peace he'd felt earlier from watching the dawn disappeared from his face.

"It certainly started out that way." The priest jousted. "Lovely outfit by the way. You certainly are a sharp dresser." He said, pointing up and down her svelte body.

She loved the compliment. "I think how we dress says a lot about us, Joseph."

Trying to humor her, he agreed. "Yes it does." He emphasized by rubbing both large hands across his protruding belly covered by the dilapidated robe. "Yes it does."

Falene was unamused.

Half paying attention, she gave him his initial instructions for the day. "Get yourself together, we're taking you on a little trip Joseph." She said, inspecting her new shoes at the same time.

Joseph paused, watching her ridiculous distraction.

"Get right on that, my lady." He unenthusiastically complied, beginning to shut the door.

Reading into his disdain for her, she held out her arm to prevent the door from shutting completely and reiterated her request. "Make sure you do, Joseph. You don't want to keep us waiting, now do you?"

Joseph nodded with contempt.

As Falene began walking away Joseph heard a male voice echoing up around the staircase.

"Falene! Get down here please!"

Joseph stretched his neck outside the door as far as it would reach and listened intently.

"Falene! Where are you?" The familiar voice called again.

Quickening her pace to a slow jog, Falene called back. "I'm coming! I'm coming!"

"That's Victor. I know it is." Joseph believed. He'd recognize his voice anywhere.

"What's he doing back?" He wondered out loud.

Falene's step quickened even faster. "See you downstairs, Joseph!" She yelled, disappearing down the staircase.

Joseph shut his door and grabbed his sack to begin packing. He began re-stuffing it with personal items he'd just unpacked the night before, making sure not to crush the scroll which he just placed inside.

"This is nuts." He said, shaking his head.

As he reached across the bed to pull the covers up, he lost his balance slightly. He'd stepped on something.

"What's this?" He reached down to feel what was beneath his left foot.

His fingers wrapped easily around the book. When he lifted it up off the floor, he saw the disturbing image of the swastika once again.

"Ah, yes. Apparently has something to do with the reason I am here."

Joseph ran his fingers over the cover, tracing the design. The book had fallen to the floor the night before during all the commotion, but found its way back into Joseph's hands yet again.

"I'm meant to have this or know about this for some reason. So, you're coming with me until I can figure it out." Without further thought, he jammed it into his bag along with the rest of his stuff.

Then he paused for a moment, to think about the recent events of the past couple of weeks. So much had happened in such little time. He never allowed himself time to decompress. As he stood there, a feeling of intense anxiety came over him. Joseph could feel his chest beating a mile a minute and misgiving take hold of his senses.

Joseph reached up to his forehead to rub it. "Uhhhhh… dear Lord."

The images of everything he'd seen and had been through polluted his mind. Rubbing his head did little to curb the onset of anguish.

So, he did what always seemed to work for him in the past. He stopped. Knelt, and began to pray.

He not only prayed for himself, he prayed for the whole world. He concentrated on sending blessings to his friend Brother David. Joseph wondered how he was doing and where he was now since leaving him at the church in Rome. Father Joseph was worried about him.

"Dear God up in heaven, I pray for your strength during this very difficult time. I pray that you reach out to my brothers and sisters and to all the animals of this planet and grant them peace during these unsettled times. I pray you speak to the planet itself and remind our Mother Earth we will not let her down. We hear her cry."

Joseph readjusted his position on his knees, his head bowed.

"As you know, I will do everything I can to help. I offer myself as your humble servant to do what you would do if you were here. I am yours and am not afraid of evil. I am not afraid to die and I am not afraid to challenge what is wrong in the name of what is right."

Just then a sharp pain shot through his head. "Ooohhhhh!" He yelled out. "Ooooohhhhh! Ooookhhh, Ghhhhhuuuuhhhhhhh!!!!!!" Joseph doubled over in unimaginable pain, pressing both hands against his temples.

He readjusted his position upon his knees.

"Please keep a close eye on my friend Brother David. He is an innocent only striving to do what's right. I'm not sure where he is or what he is doing, but please keep him safe and secure."

Again, the pain shot through his head like a bullet, making his stomach nauseous.

Joseph kept his eyes shut tight, going over his requests of the Lord, making sure he was clear on what he needed and asked for.

"Aaaaahhhhmen…" He stuttered, closing out his prayer.

He knelt in silence for a few moments longer, immobile from the throbbing in his head. He rubbed and rubbed and rubbed his head, hoping to distract himself.

Slowly, he stood. Quietly remaining there until his sight came back into focus.

In the silence, Joseph could hear arguing downstairs. Although he wasn't able to make out the words, he knew there was trouble brewing.

"There's more than just Victor down there... There's several men as well as Falene... Wait, there's another female, too." Joseph kept track of every voice he heard.

Then, everything suddenly fell silent as though the people downstairs knew he was listening.

In spite of his headache, Joseph continued gathering his things. When he was finished he left his room behind and began to make his way downstairs.

The black, ornate, wrought iron railing helped Joseph keep his balance down the windy staircase. To him, it seemed like the staircase forever spiraled downward. Joseph counted fifty-three stairs and there were more before him before reaching the lower level.

Joseph huffed and puffed, counting all the way. "Sixty-one, sixty-two... Good grief! Sixty-three...Uuhhhh!"

"There he is." Falene announced to everyone.

When Joseph finally reached the landing, he lifted his eyes to meet hers. Anatoli Vankov was there too. "Get a good night's sleep?" Vankov asked.

"Wonderful, my friend. Just wonderful." Joseph, breathing like he was having an asthma attack, placed his bags to the floor to take a rest. "No elevators here, 'eh?"

"Oh there's one." Falene admitted, pointing down the hallway. "Over there. Forgot to mention it to you."

Seeing it for himself, Joseph wasn't surprised. "Of course you did, my dear. Yep, there it is all right. Right over there." Joseph verified, placing his right hand to his chest.

"Tough to breathe?" Falene asked.

"I'll be fine. Don't you worry about me, Falene."

Swinging around on one heel to face the other way, Falene obliged. "OK, I won't. But, come on in anyway and make yourself comfortable with us." She invited, walking away toward the others.

He knew something was up.

At the back of the room, near the fireplace Joseph saw Victor standing with Jean. Jean smiled the instant she saw Joseph.

"Joseph, good morning. Please come to meet a friend of ours." Waving Joseph closer.

As Joseph apprehensively started walking over to them, he was careful not to exert too much energy so he didn't lose his breath worse.

Then he facetiously welcomed Victor back. "Victor, nice to see you again. Glad you could make it back in such a timely manner." Victor was too busy to respond.

"I can see we're not in a talkative mood, today. There's nothing new." Joseph joked with his dry sense of humor.

Between Jean and Victor a mysterious elderly man sat in a wheelchair, facing the fireplace. Victor, catering to him like a hired servant which Joseph found out of character.

As Joseph came closer, he got a better look at the disabled man. Through the crossed metal bars underneath the wheelchair, Joseph could see the lower portion of the man's legs exposed. Joseph's eyes caught just a slight bit of bare skin. There it was, clear as day. He had an unusual tattoo on his inner right ankle. Joseph squinted to see it better. From his perspective he couldn't quite make out the design, but he knew it looked pointy with several sharp edges.

"This must be your friend." Joseph said to Jean, making his way around her to see the man better and possibly identify whom it was.

Jean nodded yes, keeping a watchful eye on Joseph.

Still dressed in his bedclothes, the man's face and body glowed bright orange as the wood cracked and popped in the roaring fireplace. He sat very close to the fire and leaned inward so far toward it, it was eerie. Uncomfortably watching it, Joseph pulled his own collar away from his neck as though he himself were getting burned from the heat. Shadows from the flames created a theatrical performance upon the stranger's face, which he seemed unfazed by.

As the man stared dead straight into the fire, Joseph wondered if the man was cognizant of his presence there.

Joseph first inspected the man's physical appearance before greeting him properly.

At best guess, Joseph thought, the wrinkled old prune of a man was in his nineties. The epidermis layer of his facial skin was similar to thick, toughened leather as though the man had spent a lifetime in the sun or maybe at one time had a drinking problem.

As far as nationality went, his face was a map of the world. There was no telling where he came from. It was difficult for Joseph to make an educated guess as to his heritage. Although, if he had to render one he would say he was of Eastern European decent.

One thing Joseph was sure of, this man was surprisingly in good physical condition for a man of his advanced age who was confined to a wheelchair. He had a very tall frame with great big, broad shoulders. His arms were strong, muscles well-defined beneath his clothing. His legs were also noticeably healthy. They had apparently not yet atrophied from disuse, they too were muscular like an athletes'. As for his hair, it was silky gray, full and lustrous unlike that of someone so old.

It didn't look to Joseph like this man belonged in a wheelchair at all. Yet he was, for some reason.

"Father Joseph, sir." From a standing position, Joseph craned his neck downward at the man in an attempt to formally introduce himself.

"I know who you are." The man spoke with certitude, his voice bellowing with tremendous base.

Joseph zeroed in on him, blocking out all other ambient noise. He analyzed his speech, isolating every word, every syllable, listening for an accent of some kind.

"*Someone* has a lot of faith in you… it seems… to carry out their will." The man growled.

"German. It's German." Joseph quietly identified in his head.

"But *I* know otherwise… I know… you're going to make *us* very proud, Joseph. Not them." The man whispered, so only Joseph could hear. "You're not what they think you are. Are you?" He said, trying to make Joseph question his own resolve.

That perplexed Joseph, who was certain what he heard. "Definitely German."

Victor who was right there, smiled at Joseph, acknowledging agreement with his ally. Everyone else in the background kept his or her mouths shut during the meeting.

"Like the rest, you think you're more than what you really are. That's because you've never truly been put to the test to prove otherwise. But you'll soon see, you're merely a scoundrel who has erroneously convinced himself he's noble and principled in the name of…" Cut off by Joseph, the miserable old man stopped.

"And I think I know who *you* are, sir." Joseph revealed stoically. "It's Jan. Am I right? Jan Reichmann?"

Neither a yeah, nor a nay, formed on Reichmann's lips.

Smiling fiendishly, the crippled old curmudgeon turned his weathered face back to the crackling and popping of the glowing fire.

"There are people looking for you… But I'm sure you're aware of that, aren't you?" Joseph was sure he was right. Sure it was Jan Reichmann.

"You've been hiding out here for years, haven't you?" He pressed.

No answer.

"Hiding out here… in of all places… Newport, Rhode Island?" The priest couldn't get his head around it. "Why here?"

"How do you feel about Rhode Island, Joseph?" Instead of answering, Reichmann pumped him for information. "Any memories you want to share with us?"

Now Joseph was the one keeping his silence.

Without protest from anyone including the old man himself, Joseph bent down, forcefully grabbing the man's right ankle. Hoisting it upward from the knee, he turned the man's leg inward to see the tattoo up close.

Upon closer inspection, Joseph froze. "I knew it! A swastika! And… and… and… You savage! You heathen! You! You! You proudly wear it as a permanent badge of honor! As the devil himself would!!!" Joseph hissed, dropping the man's foot back into position on the chair's footrest.

"You are the scourge of the earth... you are! The *SCOURGE* of the earth!!!" Father Joseph condemned, pointing at him.

Repulsed, Father Joseph straightened back up, coming eye level with Pope Victor as he addressed Reichmann.

"You're boy, Victor here. You must be so proud. He's the new head of the Vatican." Joseph spat on the floor in front of Victor. "He's running the show over there! You people must love that!!!" He screamed, totally losing his cool.

Victor stared Joseph down during his rant.

"Oh yes." Reichmann gloated, fully under control. "We are indeed very proud of Victor's new appointment."

Father Joseph was nauseated by the very words.

"The Cardinals did the right thing you know, casting votes for him in the papal conclave..." Reichmann said, trying to provoke Father Joseph more so. "...They really had no other choice for Pope. Did they Joseph?"

Victor smirked arrogantly as he said it.

"I hear it was their dying wish to see Victor take over as the head of the Roman Catholic Church. Did you hear that Joseph?"

"Why you.....son..." Joseph reminded himself he was a priest and to simmer down before he did something he'd surely regret.

Reichmann had his guest fuming.

Trying to further unnerve Joseph, Reichmann revealed a tad more before being interrupted mid-sentence. "Victor's inheriting a great deal more than that, my new friend. He's..."

"Ahem!" Falene, clearing her throat and checking the time on her watch, tried her best to get Reichmann's as well as Victor's attention.

Victor nodded, understanding what she wanted.

"It's time to go." The Pontiff told Reichmann.

"Well then, let's go." He boiled.

As Joseph looked away, something fast-moving caught his eye through the window.

Outside, he saw a small black and white dog run across the back lawn of the mansion. Joseph moved closer to the window. The dog's short legs hustled along as fast as they could go. The little dog was having a great time by himself chasing bugs flying low over the grass. His tiny two-toned body hurtled itself into the air to get just the right angle to snatch his prey. A few times he got lucky, too.

"Ahhh, if only life were that simple."

The entirety of the vast back lawn of the mansion could be seen through the enormously grand windows aligning the back wall of the room.

"There must be twenty-five, thirty acres to this property?" Joseph asked aloud, only to be ignored.

His eyes covered the grounds, side to side. An incredible view of the ocean, lie just beyond the lawn. "What a view! It's truly beautiful here." He gushed, giving everyone there a backhanded compliment. "Wasted on those who live here, but beautiful just the same."

Full-length arched windows, framed in dark wood, stretching from floor to ceiling, allowed the natural light and the beauty of the outdoors to serve as the artwork for the room.

With the sound of a whistle, the frisky dog took off running toward the side lawn. Joseph tried to see where he was going, but it was out of viewing range.

Returning to the business at hand, Joseph turned to face everyone.

"So, where are we off to today? What's on the agenda?" He asked, pretending not to care.

They just looked at him and looked at each other, not sure who should answer.

"Well?" He persisted.

Falene gleefully stepped up. "Joseph. We're going to take you to see some of your old stomping grounds." She paused, her face beaming at the chance to taunt him. "Sound good padre?"

Father Joseph was now sure where he was headed. "Everything is fine by me. You can take me wherever you want and I will go." He said compliantly, with dread beginning to settle into his bones. Father Joseph was not at all happy about his impending trip.

"By the way, did you have a chance to see your friend, Brother David yet?" She teased.

"Brother David?" He bellowed. "Where is he?! Do you have him?!"

Joseph rushed closer to her, his pupils scanning hers for any hint of information about his friend. Her pupils dilated slightly, indicating she was excited by his despair.

"He's here?! Is he here?!" Joseph wailed, grabbing her by both arms, shaking her.

He frantically began searching the room. He looked behind a couch, behind large pieces of furniture and even inside an old trunk.

"Where is he?!!!" He screeched, fearing for his friends' safety. "Where are you keeping him?!!!"

Then as planned, his eyes eventually fell to the North wall of the room. There hung two very identifiable works, which mesmerized him.

"Where! Where! Where did you get those?" Joseph shouted, spittle spewing everywhere, his fists flying in the air. He put his hands up to block his face, hoping to hide his disbelief. "Unbelievable. Just unbelievable." He repeated over and over, shaking his head side to side. "Where did you get those?"

"I gave them to them, Joseph." He heard a sad, familiar voice volunteer.

Joseph turned slowly, unsure he wanted to put a face to that voice. Sure enough it was as he expected.

"David." He mouthed.

Defeat poured from David's eyes.

"David." Joseph said out loud this time, concerned. "How did you get here? What are you doing here?" Father Joseph wanted to know. "Are you all right?"

David just stood there ashamed of himself. He could barely meet eyes with Joseph.

"What do you mean *you* gave them to them?" His friend the priest begged.

"He's working with us now, Joseph." The cripple in the wheelchair had more to say after all. "Your friend really wasn't able to resist our requests for help. He's a good guy, you know. He gave us everything he could... information, documents, names, places... you know, everything."

Joseph seethed.

"Joseph, do you think you're a good judge of character?" Reichmann asked.

"Joseph, I'm so..." David tried to speak.

Falene, Jean, Anatoli and Victor all broke up laughing.

Joseph and David stood there, feeling emotionally dead inside.

Speaking up, Victor sparingly described to Joseph the circumstances surrounding David's visit. "I found him in Rome where we left him. I brought him back with me, when I returned."

Brother David hung his head in shame.

"He had both scrolls on him. Imagine that. Both scrolls." Victor laughed like he'd hit the jackpot. "I managed to convince him to turn them over to us and here we are."

Brother David kept his head lowered.

Anguished, Joseph reared toward the monk. "David. How could you do that? We both sacrificed so much and worked so hard. We had a goal. David. Why?"

Brother David's eyes began to swell.

Joseph again looked to the North wall where both unraveled scrolls hung, framed and in full view. He reached up to trace the Aramaic words with his finger. "Yashmiel." He whispered.

"There's a thir..." Victor began to speak before Reichmann cut him off.

"That's his. Let him have it for now. Let him depend upon it for false security."

Reichmann now began rolling his own chair toward Joseph and David. The wheelchair was old, looking to be from the World War II era. Its wheels, squeaky, dry and cracking from overuse.

"Keep it Joseph. Read it. Review it thoroughly and take your time with it. Make sure you digest every word and verse.

You'll soon realize you may not be able to trust what you think you learned from it."

Reichmann coughed sickly.

"Yashmiel was quite the servant, yes he was. A loyal follower of the Almighty's only son." Reichmann flattered, continuing to wheel himself slowly toward them to get close as possible.

"The knowledge he was entrusted with and which he diligently recorded was quite extraordinary, meant to serve as a sacred guide for mankind. But because of greed…" He let out another wet, wheezing cough. "…The greed of the Catholic Church which you so admire, his message was coveted and hidden from the world to preserve it's dominion over Christianity. Without it, man has blindly spiraled toward his darker side. A little ironic, don't you think?"

Joseph did question the role of the Catholic Church in this.

"I ask you this, Joseph. How can you be so sure Yashmiel accurately transcribed every word, every thought secretly ministered to him without ever once mistranslating? Yashmiel could have misunderstood some or many of the ideas shared with him." Reichmann suggested, trying to plant a seed of doubt in Joseph's mind. "He could have gotten some things wrong. Don't you think?" Reichmann tried to lead him to believe.

Joseph wasn't going to allow Reichmann to confuse him. The Nazi leader was trying to make him second guess the authenticity of Yashmiel's work as well as question his faith. He knew once he did, it would spread like a disease within his mind, body and spirit. It would be the beginning of the end of him. The devout man of God knew what the truth was and he held those beliefs vividly in his mind.

Falene interrupted the two. "Why don't we all head out to the cars and get going." She motioned to everyone, making sure they all remembered where the exit was.

Ready, they all gathered their things and headed out to the driveway where their cars were parked.

The front entrance to the mansion was imperial. Innumerable stairs cascaded downward toward the driveway.

"How many stairs are here? A thousand!" Joseph complained, carefully plotting his course down the treacherous cement stairs. He was beginning to break a sweat for the second time this morning due to a steep descent.

Completely out of shape and feeling it, Joseph needed to stop three-quarters of the way down the flight for a rest. "Oh boy…"

That's when he saw someone of the gentler sex pass in his line of view.

As Falene, who'd already long made her way down the front entrance of the mansion, sashayed across the driveway to her car, the wind caught part of the scarf she wore wrapped around her neck. Joseph noticed how beautiful it was as one end lifted off her shoulder and into the breeze. The scarf appeared couture and looked very expensive, as only Falene would wear. It was very long and thin, made of silk charmeuse. Mostly all white, a pattern of giant red flowers outlined in black, dotted the length of the scarf.

As if to have a life of its own, one free end frolicked in the fresh air, twisting and turning, creating new and interesting shapes and designs from the existing pattern. Joseph allowed himself to be taken with its beauty. As he focused, watching it whirling around in the wind, he was hypnotized.

Then, as he continued watching the scarf, it twisted in such a way so to create a very identifiable image within the black border surrounding the red flowers. It was there only for a second, but Joseph's eye caught it.

"What the…" He wondered if his eyes were playing tricks on him. He rubbed them and blinked to erase what he'd seen. Then he looked again.

There it was again, briefly. A swastika.

It reappeared for just a split second within the pattern of her scarf.

"Uhhhh…. I can't believe what I'm seeing. I think?" He questioned his own sanity at this point, with everything going on.

Just then Falene reached her car, stopping at the driver's door. She looked up towards Joseph still resting on the stairs of the front entrance, and tucked both ends of her scarf back into her jacket where they belonged.

When she knew Joseph had seen her, she took her place in the driver's seat of the same car they'd arrived in and slammed the door shut.

A flock of squawking birds flying overhead in perfect formation caught Joseph's attention. He wondered where they were going and if they thought about anything as they flew together.

"How the heck do they do that?" He asked himself, his head cranked all the way back. "Each one perfectly diagonal from the other. God it's a sight to see." He admired their natural instincts, compelling them to do what seemed so odd.

A few hundred feet from the end of the formation, one lone bird flapped its wings as fast as they would go to catch up. He was trailing, but making impressive time for his size. "And that would be me." He joked to himself, comparing the bird's current situation to his own.

Guessing which car he'd be riding in, Joseph wobbled his way down the remainder of the stairs and walked towards Falene's car. When he got there Falene was preoccupied, refreshing her lipstick in the rearview mirror.

"And some things never seem to change." He grumbled, climbing into the back seat behind her.

"Let's get this show on the road, my lady." Joseph directed impatiently.

In the rearview mirror, he could see a deceitful smile arrive on Falene's face. "Oh, the show *will* be on the road, all right."

Joseph heard the snap of a lipstick cap lock into place on the tube.

Pulling up the rear was Victor. In a clamor, he swung open the car door and hurriedly took his place in the front passenger seat beside her. He gathered his coat close to himself before he too, slammed his door shut.

That left only one available seat for Anatoli who was next into the car, taking his place in the back beside Joseph.

"Is he secure in the other car?" Falene turned to her right to ask Victor.

Busying himself with his seatbelt, Victor barely nodded yes, fumbling with his shoulder strap at the same time.

"Is he strapped in or not!" Falene lashed out, wanting a firmer answer than that.

"They're all strapped in! OK?!!!" Victor exploded. "And he's strapped in as tight as can be!!!"

There was a tense look on Falene's face. "OK then, that's all I needed to know."

Joseph wondered who the "he" was they referred to. So he turned to see who was in the car behind them.

There he found Jean seated behind the wheel in the driver's seat. She was set to drive her infirm patient Reichmann who sat to her right in the front seat. In the backseat, David, who sat alone with a desperate look on his face.

"Uhhhhh."

Joseph turned back around, his stomach turning over in sync with the engine.

"Let's go then!" Victor blasted Falene, who immediately shifted the car into drive and took off at her usual Indy car pace.

Both cars launched down Ocean Drive.

The fine natural scenery was breathtaking. The ocean in all its majesty seemed endless. As far as the eye could see, water and blue sky, meeting at the horizon.

Joseph's window, which was cracked open slightly, allowed the salty smell of the ocean to fill the car. Just one whiff reminded Joseph of his childhood.

"Mmmmnnnhhhhh.... That's so good." He delighted in the local scent. "Mmmmmmnnnnhhhhhhh... I never get sick of it. It's so full of life and earth and sea and spirit." Joseph's eyes were closed, as he slipped into another world. A world he left behind as dead a long time ago, but which again began to come alive to him now.

Rotting seaweed upon the rocks emitted a putrid yet pleasantly familiar odor to someone with fond memories of the coast.

Father Joseph inhaled with all his might again and again trying unsuccessfully to get his fill. "Mmmmmnnnnhhhhhhh… Aaaaahhhhhh. Oh God, that's so good."

He was in olfactory heaven.

"Yeah. I love that smell. I'd forgotten that smell. I just love it." He used his pudgy right hand to waft more fragrant salty air his way.

As he carried on, his window slowly raised up, shutting completely. Falene obviously had master control at her discretion in the driver's seat.

"Can't you just give me that?" Joseph groaned.

"You'll be able to revisit many memories soon enough, Joseph." Victor explained. "Why don't you just relax now. You're going to need all your strength for later."

"Oh. How's that Victor?"

Answering for him, Falene interjected. "You'll see very shortly Joseph. Don't waste all your energy on nonsense. Pace yourself."

Hearing the sound of a sputtering car engine behind theirs, Joseph turned his head around to see if Jean was still following. Sure enough, she was and followed behind by about six car lengths. "Why are they coming along with us, anyway?" Joseph asked.

"What makes you so sure they're coming with us?!" Falene reminded Joseph not everything was always as it seems.

"Well…." Joseph was at a loss.

Jean's engine continued to get louder and louder as it worked hard to make the trip.

"Reichmann. He looks like he shouldn't be leaving the house. He seems awfully frail to be out in the weather." Joseph jested facetiously. "You wouldn't want him to get sick or anything."

"Don't worry about him." Anatoli coldly told Joseph.

"Well, who will worry about him if I don't?" Joseph pointed to himself as if he really cared. "You?" He poked Anatoli in the arm.

Anatoli stared straight ahead, not amused.

"No one!" Falene confirmed. "That's the beauty of it."

Joseph looked mixed up.

Everyone in the car except Joseph snickered. He looked around at them, wondering what the heck was so funny about any of this.

"You people really like to laugh at your own private jokes a lot."

"Well, why don't you start laughing with us, Joseph." His driver requested, wearing a big red smile.

"Because, the truth is, I really don't find you guys so funny. To be honest, I really don't think this stuff is funny at all."

Falene, Victor and Anatoli all turned to look at Joseph who was growing increasingly agitated.

The exhausted clergyman reclined back in his seat, getting his temper back under control.

Sniffs in the air no longer produced his favorite familiar natural aroma now that his window was shut.

As he peered out, the scenery at least was still very familiar to him. He was in Rhode Island. Also known affectionately by the locals as "Little Rhody" or "The Ocean State". A place he knew very well.

As their car snaked down Ocean Drive, a sea gull appeared in Joseph's window, catching his peripheral vision. He turned. The bird rode the wind effortlessly, flying alongside the car just above door level. Joseph admired the bird's ability to spontaneously handle unexpected wind gusts to keep pace with them. Smiling warmly, Joseph met eyes with the pristine gray and white gull. He saw it turn its head and look at him peacefully before flying off over the water.

Memories of another time, a time before he was a priest, flashed through his mind vividly. They either warmed his heart or depressed him depending upon the memory.

This trip was already beginning to take an emotional toll on Father Joseph.

"That was a long time ago." He insisted under his breath, trying to convince himself of something. A time before the church entered his life. Before he truly turned himself over to God and way before the collar. A time he was conflicted about remembering.

As Joseph reflected, the sound of a tremendous collision exploded into the atmosphere. "Kaboooommmm!" He could hear the heart-stopping, violent sound of metal smashing, tearing and crumpling upon impact.

"Kaboooommmmmm!" Again, the forceful collision of metal against metal and the ear-piercing shattering of glass broke the peace.

Joseph immediately spun his body around in his seat to see what had happened.

"Oh! Oh! Oh no! Oh my dear! Please!!!" As a natural reflex, Joseph threw up his hands in front of his eyes to block the sight of it.

"No, David! Oh my dear!!! David, no!!!!!!!!" Joseph helplessly screamed through his car's back window.

Everyone else in the vehicle remained suspiciously still and silent as the terrible scene unfolded.

Before Joseph's very eyes, the car behind them, driven by Jean and in which David was a passenger along with the detested Jan Reichmann, was flipping end over end, along the long, windy two-lane road along the coast.

"David, no! NO!" Joseph writhed in agony, sinking down in his seat. "No!!!!!!!!!!!"

A waterfall of tears began streaming down Joseph's face as he sobbed into his hands.

"I can't believe this! Why?! Why?!!!" Joseph cried out.

The car his friend Brother David was riding in had collided nearly head-on with a large truck, traveling in the opposite direction. It was now tumbling out of control down the road behind their car.

Falene kept driving like nothing was happening.

"Stop the car! Stop the car!!!! We need to get them!!!" Joseph tugged on the inside door handle to no avail. It wouldn't open. "I said stop this car!! Stop this car right now!!!!!" He was willing to jump out if he could just spring loose.

Joseph could see David being thrown around like a rag doll in the backseat of the wreck as it continued flipping. "He must have gotten his seatbelt off…before…" Joseph speculated.

"Dear Father in heaven, please protect him…" Joseph begged the Lord for David's life.

"Falene! Stop this car!!! Let me out of here! I need to get to him!!! Please!!! Please!!!" The overwrought priest pulled again on the doors handle as hard as he could this time. It wouldn't give. He was locked in, intentionally.

"Pleeeeaaaaaaaaase!" He screamed, putting his foot up against the door, trying to push it open instead. "Is this thing welded shut or what!"

Joseph's pleas went ignored. He could see an expression of sheer satisfaction on Falene's face. Her rearview mirror had become his window into her soul.

The expression on Victor's face was much the same. As for Anatoli, he stared straight ahead as though nothing were happening.

Not soon enough for Joseph, the car finally came to rest upside down upon its roof. Jean and her front seat passenger, the Nazi, lifelessly hung suspended from their seatbelts like slabs of beef from a meat hook.

David couldn't be seen. Joseph wasn't sure where he was in the car.

Then, in a matter of seconds the car burst into flames, engulfing the entire vehicle in fire and smoke.

"It's on fire!!!!" Joseph hollered. "They're trapped inside!"

Without saying a word, Falene continued nonchalantly driving her car up the road, leaving the accident scene behind them. Joseph watched from the rear window as Jean and Reichmann came-to and frantically tried to break free from their restraints. It was no use. They were strapped in so tightly they were stuck.

Soon, the fire reached them. Jean's hair was the first to ignite. Reichmann's shirt was next. Joseph watched in horror as they fought to drive back the flames by swatting at them furiously. As hard as they tried to escape from their seatbelts, they couldn't. They were imprisoned within the inferno, sentenced to burn alive with Joseph as the witness.

Joseph moved back and forth in the back seat to get a better look inside their car. He was looking for David. "I can't see where…" He began to say. "Where is…"

He couldn't see where David was in the car or if in fact he'd been thrown. It got harder to see inside the wreckage as his car traveled farther and farther away. "Could he have?…" Joseph hypothesized where David might be.

"Oh David, I'm so sorry! I'm so sorry I got you involved in this mess! I'm so sorry!" Joseph apologized to David as if it would somehow reach him.

"Why won't you stop this car?! Those were your friends in that car as well!!!" Joseph couldn't understand what was going on.

"What are you thinking?! Why won't you stop this car!!!!"

Father Joseph punched and kicked at the doors and windows of the car. His captors, by remaining silent, rejected his requests for answers and they certainly weren't intimidated by his bravado.

"Why? Why! Why! He didn't do anything to you. It's me you want!! He… he…" Joseph lost steam quickly.

Slowly, his pleas faded to silence.

"Sometimes, friends go separate ways, Joseph." Falene explained calmly.

"Sometimes you outgrow them and you leave them when there's nothing left in it for you. That's what happened here." She stated.

"It's over. It's done. Don't worry about it anymore." Falene told Joseph, looking at him in the rearview mirror.

"You and we didn't need any of *them* anymore. They served their purpose. So… bye-bye." Falene wiggled her fingers in the mirror at him.

Feeling sickened and sleepy, Joseph closed his eyes and thought about everything. Before he knew it, he was asleep.

CHAPTER 18

HOME NOT-SO SWEET HOME

As Joseph awoke he felt stiff and sore like he'd been exposed to the outdoors all-night and had slept on cold cement.

He had. For some reason he was lying flat on his back on the ground outside somewhere. "How did I?..." Joseph was totally stupefied.

Then, a car whizzed by and he knew. "I'm on the sidewalk?! What the!!!" Rolling his head to the side, he could see cars parked along the road. "How did I get here? Where am I?" He assessed his vagabond conditions.

Father Joseph figured Falene must have dumped him here for some reason after the car ride.

He had a swollen right cheek and a scrape on his chin from whatever happened to him before being discarded here. Joseph reached up to touch his injuries. "Ouch!" His whole face throbbed.

Lying there, he massaged his back first before getting up. He waited for his eyes to adjust to the sunlight, too. "Great glory it's awful to get old. First it took me time to pee, now it even takes me time to see." Joseph griped, struggling to sit his fat body up on the side of the street.

Groggy, Joseph began to try to get his bearings. He looked around.

As he rubbed and rubbed his eyes with his fists, his vision began to come into focus better.

"Holy smokes!" Joseph exclaimed, getting his weary self to his feet immediately.

Joseph recognized where he was. He was smack dab in the middle of an old, familiar neighborhood, which until now he only allowed to exist in his mind as a distant memory.

The houses looked a whole lot smaller and closer together than what he remembered.

"I never thought I'd see this place again." He shuddered, dusting his clothes off.

Everywhere Joseph looked, memories came flooding back.

Joseph was in Providence, Rhode Island. A place he swore off years ago because of what happened here.

"That's the house you grew up in, Joseph." Sneaking up behind him, Falene directed Joseph to a three-story tenement a short distance away.

"Aaaaahhhhhhhhhhh!!!" He screeched, losing his balance.

"Don't do that!!! I hate that!" Joseph reprimanded her.

The run-down white triple-decker with black shutters in the city's Federal Hill section was falling into disrepair. Its paint, blistering and peeling away from the siding. The whole exterior of the property looked and felt dirty. On one side, a lone, ambitious but half-dead brown vine grew up to a second floor window.

Not that it was ever a palace, but it was never this shabby as far as Joseph could remember. Nonetheless, it was Joseph's boyhood home.

He fixated on it, allowing his memory to take him back to his adolescence.

That's when Falene took her opportunity.

"Remember threatening to throw your younger brother off the third floor balcony?" Falene reminded the priest of his younger, more carefree days.

Without realizing what she was doing, Joseph began to laugh heartily. "He was so scared. He thought I was really going to do it." He reminisced, smiling up at the very same balcony.

"Your mother came to the rescue, I believe?" She covertly nudged.

"Of course she came to the rescue. Peter was always the favorite. You could never mess with Peter. He was the baby." Joseph lovingly shared, without a single bit of jealousy. "We all loved him so much."

Joseph's eyes scanned his childhood home from roof to foundation. "It's so dilapidated now. No one is taking care of it."

His eyes rested on the side of the house, and specifically on one of the windows on the third floor. "That was our bedroom. Right there." He pointed to it.

"Our?" Falene asked, looking for clarification. "You shared it with Peter?"

"Yes, with Peter." His speech slowed, depression beginning to sink in.

"Do you ever think of him now?" Falene pried.

"Every day." Joseph admitted heavyhearted. "Every day of my life."

There's nothing Joseph wouldn't do to change the terrible things that happened in that house so long ago but he couldn't. What was done was done. That's why Joseph left Rhode Island, to start over.

Wearing his heart on his sleeve, Joseph let out a long sorrowful sigh. "Uuuuhhhhhhhhhhhhhh…"

Everything seemed to be happening in slow motion. Joseph still couldn't believe he was here.

"Why? What does this mean?" Joseph tried to figure it out. "Why bring me here?" He racked his brain for answers, trying to get ahead of Falene, Victor and Anatoli.

Then he heard a car idling behind him. He turned. Behind him, the car he'd been riding in sat parked with its motor running. Inside, Victor and Anatoli awaited patiently for Falene to return.

"What are they doing?" Joseph asked Falene.

"They're waiting for me like good little soldiers. We have some stuff to do. So, we're going to be leaving here shortly." She said.

"Oh? Where are we going?"

"*We're* not going anywhere, Joseph. *I* am going with *them* and *you* are staying right here." She instructed.

"What do you mean I'm staying?!" Joseph rebuffed the idea.

"Doesn't God Damned matter why!!! You're staying! That's it!" Falene tore into him. "No more questions!"

Joseph was taken aback at the thought of being stuck here of all places.

"How?!... What am I?... What?!!!" A what, a how, a why, a when... anything would do. "What am I supposed to do here?!"

"That's it Joseph! You're on your own now!" Falene rudely started walking toward her car, without answering him. "Good luck, too!"

"What the... I can't believe this!" Joseph's words all ran into one another.

Joseph spun around looking again at his surroundings, wondering what the heck he was meant to accomplish here.

He called out to her again. "What am I supposed to do?! I don't get this!!" His arms outstretched to her for some direction. "Anything?!!!"

In her usual style, without turning around, Falene shouted to him. "Just follow your gut instincts and see what happens! Those are the rules!" That was the only information she'd offer.

"The rules?!" He yelled. "The rules?! The rules for what?!" Joseph knew he would have to find his own answer to that question.

"But... Wait! Wait! I can't!!!..." It was no use. Falene wouldn't listen, she wouldn't turn around and she would offer no more help. She casually walked off, getting into her car and driving away with her contemptible passengers.

Anatoli condescendingly waved good-bye to Joseph from the backseat.

"I can't just...!" Joseph's cries fell upon deaf ears. The car's engine revving so loudly, it drowned him out.

Falene's car noisily rolled out of earshot and eventually out of his line of sight.

"God she's a nightmare! A total nightmare!" Joseph shouted to the sky.

There he was, left all alone without a clue as what to do.

"I don't believe this. This is utterly absurd!" He declared, scratching the top of his head, eyeing everything around him. Even the street smelled the same. He didn't know this street ever had a smell until he recognized it now.

He pivoted on the balls of his feet, starting to feel a little insane as he looked around. "I don't know what to... I just don't know... I..."

A succession of words spilled out of Joseph's mouth with no rhyme or reason.

Then, something suddenly interrupted his random chaotic stream of consciousness.

A small dog jumped up on his right leg, staring up at him with big brown eyes.

"Well hello there..." He cooed, looking down. Joseph loved dogs. He loved all animals.

The sight of the dog changed Joseph's mood. "This is a pleasant surprise."

Joseph welcomingly reached down to pick up the small dog. "What can I do for you?" He asked, petting him adoringly.

Now eye level, the dog answered him with a few ambitious licks to his nose. "OK, I know that's an answer, but I don't know dog language, so we're going to have to figure it out." Joseph laughed, wiping his face.

"You need a new friend?" He could feel the dog's little stub of a tail whack against his side as he spoke to him.

"I'll be your friend." Joseph promised the little black and white pooch.

"Boy you're cute, and friendly too." He tucked the compact canine under one arm and began to carry him with him as he walked with trepidation toward his childhood home.

"Wait a minute... Are you a boy or a girl?" One quick peek and he had his answer. "Uh, you're a boy all right!"

As Joseph carried on with his new friend in his arms he came upon a well-dressed man who wore a great big smile on his face, standing at the corner.

"Hello Joseph." The fellow spoke warmly.

Joseph relaxed a bit once he realized who it was. "Well, hello Glenn."

The last time Joseph saw Glenn was in that church in Rome that fateful day. The day it was decided by Glenn that Joseph was the one he had chosen to go with Falene. Joseph remembered accepting, willingly. It was a defining moment for the priest. Perhaps, the most defining moment of his entire life.

Now here they were together again. Joseph wondered why.

Joseph's pet companion started suddenly wiggling his way free from Joseph's grasp for some reason. Once liberated, he plopped down to the ground, trotting to Glenn's side.

"Guess he's yours." Joseph said as the pup loyally took his place by Glenn's feet.

Glenn just smiled, looking down at his trusted little pal. "You can't beat 'em. All animals, whether it's dogs, cats, horses, reptiles, birds or fish, they're all a true expression of God." He commented.

Joseph couldn't agree more, watching Lucky make his way over to his old house.

"Lucky!" Reprimanded Glenn. This was precisely the time Lucky decided to take a bathroom break on the foundation of Joseph's childhood home.

"An expression of what, again?" Joseph repeated half-laughing grabbing at the little mutt.

Both men chuckled, but couldn't get mad.

Lucky whipped his head around, pretend-biting Joseph's hand as he tried to scoot him away from the house. "Oh, you're a big faker. I know you're a faker. You won't bite me." Joseph joked.

Lucky put on his best, big dog show with growls, play bows and jerky quick maneuvers to escape capture.

The more Joseph called him a faker the faster Lucky's tail wagged. They were having fun together.

"Yeah. Most of the time they're a true expression of God. Sometimes, they're just kooky." A newly embarrassed Glenn suggested.

Both men got a kick out of the dog.

"I think he was meant to be a comedian, not a dog." Joseph clowned.

"Well, that's really not my department, Joseph." Jested Glenn.

Lucky was a pleasant distraction for the moment, but the inevitable loomed over their heads.

"So, what are you doing here?" Joseph asked, growing concerned. "Should you even be here?"

Glenn also turned more serious. "I just wanted to see you one last time Joseph, before everything gets underway."

As Glenn's parched mouth opened to speak, a loud, annoying horn blared from the main road. "Beeeeeeeep! Beeeeeeeeeeep!! Beeeeeeeeeep!!!!"

Both men and the dog snapped their heads toward the direction of the honking.

"Sheeeeeee's baaaaaaaaaaaack..." Joseph sang.

"Let's move along!" Falene bossed Glenn. She returned, very pissed off.

"There's no interfering from this point on! You know the rules!" She scolded Glenn from her driver's seat window as though he were breaking some secret pact.

"Beeeeeeeep! Beeeeeeeeeeeeeeep! Beeeeeeeeeeeeeep!" She wasn't letting up. "Get out of here!!!" She waved him off with her left hand.

Lucky started barking his head off at all the commotion.

Egging the dog on all the more, Falene laid on the horn. "Beeeeeeep! Beeeeeeeeeeeeeeep! Beeeeeeeeeeeeeeeep!"

Glenn nodded in her direction and took a few steps back, away from Joseph.

The horn stopped.

"What are you doing?! Why are you listening to her?!!" Confused, Joseph pleaded. "You don't have to get away from me. I want you here!"

Joseph could hear scuff sounds from the bottom of Glenn's shoes as he carefully backed away from him. He could picture the long gouges the cement dug into the bottom of Glenn's soles as he slowly dragged his feet away.

"Yes, I do Joseph. I do have to leave." Glenn acknowledged.

From their vantage point, they could see a scowling Anatoli still seated in the backseat of the car.

Glenn took another step backward, away from Joseph.

"That's it! Just like that! Keep going!" She used her bony finger to imitate Glenn moving away from Joseph. "There 'ya go, keep moving!!!" She cackled, barking orders at Glenn.

Joseph also noticed that Victor was suspiciously absent. "Where's the big guy? He was in the car with us when I was riding with them down here and now he's gone. I wonder where they dropped him off?"

Glenn didn't answer, knowing he had to get a point across quickly and get out of there.

He looked at Joseph one last time, putting his hand on his shoulder.

"Joseph. Listen to me. I have to be brief and to the point, so listen up. Remember, no matter what happens, be true to yourself… always. Trust your instincts, be clear about your principles and…" Their conversation again interrupted by the blaring horn.

"Beeeeeeeeeep! Beeeeeeeeeeeeeeeeep!!!!! Beeeeeeeep! Beeeeeeeeeeep!!!!!"

Falene screamed wildly, holding her horn down. "Give it up Glenn! Move out of there! What the frig!" Her face becoming more distorted, the angrier she became.

"Beeeeeeeeeeeeeeeeeeeeeeeeeeeeeeeeeeeeeeeeeeeep!"

Glenn yelled above the din. "Never, ever give up what you believe in Joseph! No matter how badly you hurt! No matter how badly you fear! Never, ever give up what you believe in! Hold on to that… and it will carry you through! Don't forget that!"

"Beeeeeep! Beeeeeeeeeeeep! Beeeeeeeeeeep!!! Beeeeeeeeeep!!!!"

"Good luck, my son!" Glenn hollered over the horn blasts.

Covering his ears, Glenn trotted down the street, his faithful friend at his heels.

"Glenn, wait!" Joseph called to him. "Wait! I have to know what I'm…???"

"Beeeeeeeeeeeep!"

Glenn couldn't hear him. He called out to Joseph one last time. "Follow your heart, always! Always!" Glenn's voice trailed off as he disappeared down an alley. "You'll always know the right thing to do, just listen to yourself!"

Before Joseph knew it, Glenn and Lucky were gone.

"Thanks!" Falene yelled. "You're a pal!" She shouted from the car, waving indignantly in Glenn's direction while staring straight ahead at Joseph.

As soon as Glenn was out of the picture, Falene seemed satisfied.

She relaxed her defensive posture and began pulling her car away slowly. She looked in all directions, making sure Glenn wasn't lurking around a corner, bent on returning to speak to Joseph.

Sure enough, Glenn was gone.

"See 'ya Joseph. Take care." She mocked, before driving off in her car with Anatoli. "Tell dear old dad we said hello."

That remark made Joseph feel ill.

Joseph was left completely alone to figure things out for himself. No friend, no dog, no one around him whatsoever. Not even an enemy to trade barbs with.

Hopeful, he considered his circumstances. "Well, I might be alone but at least I know my way around." He said, taking a few steps closer to his past. "Maybe, I'll just stumble my way to finding my mission here."

As Joseph came to the front stairs of his former residence, he dreaded everything about it. "Yep, this is the old homestead all right." He attested.

"A real house of horrors." He let his eyes fall to the cement stairs leading up to the front door. They were disintegrating from exposure all these years.

Before he took his first step, he kicked away some of the large chips of debris settled atop each individual stair. Beneath the chips, pulverized cement as fine as sand.

"What a mess this has become. I remember when these were brand new." He recalled, scanning the flight of steps from top to bottom.

The exhausted priest kicked away another hunk of concrete which left a thick white powdery streak across the bottom of his trousers.

"Ohhh. Darn it." Joseph slapped away at his pants to free the crushed cement fragments from the fabric. As he did he could hear the smaller chips rain down to the ground.

Over the decaying steps, Joseph wobbled up to the landing, peering into the window of the front door.

There, in between the part of an old, tattered nineteen-sixties brown and orange curtain he saw the kitchen floor littered with old newspapers and trash. Everything else inside, the counters, the teapot, the wooden table and chairs were all dingy looking.

"Ugh. What a disgrace!" Everything was unkempt and in deplorable condition.

Joseph tried the knob to the front door and surprisingly, it was unlocked. "This is entirely unusual." He stated, turning the large, blackened, non-descript brass plated doorknob further until it clicked and released.

The ease of entry unnerved him. He didn't trust it for some reason.

He pushed the door open cautiously, looking and listening for any sign of danger.

Nothing.

He waited a few more minutes.

Still, he heard nothing.

Joseph wondered if anyone still lived here or if it was abandoned.

When he felt secure enough, he took a few steps inside, keeping his wits about him the whole time.

He listened again for any suspect sounds. Nothing. Only the eerie melody of wind blowing through an open or broken upstairs window.

Joseph's senses followed anything that moved or made a noise. He didn't need any more surprises.

For now at least, he felt out of harm's way.

And there he was. Father Joseph had somehow managed to return to a place he swore off so long ago. He thought to himself that this must have something to do with his mission here so he remained open to whatever might come his way.

He took a few minutes to compose himself. He wasn't really prepared for this and wasn't sure what to do next so he just went with it.

This was a long dead and buried topic for Joseph, until now. "This must be a time of reckoning in some way." He speculated.

The abused and neglected boy who once lived here in shame, but who was now all grown up and a priest of all things, was in such a state of shock that his thoughts involuntarily came out of his mouth without permission from his brain. "I can't believe I'm here."

The terrible memories came flooding back. "I just can't believe… I never wanted to come back to this… this, hellhole."

Father Joseph circled the perimeter of the kitchen, closely inspecting everything.

Relatively innocuous house wares such as the toaster, the oven, dishes in the sink and even the worn wood flooring beneath his feet all brought some level of pain to Joseph as he viewed them. With that pain, Joseph challenged himself to rise above it and find a way to reconcile his sad memories and put them behind him once and for all.

"So be it then." Just like that Joseph accepted his current situation as a necessary evil and as a means to an end.

"Bring it on. Bring it on!" He roared defiantly.

Looking around at the kitchen, which played such an important role in his life as a youth, he realized his memories were flawed. Everything was much more modest than he'd remembered. This is where on good days; the family congregated, cooking, eating, socializing, etc. "It looks so much smaller than what I remember." Joseph realized growing up he had a false sense of grandeur about his house, even though his experience there was a tormented one.

"Growing up, I guess we all feel like our home is special in some way, important or something… and much richer and more grand."

The discombobulated priest, so far away from his protected fortress at the Vatican, tried to figure out why he expected his house to be nicer when his recollection of it was a nightmare.

"It's just an ordinary, plain, small, unpretentious home. Now the outside reflects what it always felt like to live inside." He saw the irony. "Hell."

Joseph's eyes made their way to the adjacent room and to the decorative wooden banister, which followed the staircase to the upper levels of the house, including his old bedroom, which he shared with Peter.

"Now, there were some good times." He reminisced with a frolicsome expression. "We had our own little world going on in that bedroom, safe from mom and dad and our depressing reality." His smile widened. "We were a team, The Mighty Brothers. Do you remember that Peter?" He spoke directly to his brother's spirit, now with God.

Joseph wanted so badly to go upstairs to see his bedroom again but he held himself back, not knowing if he could really take it.

That's when an unexpected houseguest startled him.

Looking still spry as ever, an old man in his very late eighties leapt his way up the same crumbling front stairs Joseph just navigated. He called out to Joseph through a long, silvery mangy beard.

"Joseph, I know that's you! Joseph, is that you, you little rascal?"

He knew the voice. "That couldn't be…" Joseph rethought it.

The man called to him again with strained, raspy vocal cords. "Joe!"

Joseph rushed to open the front door, which had shut behind him. When he did, he received the greatest gift he could have ever hoped for. He knew who the visitor was. It was a neighbor he'd grown up around and who knew the family well and who frequently saved he and his siblings from the misery of domestic violence.

"Mr. Buonopane! Oh my goodness! You still live here in the neighborhood!" Joseph was elated to see him. This was a real treat.

"Joseph, it is you! Why you little devil! Where have you been all these years? I wondered..." The man shrieked with delight, seeing it really was his little chum from decades before. He shuffled inside, clearing the threshold and shutting the door behind him.

Joseph threw his arms around the elderly gentleman, giving him a great big bear hug.

"How are you Mr. Buonopane?" Joseph squeezed him tightly around his middle. "I've missed you, you know. So many times over the years I thought about you."

The old man whose vintage clothing hung off him like he was a scarecrow, looked up at Joseph whom he still saw as a kid, with great pride. He could picture him riding his bike around the neighborhood, like it was yesterday.

"Look at you, Joseph. Why you're a..."

His skinny fingers with protruding blue veins reached for and grabbed Joseph's cross, which hung around his neck. Mr. Buonopane's hands shook as he brought it closer to his aging eyes to see.

"A priest!" Joseph exclaimed. "Can you believe it? Me! A priest?!"

"Well how about that! I'm so proud to know 'ya, Joseph. I really am. I always knew you'd turn out OK. I really did." The kind man with a face that looked like a sunken-in apple and with just as many deep-set lines, smiled proudly at Joseph. His tenderhearted grin was as honest and good as it got.

"I am so glad to see you!" Joseph gushed, his hands firmly clamped onto his visitor's shoulders.

"You were always so nice to us Mr. Buonopane. You always were." Joseph looked his old acquaintance over, so happy to see him again. Much time had passed since he'd last seen this man, but time hadn't changed who he was. Not one bit.

It was a fine reward during such a difficult time.

"You probably don't know this, but I think you saved our lives many times when mom and dad got... out of control." Joseph reminded appreciatively.

"Oh, never you mind about that. It was hard times. That was a long time ago." Mr. Buonopane reached into his pocket for a dirty cloth handkerchief to wipe his nose.

Joseph swore he remembered the same handkerchief from when he was a child. It didn't look like it had ever been washed in between then and now.

Mr. Buonopane blew his nose loudly into the handkerchief.

"You looking for your father, Joe?" Mr. Buonopane asked, assuming that's why he was here. "Is that why you came back?"

His eyes were no longer bright and clear with a distinct black ring encircling his gorgeous bluish-green iris. They were now cloudy and dim. It was evident he had trouble seeing. Still, they were the most beautiful eyes in the world to Father Joseph.

"I wasn't really sure if he was even still..." Joseph stopped. "To be honest, I really don't care if..." He stopped himself again.

Mr. Buonopane didn't read between the lines of what Joseph was saying.

"He's at Ocean State Hospital, Joe. You should go see him. It's just him now. Everyone else is gone." The old man offered what Joseph had been wondering but didn't want to ask. "I bet he'd want to see 'ya, Joe."

Joseph didn't want to react negatively about his father to Mr. Buonopane, so he smiled subtly, thanking him for the information.

He also wanted to make sure while he had this opportunity to let his former neighbor know just how much he'd meant to him when he was little. Joseph had always regretted never telling Mr. Buonopane how much he appreciated what he had done for him and his family.

"You were an angel to us, Mr. Buonopane." Joseph said, looking back into those very aged but radiant eyes.

Mr. Buonopane bowed his head out of humility. Being so modest, he found it uncomfortable to receive such a generous compliment.

"You treated us like your own children when my father would brutalize us. When us kids couldn't take it anymore, we'd run to your house and you would take care of us and let us stay the night." Father Joseph reminded him of his graciousness.

Mr. Buonopane silently nodded his head.

"You fed us, gave us a roof over our heads and gave us love. We slept over so many times, I can't count how many. You even gave us our own personal blankets and pillows to keep there." Joseph became emotional thinking about it.

"I'll never forget it, sir. Never. You really did save our lives. Your example helped me become the man I am today and I am proud of that fact." Joseph's gratitude revealed itself through reddened eyes.

"Oh, you never mind about that!" Mr. Buonopane dismissed, as though he didn't do anything special. "I know it was hard. But you have to do your best with what 'ya got, kid." The elderly gentlemen's Italian accent came out when he was nervous. "I always knew you'd be O.K. Joe. You were the strong one. I didn't do anything. You did all the hard work. Up here." He tapped Joseph on the temple with his fingertips.

Both men beamed with admiration for one another.

"Did I ever thank you?" Joseph asked.

Mr. Buonopane didn't know what to say.

"If I didn't, I want to thank you now… from all of us, especially Peter." Joseph reached out to grab Mr. Buonopane's hand.

Mr. Buonopane was so proud of what a fine man Joseph had become. His crinkly smile was as wide as his mouth would allow it to go, displaying his brown, stained, crooked teeth.

"I want to say thank you for all you did for us and I want you to know how sincerely I mean it Mr. Buonopane. I love you. I know God was at work when you came into our lives. It wasn't coincidence and it wasn't an accident. God sent you to us to help us and you did. You did as you were meant to do and good things happened as a result. Thank you." Father Joseph said, meaning every word. "Thank you for knowing the right thing to do… and actually doing it. It saved lives. Truly saved lives."

Mr. Buonopane was overwhelmed.

"If there's anything I did that helped, Joe... then... Prego!" He answered in Italian. "You are welcome!" He was such a happy-go-lucky old geezer. "Very, very welcome!"

With that, Mr. Buonopane excused himself from the house, to go back home. "If you get a chance, come back to see me Joe. I'll make you a cup of my famous espresso a'la Buonopane and we'll sit and have a chat." He said, turning to head out the door. "Now, go see your dad kiddo. He'll want to see 'ya."

"Thank you, I will." Joseph accepted the invitation to return for a visit; sure he wouldn't ever be back.

He watched as Mr. Buonopane slowly strolled down the sidewalk, toward his house a few doors down.

Joseph exited as well, shutting and locking the front door of his old house behind him.

"Which way..." Father Joseph tried to remember where exactly the hospital was located in relation to where he was in the city right now. He pointed in the direction he thought he should head. "East a few blocks, then South." Joseph guessed.

He took off on foot for Ocean State Hospital as Mr. Buonopane had suggested.

The hospital was not far at all, less than two miles. He kept walking in its general direction until he stumbled upon it.

Oversized, shiny metal letters running along the roof of the building read, Ocean State Hospital. "And sure enough, here we are. Not a bad sense of direction for a guy whose been away a long time." He patted himself on the back, figuratively.

Father Joseph walked in through the main entrance's revolving turnstile door. "Now where can I find the..." He wandered aimlessly, searching the lobby.

The Information Desk was straight ahead. "Ah hah."

He stopped there to get the status of his father's condition and room number. Then he hopped onto the nearest elevator, punching the button for the seventh floor. "Didn't think I'd be doing this today."

The elevator hoisted upward quicker than what Joseph was used to. He swayed. To stop himself from falling, he braced himself against a handrail, which ran along the inside of the car.

Within seconds the elevator stopped, chimed and its doors slid open horizontally before him. A large, silver 7 was affixed to the wall across from the elevator. "Seventh floor, here we are."

Before getting off, Father Joseph concentrated on his breathing. "O.K. Joseph, this is a big one now." He said to himself. "Get your mind ready. Get yourself together." He drew in a long, deep breath.

When he felt he was ready, he stepped off the elevator and on to the Intensive Care Unit of the hospital.

"He's here." Father Joseph knew his father was somewhere on this floor, he could sense it. Chills ran up his spine.

Joseph closed his eyes for a moment of silence and a final prayer before confronting one of the main demons from his past, his own father.

He obediently bowed his head.

"Dear God, I don't know why this has been placed before me. Why have I come back to revisit this chapter of my life? I was done with this a long time ago. Truly put it behind me. Please help me to understand. What is left to do here?"

Another set of chills traveled up his back. "I can feel him." Joseph attested. "And he can feel me, too. He knows I'm here." Getting the creeps, Joseph opened his eyes. He looked around, disturbed with fear and then closed them again, resuming his prayer.

"The mind-numbing abuse I suffered at the hands of my father as a child was life-altering. He was the spirit of evil, disguised as the man I believed intended to raise me to be a good, strong man. But, he manipulated me instead. In retrospect, I see how sneaky he was to use my naiveté against me, to warp my sense of reality. My father cruelly used his position as the head of our family to emotionally crush those of us who thirsted for his love and guidance. His intent was to annihilate our confidence, our will. For a long time in my family, everyone's hearts were broken. I personally struggled for years to find myself through the pain... to find my purpose, so I would have a reason to live. Through much hard work and prayer, I did. I found my passion, and my mission in life. Your love and compassion replaced the darkness, hurt and resentment which festered within my heart." Father Joseph felt God's love embrace him. "I thank you."

Another deep breath.

"Once I was old enough to unmask and expose my father for the coward he was, I never sought revenge on him my Lord. You know this. I left that to you, to do with him as you see fit. I simply walked away, a man of peace and never looked back. Marched on... to find my own way in this complicated world. I viewed my nightmarish experiences with him as a necessary evil; you must be trying to teach me something. In time, I realized that my lesson was to learn how to overcome the most threatening circumstances and to use those negative experiences as a motivating factor for becoming a better human being. To make it a priority to help others who are also in peril. It taught me the only correct solution to any problem is absolute and total dedication to your passion, whatever that may be. That will always lead you in the right direction. It made me the man I am today."

Joseph cited one of his personally favorite orisons authored by Reinhold Niebuhr. "It taught me... to seek... the serenity to accept the things I cannot change, the courage to change the things I can and the wisdom to know the difference."

Not letting it distract him, he listened as a patient's bed was wheeled down the corridor by hospital staff chitchatting with each other.

Even though Joseph was confident of his resolve, he feared what he might say or do in the company of his father whom he still detested so greatly. As a child, Joseph frequently wished his father would die because it would have been easier on the family.

"So if this is your will, then let it be done. I know you have a plan for me even though I don't know what it is. I will surrender to it. I am your humble servant."

He looked down the hallway in the direction of where he thought his father's room might be in ICU. Goose bumps formed beneath his skin, just thinking about seeing him again.

"What doesn't kill us, makes us stronger. So we can positively impact the lives of our brothers and sisters." Joseph reminded himself how important this was. "My mission in life is to preserve the goodness of this world. To create more and to continue this work until I draw my last breath." He affirmed.

He also appealed to God to help him quickly decipher his purpose here and asked for the strength to be able to do the right thing under the circumstances.

"Amen." His prayer was with the Almighty.

Father Joseph anxiously walked down the hall toward the patient rooms in the Intensive Care Unit.

He could hear the sounds of illness all around him. Sick people coughed, sneezed, moaned and groaned. Some desperately called for nurses. Others summoned hospital staff to their bedsides, by pressing a button, which caused their room lights above their doors in the hall to flicker on and off, like fireflies.

A bit of a hypochondriac, Joseph couldn't stand it. "Ack!" He covered his nose and mouth with his collar. Joseph once read in a medical journal that a single sneeze could spray droplets infected with bacteria and viruses as far as three feet.

"Good grief! If I get out of here without contracting something life-threatening, I'll have really done something."

The managing nurse reading medical charts at the nurses' station frowned. "Mmmnnnhhhh-Hmmmnnnnhhhhh." She disapprovingly murmured under her breath.

Joseph kept his hands shoved deeply into his pockets as he walked. He didn't want to accidentally touch something infected, transferring it to him. He knew bacteria such as Staphylococcus aureus could survive for weeks on surfaces.

The smell from commodes, yet to be emptied, sitting out in the corridor made Joseph feel sick. "Oooooooffffffffffffff…" Nauseated, he turned his head away. "Offensive."

He strode quickly as possible to escape the sight of it and the odor.

It was all he could do, not to remark.

"Foul..." The word unintentionally slipped from his lips within earshot of a young nurse. She inertly turned in Joseph's direction but had no real reaction to his criticism.

Father Joseph kept going, checking room numbers on both sides of the hallway.

Peeking into patient rooms along the way, he could see the infirm lying in their beds, like zombies. Some had company, most didn't. It was depressing.

Then, he finally came upon what he was looking for. Room 704. The nameplate hanging eye-level on the wall outside the room confirmed it.

It read, **Joseph Maggiacomo** in bold black text.

Father Joseph's feet fell still before the door. His heart and mind grew heavy with stress, making him feel a little sleepy.

Joseph reached up to trace the letters of his father's name with his forefinger. "Joseph Maggiacomo. After all this time, we meet again." He said regrettably, reminding himself to remain open-minded about God's unforeseeable plan for him.

Another round of chills shot up his back.

"This better be good..." He joshed under his breath to his Creator.

Joseph knew he had to enter, but he felt conflicted. After all, with good reason, he'd hated his father with a passion for as far back as he could remember. He never wanted to see him ever again. Yet, Joseph knew, he must have arrived at this personal crossroads for a good reason. This must be where God wanted him. So, going in, facing his father and dealing with whatever occurred as a result was his destiny and therefore, the right thing to do.

"Is there a lesson here or is it a test of some kind?" He considered both possibilities.

Father Joseph knew it wasn't his business or right to know the reason he had to do this today. That was only for God to know. Joseph knew his sole responsibility in this world was to serve as a proponent of peace through any situation he encountered. No exceptions. He was committed to this.

Still, he wondered if visiting his father after all this time was the right thing to do, for him or his father.

Then he remembered what Glenn told him. He recollected the brief conversation he had with him just earlier in the day. Glenn said… "No matter what happens, be true to yourself… trust your instincts… follow your heart, always." Father Joseph believed this.

Holding his breath a little, Joseph took one step forward and pushed the door to his father's room slightly ajar by its silver handle.

He listened.

The only sounds he could hear come from the room were the blips and bleeps of complex-looking monitors and the distinct pressurized rise and fall of a ventilator.

No voices.

Joseph pushed the door open further, sticking his head inside.

From what he could see, it was a private room. There was only one bed, surrounded by sophisticated medical equipment. Like cobwebs, white and gray wires, criss-crossed each other in a fine network, from one medical device to another.

Resting in that hospital bed inside the room, a man whose identity was concealed behind a tangle of cables.

"Oh my! Is that him?" He gasped, leaning closer.

Something at the foot of the bed caught Joseph's eye. There, a pair of old, pale, skeletal feet poked out from beneath a cheap hospital blanket. They didn't look familiar.

Joseph courageously walked into the room, allowing the door to swing shut behind him.

Now inside, he could get a look at the patient up-close.

Joseph tensely walked up to the bed and then went numb.

"Oh dear." He said, shocked. "You're…"

Appearing to pathetically weigh only about a hundred pounds, it was a much older, much grayer, much weaker and much more vulnerable man than he remembered.

"It *is* you. But you're so old now." Joseph said in disbelief, standing there like he was looking at a ghost. "A frail, sickly, worn out you, but it's you nonetheless."

Father Joseph never intended to deliberately lay eyes on this man ever again. Yet, here he was. It was surreal.

A flexible plastic tube had been inserted into his father's trachea, providing mechanical ventilation. "Wow. You can't even breathe on your own." A ventilator now moved breathable air into and out of Joseph's, father's lungs for him.

"Geeeeez."

His father's bony framework was covered up to his neck with a thin, light powder-blue blanket trimmed at the top and bottom with shiny satin in a darker shade of blue. His beard had a few weeks worth of growth. His severely wrinkled complexion was white and pasty and pitted, an indication of just how much he abused himself by drinking and smoking his entire life.

"I swear I can still smell Kool menthol cigarettes and Scotch when I look at you." The sight of his father brought Joseph right back to the unpleasant sights, sounds and smells of when he was a kid.

By the looks of things, his father appeared to be holding on to life by a thread, if that.

Gathering up the strength to try to respectfully address a dying man he admittedly loathed, Joseph gave it his best.

"Are you awake?" He asked softly.

His father's eyes remained closed. He did not or could not answer.

"He's in a coma." A quick-speaking, overworked nurse said, dashing around the priest to get to her patient. Joseph was so distracted seeing his father in this condition, he never heard her come into the room.

Jumpy, Father Joseph hopped in place. "Oh! You scared me!" Embarrassed, he snickered nervously. "I didn't see you there. Hello."

Then, his brain finally caught up with what she said. "A coma?" He repeated.

"Yes, doctors have expected him to pass for a while, but now..." The caretaker pointed to the orange tabby cat lounging by his father's side on the bed. "...The end seems *very* near."

Joseph hadn't even noticed the cat there.

"Oh my goodness... she was there the whole time?" Joseph knew he had sensory overload if he never heard her come into the room or saw the cat sitting right there on top of the bed alongside his ailing father.

The nurse hurriedly exchanged one intravenous drip bag for another and took vitals from her patient as she informed Joseph of his father's condition.

"That's Tiamat." She pointed to the cat again.

Tiamat swiveled her head toward the nurse when she heard her name.

"We don't exactly know how, but Tiamat seems to know when a patient is at the very end stages."

"How's that?" Joseph asked, doubting the reliability of a domesticated pet to predict such things.

The cat began to purr loudly, rolling onto her back, as the attendant explained.

"She lives here. She usually stays with us at the nurses' station all day long. We have a spot for her behind the desk but every so often, for no apparent reason she gets up and walks to a patient's room. She'll jump up onto their bed and stay with them, sometimes for days, until the moment they die. Then, she jumps down, leaves their room and comes back to her own bed at the nurse's station."

Her eyes darted back and forth between the cat and Joseph as she explained the feline's significance in the room.

Joseph noticed the nurse spoke with her hands, leading him to believe she might be of Italian descent and a local from the area. After all, Rhode Island did have a large Italian-American community, especially where he grew up.

"Usually, when a patient gets a visit from Tiamat, we know they have approximately forty-eight hours to live. Unofficially, it gives us the chance to notify family so they can make the proper final arrangements." She said.

Joseph was creeped out. "Ah hah."

The nurse carried on. "Somehow, some of the doctors around here believe, she can predict death. Hypothetically, they think dying patients may emit a gas *we* can't detect, but that she can smell. If that's the case, they feel she is either attracted to the smell for some reason or knows it means the person is dying and needs companionship."

Joseph couldn't believe what he was hearing but gave her the benefit of the doubt. "OK."

"The nurses feel it's definitely the latter. All of us around here think she's comforting patients before they meet death." The nurse's voice cracked as she spoke. She reached over, rubbing Tiamat's furry belly.

"You're a good girl, hah?"

Tiamat purred with contentment, but stayed right by Joseph's, father's side.

"Are you here to administer last rights?" She asked Joseph.

"No." He replied, doleful.

Curious, the nurse pressed further. "Did a friend ask you to come to pray over him?"

Joseph didn't answer right away.

"I'm his son."

"Oh!" She said, ashamed she didn't consider that. "I'm so sorry. How ignorant of me. I didn't realize. It's just... we didn't think he had any living relatives. No one has been here to see him since he arrived and that's been quite a while. So we just thought..." She searched for ways to correct her blunder, but then decided it best to just quit while she was ahead and shut her mouth until she was spoken to. "I'm so sorry."

"Not to worry. Not to worry. It's understandable." Joseph graciously pardoned the misidentification.

He was more interested in learning about his father's condition. "Exactly how long has he been in a coma?"

"Uh, let's see..." She counted on her fingers, trying to put a number to the weeks he'd been here. She added carefully before speaking again.

"Oh, one, two... about three months or so."

Joseph looked at his father, comatose in the hospital bed.

"The doctors believed he was going to pass away months ago, but he's still here. Now they think he's hanging on for some reason, maybe waiting for someone special to come and say good-bye." The nurse looked at Joseph like he might be the one.

"That happens more often than you'd think." She shared, turning her attention to a medical chart chained to the foot of the bed.

"What do you mean?" Joseph asked, unclear.

The nurse was happy to clarify as she scribbled numbers, measurements and information onto his father's chart.

"In *some* cases..." She emphasized. "... patients who are so close to death linger beyond what is scientifically explainable."

She and Joseph both glanced at his dad as she expounded.

"It just seems, more often than not, they linger because they're waiting for someone in particular to show up."

"You have my attention." Joseph encouraged her to elaborate.

"I just get the feeling that maybe they're waiting for someone they need to make peace with before they allow themselves to go. That there's some sort of unfinished business they need to take care of before they leave this world. I'm convinced of it." The nurse was very sure about her thoughts on this.

"Again, I don't have a medically sound explanation for saying this, but all I can tell you is, I've seen this before and so have my co-workers on this floor. It is rare but it happens."

Joseph listened respectfully to her personal experience with this unexplainable phenomenon.

"So many times, after that special individual shows up and makes peace with the patient... they are able to finally let go." The nurse smiled compassionately. "It's really a beautiful thing."

All this was new to Joseph. "Really?"

"Really." She said convinced, placing the completed medical chart back where it belonged.

"I'll leave you two alone now." The nurse excused herself.

An intense burst of fluorescent light entered the room as the door swung open and she exited, but gradually shrunk as the door slowly swung closed. Joseph's pupils constricted to pinpricks.

There he was, left there alone with his father.

Now, the only available light in the hospital room left to see by was from a small reading lamp fastened to the wall behind his father's bed. It cast a faint putrid greenish-colored light, illuminating the top of his father's head as well as his face and neck. The backlighting made his father look like a ghoul. It was barely enough to be able to see around the room.

It took a minute for Joseph's eyes to adjust.

There he lay before Father Joseph. The merciless Joseph Maggiacomo, weak and helpless in a state of unconsciousness. The tables had turned on him. The once depraved conqueror of women and children was now at the mercy of his caregivers.

"Boy, he'd really hate this." Joseph thought to himself.

Joseph also thought about how pitiful it was for his father to have spent all the wonderful years of life he'd been blessed with, being a scornful human being who intentionally poisoned everything he got his hands on. Now, here this man lay at the end of his life. All chances given him to change course, used up and wasted.

Reaching behind him, Joseph felt for the seat of a chair. He grabbed one by its edge, dragging it across the floor up to his behind so he could sit by his father's bedside.

"It's been a long time, dad." Joseph said, scooting closer. "A long time."

He placed his elbows up on the chromed steel bedrail, which felt wobbly beneath his arms.

Joseph had mixed feelings about being here. His father was the worst man he'd ever known. Truth be told, he hated him.

As Joseph sat there, looking down upon his father, he reflected back to his younger years. He remembered the few but cherished good times he had with his mother and his siblings. Times that his father would inevitably ruin with his hateful disposition, his divisive personality and cruel intentions. Eventually, those good times with his mom and brothers and sisters came less and less frequently until they ultimately disappeared forever. That's the way his dear old dad wanted it.

"Dad. I know you can hear me." Joseph began a one-sided dialogue.

"I know you can hear me and I want to talk to you." He said.

"It's been a long time, you and me. We haven't seen each other in so many years."

Before he got into what he wanted to say to his father, Joseph reached up to clasp the cross still hanging around his neck. It was last touched by one of the most wonderful men he ever knew. Mr. Buonopane. Now, ironically, Joseph would use it as comfort whilst in the midst of the worst man he ever knew.

Father Joseph said a quick prayer. Then he thought for a moment, wanting to be clear about what he was about to say and why.

His hand trembled as he began to speak to his father in a very direct tone. He spoke as a son this day, not as a priest.

"You were not a good man dad." Father Joseph said honestly. "Truth be told, you were the devil incarnate." His truthfulness felt liberating.

"When I first saw you laying in this bed, I wanted to leave you to rot. To rot, because that's what you did to me, mom, Peter, Dante, Maria and Josephine." An all-encompassing loathing filled Joseph's heart. He was so full of resentment for his father; he could feel one of his cardiac valves fluttering.

He concentrated on getting his breathing under control to help with the angst.

"You know, I feel you deserve to spend eternity in hell for everything you did to us."

Joseph meant every word he said.

"Mom was such a sweet woman. I loved her so much." Joseph felt sad remembering his mother.

"I know your consistently malicious mistreatment of her caused her mental illness. Doctors diagnosed her with schizophrenia, but I know it was your relentless torment that broke her down." The priest felt justified confessing to his father what he'd been feeling all these years.

"Toward the end dad, mom was so sick. She was on so much medication. It broke her... your disappearing act every weekend. Not to mention your cheating, your lies, your drinking, your gambling, everything... it just killed her, emotionally. Eventually her body responded to what she'd been feeling inside for so long and... gave up." Joseph hoped for some sort of subconscious facial reaction from his father to let him know he heard him.

"She wanted so badly to be perfect for you so you would love her. You knew you had her, because she loved you so desperately. She loved you more than she loved herself and that's why, after decades of being rejected and used and abused by you and never being able to obtain your love, which you always held just out of reach, she turned on herself. You used her love for you against her and made her hate herself."

Joseph's father began breathing harder as if he really could hear him.

"What you did to us kids, no father should ever do to any child. It was inhuman. You were a real sadist dad, a real sadist." Joseph tongue-lashed.

"I've hated you my whole life for it." He'd always wanted to tell his father this, but never had the courage when he was younger. "Never once, in my entire adult life have I had a single kind thought about you. Do you know what that does to a person? When it's their parent they're thinking about?"

Father Joseph thought back to when he was about thirteen years old.

"Remember, we'd watch the fights as a family, dad?" He asked.

"All us kids would gather in the living room in front of the television set and you would sit in your chair behind us. We'd be excited to sit together as a family to watch an event. About halfway through, you would get us kids to pretend we were the boxers and compete against one another." His lip quivered at the thought.

"You used to pit us against each other to fight! You would pit one child against the other so you could see us fist fight. You would pretend whoever won the match would win your favor. You sick barbarian!"

Joseph stared at his father. "We would get really hurt! It would turn vicious among us! I remember splitting Dante's face open once. Mom was screaming for us to stop, but you wouldn't allow it. We all started to hate one another!"

Joseph's father never made that facial expression he'd hoped for.

"It was your way of messing with our heads, of controlling us. You got us to compete ferociously against one another to try to get close to you. Even if we won, thinking you'd finally love and respect us for it, you'd then turn on us, telling us we cheated or something stupid like that. Again, you kept the prize just out of reach so we would turn on ourselves. There was no winning… everybody was a loser in that house. That's just one example of how you manipulated us."

From his anxious breathing, Joseph knew his father could comprehend every word he said although he couldn't speak. Joseph felt a sense of relief from that.

"It made you happy to watch your kids tear each other apart. You treated us like you resented us for being born. We all felt like you hated us but you really must have hated yourself, dad." The worthless light shining down on his father's head, cast shadows upon his father's face, making him look demonic.

"Our family was torn apart. Your other children were crippled with mental illness because of it and mom…" The next words were difficult for Joseph, even after all this time.

"Mom… she… eventually took her own life to escape the mental torment she didn't know how to deal with." Joseph clenched his cross even tighter for support. His face wrinkled with pain.

In the hallway, Joseph could hear nurses walking past, so he kept his voice down. He didn't want them listening in on this.

"I bet that was the ultimate for you, wasn't it?" He whispered insultingly, wondering if that's truly what his father had been striving for.

"You took a life dad." Joseph blamed. "You may not have physically ended her life, but what you did to her emotionally was just as criminal, just as sinful and yes, you took a life. Were you proud of yourself for that? Or wait. It wasn't your fault. Right? She was sick. Your famous line."

Father Joseph's eyes filled with tears.

Then, Joseph decided to share with his father where he'd been all these years. "Remember when I left home dad, when I was 18-years-old?"

Joseph couldn't believe himself how long it had been.

"I left seeking comfort, healing, hope, peace and self-fulfillment." He explained, knowing this information would greatly annoy his father if he were conscious.

"I wasn't going to let you define for me what life was or what my life was going to become. I wasn't sure if I'd find it or where it was… but I knew it was all I wanted and therefore I had to try my hardest to find it for my own sanity. Because, if it existed on this earth I wanted to see it, feel it, live by it and show others. Somehow I knew… I would be led to it."

Sharp points on Joseph's crucifix were cutting into his hand from squeezing it so tightly.

"I really have you to thank for it dad, believe it or not. The desperate situation you put me, put all of us in, forced me to leave home, seeking the exact opposite. I wanted to find the Mr. Buonopane's of the world. I wanted to understand that mind, that philosophy. I didn't want to live if I couldn't live that way. So, I *had* to seek it out. It became my mission in life." Joseph knew his father always thought Mr. Buonopane was a wimp for how kindly he treated his wife and kids.

Then he shared what he knew his father would never want to hear.

"Guess what?"

Long pause.

"I found it, dad. I found it! I found comfort, healing, hope, peace and self-fulfillment… everything I longed for."

Peace and calm came over Joseph.

"Guess where?" He knew his father would be dumbfounded. "…At Vatican City in Rome."

Joseph smiled with pride.

"I found it simply by following my own sense of what was good and right for me. When I left home, I found a place to stay with a longtime friend. I took care of my health while I was there. I befriended kind, honest people to share life experiences with. I read great literature. I kept journals of my experiences. I helped others in need when I could and I stuck to those very basic, but healthy and positive pursuits. I kept it simple, but all good and well… one positive thing led to another and before I knew it, I found myself in Italy at the Vatican. It just seemed like one good decision led to another and to another and so on. Until… I found what I'd truly been searching for in my heart. That's when I had an epiphany and I knew God was responsible for leading me to my greatest want. I found God at that very moment dad. Then I found myself. The real me."

His dad's breathing seemed to calm some.

"And… You'll never believe this one. I studied to become and am now a priest dad. I'm a priest now. I've devoted my life to God. Now I lead others to hope when they are in their greatest despair. I am so abundant with thankfulness for my own blessings that I am able to give back in a meaningful way and spread joy back into the world. I've come full circle."

No one was more proud of his or her accomplishments than Joseph.

"I am where I always wanted to be. Where I begged the Lord Almighty to be. Do you know how this happened to me?" He asked, knowing his father could only listen.

"I first had to slay my dragon. Something inside me wouldn't let you finish me off the way I watched you finish off everyone else in our family." Joseph spoke with conviction.

"I was determined to find my purpose in life and rise up against you; but rise up against you in goodness, as you rose up against us in wickedness." Joseph's thinking was profound.

"If I could save one of us from systematic annihilation by you, I figuratively would save my mother, my sisters and my brothers. I would stop the buck with me." He glared at his dad. "I could begin to create love in the world."

Joseph smiled with his next sentence. "And I did."

"What's so strange about it is I have you to thank for it." Joseph understood that sometimes in life our blessings or lessons come in really strange packaging.

"By being the man and father you were, you took me to the lowest point a human being and a child can reach. I found myself in great despair with no hope in sight. It was then that I realized, to survive it, I had to reach into the deepest recesses of my soul, of my character, to find the tools to combat such an overpowering force. Out of a survival instinct, I found them. I found the tools. All they were… were… to love myself and to love others and to love the world around me at all times. Then, enjoy the ride. Life will dutifully carry you to exactly where it is you need to be."

Joseph gleamed. "Amazing, hah?"

"Through your torture, you awakened the part of me, which I didn't then know existed, but which needed to surface for me to survive. You created me! The true me! I guess I had to face the devil himself to bring it out of me. It was a live or die thing, dad. I chose to fight as hard as I could for life. That's how I was reborn, the man before you now."

Caught up in the moment, Father Joseph started preaching louder out of gratitude, when two pair of footsteps in the hall stopped just outside the hospital door.

He paused.

Not to attract further attention, he quieted down.

"You were such a monster to us dad, you made me want to be the exact opposite of what you were and I did it. Ironically, you defeated yourself and your mission by unintentionally creating me."

That's when Joseph had a light-bulb moment.

He knew there was a reason he was here and he had to figure it out to move forward with his destiny. "It must be to remember something? To think about something?" He wondered to himself. "Or, maybe to remind myself of who I am, what I went through to become the man I am today?"

As his father's breathing continued to slow down, Joseph concentrated on this.

Then, without much effort, he finally understood why he was here.

He drew in a really deep breath.

"Dad, I know you've been hanging on for some months now. I know why." Joseph released the cross he'd been clutching the whole visit and extended his hand to embrace his father's. He laid his large, burly palm directly on top of his father's hand and wrapped his fingers around tightly, sympathetically. The sight of this was surreal to Joseph.

"Dad, you were an awful wretch. You did some really terrible things to your family and I know you know that." Joseph said. "Things that can never be erased or fixed."

He thought carefully about his next sentence, enunciating each word perfectly and clearly.

Another deep breath.

"I forgive you, dad." Joseph said, meaning every word of it.

With those words, a great weight seemed to lift off of Joseph's mind and spirit. A flood of emotion flashed through his entire body. He held his breath to prevent tears from falling.

"I forgive you dad, for all those things and I love you." He added, squeezing his father's hand tighter. "I know you did what you thought you must to survive yourself."

Knowing these next words were lies, Joseph said them anyway out of compassion. "I spoke to Dante, Maria and Josephine today. We talked about everything that happened in our family. They forgive you as well. They wanted me to tell you that. I told them I was coming to see you today. They wanted me to tell you they love you and they forgive you, too." He knew his father needed to hear that. "Everyone is doing really well and they are at peace in their lives and they wish you peace."

The truth of the matter was that Dante had become a recluse, living on the streets. No one knew where he was now or whether he was dead or alive. Shortly after he took off he cut off contact with the family. Maria was still a resident of the state mental health hospital, where she was committed at the age of thirty. As for Josephine, everyone knew where she was living, but she wanted nothing to do with any family members and rejected any communication whatsoever.

After what everyone lived through, no one ever wanted or produced any children.

Joseph communicated what he felt was humane under the circumstances.

"They love you dad. We all do. We know you did the best you could." He said lovingly. "Even Peter, God rest his little soul. I know he's in heaven waiting for you right now and he forgives you, too."

A third pair of nurses' shoes stopped at the door for a listen. Joseph didn't care anymore who heard what.

"I know you're sorry. I know that's why you couldn't leave yet. I know, you know, you were horrible and you can't leave until you make peace with us." Tears streamed down Joseph's face.

"Dad. You can go now. It's OK. You can go now and we're all OK." Joseph nudged his father's hand as a sign he was free to pass with his blessing. "We all want you to know it's OK to go… we love you. We forgive you and we all want you to know you can leave in peace."

In a loving and forgiving gesture as a son and as a priest, Joseph removed his crucifix from around his neck and placed it over his father's head.

"Dad, this was blessed by the Pope himself. May he rest in eternal peace. I've been wearing it ever since I became a priest. Now I give it to you, for protection, my father. May you walk with God in death as I do in life. God Bless."

Almost instantly, his father began laboring to breathe.

Joseph leaned back in his chair, away from his father as nature took its course.

Everything was happening so quickly.

Joseph watched as his father's chest rose with one last dramatic demand for air.

"Dad." Joseph was but wasn't sure what was happening. He leaned in.

All on his own, Joseph's father sat up slightly in his hospital bed. His lifeless eyes popping open, staring straight ahead at the wall. Out of nowhere, a faint golden light shined upon his face as he held that one last precious breathe.

"Dad." Joseph said, gently. "It's OK. It's OK to go."

And then it was over. His father finally let go.

With one final exhale; his father closed his eyes and softly reclined back in his bed wearing a peaceful expression.

"Good-bye dad. Good-bye. Until we meet again."

Joseph pressed a button, calling for a nurse before administering last rites over his father.

Within minutes, the door swung open and a member of the medical staff appeared.

While the door was still ajar, Tiamat took the chance to sneak back out of the room, knowing her job here was done.

"Yes?"

"I think he… I think he's… He's gone." Father Joseph told the nurse he'd spoken with earlier.

She quickly pulled out her acoustic stethoscope and listened for a heartbeat. "Nothing." She placed the stethoscope's diaphragm on the opposite side of his father's chest to listen for heart sounds. "Nothing."

Then one last time, placing her device directly over his heart, she listened, looking at her watch. "Nothing."

Joseph already knew he was gone. This was merely hospital protocol.

"I'm sorry sir, but he's passed. I'm so sorry." The nurse wrapped up her stethoscope and offered her condolences.

"I'll leave you alone with your father for a moment and then the doctor will be in shortly to confirm the time of death. I'm so sorry for your loss, Father." She said before she left.

"Thank you very much. You're very kind; and thank you for watching over my father these past few months."

Joseph felt differently inside as he stood there. He felt as though a part of his soul had awakened from a deep slumber.

Father Joseph took his father's hand in his for the second time in his life and the very last. "Good-bye dad." He said.

"I thank you for everything you taught me."

CHAPTER 19

THRESHOLD OF THE APOSTLES

In Rome it was scorching hot this time of year although the locals seemed perfectly comfortable with the temperature. Over the centuries their skins had grown tolerant of the blistering sun.

This season called for vast stretches of clear, blue skies, which allowed blazing sunshine to persistently singe the earth all day through.

The Mediterranean climate, which characterizes the country's coasts, was an attraction for tourists from all over the world, especially the West. They flocked here for the art, the culture and the food and after about two weeks, they went home to brag to their envious friends about their adventures overseas. That was the best part.

Within the city, thick humidity hung at street level as compact cars whizzed by, beeping their horns, dodging each other and pedestrians.

Raucous Italians hollered over one another, their voices echoing in the streets and in the alleyways. It was hard to tell if they were yelling at each other or just excited about what they were talking about. It was simply how these folks communicated. It distinguished them from other cultures.

Restaurants and outdoor cafés lining the city's huge majestic squares such as the Piazza di Spagna, Piazza Venezia, Piazza Navona and the Fontana di Trevi were bustling with men, women and children. Each person, zestfully, taking the time to enjoy life minute by minute, amidst the 17th century architecture.

Here, aromas from competing eateries commingled with the humidity, amplifying the smell of savory ingredients and juices to those in the immediate area and on the streets.

Vacationers were doomed to add inches to their waistlines when they came to this part of the world. The food, so delicious, even the strictest dieters succumbed. Everyone overate, beyond his or her wildest nightmares, loving every bite of it.

Today was like any other day for Italy's capital city, except for the fact it had a repeat visitor.

One it could do without.

Handsome and tall, with thick, black, wavy hair, he walked with a swagger. A hat and sunglasses used to disguise his identity.

No other person on the street had such blatant self-confidence.

Those who noticed him walk by got the sense he was unapproachable. He appeared cold, distant and unfriendly. From his body language, it was clear he didn't want to be bothered. Staring straight ahead, his feet kept perfect pace, making sure not to acknowledge anyone.

Everyone who saw him, thought to himself or herself. "Definitely a foreigner." He wasn't warm and inviting like the native Italians. From where he came, was anyone's guess. His coloring and bone structure could be a mixture of many nationalities.

There was something about him though, something uncomfortable. No one could put his or her finger on it.

Dressed in a traditional priest work cassock to be overlooked and blend in with the general public, Pope Victor made his way on foot through the winding streets of this ancient city. He was still so new to the Papacy; most didn't know his face well enough to recognize it yet.

Victor enjoyed traveling virtually unrecognizable. He knew he could get more done with the benefit of anonymity and expertly used it to his advantage.

As he walked, he drank in the sights of Rome, rich with history. Not to mention, much of it violent.

He kept his mind busy as he marched forward, by recounting its growth and development through bygone times. There was a special place in Victor's memory, where he tucked away only the most distasteful details of one period.

Tapping into it, he thought back to one of his favorite epochs, The Roman Empire.

"Now that era was a work of art." The Pontiff romanticized.

Its success dependent upon military conquest, commercial predominance and assimilating neighboring civilizations.

As Victor thought about its significance to his ultimate mission, the green flecks, which lived within his brown eyes, began to breathe life again.

"Magnificent, just magnificent." He cooed.

The Holy Roman Empire had achieved so much.

For nearly one thousand years, Rome's dominance expanded over most of Europe and the shores of the Mediterranean Sea, during which time it was the most politically important, richest and largest city in the Western world. The memory of its dramatic accomplishments brought tremendous satisfaction to Victor.

He also reminisced about one of Rome's greatest iconic symbols.

The Colosseum.

One of the largest amphitheaters ever built in the Roman Empire; it was erected for the perverted pleasure of Roman spectators who used it for senseless, gory gladiatorial games and public spectacles. Men equipped with barbaric weapons were pit against wild, exotic animals in a fight to the death. In a kill or be-killed situation, man and beast spilled their blood in violent combat before a live audience of nearly sixty-thousand to save their own lives.

It is believed over five hundred thousand people and over a million wild animals died in the Colosseum.

"I always had the greatest ideas, didn't I?" Victor bragged.

He could still hear the crowds cheering as the bloodbaths unfolded before them.

"Remember how great it was?" Victor spoke directly to the hundreds of thousands of deceased souls he was spiritually connected to, who observed the slaughtering at one time or another. "Remember the theatre of it all?"

He felt a weak flow of energy surge into his body, which meant he'd been heard and answered by them.

Satisfied, Victor now allowed room for Providence and the important business he left behind to creep back into his thoughts.

Pope Victor felt secure knowing everything there would be handled appropriately by Falene and Anatoli. They had perfect instructions there, while he took care of things here.

He trekked through Rome for hours more. His feet never tiring even though his shoes told a different story. Dirty and cracked at the toes, Victor's dull, black leather shoes looked more like he'd been living on the streets for years rather than the wardrobe of a sitting Pope. But then again, it only added to the authenticity of his disguise.

Plodding along, Victor allowed himself the worldly pleasure of all five senses. It was too long ago he had this opportunity. He couldn't resist.

As he walked, he focused on what had been denied him for so many years, the delightful and amusing diversion of sight, sound, smell, taste and touch. It could only be found here, on earth.

And he was here, so why not.

Victor took in the breathtaking beauty of the many marble sculptures surrounding him on the street. Artistic genius, everywhere he turned. The intense passion the artists felt while creating their great works of art permanently bathed the pieces with a positive energy. That energy, still present to this day and sensed by anyone observing the works. The seed of inspiration was firmly and successfully planted here.

It was the unnamable *thing* that attracted students from across the globe to come here to study art.

Victor was keenly aware, unlike mortals, that this unnamable *thing* had been in existence since the beginning of time and was responsible for infusing human beings with inspiration and moving them in a positive, productive, healthy direction. Exactly what he had been working to abolish for just as long.

He could feel pangs of outrage as he looked at one sculpture in particular and was impressed by it.

Victor understood that anything conceived and created or given out of love, sincerity or passion leaves behind a permanent positive energy marker. A unique act that, for eternity, can never be replicated or destroyed, remains in existence forever and enhances the overall goodness of the world.

And it worked in direct opposition of he and his objective.

It reminded Victor of one of the most renowned artworks of the High Renaissance, which had the same effect on people. The frescoes Michelangelo painted upon the ceiling of the Sistine Chapel in the years 1508 to 1512. Although Victor wasn't currently standing in the best-known chapel in the Apostolic Palace, he could recall its images from memory as though he were.

Its strong and rich colors, intense and expressive images and exquisite qualities filling every crevice within Victor's mind.

Commissioned by Pope Julius II or the Warrior Pope, as he was more commonly known, the Florentine master Michelangelo created the finest masterpiece in the world, according to many critics.

And all for a Pope he reportedly loathed. The two often clashed about the design, content and scale of the project. Michelangelo who never truly considered himself a painter and whose passion, without question, lay with sculpting, was resentful of the project because he wanted to sculpt, not paint, but Pope Julius II wouldn't allow it.

Pope Julius II was a man Victor knew well, cut from the same cloth and one of the biggest let downs in history, according to Victor.

Victor's muscles stiffened, just thinking about him.

Pope Julius II was delivered during his time for one purpose and one purpose only, to straightforwardly interrupt the greatest artist of all time. Thus stemming the tide of awe, inspiration, love and freedom of creative expression into the world.

He was sent to misguide, hamper and foil Michelangelo's creativity and God given talent so that he and his work would never develop into its true potential. Simple.

Pope Julius' decided strategy… Prevent Michelangelo from pursuing his passion of sculpting and force him to paint. The sitting Pope felt it was impossible for success to breed from indignation and frustration.

So he thought.

Considering his disappointing undertaking Michelangelo through his faith resigned himself to his assignment. He remained dedicated to the vision even though it wasn't his desire, and expanded and challenged his artistic capabilities. In doing so, his genius was inadvertently revealed by bringing to life the majestic works of the Creator through paint. The treasure unveiled in October of 1512 secured Michelangelo's place in history as arguably the greatest artist of all time.

Since, millions of people have been influenced by his work and the world became a better place because of its creation.

Victor viewed Pope Julius II as a total failure and his time spent on earth a complete waste.

"What a callous plan!" Victor recalled with contempt. "You should have crippled his hands! It would have been as simple as that!" Victor brought both hands up to his face, outstretching his fingers like claws. "How didn't you know to break his fingers?!"

He was so furious Pope Julius never thought of that. "You should have crushed those hands you stupid bastard!"

Still so pissed off about this, he had to redirect himself to the sense of smell just to forget about it.

Victor's nose instantaneously caught the scent of many delicious foods coming from all directions.

His mouth watered for the culinary fare searing, baking and grilling to perfection in restaurant kitchens on every block. Everything the Italians did was steeped in passion, especially their cooking.

"Ooohhhhh, that smells gooooood." He drooled, fantasizing being able to taste everything all at once.

That's when he came upon a pizzeria named, Cataldi's. Victor got a whiff of a fresh Neapolitan pizza baking in a stone oven over an oak-wood fire inside. He swore he could taste the ripe San

Marzano tomatoes from where he stood. Peering into one of the pizza parlor windows, Victor could see the hardworking owner's wife, setting up tables for the dinner rush.

Victor smacked his lips. "Mmmmmmmmmmmmm. Mmmmmmm." He was starving, but knew he didn't have the time for a sit-down meal.

A few blocks away, the Pontiff decided to stop again at a sign reading, *Il Sorbetto.* The gelateria ice-cream shop boasted *gelato fatto en casa*, or homemade gelato.

Victor scanned the bewildering array of flavors from behind the frosty glass of a cheerful, refrigerated gelato case gleaming on the sidewalk. There were so many concoctions.

"Let's see…" He tried to make his selection quickly.

Victor decided to take a gelato to go to satisfy his hunger temporarily.

When the waitress approached, he pointed to his favorite flavor. "I'll take one, please." He ordered over the top of the counter.

A pretty Italian woman prepared his order, took his money and handed him his Cappuccino flavored Italian ice cream on a cone. Two tower-shaped wafer biscuits stuck out of the top of it.

"Grazie. Buonasera." She said, handing him a napkin as well.

Victor snatched the cone from her grasp. One deep, long, lick and he was in bliss.

"Mmmnn! This is good, so very good. Nothing like it in the world." Every pass of the tongue was a cold, sweet, pleasurable human experience for him.

The waitress, not sure what to make of him, politely smiled and went about her business.

Victor took his cone with him and began pounding the pavement. "Arrivederci. Grazie." He waved over his shoulder as he left.

It seemed he'd been walking at least a mile and Victor hadn't encountered anyone else on the street.

He entertained himself by losing himself within the deliciousness of his gelato. He continuously spread and smooshed the ice cream's flavorous consistency between the roof of his mouth and his tongue, dissecting all the ingredients within the semi-frozen dessert.

"Milk, espresso powder, cornstarch, coffee beans, sugar…" By taste alone, Victor broke down the recipe.

His tongue pinched a bit from the cold.

Then, finally, Victor spotted someone up ahead.

Approaching him in the opposite direction was an attractive couple. The man was about thirteen years the woman's senior and both were short in stature. She had fair skin, long strawberry blonde hair and blue eyes. He had a receding hairline of salt and pepper, an olive complexion and large, bulgy, dark eyes. They were holding hands and speaking lovingly to one another in one of the most romantic languages in the world, Italian.

It was enough to briefly take Victor's attention away from his tasty treat.

Proclaiming their undying love for one another, they stopped mid-block, took each other in their arms and sealed their declaration with a soft, sensuous kiss.

Victor watched them as their arms and hands found the curves on each other's backsides. These two were very talented at writhing their bodies around each other like twisted tree trunks. They were sexually expressive and very into one another.

"Uh, brother." He said disgusted, watching them maul each other.

As he studied them, Victor focused on a secret the man was hiding from his girlfriend.

"Well, well, well…"

Victor took another deep, long lick before messing with the woman.

He waited until he got close enough to the engrossed couple before speaking. He wanted his messages to reach her subconscious, remaining with her throughout her relationship.

"Wait about a year honey, see what he puts you through." Victor cruelly whispered under his breath.

One of the woman's eyes popped open. Subliminally, she caught something.

"Let's see how you feel when he comes home from work one day and you see he's not wearing any underwear." Victor spoke ever so softly by her ear as he breezed past her. "You'll know he's lying to your face when he tries to explain why when you confront him." A tiny droplet of gelato flew from his lips and landed on the collar of her dress as he spoke.

"It'll screw you up for a long time. A long time." He warned insidiously. "There's a deep dark secret he has, you know. It's the reason he smokes so much marijuana and always seems so distant and depressed. A really dark, dirty secret he doesn't want anyone to ever find out, especially you."

The woman knew she heard the passing priest say something that made her feel uneasy, but she didn't know what. She lifted her head away from her lover's kiss and looked at Victor to see if he would repeat it, but he wouldn't.

She was too enraptured to care about what she might have heard, returned to her boyfriend's lips and forgot all about it.

Victor, now past them, concluded his forewarning in a low voice. "You'll see." He said. "You'll see. It's going to hurt real bad." He related. "It'll hurt real bad, when you find out how and why he was using you."

Victor threw the last bite of his cone down the hatch.

"Those bruises you saw all over him that time. Those bruises he told you were from working out?" Victor reminded her of the explanation her boyfriend gave her, that never quite felt right.

"They were teeth marks."

The woman looked up again, believing she heard him say something else disturbing, but didn't hear it clearly enough to say what it was. But by then, Victor had made his way at least another entire block down the street.

"Stupid bitch." He mumbled.

In the distance, Victor could now see Vatican City, the sovereign territory of the Holy See and the smallest nation in the world. It was not very big, just one hundred-ten acres, but all of it a thorn in Victor's side.

He knew it would be hard for anyone not to be electrified by the sight of it, although it did nothing to stimulate him.

"The only religion to have representation in the United Nations." He acknowledged begrudgingly.

The tiny statelet, bold and glorious, was just about half a mile away.

"You're a non voting member state though." He pointed out, comforted by that fact.

Victor arrogantly made his way in its direction, one step at a time. The closer he drew, the heavier his feet became.

He tried to smell it from where he was.

"Mmmmmnnnnnnhhhhhhhhhh." Victor's nostrils opened wide to take in as much air as possible.

When his lungs filled to capacity, he held it. He was searching for the presence of his favorite smell. Depravity. If depravity existed within the walls of the Vatican in any form, he would detect it.

He exhaled. His lungs now ready to expand further.

Pope Victor breathed in again, harder this time and concentrated.

"MMMMMMMNNNNNNNNHHHHHHHHHHHHHHHH!" His large chest rose impressively.

Then his dark eyes opened slowly, cautiously. He looked around, sensing something.

"Ahhhhhhhh…haaaaaahhhhh." Victor's suspicions were correct. "Manipulation. How beautiful a thing it is." His olfactory nerves strengthening once he caught the stench of it.

Smelling it empowered him.

Again, he inhaled.

"MMMmmmmmmmnnnnnnnhhhhhhhhhh!"

"Yes. Yes. The sweet fragrance of moral corruption and wickedness. In one form or another it exists everywhere. Even where you least expect it, which is exactly as it should be." Enthralled, Victor confirmed the work of him and his allies, penetrating the most sacred of places.

He got his fix. For now.

"La Citta Eterna!" Victor called out for all of Rome, the eternal city, to hear.

"La Citta Eterna." He loved the name. He loved saying it.

"There is another place, far from here, with this very name!" Victor looked around to see if anyone was listening.

"Another place! Where I come from! It is also an Eternal City! Built upon the wasted carcasses of its devoted sons and daughters!" He heard his own powerful voice echo off the surrounding homes and buildings.

"And where I want you all to join me!" Victor implored the city and its faithful to unite with him.

"Threshold of the Apostles! I call to you!"

"Caput Mundi! Hear me!"

"La Citta Dei Sette Colli! Awaken!"

He absorbed the life force of the nearly four million residents surrounding him within the metropolitan area. Their energy spontaneously and collectively surging into his body upon command.

Victor decoded the heart and mind of every one of the souls here. He knew their every thought, their every wish and their deepest darkest secrets.

"Hmmnnnhhhh. Very interesting." Victor commented, unraveling each individual mystery.

How unaware they all were, that under the laws of the universe, the very essence of who they were could never be concealed from those who knew where to look.

Those such as Victor, who was able to use this knowledge to his advantage.

To the untrained eye, people were only what they revealed themselves to others to be. By baring only the parts of themselves they were willing to share, they were able to mask their past, their objectives, and their desires from one another.

To the trained eye, such as Victor's, they were as transparent as water from a natural spring. Victor spiritually stripped everyone naked.

The key, he knew, listen not only to what one says. Know where they've been. Ask where they're going. See what they do. Watch their actions. Closely. Very, very closely.

Many people are masters at saying all the right things to attain their goals. It's what they *do*, which often discloses their true intentions. Thus, their true identity.

People are often more articulate with their actions than with their words and Victor understood this implicitly.

He sorted through each soul one by one, in a flash. It wasn't long before a subtle look of satisfaction washed over his face.

"I think you all will rise to the occasion, rather smartly." The rogue Pope felt, based on what he knew so far.

Then Victor turned his attention back to the Stato della Citta del Vaticano, its territory consisting of a walled enclave within Rome.

He focused on St. Peter's Basilica, the iconic dome, which dominates the skyline of Rome. Its image reflected in Victor's pupils.

In native Italian, he called out to the religious superpower. "La Santa Sede!" His eyes, sent daggers toward the largest church in Christianity and the burial site of its namesake Saint Peter, one of the apostles of Jesus.

He stopped for a second, beholding it.

"La Santa Sede!" He yelled at the top of his lungs. "La Santa Sede! Hear me! Hear me now! It is *me* they worship now! Not thou!"

A long stretch of glistening saliva clinging from his lower lip extended down to his chest. A wet stain marked the spot on his shirt.

Pope Victor wiped his chin, feeling something wet there.

Some locals, who'd settled into their homes for the late afternoon, peeked out of their windows to see what the commotion was. When they saw Victor down on the street, they dismissed him as a mentally ill person dressed up like a priest, acting out. It was blasphemous, but not entirely unheard of. Everyone returned to what they were doing.

Victor brushed a dangling lock of hair hanging down from his forehead, back into his black, lavish mane.

Adrenaline coursed through his veins as he contemplated his new home, the Apostolic Palace. His heart beat harder than ever.

"Here, is where I am ex officio! I am ready to take my seat here, and faithfully carry out the will of the crowned head of the lower world so that I may then take my rightful place in eternal life!" Pope Victor roared, his eyes burning into the side of the edifice.

There was still so much work to be done. Victor knew everything had to go according to planned before this transition could take place.

"You have all arrived at a personal and spiritual crossroads." Victor apprised the public.

His heartbeat slowed to a normal, steady rhythm.

"The moment is finally here everyone. Are you ready?" Victor wondered *if* and exactly how ready they all really were for the challenge they were about to receive. Or more specifically, the challenge Joseph, who was selected to represent them, was about to receive for them.

The Pontiff kept walking until he came not to the private entrance of the Vatican… but to police headquarters.

This was his first stop.

"Hmmmnnnnhhhhhh." Pinching his chin, he deliberated his plan of attack. Then, walked over to the building's south wall.

Through a vibrating glass window, Victor saw a tired looking Chief Morgera watching television with the volume turned all the way up.

"Wow that's loud." Victor felt the glass tremor with the tips of his fingers.

The Chief sat there in his office, zoned-out, watching the news. Victor could see from the lower third graphics on the screen, reports of world food shortages and a potential pandemic topped the broadcast.

Now that he knew where Chief Morgera was, Victor walked around the other side of the building.

No one saw Victor walk up the stairs of the main entrance, saunter through the front doors of police headquarters, sneak past the front desk and float down the hall like an apparition, to the Chief's office.

Once there, Victor casually poked his head around the Police Chief's opened door.

There his prey sat. The TV's audio blaring, filling the hallway.

The television news anchor read her stories flatly.

"Today the United States Environmental Protection Agency announced that seven commonly known varieties of fish in the Atlantic Ocean are expected to become extinct within the year, if protections are not put into place to preserve the species. Officials are blaming over fishing and pollution as the causes."

Victor rolled his eyes.

"In other news..." The anchor began her next story.

"Deaf bastard." He insulted, hoping the Chief could hear him. The Pope looked around to see if the din of the television bothered anyone else.

Everyone in the police station appeared completely undisturbed by the annoyance, going about his or her business.

"You're all probably deaf at this point, anyway." Victor guessed, watching the staff indifferently bustle about.

From here, Victor could see Chief Morgera better. Elbow up on his desk, the Chief rested his chin in the palm of his hand, and just stared at the boob tube.

Victor watched him, watch the news.

Again, the female news anchor's voice blasted from the tinny speakers on the front of the Chief's cheap television set.

"Tonight, police are on the lookout for a suspect wanted in a heinous crime here in Rome."

Chief Morgera looked down at his desk. There, a file sat with the name, Roberto Indeglia typewritten on the tab.

The anchor continued. “Forty-two year old Roberto Indeglia, shown here on your screen is wanted for the murder of his boss, fifty-seven year old Pietro Angelone. Back in 2008, Angelone who was an avid horse racing enthusiast and racehorse owner, hired Indeglia to train his three-year-old thoroughbred Black Knight for competitive racing. Sources close to the two say Indeglia and Angelone often clashed on equine healthcare issues such as steroid use. Late yesterday afternoon, Angelone was found trampled to death in Black Knight’s stable. Police say it looks like a case of foul play and that Roberto Indeglia is their primary suspect. His location at this hour, investigators say, is unknown.”

With a great big sigh, the Chief grabbed the file and placed it on top of a heap of other work piled atop his desk.

As Victor spied on Morgera, he could sense the sadness within him. Crime was this man’s life. It was what he lived, breathed and thought about every minute of every day. His entire life revolved around his police work. To date, it had cost him a marriage, his family and a significant portion of his happiness. It had turned him into a cynic.

“Very nice.” The Chief’s fate put Victor in good spirits.

Standing there, Victor rapped on the door to get the Chief’s attention.

Knock! Knock! “Ah-Hem!”

The Chief jumped in his chair.

“What the…” As he jolted, the vibration from his body caused a pencil on top of his desk to quake, and begin rolling straight across the top. Morgera shot his arm out toward the outer edge of his desk. His fingers and hand fully outstretched, forming what looked like an eagle’s talon. He wasn’t quick enough to catch it before…

“Whap!” It hit the floor, rolling out of sight.

“Come on!” He yelled.

Chief Morgera looked under the desk immediately to see where it went.

“Uhhhhhhhhhhhhhhhh.” He couldn’t find it.

"Just a min…." Morgera held his visitor off with his index finger up in the air as he continued looking. "…ute."

"Come on! Where are you?" The harder he looked, the more impossible it seemed to find.

Victor watched the whole ridiculous situation unfold like a bad cartoon.

Punching the top of his desk, Morgera rolled from side to side in his swivel chair, searching for the elusive writing instrument on the floor.

Again, Victor knocked to get his attention. Knock! Knock!

"Ah-Hem!" With raised eyebrows, Victor implied his visit was of much more importance than a stupid pencil.

"Uhhhhhhh, wait a…" The Chief tried to get himself together and look more professional.

Squeaking beneath him with every twist and turn, the well-worn wheels of his chair.

Semi-composed, he rolled closer to his desk.

"Come in!" He invited with an exasperated tone. Morgera had given up on his pursuit of the lost, insignificant piece of wood. He pulled another from his top drawer and placed it on his desk near the mound of work related files.

"Come in! Come in!" He welcomed Victor, a little more inviting this time.

Victor entered.

"Why thank you!" Victor expressed sarcastically.

Morgera glanced down at the floor one more time just in case he missed a spot.

Not a single pencil in sight.

Victor's attention also turned toward the floor.

He bent down exactly where he was standing. When he came back up, Pope Victor lifted the lost pencil off the floor with his hand and held it eye level for the Chief.

Chief Morgera stared at it, expressionless. "Where the heck? How did you…" He couldn't believe it'd been in plain sight the whole time.

Victor placed it down on his desk before him.

"There 'ya go. Wasn't so hard to find from where I'm standing."

"Thanks, I couldn't see…" The Chief leaned over and looked back at the floor, wondering how he could have missed it.

"Anyway. To what do I owe this unexpected visit?" The Chief asked, straightening up the mess on his desk. "We didn't call you back in for questioning."

Victor took a seat before being offered one. He was slow to sit, as though he were thinking about how to broach the topic. He glanced briefly at the TV, still blasting, behind his head.

"Wanted to see how you were doing with the investigation?!" He yelled, competing with the television.

Victor was testing the police Chief but it was hard to communicate with each other with the volume so loud.

"Hey, can you turn that down?!" Victor hollered across the desk, pointing back at the television set. "It's really too much!" He indicated by blocking his sensitive ears with his hands.

"Yeah sure!" The Chief yelled back, nodding in agreement. "Got a bit of hearing damage!" He explained, pointing to his right ear.

"Long time ago, my partner and I got into a shootout with a Camorrista on the West side of the city!" Morgera chuckled faintly as he remembered. "And, well, Antonello didn't think anything of firing his gun right beside my head!"

The Chief shook his head. "Rookie mistake! Kid was all charged up!"

Morgera reached for the remote sitting on a chair beside his desk and pointed it at the TV.

Turning around again, Victor saw the bars on the bottom of the television screen decrease until it went mute.

"Thanks. My hearing thanks you." Grateful, he removed his hands from his ears.

The Chief placed the remote back on the chair and got right down to business.

"So, what investigation 'ya talking about?" The Chief asked facetiously. "We've got a whole bunch of 'em going on right now."

Victor smiled a fickle smile and waited a few seconds. "I think you know which one I'm speaking of." He nodded, knowing the Chief knew exactly what he was talking about.

The Chief returned the simper.

"Oh, *that* investigation. The one I'd called you here to discuss not so long ago." He conceded, his affected smile never leaving his face. "The one in which you had such limited information to share with us?"

The two played a cat and mouse game with each other.

"Yes, *that* investigation." Victor emphasized.

"Well, we're still interviewing people and gathering evidence. The investigation is currently in its preliminary stages right now. However, we do feel we already have a solid case against our primary suspect." The Chief tapped his fingers on his desk, the ball firmly placed in Victor's court.

The two stared at each other across Chief Morgera's desk.

"Anything new to tell me? Anything you may have forgotten, which you now remember?" Morgera asked Victor, now testing *him*.

"Remember who you're talking to, Chief Morgera." Victor disciplined, putting the police chief in his place.

"Oh, I know *exactly* who I'm talking to. Just remember who *you're* talking to." The Chief reminded Victor of the importance of his position as well.

In silence, the two took a moment to size each other up in the seconds that passed.

"I've told you everything I know, everything I remember." Victor answered in a high-and-mighty tone.

Rome's top cop felt Victor underestimated his intelligence.

"Can you explain then, how, before each slain Cardinal, we found a slip of white paper. On that paper, your name written in your own handwriting?"

"So?" Victor challenged.

"So?!" The Chief shouted.

"It was written in *their* own blood!" Morgera divulged. "That's what!"

Victor remained calm.

"Prove it." He said stoically, untroubled by the findings.

Chief Morgera couldn't believe the audacity. He sat there, dumbfounded.

Morgera slid open the top center drawer of his desk and pulled out a witness sign-in sheet secured to a clipboard. He threw it across his desk at Victor. In midair, it spun one hundred eighty degrees and landed on the other side of the desktop, facing Victor.

"That's how I can prove it!" The Chief insisted, pointing at it.

The Pontiff leaned forward, scanning the document.

On it, Victor saw where he'd dated and signed it the last time he was here. It provided investigators with a perfect handwriting sample to compare evidence to.

"So." Victor said.

Morgera slammed his top drawer shut.

"So?!" The Chief couldn't believe Victor's arrogance in light of the damning evidence.

"So?!" Morgera repeated.

"So this proves it was your handwriting on all of those slips of paper. Your handwriting, in *their* blood!" Chief Morgera inadvertently revealed exactly how much condemning evidence they had against him. "You made it look like the Cardinals voted for you… that *they* willingly wanted to seat you as the next Pope. But really, it was you voting for them, so you would become Pope!"

Victor didn't say a word. He intentionally sat there emotionally unstirred as Morgera worked himself up into a lather.

"We all know how you got their blood!" It was all so obvious; Chief Morgera thought Victor should just admit it and get it over with.

"How's that?" Victor whispered, looking down at his hands as he pushed his cuticles back with his fingernails.

A wet ring of saliva lined Morgera's lips. "By slitting their throats and their wrists!!! That's how!!!"

An annual calendar placed at the center of his desk received a generous spray of spittle. The more incensed the Chief grew from

Victor's indifference, the more saturated his calendar became. Within the numbered blocks, boldly outlined in black, some of the appointments marked in ink began to run from a steady dousing of sputum.

The brawny cop pounded his fist on top of his desk, shouting every word he said.

"YOU slit their throats and their wrists, didn't 'ya?!!!" Morgera's eyes boring holes into Victor's face as he unofficially indicted him in the slayings.

Glancing up from his crude self-manicure to meet the Chief's eyes, Victor offered a flimsy alibi. "Maybe I was set up."

Chief Morgera fumed at the swipe at his mental skill.

"I was engaged in Church business at the time of the killings, Chief Morgera. My staff can vouch for me." The Pope backed up his explanation with witnesses.

Morgera leaned forward. His round, basketball of a belly crushed against his desk.

"Set up?" He turned to look out an office window for a quick break from the insanity. Beneath his weight, the wheels secured underneath his chair legs squeaked.

He watched as a Redstart bird landed and sat along the ledge outside his office window. With grey upper parts, a black face, orange breast and belly and red tail, Chief Morgera figured it must be a male. He listened as it sang a squeaky warbling song. Its call, repetitive and softly whistled.

"Hweet! Hweet!"

The Chief listened to the bird for about a minute before turning back to face the savage before him.

"Set up? You expect me to believe with everything I have against you… you were set up?" The Chief looked flabbergasted that Victor considered he would ever buy such a lame hypothesis.

Morgera pointed his finger straight down, in the dead center, of the top of his desk. He was referencing what else lie inside the top drawer.

"This tape here. The tape that news crew shot. There's more on this tape than you think." The Chief knew he'd already revealed too much. He couldn't help himself.

Victor remained stone-faced, although he knew exactly what Morgera was referring to.

"All I need is on there! It's there!!!" Spittle now overshot the top of the Chief's calendar and landed on the exposed portion of the desktop just before Victor.

The Chief picked up the pencil Victor had just recovered for him and hummed it against the wall.

Smack! The sharpened lead tip of the pencil snapped off first, hitting the floor before the pencil itself did.

"I'm just waiting for the handwriting analyst to officially confirm what I've already confirmed for myself. She needs to finish her report. Establish that that is indeed your handwriting and guess what? You're done!"

The newly appointed Bishop of Rome spoke again so softly, the Chief had to read his lips to make out what he said. "Like I said. You'll have to prove it first."

Victor's insolence ticked the Chief off.

"Prove it?!!! You killed the Cardinals and then used their blood to vote for yourself to rise to the top of the Catholic Church!!! I can prove that!" The Chief was sure of it.

"Why?! What for?! You've got to have some sort of sick plan or something! You must want to hold that position for some specific reason! To carry out a mission of some kind?!!!" He interrogated out loud.

"I can prove the *how*!!! The *why* doesn't matter. I've got you."

Some of the office staff began to look. Others had been watching for quite a while.

"What I'm just curious about is... what for? Was it worth it? *Why* did you do it? Are you just nuts?!" The Chief proposed the questions, knowing he'd never get honest answers from a sociopath.

As the Chief continued yapping, Victor looked to the messily stacked pile of files sitting upon Morgera's desk. His eyes following the heap downward, until he came across what he was looking for.

From where he sat, he could make out the typewritten tab on one of the folders. In bold, it read, **Pope Victor**. He counted how far down the pile it was.

"Eleven." He mouthed, counting again to make sure.

"Yep. Eleven."

Morgera knew he had to get himself back under control. He took a deep breathe and tried to engage Victor again.

"Just tell me why? Was it for the fame? The fame of being Pope?" The Chief honestly wanted to know why someone would do something like this.

Victor repeated his position. "Like I said, I don't know who did this or why. I've given you all the information I have. I have nothing else to say."

"When I get that report back, you won't be so smug, Holy Father." The Chief said, leaning back in his chair. "Holy Father… dressed as an ordinary priest for some unknown reason."

The two continued their verbal tennis match.

"It's ironic you're here. Because all we're waiting for is that report from our handwriting analyst. Then we'll announce our findings to the media, confirm we have enough for an arrest and bring *you* into custody. So, good thing you're back in town." Morgera peered at Victor, letting him know who the smart one really is.

"The media is going to love this." He jabbed.

"I guess my instincts were dead-on, I came to see you in the nick of time." Victor coyly played along.

"Guess so."

Both men were barely able to contain their resentment for each other. It was all they could do not to leap over the desk at one another.

Victor had had enough at this point. He stood up. "You call me when you get that report, Chief. You hear me?"

"Oh, we'll be ringing your bell, all right. Don't you worry about that." Chief Morgera patronized with a laugh.

Victor started laughing at him, instead of with him. "Enjoy that laugh my friend. It's going to be your last one."

"Is that a threat?!!!" The Chief barked.

"Yes, it is." Victor answered bluntly. "Oh yes it is."

Morgera shook his head, believing Victor to be the type to say anything outlandish to get him riled. He didn't take the threat seriously.

Victor nodded a good-bye to his new adversary but gave him the once-over first before leaving. "The next time we meet, it won't be so pleasant you know." He told him.

"Oh no it won't." Morgera agreed for his own reasons.

Victor walked over to the door. Standing there in the threshold of the doorway, he left the Chief with one final thought before he walked out. "You know where to find me, and remember, I know where to find you."

Chief Morgera felt his blood run a bit cold after Victor said it.

"On that note, I have a meeting to keep, so I'll be going. See you again, real soon Chief."

With that, the Pontiff turned, exiting the office.

The Chief had nothing to counter with.

The entire station was dead silent as Victor walked out.

With his impaired hearing, the only sound Chief Morgera could hear was the muffled chatter of his staff whispering behind their cubicles. That and Victor's long, hard steps crashing down on the tile floor in the hallway as he made his way out of police headquarters.

CHAPTER 20

MAN'S INTERNAL STRUGGLE BETWEEN GOOD AND EVIL

Father Joseph finally had some time alone after ducking inside a local hotel.

He'd walked quite a distance from Ocean State Hospital, after saying good-bye to his father for the final time.

The whole experience was still a blur in his mind.

"Did I really just visit my father? *And* forgive him? *And* then watch him die right before my eyes?" He asked himself in total disbelief, yet grateful at the same time for the chance to make peace with the situation.

"Incredulous." Joseph shook his head. "Just incredulous. Never say never."

His feet were throbbing from the hike to and from the hospital. It was a heck of a workout for a guy not used to a lot of exercise.

Joseph briskly marched through the lobby, past the concierge and up a flight of stairs. Searching for a place to rest, he opened a random door and went inside.

He found himself holed up in an unoccupied conference room at the illustrious Aviatrans Hotel in down-city Providence. A local Armenian family owned and operated the five-star property for decades and it had been passed down to relatives for generations. It held a distinguished history and reputation and serviced only the most discerning clientele.

"Ouch! OK, OK, I hear you! You've had enough. OK." The priest hobbled a few more steps to a nearby chair.

He sat. "Ahhhhh... That's it. There we go."

Finally able to take a load off, Joseph removed his heavy, size thirteen leather shoes, dropped them to the floor and began rubbing the bottoms of his feet hard. "Oh, that feels good. That feels good." He admitted with pleasure, flexing his toes up and down.

Beginning at the soles, Father Joseph massaged his feet upward, moving along the arch, making his way to the balls of his feet. Here, he could feel thick, calloused skin through his thin, inexpensive, dark socks.

"Oh, mama." He rubbed and rubbed, applying pressure to increase the pain. Until, it subsided slightly from the deep stroking. "There we go. There we go, you poor things."

Joseph gave in to the relief. His eyelids heavy and barely still open, his eyes began to roll back into his head.

As he kneaded, he thought about how his relationship with his father ended after all these years. A conclusion, Joseph could have never imagined.

"Did that *really* happen?" Father Joseph asked himself again out loud, shaking his head to clear out any cobwebs. "Am I dreaming this stuff?"

To the contrary, he knew that everything that had happened was very real.

Joseph kicked his shoes out of the way and out of sight. He didn't want to lay eyes on them for at least another month, no matter how unrealistic that seemed right now. "Torturous things! Like penance."

"When they say life is full of surprises, they aren't kidding." The priest found himself remembering his dad fondly now, instead of in the bitter way he had for nearly his whole life.

He smiled with love and peace in his heart, finally.

"Thank you for that..." He whispered gratefully, for only the Lord to hear.

Father Joseph bowed his head in prayer.

"Dear Lord, since I can remember, I begged you to release me from the pain my father caused me during my life, but it never seemed to completely go away. I was haunted by the memories of him and my family life every day and with nightmares during every night. I couldn't grasp why you wouldn't erase that pain so that I could go on with my life. That sadness plagued me relentlessly, yet all I sought was harmony." Joseph was ashamed of himself for not realizing why until now.

"I see why now, Heavenly Father. I see why. You were leaving it for me, for me... to take from myself." He understood humbly. "I never fathomed that possible, until now."

"I prayed for my pain to be removed, instead of asking for insight into what lesson it was teaching me. I prayed for my pain to diminish, instead of asking for the strength to deal with it and get through it. I prayed for my pain to disappear, instead of asking for guidance to help me find a path to forgiveness and love and peace."

Father Joseph saw clearly, he'd been praying for all the wrong things all along.

"That pain was there in my heart for a reason. It had to live within me to teach me things so I would awaken spiritually. I needed to ask myself questions such as... How did the pain get into my heart and my head? Why did I let the pain in and stay within me? What did the mental pain do to me physically when I allowed it to invade my spirit? How could I use this pain in my life moving forward? And finally, the most important lesson... to learn how to drive out the heartache permanently, through positive, healthy and productive thoughts and activities."

Joseph knew he finally got it.

"I understood all of that today, all at once, in my father's hospital room during one visit. You know what? It was worth the struggle to arrive at this enlightened state. It took me a while to get here. But, I'm here!"

The clergyman was proud of his spiritual accomplishment. He drew in a long, deep breath and released it. He knew with certainty he would experience no further fear or sadness regarding the history he had with his father. The newfound solace it brought into his life was invaluable.

He continued his prayer of gratitude.

"That's exactly what you wanted for me, I know it is. You always wanted love and peace for me. I had to earn it through my own personal self-discovery for it to have any deep, spiritual meaning. Otherwise, it would be worthless. This way, I would truly *own* the experience and make it an integral part of my being. Therefore, I would possess sincere compassion for others and remain dedicated to your work the rest of my life."

Joseph thought about that. "Well, I guess, anything worth having is worth the hard work." He acknowledged the obvious.

In his bones, Joseph felt the tremendous love and respect God had for him and the love and respect that God wanted Joseph to have for himself.

Joseph also knew that God had given him the time he needed to find his own way, sure he would. Father Joseph was thankful for the generous opportunity to find his own way in his own time, elated he finally did, knowing it came at a critical time.

"If you'd have taken my pain from me as I begged you to, that would have been you doing the work for me. Not me doing the work for myself. Therefore, I would have experienced a false sense of healing. I would have been doomed to repeat my mistakes over and over again until I figured out why. That's *if* I ever figured it out, before my time on this earth ran out. I'm here to learn and therefore earn life's bounty. I see today, I have."

Joseph knew to be thankful for the mercy the Lord had shown him.

"Thank you Lord, for allowing me to stumble and fall before your feet as I blindly navigated my way to inner peace. It has brought me the love, peace and closure I so desperately sought. Now I will take this knowledge and use it to better focus on doing your work and keeping your spirit alive in the eyes of all those I meet."

Father Joseph traced the shape of the cross over his body and concluded his prayer in Latin.

Joseph touched his right hand sequentially…

To his forehead. "In nomine Patris."

His chest. "et Filii."

Both shoulders next. "Spiritus Sancti. Amen."

Father Joseph raised his head from prayer and looked around the vacant conference room where he was safe and sound and all alone.

"May Christ's words be in my mind, on my lips, and in my heart." He added, blessing himself.

Joseph didn't think anyone saw him sneak in here. He was glad for that. "Finally, some peace and solitude. A place I can get some work done."

This room was quiet and secluded, far away from the chaos of check-in downstairs. There were nice long buffet tables to work on. Joseph knew his time was limited, so he had to work fast.

Joseph carefully pulled his secret stash out of a back pocket and placed it on the table before him.

"At last, I can take a good look at you without being chased halfway around the globe." The scroll easily slid out of its hiding place. "There we go, easy does it."

It was a little more beat up and crumpled, than when Joseph first got his hands on it, but at least he still had it. He was grateful to have at least one copy he could read.

"English. Thank heavens for small miracles."

Father Joseph fussed over how to best unfold the delicate, brittle document. Once he did, he painstakingly smoothed out the wrinkles in it, making sure not to further wipe away any of the writing or the artwork.

With a meticulous eye for detail, Joseph noticed the copy he had was made using materials, which appeared to be from the Christian era. Yet he knew his copy was replicated from the original in nineteen-twelve as indicated at the bottom right hand corner. He questioned where the forger would have secured such rare materials.

"… Whomever did this, wanted it to appear authentic." He theorized.

"I'm so sorry I had to fold and jam you everywhere imaginable just to keep you with me." He spoke to it, like it was his new best friend. In some ways, it was.

"The traveling took a toll on you. I can see that." Father Joseph stroked the crumbly edges of the work. A few pieces broke off in his hand.

"Oh gosh. This isn't good." Joseph rubbed the coarse pieces between his fingers, watching them pulverize to dust as he did.

"Well, would you look at that." He examined, holding the bits up to his face.

Joseph pushed the scroll further up the table so he didn't accidentally lean on it.

"OK, let's see here. I need to read it again and try to decipher all of its hidden messages before it falls apart completely." Joseph took care to handle the ancient record as delicately as he could because of its condition.

With his bear claw-like hands he patted the old canvas down gently on the tabletop so as not to break it apart further, so he could best read it.

There it was before him. Still more intriguing than anything Joseph had ever seen.

His intellectual and spiritual curiosity was sparked. "You are, for certain, one of the most beguiling yet debatable *things* I've ever come across."

Father Joseph suddenly forgot about his aching feet, which had now expanded a whole shoe size since being liberated.

He took a moment to just sit there and take the work in as a whole. The scroll was a significant piece of history and it had fallen into his hands, it seemed, through fate. Joseph needed to know why.

"Incredible." Joseph had to make sure to keep his emotions in check. Becoming overly emotional confused people. He couldn't afford to make a mistake this far along in his journey.

Before he began, Father Joseph did what Father Matthew did back at the Vatican when he first showed him the scroll and read it to him. Joseph traced the words with his fingers before annunciating them aloud.

Father Joseph also made sure to keep his voice down, so as not to draw unnecessary attention to the conference room.

He turned his attention to the left side of the map, the side Father Matthew was originally reluctant to translate into English from Aramaic for him to keep him from harm and then did as he was ordered.

Joseph wondered where Father Matthew was today and if he was all right. "I sure hope you didn't get caught up in this mess." He prayed, promising himself to consider Father Matthew's personal opinions of what Yashmiel was trying to say in his writings, along with his own ideas, to try to arrive somewhere at the truth.

The scroll had deeper meaning for Joseph now with all he'd experienced since learning of its existence.

He began reading in a normal conversational tone and thought hearing his own voice might trigger new interpretations and therefore more clues.

"The true depth of man's soul will remain secret until it faces its ultimate challenge."

Joseph looked up from his reading. "I guess, none of us know what we're truly made of until we're put to the test."

He pondered the meaning of the first line.

"Perhaps, deep within an untapped part of the human soul, lies a dormant inner strength which has never before been summoned to awaken. An inner strength, present since man's first breath but never beckoned, able to be roused from its slumber only when the circumstances are so grave, there is no other recourse but to wake, surface and fight."

Then moved on to the second line.

"The human spirit is capable of great suffering and great triumph and the time will come for it to rise or fall amidst the shadow of its creator." Father Joseph put much thought into this one, tracing the sentence a second time with his fingertip.

"Hmmnnhhhh. Perhaps, the world has never truly seen the degree to which a human being can withstand abuse, torment and suffering. We *think* we have. Maybe the world has also never witnessed the absolute and total power of the human spirit in its full splendor. We *think* we have. Now, if I'm reading this correctly… I would say the time has come for mankind to be tested, calling forth that unconquerable primitive inner strength, so that man may once and for all raise his head to the Lord and truly be seen and judged for all that he truly is or is not."

Joseph considered it a viable possibility.

"A test." His bushy eyebrows lifted.

"A test, the likes, no one in present day could ever conceive." The fact that mankind, of his own hand, had come to this crossroads made Joseph feel more despair than he'd ever felt.

He knew it was *he* this tremendous burden fell to. He'd willingly assumed this responsibility in the cathedral that day with Glenn and was glad he did.

"Will the true resolve of the human spirit be lured out of the darkness with a test of some kind? Dependent upon how man responds, translation how *I* respond, mankind will rise or fall... Or, live or die, as a result?"

Joseph wasn't sure he was entirely accurate in his interpretation of the scroll's coded messages. But his instincts told him he was on the right track.

His eyes glanced down again to the ancient document before him.

Viewing the work as a whole, Father Joseph tried to get the big picture of what Yashmiel was trying to communicate here.

"Hidden within its prophecies, this mysterious writing poses a profound question." Joseph saw it in plain sight secreted within the text.

He lent voice to the question begging to be asked.

"Who is man?"

The faithful servant of the Lord asked himself the same question. That wasn't the only question the scroll put forward to its reader. There were more.

Joseph vocalized the others.

"Is man inherently good or evil? Would man accept suffering so great, so powerful, it could wipe him off the face of the earth? Would he sacrifice his own life to save all of mankind? Is man really that good? Would he relent, saving himself, therefore damning mankind for eternity? Therefore, that wicked?"

The questions clamored around inside Joseph's already crowded mind. It was a lot to process.

Joseph knew of only one who ever answered that question and backed it up with his actions. Jesus Christ.

"He did it for us. Would we be willing to do it for ourselves?" Joseph asked himself.

The next part, he felt he understood.

"There will be great affliction before the earth may know world peace." Joseph made a wry face.

"This is definitely referencing today, the present. The world is in a complete mess because of man's actions. This is the time we're living in."

Joseph gave the following sentence the weight it deserved.

"When the victorious one stands alone, it will signal the end or the rebirth of the world." The very thought caused Joseph to feel nauseous.

Based on his understanding so far of the scroll, he knew what this might mean.

It didn't mean a battle between two mortals, where an inherently good person and an inherently bad person would clash, with one ultimately rising as the victor.

It meant a battle between the representatives of heaven and hell. Good and evil.

"Good and evil. The two forces present within the mind, body and spirit of man, which have been vying for his soul since the moment of original sin. Man has worn two faces ever since."

Joseph could see man was losing this battle on a global scale.

The theologian brought the scroll closer to his face.

He had a revelation.

"Oh my! That's where the war will occur! Within man! *One* man." Father Joseph was catching on brilliantly to what Yashmiel was trying to say.

"It's going to be one man against himself. When the dust settles, the world will see which is victorious. Man's good side? Or, his evil side?"

His brain kicked into overdrive.

"This is about man's internal struggle between good and evil. The battle everyone wages within himself or herself daily." Joseph declared.

"Dependent upon which side of man reigns supreme... All of mankind will be turned over to *that* respective dominating force. Heaven or hell. Man will either be given a second chance or be annihilated as a result. Hence, the end or the rebirth of the world."

Nervously, Joseph rocked back and forth in his chair.

"The very essence of man is about to be tested. Tested for purity of heart." He was confident of that from the reading. "To see where he is to be seated for eternity."

He grew increasingly wretched when he contemplated how ugly and corrupt man had allowed himself to become through his own free will. Joseph saw with clarity, the peril man had put himself in.

"Man's soul currently hangs somewhere between heaven and hell." Joseph stated conclusively.

His eyes froze where they were on the scroll.

"A cleverly designed test will pit man against himself. Putting in competition, man's good side against his bad side. To see, which side of man is mightier? His good side or his evil side. Which determines... If we're worth keeping around."

If the Good Father thought about it too long, he knew he'd have a nervous breakdown. So he carried on with his work.

Finally, he read the last line.

"The fate of the world lies with the purest of heart." He traced the sentence with his index finger several times.

Joseph's eyes unfroze and lifted from his reading. "He who is strong enough to stay the course of goodness and righteousness... When he has nothing to gain and everything to lose by doing so. It is *he* who can save the world. *He* who shall inherit the earth."

Father Joseph's melancholy heart started to brighten a little.

He knew that *great triumph* lived inside every man, woman and beast upon the earth. This is what would make all his efforts worth it.

"They just need someone to remind them who they are." Joseph reaffirmed to himself.

"I can show them."

That was it. He was done with his research. The time had come for Joseph to do what he needed to do.

Now if only he knew where Victor, Falene and Anatoli were.

CHAPTER 21 -- REVENGE IS MINE

Safe and secure inside the pontiff's private quarters at the Vatican Victor kept to himself tonight in his sitting room.

After his disturbing visit with Chief Morgera the other day, he intentionally slipped back into his official residence without ever letting anyone know. He'd inconspicuously left and come back several times over the course of three days with no one ever detecting a thing. That was key.

There he sat, unshaven and bare-chested. His trousers undone at the waist, zippered down all the way. Lounging back on his couch and with his feet resting up on the arm of a nearby chair, Victor pointed a remote control at the television.

"Let's see if we've made the news." The unblessed said.

His outdated television took a moment to warm up. The volume came up immediately. The images were almost unnoticeable. The faint picture slowly but steadily brightened until it fully illuminated to its capacity, which was still rather dull.

Just as he expected and just what he was waiting for.

A busty, blonde news anchor, poised to deliver what he knew would be the year's most notorious news story. Her glossy red lips jumped off the screen at him.

"Come on baby." He rubbed his chest, fantasizing what it would be like for her to perform oral sex on him.

Quickly proofreading the bloodcurdling details of the two spine-chilling murders in the city made her noticeably uneasy.

A barbaric smile replaced the lower half of Victor's face.

"That's it sweetheart. Go ahead. Read it."

Victor's hand snaked down the front of his stomach, gliding over the curly dark hair covering his lower abdomen. He reached down between his legs. With his fingers, he lifted the elastic waistband of his underwear, so his hand could make its way inside. He took a firm hold of himself as he watched the broadcast.

He listened intently, while focusing on the sexy broadcaster's glistening; plump, ruby lips deliver the details of the homicides.

"Mmmmnnnnnnnn." Victor moaned.

"Investigators are calling our next story the most gruesome crime, law-enforcement has ever seen in the history of Rome. Coincidentally it was committed at Police Headquarters." She nervously adjusted herself in her seat before reading the copy, which followed.

"We want to warn you at home, the facts of this story are extremely disturbing. You may want to have your children leave the room at this point in the newscast."

She paused so the viewing parents could shoo their children out of the room.

"Rome's Chief of Police, Leo Morgera and the department's handwriting analyst, Antonella Castiglio, both shown highlighted here in this group shot of the entire force, were found brutally slain and dismembered inside police headquarters earlier today."

"Mmmmmnnnnnnnnnnn." Victor groaned again, gripping himself tighter.

The bombshell with a resonating broadcasting voice took a moment before delivering the rest of the troubling story.

"Due to the graphic nature of the crime scene, we are not able to show you the video taken from inside the station where the killings took place. But, what you at home are seeing on your television screens right now is an outside shot of the Rome Police Department. The Chief's bloodied office window tells part of the story."

"Oooohhhhhhh." Victor's eyes rolled back into his head. He shut his eye lids as he listened to her describe to her audience what happened.

"Authorities say, it appears Morgera and Castiglio unsuccessfully tried to run to the window to escape their attacker when they were chased down and overcome."

Victor took a quick peek.

A shot of a smeared, bloody handprint stained the glass. From the petite size of the hand, Victor knew it was Castiglio's.

"Blasted women! Gotta make a big show about everything!" He spat a sharp peppercorn granule he'd loosened from his gums onto the floor.

With his free hand, he took a swig of amber liquid from a tall glass sitting on the coffee table in front of him. While his other hand kept hard at work.

The seasoned journalist glanced at the monitor to make sure the right video was synched up with the story.

"According to Deputy Police Chief, Giuseppe Bianchi, who now serves as Interim Police Chief and lead investigator, both were found dead and dismembered inside the Chief's office. Chief Morgera was found with his head, left arm and right leg severed."

"Uuuuuuuuhhhhhhhhhhhh!!!" Victor tried to hold back.

The anchor coughed as though she were going to throw up.

"And, Castiglio, was also found with her head, left arm and right leg severed."

She paused again.

Victor's body started to tremble.

"Bianchi tells us, Morgera's body was found with Castiglio's head sewn to his neck. With Castiglio's left arm sewn to his right leg. And, with Castiglio's right leg attached to his left arm."

Offset, a male voice called out to the anchor. "You gonna be all right?"

She ignored him and continued.

"Antonella Castiglio's mutilated torso was also found in the same gruesome way. She was wearing Morgera's head. With *his* left arm sewn to her right leg. And, with Morgera's right leg attached to *her* left arm."

"You sure you're gonna be all right?" The voice returned.

She nodded she was fine.

"Both had been disemboweled. The bowels of each shoved down the throat of the other and their mouths sewn shut."

The newswoman reached up to her pouting lips with her fingertip. She felt ill.

"Who says the news is depressing?" Victor stuttered, shaking violently and breaking a cold sweat.

"Whoever did this also ransacked Chief Morgera's office, taking files and evidence with them. So far, no arrests have been made. We'll have more for you as investigators continue to release information to the media."

The anchor looked relieved to reach the end of the story as Victor reached his own conclusion.

It was just as he planned. Everything was going perfectly.

Pope Victor looked again to the coffee table in front of him.

There, in plain sight, a folder with his name **Pope Victor** typewritten on the tab. Next to it, a video tape as well as a clipboard with papers secured to it. In a pile next to that, some white pieces of paper with red writing on them. All of it covered in thick, dark-red blood.

"Told you I knew where to find you." Victor mocked the deceased's conceited decision to ignore his fair warning.

Again, that telling smile stretched across his face.

"*Now* let's see you prove it, you fool! I warned you!"

Victor got up from the couch, pulling his pants up and holding the front closed tight around his waist. He headed for the bathroom. But stopped, hearing something outside.

Crack! Kaboom!!! Followed by a bright flash of violet light.

He walked over to a window, turning an ear to the outside. Victor could see it was darker than usual for this time of evening.

Craaaaacccck!!! Kabooooooom! Boom!!! Another blinding flash.

"There it is again."

A fierce storm was moving into the region. Thunder and lightning rolled across the night sky.

"Looks like we're going to get a good one." He said, wondering where Falene and Anatoli were at this hour.

CHAPTER 22 -- TELLTALE SIGNS

Tommy's short legs dangled down off the couch. He sat there as usual mesmerized before the blasting television set.

He swung his legs out wildly, one by one. Each foot suspended in mid air for a few seconds, before crashing back to starting position. Bam! Bam!

He did this over and over repeatedly. The lower front portion of the sofa taking a pounding from the backs of his shoes.

The boy was totally hypnotized by the show he was watching.

Bam! Bam! -- Bam! Bam! His feet began to get rhythm, destructively kicking the couch like this. It was involuntary. A command he sent to his brain twenty minutes ago, looped, over and over.

The kid was operating totally on autopilot.

"Turn that thing down!" Terri hollered from the kitchen, busily making her son lunch.

Tommy pretended not to hear.

She waited.

"I said!..."

"OK, OK!" Tommy yelled back, sitting up slightly to reach for the remote. He pointed it across the room at the television, and immediately decreased the volume.

"I'm turning it down!" He reluctantly yielded to her demand. After all, she was in charge of lunch.

As he held his finger down on the volume button, his greasy finger accidentally slipped off, hitting an arrow up button to change channels.

The television switched to black.

"Whoops." He tried to make a quick save, but it was too late. The station switched from cartoons to a news program.

"Oh no!" Tommy howled. His right arm flapped up and down in the air out of frustration. As he did his grip on the remote control loosened. Off it went, sailing to the floor, bouncing out of sight.

"Oh, frig!" He shouted, trying to follow it with his eyes.

His enforcer disciplined from the other room. "Tommy, what did I tell you about your language?!"

Flustered, Tommy took a long, deep breath.

"I know. I know. I'm sorry!" Tommy apologized, rolling his eyes at the same time because he knew she couldn't see him.

"Frig…" The boy whispered, out of earshot. "Where is it?"

Tommy balanced his body's core on the seat cushions of the couch. Lying on his stomach, with his legs back and up in the air, he hung his upper body off the front of the furniture like a stuntman, looking for the remote control on the floor. He checked under the sofa, around some toys scattered on the floor, under an old pizza box, and everywhere else in sight until the TV took his attention away.

Even though the volume was still turned down, Tommy could make out some of the narration to the story.

"Is this the last untouched place on earth?" The deep male voice asked viewers' opinions. "Some say it may very well be."

Tommy flipped himself back up, and sat on his bottom.

Shots of a lush, green, foreign land with wild animals filled the television screen. "Wow!" Tommy shrieked. "That's so cool!"

Tommy was awestruck by the program, which came across his television set purely accidentally.

Tommy's family never had the money to visit such a place. Heck, he'd never been to Disney World on his mom's single-parent salary.

He searched one last place for the illusive electronic gadget, behind one of the coffee table legs.

"There you are! Gotcha!" The boy snatched the gizmo off the floor with a death grip, pointing it back at the television.

"Let's see here. What are they talking about?" He was dying to know where this place was.

And up the volume went again.

"Tommy! What did I just say!" Terri raised her voice again from the kitchen.

"Mom! Wait! Ya gotta see this! Look! Come here!" He persisted. "Mom! Hurry!!!"

Barely wiping her hands dry with a dishtowel, Terri immediately left her chores in the kitchen and jogged into the living room to see what the heck was on TV that had Tommy so excited.

"Look!" Tommy shouted, pointing to the television.

Terri found her glasses on top of an end table next to the couch and quickly shoved them onto her face.

Terri saw the images of that lush, green, peaceful place on the screen.

"Oooohhhhh... That's nice Tommy. Where is that?" She asked him.

"I don't know. I just put it on by accident." He answered. "But I like it there!"

"Yeah, I do too." She confessed.

Just then, as if by request, bold text popped up at the lower left-hand corner of the television screen. It read simply, Asia.

They were looking at aerial pictures taken from a helicopter somewhere over the continent... in the jungle.

From the video, Terri and Tommy could see a crude village below. The remote settlement, tucked away within the most isolated part of the wild impenetrable land, sat upon a ring-shaped clearing. Shabby teepees dotted the dirt floor of the modest colony. What appeared to be four-hundred-year old trees surrounded the village, forming an imposing border. The towering trees and vegetation of a prehistoric-age era dwarfed everything else in comparison.

There was something special about this place; neither mother nor son could put their finger on it. It was of this earth, but didn't seem so. It was tranquil, undisturbed and inherently good and holy.

"That's really a beautiful place." She told Tommy. "It's like heaven on earth." A feeling of peace came over her as she watched the story.

"It is." He agreed, gaping at the TV.

"I'd love to go there! What an adventure that would be! I could swing around on the trees with the monkeys!!!" He announced with a beaming smile. "Since we can't go to Disney World.... Can we go there?" Tommy begged, using his best puppy dog eyes to try to sway her.

Terri turned to her son sympathetically and with a tad of guilt. She reached out, putting her arm around him.

"Well, I sure wish I could take you there, honey." She said, brushing his hair out of his eyes. "Right now, we have to concentrate on getting you better." Cradling his head in her breast, she compassionately reminded him of his illness. "When you're better, Tommy. When you're better. I promise. I'll try to find a way." Terri kissed the top of his head.

"Oooohhhhhhh." He twisted away from her, subtly telling his mother he was getting too old for this sort of thing.

Both returned their attention to the story at hand.

"Researchers *are* calling this the last untouched place on earth." The news anchor read.

Terri detected from the newsperson's tone, this was going to be a sad story.

"Ohhhhhhhhh..." The skin between Terri's eyebrows wrinkled, creating that deep groove in her forehead, which she'd been trying so hard to smooth out with anti-wrinkle creams.

She hated news stories like this. They made her feel bad for days. The very reason she didn't watch the news much anymore.

"We're going to hear something terrible in this story Tommy. I just know it and it's going to ruin the rest of my day." She huffed.

Thinking about the attitude she'd just shown her child, she changed her tune to a more optimistic one. "But, we have to be informed about the world around us. If we're not, we're like lambs to the slaughter. If we arm ourselves with information, we can make a difference. Right?"

Tommy looked up at his mother and smiled. "Right."

"So, let's see what this story is all about. Maybe we can make a difference in the world somehow, Tommy." She tapped his nose.

The news story continued.

"Dozens of villagers, living here in this far-removed settlement in the jungle have simply vanished. According to anthropologists and activists, this so-called *uncontacted* or *lost* tribe, was fully aware of the outside world, but chose isolation for as long as they've been in existence. Although Western society was well aware of their existence, they were left alone, preserving their autonomy and distinctiveness."

Both adult and child were riveted by the report.

"Now, it appears they have either fled from companies illegally encroaching on their land looking for oil and/or timber. Or, they were killed off somehow."

Tommy got upset when he saw previously recorded images of the primitive people peacefully going about their business. The group was photographed several years ago by the local government during a reconnaissance flight.

"Why would anyone want to hurt them?!" He asked angrily.

Terri put an arm around him for comfort.

"I knew it was going to be bad." She said low enough so he couldn't hear.

The news piece didn't stop there.

"Scholars in this field say it's common for a group like this to decide to flee deeper into the forest to avoid the disease and violence that comes with contact from outsiders. But, it wouldn't be common for them to leave everything behind as they had."

A telephoto lens zoomed in on the shabby teepee style tents and large iron cooking pots left below.

Terri and Tommy leaned in toward the TV to get a better look. Something about this news story had them unnerved.

"The Indigenous Peoples Foundation, says this uncontacted group is the last one of its kind in the world. Representatives from the Foundation have trekked on foot to the sight for evidence explaining what might have happened at the camp. They report what they've found on the ground."

Next was a sound bite from The Indigenous Peoples Foundation Spokesperson, Avis Gallagher. She was an older woman in her sixties, heavy-set with short, curled, golden blonde hair and hazel eyes. She spoke about her observations with great pride.

"Well, what we've found here is truly very unique." Her eyes darting around, searching to find the right words to describe what she'd seen.

"The only way to describe it is.... A heaven on earth. A modern day Garden of Eden of sorts." Gallagher paused.

Terri and her son looked at each other. "Didn't I just say that?" She asked Tommy.

He nodded in disbelief.

"There are varieties of plant life here never before seen by modern civilization. As well as, animal, fish and bird species also never before seen or recorded by Western society."

"Oh my God, mom! I have to go there!" Tommy demanded relentlessly. "I have to see that! I swear, if I go there, I'll get better and never be sick again!"

Terri ignored his pleading as she listened to Gallagher proceed with her findings.

"We've been here for days, inspecting the village, sifting through the remains left behind by the villagers and making some pretty astonishing observations. While here, the Foundation has discovered, the primitive people who lived here, lived here in harmony with each other, the animals, birds and plants. The people and the animals are or were, amazingly, all vegetarians. So, believe it or not, there is no food-chain hierarchy here. All lived off the land, and lived together in perfect harmony." Gallagher was visibly titillated by her own fascinating discoveries.

"Here, the birds and the beasts, all unafraid of human beings, come right up to you, to investigate you. They're NOT afraid!" She emphasized. "It's as though they never learned to be afraid. Never had a reason to be and are just as interested in learning about you as you are about learning about them."

"Wow..." Terri couldn't take her eyes from the screen.

"It's truly, truly paradise." The spokesperson reported from the site.

As Gallagher excitedly rambled on during her interview, a small bird brightly colored red, yellow, blue and black flew to her, landing upon her shoulder.

"See!" She exclaimed. The bird craned its neck to get a better look at her.

"Stay here Tommy, I'll be right back." Terri hustled to her bedroom, returning quickly with a Bible. She had an idea.

She sat right back down on the couch next to Tommy, furiously sifting through the pages.

"Keep watching Tommy. Then we'll talk about it." Terri instructed.

Not a word from Tommy. He was too focused on anything and everything Gallagher had to say.

"This is what we know." Gallagher summarized.

"What we don't know is what happened to the tribe that lived here. There is no evidence of murder, no evidence of the group packing up and relocating. No evidence of anything really. It's almost as if they vanished into mid air." The spokesperson confirmed. "The question for now remains, where did these people go?"

The news anchor tagged out the piece.

"Again, that's Avis Gallagher from The Indigenous Peoples Foundation at the site of the missing *lost tribe*, in Asia, thanks Avis… Now, big news in the Mid-West today as floods…"

That was all the world would learn about that story today.

With the remote control now firmly in mom's hands, the volume steadily decreased until mute.

"What did you think of that story, Tommy?" She asked him seriously.

"Cool! I want to go there!" He said, bouncing on the couch.

Terri marked a spot in the Bible by wedging her fingers between the pages.

"Tommy. Remember how, in the story, they showed the big, old, impressive trees surrounding that remote village?" She asked him if he'd remembered that fact.

"Yeah?" He answered, unsure of what she was getting at.

"They seemed to be an important part of that village for some reason." She pointed out. "Just looking at those pictures, it was obvious those trees had some real significance to those villagers."

She spoke quickly, using her hands to illustrate what she was talking about. "Well, I'm not sure if this has anything to do with that village, but…" Terri hesitated.

"The trees in the Garden of Eden held the secret to life and healing. The Garden of Eden we know from the Bible, Tommy."

He looked at her blankly. "Uh-huh?"

"I think that's what those trees might have meant to that tribe." She looked to him for his opinion. "They may have settled there for a precise reason. There may be an energy there or something they were drawn to." Then Terri realized she was speaking way over her son's head.

She opened to the page she'd marked with her finger, reading to her son directly from the Bible.

"Listen to this Tommy. Here in Genesis 1:29-30 it says… When God blessed Adam and Eve in the Garden of Eden, he said to them: I give you every seed-bearing plant on the face of the whole earth and every tree that has fruit with seed in it. They will be food for you. And to the beasts of the earth and all the birds of the air and all the creatures that move on the ground – everything that has the breath of life in it – I give every green plant for food. And it was so."

Tommy still found himself dumbfounded but tried to follow. "OK."

Terri pointed to the TV. "The spokesperson said, all the people and the animals there are vegetarians! There is no food-chain hierarchy there."

"Yeah?" Still not catching on, he made a face.

"That's not normal, Tommy! That's not how things are in *our* world. In our world, we see man killing man, man slaughtering animals for food, animals killing each other to eat. But that's not what's going on there! WE don't live together in harmony! Why?"

Tommy's mom poked her finger down at the Bible. "That place they showed… in Asia… It's just like in the Garden of Eden."

She knew she had to explain further.

"In the beginning, Tommy, God gave man the entirety of creation. Man had the authority to rule over the land and all its inhabitants. It was perfection, just like what we saw on TV, but it was ruined by original sin. The sin committed by Adam and Eve." She spoke slower, so Tommy could follow.

"You mean the apple thing?" He asked innocently.

"Yes, the apple thing. You see, without the innocence of Adam and Eve, man lived in sin," she explained.

Terri began at the beginning again, to try to help Tommy see the connection she was trying to make.

"When God created the earth, in the beginning, there was a perfect balance in nature. The earth was perfection. All its inhabitants, including man, beast, fowl and plant, lived in perfect harmony with each other. Until, man lost his authority over creation because he chose sin in the Garden of Eden." She jogged his memory.

"Uh-huh." Tommy got this part.

Terri thought back to the details of the news report and to the facts within the Bible sitting in her lap.

"Everything in the Garden of Eden was perfect. Just like in that village. Perfection. Harmony." She saw the report play over and over again in her mind.

She looked down at her Bible again, speed-reading.

Then looked up, putting what she'd read into her own understandable language.

"Because that village is so isolated from the rest of the world, the villagers were able to maintain that perfect balance in nature… Right there at that spot."

Terri could feel a charley horse coming on. Anytime she was under stress, she'd get stiffening and cramping of the leg muscles. She reached down to massage the calf muscle in her left leg without letting it break her thought process.

"But in the rest of the world, man who has free will, continued a path of wickedness. That's why, so very long ago, God decided to flood the earth and destroy man and every living thing on the planet. Only Noah, his family and two of every kind of animal were selected by God to survive and replenish the earth. Noah and his family were like Adam and Eve, beginning things again."

Terri thought to herself. "This would explain why the animals didn't kill and eat each other in the ark. Because they were not meat-eaters at this point."

Tommy stared blankly at his mother who was on a roll.

"Following the flood, with that new world order, God allowed for the eating of meat. Man was refused more and more of the natural perfection of the world as he continued delving to his dark side. Look where we all are now."

Terri looked at Tommy's face. All of what she said was lost on him.

"OK Tommy. Never mind. I'm going to get back to the kitchen and fix your lunch."

She got up off the couch, heading to the kitchen with her finger still stuck in her Bible.

Tommy forgot about the whole thing and switched the channel back to cartoons.

"Thank God. I just liked the story. I don't know what she was talking about." He murmured under his breath.

His mom, now alone in the kitchen, talked to herself.

"Could that be it?" She asked herself.

A teakettle whistling in the background couldn't distract Terri from her thoughts.

"Since the flood, God deemed it fit for creation to eat each other. Perhaps, because of man's sinful ways?" She wasn't sure she was right.

The whistling teakettle finally caught her attention.

As she poured herself a cup of tea she could hear the television set too loud again. Tommy was back watching his cartoons at full volume. She didn't care.

She sat down to the kitchen table with her teacup in hand, thinking about the ideas inundating her mind. A fourth teaspoon of sugar, shoveled into her drink.

"Ohhh! NO!" Terri walked over to the sink, pouring it down the drain.

She started over again with a different cup, new teabag and fresh hot water. Back to the table she went.

"God destroyed us twice." Terri tried counting it out, making sure she had it right. This was confusing stuff. The most she had to concentrate on, on a regular basis were the daily specials at Harry's Lunch Spot here in exciting Nebraska.

"The Adam and Eve original sin thing." She held up one finger. "That changed the essence of who man was forever. But God gave man another chance. He could live, but he'd live with the shame of sin. That's how he was destroyed the first time."

She was clear on that point.

"Then, even after being given a second chance, man used his free will to continue to make sinful decisions. That's why God eventually decided to flood the earth, starting over with Noah, his family and all the animals on the ark. That's how he was destroyed the second time. But, again, given another chance." She held up a second finger.

"Reason? We're all idiots who can't appreciate what we've got! Now, we're all so brilliant we're working hard on strike number three!" Terri took a sip of tea to calm down.

"I think I'm on to something here." She figuratively patted herself on the back.

"If we watch the news these days, it's clear, we're being wiped out again… Because of our greed, sloth, wrath, pride, envy, gluttony and lust." She desperately craved a cigarette, but it was one of the many vices she'd given up as a plea bargain with God to save her son's life.

If she spoke any faster, she'd speak in tongues. "OK, so we're all losers who don't appreciate anything, pollute our earth, kill each other and our animals, commit crimes against each other, destroy God and screw up anything we get our hands on."

She lowered her voice so Tommy wouldn't hear her tirade.

"Yup! That's human beings all right. That's us!" Terri's fingernail nervously tapped the top of the table.

"We deserve to die. We really do. Yup. We really do. We stink! We don't even deserve another chance."

Realizing she'd gone off on a tangent, Terri refocused.

"That camp on the news looks and sounds a lot like a present-day Garden of Eden. Not *the* Garden of Eden, *a* Garden of Eden. The trees, the way the people lived among nature and the animals." Every image, each bit of natural sound, everything Avis Gallagher said, was burned into Terri's memory. She felt she was meant to see that story.

"Those people represent the last good, pure souls on the earth, living as man was originally meant to. Now they're gone." She said, greatly disturbed by their mysterious disappearance.

"Where did they go?" There was no way for her to know.

Then she had a profound thought.

She glanced back down at the Bible, reading.

She spoke to the Lord in her head. She didn't want to scare her son more than she already had.

"Dear Lord, I believe we are in our final hour here on earth again, because of our wicked ways which we can't seem to mend."

A tear began to roll down Terri's cheek. She wiped it quickly, wondering if it cut through her make-up, leaving a water streak.

"I believe that tribe I saw on the news today is a sign of some sort. A sign we have sinned to capacity, destroying the last beautiful, pure spot on earth which represented your original plan."

Another tear. This time, falling from the opposite eye.

Terri didn't bother to wipe it this time.

"Is it too late, my Lord?" She asked him, knowing he always answers her prayers in one way or another and if she doesn't understand his communication regarding a particular matter, she has faith in leaving his will to Him.

"As you sent Jesus to redeem us from our sins, restore our hearts and give us another chance at eternal life, please send another to light the way for us. We have lost our way Father. Someone out there among us can show you the true heart of mankind. Please help them to come forward and show themselves." Terri prayed.

"During the hour of our need, who may show our true heart to you, as Jesus once did, Oh Lord? Only you know who that may be. Please help them find their true destiny." Now she was pleading with God.

Terri also silently called out to the world at large.

"Who among us has the strength to reveal a pure heart, while fighting the devil himself?" She asked.

"All the earth groans for this person to come forth, so that we and the animals can again eat of the land and not of each other under a cloud of sin." The single-mom now with her head bowed over her table prayed harder than she ever had.

"Let the lion and the lamb lie down together. Let man have no desire to hunt or kill anything."

Terri could hear Tommy changing the channel on the television set again. She knew he was searching for more on that story they'd just watched together.

"I pray to you, Oh Lord, that one among us may rise up against the Beast, representing man's collective heart, not the spoiled soul of the masses. Let him see to it the devil no longer roams this earth but is chained and cast into hell along with those who demonstrate allegiance to him."

Terri made the sign of the cross over her body with her right hand.

"Lord, I know you've started over with us for the last time… and rightfully so…" Her prayer was interrupted.

Terri recognized the broadcaster's voice coming from the other room.

The volume, still blasting, allowed her to hear every word.

"A typhoon in the Philippines has left three-hundred dead with the death toll expected to rise as hundreds more go missing." More bad news on top of bad news. "This, as tornadoes continue to rip through the Southern part of the United States on a daily basis. This year alone, eighty-nine people have died in this country as a result of the intense and highly destructive storms."

She put her head in her hands, as she listened. Tommy tuned in to yet another station.

"Rising gas prices are putting working class families out on the street…" The reporter informed the viewing audience.

Tommy hit the remote again, inviting into their home, more dreadful accounts of what was happening in the world.

"Doctors are calling it a medical mystery. In the past year, the number of patients diagnosed with cancer has quadrupled. Not only has the number of cancer patients worldwide skyrocketed dramatically, their mortality rate has increased by thirty-seven percent."

Terri knew she could have listened for hours, but the information would have all been the same. Bad news. She let out a long, sorrowful sigh. "Uuuuuuuhhhhhhhhh."

She petitioned the Lord with every fiber of her being.

"This is it. I know it is. I see the signs of our impending doom, which we've created of our own free will. I pray the right person finds their way to where they belong, so that the true nature of the human spirit may be revealed, for the sake of all of us. Amen."

Terri quietly ended her sincere prayer.

When she looked up, that's when she noticed Tommy's lunch still sitting over on the counter.

"Oh gosh."

Up from the table she sprang, grabbing the plate.

"Come on Tommy! Lunch!" Terri called out.

Tommy leapt from his place on the couch and came bounding into the kitchen.

"Did I hear, lunch?!" His perky face always made his mother smile.

Tommy took a seat at the kitchen table before his bologna sandwich.

"Ouch!" He looked to his left front pants pocket.

"What's the matter? Are you all right?" Terri asked, looking for a reason for the "Ouch!"

"It's this, this thing you gave me here!" Alarmed and confused, Tommy jumped up from his seat, pulling the stone Terri gave him from his front, left pocket. He threw it onto the table like it was a hot potato.

"Ouch! It's hot!" He screamed, rubbing his hands together.

Terri knew immediately it was the stone Glenn had given to her at the hospital.

"What do you mean it's hot?!" She came over to inspect, not believing him.

"It's hot! That's what I mean. It's actually hot!" He persisted, backing away from the table, afraid of it.

As Tommy looked down at the rock on the table, he saw it was primarily black now, with only a single tiny spot of dark blue with green and while trails running through it.

A safe distance away, with his feet planted firmly on the kitchen floor, he leaned in. He saw yellow squiggly lines drawn all over the stone.

"It looks like... like a... a... puzzle." He remarked to his mother.

Yellow lines forming the shapes of puzzle pieces were all over it.

"It changed into a dark puzzle of some sort!" Baffled by what was going on, Tommy immaturely yelled his sentences.

Terri had to grab her glasses again to see. "Just take it easy Tommy. Let's see here." She scrutinized the rock.

"Oh my God! It did change." She confirmed for herself. "It lost its primarily blue and greenish coloring." She looked at it from all angles. "It used to have those ugly black blotches on it, remember Tommy?"

"I remember, yeah!"

"Now the black spots seem to have taken over. There's just a little blue and green left and it's divided up into puzzle shapes by these yellow lines, here." She pointed out with the tip of her finger.

Both had their faces as close as they could get to it without touching it.

With her fingernail, Terri flicked the rock over to examine the bottom of it. There, in ancient Aramaic writing, the name Ara appeared glowing as though the sun were shining through it.

"Look at that, would you?" She gawked. "Ara." She repeated the name Glenn told her. "King."

"Tommy, where did you put this down since I gave it to you?" She asked him.

"Nowhere mom! It's been in my pocket the whole time." He insisted. "The whole time! I swear it!"

Terri lightly touched the stone to see if it was still hot. It was roaring hot.

"Ouch!" She yanked her finger back, and stepped away.

"See, I told you it was hot! You didn't believe me." Tommy teased.

"Well, what the…" Terri didn't know what to make of this. "Hmmnnhhhh. A puzzle. Why a puzzle?"

She thought to herself.

Then she asked Tommy.

"How can it be a puzzle if all the pieces of the puzzle are present and they're all put together? The stone is solid. Doesn't this mean the puzzle is solved?"

Tommy shrugged his shoulders.

Neither had a good explanation for what they were seeing.

CHAPTER 23 -- A PERPLEXING DISCOVERY

Joseph wondered if Falene and Anatoli were still here in Providence. He had no idea. If they were, they weren't interested in him right now. They had a way of finding him when and if they wanted to.

"Don't care if I ever see you two sinister miscreants again." He declared, just in case they were listening somehow, some way.

He knew he would, unfortunately, eventually be in their company again. That's why he had to make progress now.

Joseph was still working, secretly tucked away inside a conference room at the Aviatrans Hotel and time was of the essence.

Before he put the scroll away, he decided he better make sure he observed everything he could from it and reread the right side. He didn't know when he'd have this much time again to try to decipher its meanings.

Feeling he now completely understood what was on the left side of the map, he wanted to be sure he didn't overlook anything else important on the right side.

The previous opportunities he had to review the scroll were far between. In each instance he was in a huge rush against the clock. Never, did he have the time to closely scrutinize the map at the center. Father Joseph knew the drawing must contain major clues to the scroll's messages. He needed to find out what they were quickly as possible.

Joseph looked closer at the sketch. The continents and their positions were all geographically accurate.

"Not bad for a guy living over two-thousand years ago."

The astute priest remembered his dear friend, Father Matthew explaining it to him after leading him to that secret room at the Vatican, while they awaited word of the Pope's grave condition. The pontiff was near death, but still alive then.

It seemed a lifetime ago now.

Father Joseph remembered Father Matthew emphasizing with great emotion, the importance of the chart at the middle of the scroll, saying. “Yashmiel drew this crude map long before the oceans and the continents of the world were charted. There was no way for Yashmiel to know the positions of landmasses and large bodies of water back then, yet he was able to accurately draft a map of the world!”

Then insisted to Joseph how. “Because Christ revealed it to him, that’s how! He did so, to prove that Yashmiel walked with greatness.”

Joseph would never forget those words.

He was certain the map was significant to this work for additional reasons than what Father Matthew had already discovered. What, Joseph hadn’t yet found out.

As Father Joseph studied the picture closer, he noticed the map had a faint jagged border drawn all the way around it. Most of it was worn away, barely still noticeable.

“I missed this the last time I looked at it.” He admitted, leaning in, making sure his eyes weren’t playing tricks on him. “Probably because it’s hardly observable.” He squinted.

Joseph had to trace his finger along the faint lines of the existing border, connecting them with the bare spaces in between, to make a mental picture of what it was supposed to look like.

“Ah-hah. I see. Well, this is an odd shape.” He thought, tracing it. “It goes all the way around the map.”

More details of the scroll surfaced, the longer he looked at it. He saw there were other long-faded lines covering the diagram. “These here, I didn’t see these before.”

Barely there squiggly, odd-shaped lines were drawn over the landmasses and the oceans within the map itself but they were so dull they too were hardly noticeable. Joseph had to really look closely.

He used his finger again to trace where the lines began, ended and where they should connect.

“It… it… it… looks like puzzle pieces?” The confused priest still wasn’t sure what he was looking at.

"This map looks like it's divided into puzzle shapes."

Joseph mulled it over.

"Why? What the heck is that about?"

Trying to piece it all together, Joseph reviewed that irregularly shaped border again, which encompassed the map at the center of the scroll.

"Is that supposed to represent, the shape of the world? Maybe Yashmiel thought the world was flat and shaped like this?"

Joseph answered his own question. "Obviously Yashmiel had knowledge long before his time. He's not going to be able to draw a perfect replica of the world and not know it's not flat." That explanation was out.

He ran through a list of ideas in his head. "… It kind of strikes me as a boulder or a rock." He speculated, leaning back in his chair.

"From a distance, it looks like a large stone." Joseph imagined what it would look like if it were in color. "Deep dark blue… Where the oceans are." He mentally shaded those zones in blue. "There would be greenish-brownish patches, here… Here… And here, where the landmasses are." With his finger, Joseph imaginarily colored-in the areas representing land. "Clouds floating overhead would carve up the entire picture with random white trails." He had a colorful image of it in his head.

Another possibility.

"Or… Perhaps it's meant to represent a tablet. Like what the Ten Commandments were chiseled upon." He thought that might make sense.

There was no way to be sure.

"Well, it's information I didn't have before. Complicates things far worse, but… I'd rather have more information than not enough."

He moved on.

Joseph revisited the right side of the map now. He noticed there was a lot more writing on this side than the other.

"Why?" He wondered. "Was it of greater priority than the left side?"

Joseph lightly floated his finger along the top of the ancient script.

"OK, let's see here." He said, circumspectly.

Bringing his chair closer, his midsection pressed up against the edge of the conference table as he slid the scroll slightly toward him with both hands.

He began to read.

"When man has emptied his soul…" He stopped abruptly. The hair at the back of his neck stood on end and goose bumps rose on his forearms.

Something suddenly felt different in the room for some reason. A new energy had come into the conference room he occupied. Joseph could feel it in his bones. It was an unseen entity. He couldn't see it, hear it or smell it but he could clearly feel the presence of someone or something watching him there.

He looked around, scared to death.

"No one has come in here." Deeply unsettled, Joseph questioned his own sanity at this point. "Have they?" He surveyed the entire room again.

"Falene?!"

Dead silence.

Next, calling the name of her lackey. "Anatoli?!" He shouted, listening for a response of any kind.

No one was there, at least physically.

The undeniably strong, powerful presence *was* there, but in nonmaterial form; watching Joseph with the scroll from a dimension he couldn't comprehend intellectually.

"What do you want?" Joseph asked bravely.

No answer. No sign.

"Please tell me why you're here." Joseph implored.

Strangely, the quiet existence, which filled the room didn't feel threatening in any way to Joseph. From where it came or what it wanted, Joseph had no idea.

"Perhaps you're here as a guardian of this scroll, here to protect but not to intervene?" He posed.

Still nothing.

Joseph knew if the *being* wanted to hurt him it would have done so by now. He didn't get that feeling. That's not what it wanted.

So Father Joseph let it be, as it let him be.

Together, they would occupy this space at this time.

He began to read again, feeling more at ease now.

"When man has emptied his soul of his own free will and the world cries amidst tremendous domestic and international conflict, a seraph will be summoned by God to walk the Earth."

Joseph considered that first line. He knew the world was in a state of self-destruction and imminent disaster because of man's actions. He got that.

"… A seraph among us?" He reread the line. "Glenn. OK. That's him." He was glad to know at least this much.

But there was more. Much more.

"This visitor among men will search the world over, with his nemesis by his side, for the last pure soul on Earth who is blessed with a holy bloodline. It is within this sacred person among men, where hope for mankind lives in its purest form. This natural "monarch" of man has the potential to triumphantly rise up against sin in the name of the father and is why they are sought equally by the angel and the Archfiend."

Joseph kept his mind open. He separated what he knew for certain from what he was unsure of. This way he could try to keep things straight in his head.

He was clear who the visitor or "angel" was, Glenn and who his nemesis or "Archfiend" was, Falene, and that Victor and Anatoli were here helping her. Joseph also had been made aware that Glenn and Falene had been searching for *the last pure soul on Earth who is blessed with a holy bloodline.*

Him.

Glenn had ultimately selected him to represent the true inherent nature of man after scouring the world over. It was within him, Glenn felt, where hope for mankind lived in its purest form.

"How am *I* blessed with a holy bloodline?" Joseph heard the cock-and-bull explanation Glenn gave Falene that day in the cathedral when he was turned over to her but that didn't hold water. Joseph had no idea how, but he knew there had to be another way he was *blessed with a holy bloodline* and it wasn't the way Glenn said.

"Was Glenn holding something back from Falene?" Joseph pondered the possibility Glenn told Falene the truth, but not the whole truth.

The energy from the invisible entity in the room intensified.

Joseph gave another quick sweep of the room with his eyes.

Then his thoughts turned to his dearly departed, old friend, the Pope. The real Pontiff. The one who'd dedicated his life to the Roman Catholic Church and had passed away only recently.

Some outrageous ideas passed through Joseph's mind.

"No. He couldn't have. Could he?" Joseph questioned aloud.

"The only way I could see this being possible is if, he... There's no way he did!" The priest stopped himself short of blasphemy.

Father Joseph blew off his thought as ridiculous but returned to it immediately because it was the only viable explanation he could think of.

"Did the Holy Father name me a Cardinal in pectore?" Joseph had a hunch this could explain things.

"Did the Pontiff exercise his right to name me a Cardinal in pectore? In other words, to protect me from harm, secretly reserved my name in his heart as one of his Cardinals without ever telling me or anyone else?" Only the Pope knew this answer and he took it to his grave.

"This way, I'm not bound by the duties of a Cardinal and don't possess any of their rights or privileges. Thus protecting my identity. I would be a Cardinal nonetheless and therefore... Of a holy bloodline?"

Joseph couldn't believe it. If this were so, then he truly did fit the description of the prophesied person in the scroll.

His eyes scanned the next line quickly and ironically, it focused on the Pope.

"This time on Earth will be recognized when an exalted holy spiritual leader dies in the West and is replaced with a fork-tongued rogue." He read. There was no mystery here for Joseph.

"This has come true." Joseph nodded, affirming the prognostication. "Victor." He scowled.

Just a little more to go before he'd digested the entire scroll.

"As the jewel of heaven and his vixenish shadow lay their feet upon blackened soil, scourged from waste and natural disaster, they will see desperation in the eyes of man. When the last spirit turns foul, so will the Earth turn foul and furious with rage. Unless the chosen one recognizes their destiny, man's eternal damnation will be set into motion and it will be the beginning of the end of the world."

The scroll's messages were finally beginning to make some sense to Joseph. He checked-off what he knew at this point for clarity.

"OK, so... The world and mankind as a whole has come to a crossroads. Check. A representative from heaven and one from hell are here. Check. Their mission is to find the last pure soul, blessed with a holy bloodline. Check. That's when the content of mankind's collective heart will be measured... *that* will determine the fate of civilization."

Joseph stopped his reading there.

"Yet to be checked." He gulped, looking grim.

"No pressure... No pressure. No need to get nervous here, Joseph. No big deal. You can do this."

The last line, Joseph read totally spent.

"Until then, the sun will continue to warm the Earth and hope will live until the last spirit knows not God."

Joseph didn't need to reread anything. He was done. He had all the information he needed now.

He looked up from the scroll for the last time. "It is a time of rebirth or of annihilation for this world." Joseph authenticated. "Rightfully so."

The priest was done with his work for now.

Joseph searched on the floor for his shoes. He began gingerly putting them back on as he packed up his things. It took a while for him to cram his big, fat feet back into those old shoes. They hurt so badly and had swollen during the short time they were free to breathe.

"Ah, come on. In 'ya go!" He ordered. The severe pain in his sore feet came back the instant they returned to their confinement. "Ouch!" Joseph yelped.

"How do women do it in those high-heeled things? Like what Falene wears?"

Then it occurred to him. "That's because they're a design of the devil! Satan invented those things!"

"Ouch!" His feet felt like they were being bound with wire.

When he finally successfully wrangled his shoes back on his feet, Father Joseph folded the scroll tightly into a square and re-stuffed it into his back pants pocket.

He used both hands to hoist himself off the chair.

"As for you whoever you are…" He paused, gazing about the room to speak to the unnamed. "Thank you." He said kindly.

"Thank you for being here. Thank you for protecting what I am trying to protect."

No response.

"You have my word, you'll have my best and I won't let you down." He offered.

With that, Joseph left.

CHAPTER 24 -- UNITED FORCE

Victor hurriedly cleaning himself up at the sink in his bathroom heard someone at the door.

Knock! Knock! Knock!-Knock!

"Just a minute!" He shouted from the washroom. "Be right there!!"

Victor shut the water off and hung his bloodstained terrycloth hand towel back up on the hook mounted to the wall.

Inspecting himself in the mirror above the basin, he saw he looked a little cadaverous. So, he placed a palm on each jowl and roughly rubbed his face in circular motions, to give his cheeks a natural glow.

"There we go. Much better." He said, slapping his face on both sides.

His overweening pride was firmly in place.

Victor could hear the muffled, nervous banter of two people through the walls, but couldn't identify the voices.

"Get over here! We have to… He's inside. Let's go!" He heard one of the voices chastising.

"OK! OK!" The other voice complied, followed by sluggish footsteps.

Based on what he overheard so far, Victor knew he had a male and a female caller.

"Hmmnnhhh." As he strained to listen, a deep trench vertically etched into his glabella.

Knock!! Knock!!! Knock!!!!! Knock!!!-Knock!!! More rapping.

Whoever it was, was very impatient.

"Coming!" He promised, trying to get himself together and to the door quicker. "I'm coming!! Just a minute!!"

First making sure he was dressed appropriately, he dashed out of the bathroom and to the entrance hall of the Pope's private chamber. Once there, he swung the front door open.

There they were. His myrmidons.

"Ciao, Vittorio!" Falene saluted obnoxiously, in her typically theatrical manner. She raised her right arm at a forty-five degree angle above the horizontal and slightly sideways to the right as though she were indicating loyalty to the Nazi Party or greeting scores of fans.

She and Anatoli had finally made their way back to Rome and to the Vatican from Providence, Rhode Island.

"Guess who's back in town?!" His well-coifed ally clowned. "And glad they are!"

"Well… I can see who." He stated unenthusiastically, opening the door wider.

"Come in."

Victor stepped back two steps and extended his left arm into the room, disingenuously welcoming Falene and Anatoli into his living quarters. As he did, he turned his head away so they wouldn't see him yawning.

"It's good to be back where we belong!" Falene rudely walked past her host without visually acknowledging him.

"I'm glad you both finally made it back here." Victor said, slamming the door shut.

"Yeah well… The job there is done." Falene sassed, as all three made their way to the sitting room.

After throwing her a look, Victor walked back to the adjacent bathroom to check himself in the mirror one more time.

"It's about time you two returned! I had to do most everything here myself!" Victor excoriated his guests from the john.

Falene picked up on Victor's vexation.

"Poor baby! Nice to see you too!" She teased sarcastically, finding a plush chair to retire to. "As you'll recall, *we* had important work to do as well." She reminded him strictly.

"And… Uh… Let's not forget who's in charge here, Victor! OK?!" She pointed to another chair across the room where Anatoli should sit.

Anatoli took his seat immediately upon her nonverbal instruction.

Victor, half leaning out of the restroom doorway, wanted to be immediately brought up to speed on everything. "Anything to tell me?! What's going on over there?!" He was referring to Joseph and the situation in Rhode Island.

Falene turned in his direction, glancing at her fingernails first before answering.

"Well, he was still there when we left." She began. "But… Uh… He…"

Victor reached his boiling point as Falene dilly-dallied with the details.

"How did he deal with his father?!!! That's all I want to know!!! How'd he do with that God Damned father?!!!" Victor was unable to temper his indignation.

He grew more furious the longer he had to wait for her to tell him what happened.

"Well!!!!!" He roared. "What happened!?!" Victor was starting to lose his voice from screaming so loudly at her insolence. "We don't have much time left! I need to know!"

Falene took in a deep breath and told him the news.

"He forgave him, Victor." She shook her head, disbelieving it herself. "He forgave that rotten bastard. After all he did to him. He forgave him."

Victor's face fell when he heard it.

"When it came down to it, Joseph found it within his heart to forgive his father." Falene shared with defeat in her voice.

Anatoli squinted his eyes shut as if bracing for impending doom.

Victor was rendered almost totally speechless. This wasn't what he expected to hear.

"He…? He…? He…! You can't be serious?"

After a few moments, Anatoli opened his eyes and relaxed how tensely he held his body. A piercing pain shot through the upper portion of his right shoulder as he did.

"Why no emotional outburst?" Anatoli wondered after Falene told Victor such ungratifying news.

Falene felt she should explain the situation to give Victor better insight into Joseph's mindset during his visit with his father.

"I am serious, Victor. Joseph forgave his father. He did. His father was able to pass peacefully because of it."

"Cock Sucker!" Victor screamed, punching the bathroom wall with a closed fist. "Now what?!!!"

"Are you going to calm down?!" Falene yelled back, leaning forward in her chair. "Because you need to listen to this!"

Holding his stinging hand up to the light, Victor examined all four bloodied knuckles on his right hand. The flesh on each jaggedly split open from the impact. His whole hand started to swell right before his eyes.

"Pay attention to me!" Falene insisted. "This way! Over here!" She motioned.

"Go ahead!" Victor disrespectfully flicked his other wrist at her to shut her up. "Go ahead! I'm listening!!"

"O.K. then!" She continued. "Now listen!"

"Joseph has moved toward an enlightened state. It's as basic and simple as that." She apprised Victor. "We need to understand this."

"How? What do you mean by that?!" Victor was lost.

"Again, just listen and I'll tell you everything." Falene assured.

"O.K. Go ahead."

"So… Basically… We got him there, to Providence and to his childhood home. Blah, blah, blah. Eventually Joseph finds his way to his father in the hospital as we'd hoped and that's when Joseph revealed his true character or at least part of it."

"I'm listening…" Victor said, with greater self-control.

"Well, when the moment came, and Joseph's father was ready to pass, Joseph didn't try to fight the darkness within his father or within himself for that matter. Rather, he surrendered to it."

"O.K.?" Victor allowed himself to lean further out of the bathroom doorway to better hear.

"Father Joseph was able to humbly accept all experiences with his father, especially the perceived negative ones from years past, as right and indispensable to his evolvement and allow them to finally pass over him. Understanding, they had a temporary but necessary place within his life, which allowed him to further evolve and thus exist on a higher plane. In doing so, Joseph became the true light of *being* and he found peace within it." Falene explained.

All Falene heard coming from near the bathroom was. "Mmmnnhh. Hmmnnhh. Mmmmnnnhh. Hmmnnhhh."

"In the end, oddly enough." She said. "Joseph didn't try to attack his perceived attacker in an attempt to prove his very own existence worthy."

She looked down at her feet and whispered the next thought so Victor couldn't hear. "Like we thought he would."

Falene looked at Anatoli who was sitting there quietly.

"Joseph seems to have a fundamental understanding of universal law. That is, that he *is* worthy simply because he exists."

Victor saw Anatoli nod his head.

Falene's voice grew raspier as she fully conceived what had truly taken place. She reiterated her points more concisely for all their benefit.

"Joseph didn't attack his father for his perceived offenses because he didn't want the negative attributes he believed his father possessed to move into him by bolstering their importance, significance and presence within his own mind, body and spirit. He didn't resist what had happened between them so long ago, so that the anger and the hatred and the resentment he carried for so long couldn't strengthen and continually manifest within him."

Although Victor made little to no sound, Falene knew he hung on her every word.

"In the end, at the time of Josephs father's passing, both father and son were endowed with a strengthened inner peace following Joseph's forgiveness of his father, his father's acceptance of that forgiveness; and finally his father being able to forgive himself for his own actions born of anger and all that is negativity."

Bright red blotches began to appear on Falene's chest and neck the more upset she became from talking about the goodness that transpired between Joseph and his father.

"They say those who suffer the most in their lifetime often are destined to become the most enlightened among man, forced to seek true inner peace in the midst of unbearable emotional and physical pain. Some go on to become the world's spiritual teachers and great healers." Falene made sure Victor was aware of this very important fact.

He coughed sickly upon hearing this.

"But others, who *cannot* rise above it, as we are already keenly aware, typically become addicted to drugs or alcohol or another vice. They are more susceptible to slipping into severe depression. Go mad, or most commonly... Become stronger, smarter, more sinister replicas of the monsters they suffered at the hands of. Therefore, creating more sorrow for themselves as well as others and the whole of the world."

Falene smirked; displaying the pleasure she got from knowing many fell into that category. "The perfect reaction to an unerring action."

She quickly returned to the subject at hand, before veering too far off topic.

Falene directed Victor and Anatoli's attention to the more recent past, which would help them better understand what she was trying to say.

"See a person like Wei-Xing? She *was* able to rise above the obstacles and challenges placed before her."

Upon bringing the subject of Wei-Xing up, Falene suddenly felt the onset of hot flashes. She lifted her hair off her back to get some air.

Tiny beads of sweat began to surface along her forehead and at the nape of her neck. Holding her hair up with one hand, she fanned herself with the other to try to cool off.

She continued. "A great spiritual teacher Wei-Xing, maybe one of *the* awarest souls known to this earth. As we well know…"

Her eyes darted between Victor in the other room and Anatoli sitting across the way. She was checking to see if they were indeed listening. They were.

"Wei-Xing's village lived through a time of great suffering many years ago. It was during this time that she personally met with an unspeakable fate. An inescapable course, most would have elected suicide over."

Falene watched in her mind's eye as Wei-Xing was subjected to severe physical and emotional pain and brutality.

As she poured over this particular chapter of Wei-Xing's life, Falene gave a blow-by-blow to her accomplices.

"… This woman, Wei-Xing. It was a lifetime ago now, but when she was younger, she met with hell on earth, the likes of which, few human beings have ever known. To get through it, Wei-Xing had to delve into an untapped part of her soul, to a place she never knew existed, to search for the inner strength to survive. That's when she had her awakening and arrived at an enlightened state. Most others would have succumbed to their dark side, after living through what she did." Falene begrudgingly acknowledged Wei-Xing's fortitude.

"She didn't. She fought. She fought hard. She blindly walked into and through the darkest of storms. Her only guide, faith in the grace of God. Convinced she would eventually be led out of her torment on the wings of angels, Wei-Xing accepted her fate as it dragged her through the bowels of the nether world. She limped on, until she found the light at the end of the tunnel. And she did."

Falene detested Wei-Xing's personal success because it represented the best of mankind.

"She used her experience and that knowledge to help Glenn. She was the one who pointed him in the right direction." Falene highlighted.

"Wei-Xing was able to pass on some very useful information to our adversary. Information, which made her extremely dangerous to us and our mission. Information Glenn wisely understood and used to his advantage. That's how Glenn found and decided upon Joseph."

An energized stillness befell the room.

Falene stated her case astutely. "People, whom through tremendous adversity, are reborn from the womb of peace are the most shielded from us. They become impenetrable."

Without saying a word, everyone there, Victor, Falene and Anatoli thought about that.

"Wei-Xing and Joseph have the same mother." She said. "Their souls originate from the same *source*. They were both born of the womb of peace." The corners of Falene's mouth turned downward.

"In this way, they are one, and the same." She had proven it true to herself. "It makes them… Dare I say, nearly invincible."

She let her cohorts process this.

"That's why she had to go." Falene waited for a reply from anyone in the room, confirming the good news. "Right?" She looked around.

"Right?!!"

Victor and Anatoli remained quiet.

"She better be!"

Falene looked at Anatoli who was too busy inspecting the tangled fringe on the edge of the carpet to hear her. She shook her head in disgust.

"Like Wei-Xing, Joseph is different. We need to understand this." She focused her eyes way across the room on Victor and then again on Anatoli who had finally tuned back in.

"Rather than succumb to his insurmountable circumstances. He too, rose and evolved to the next level." Falene pointed out. "Joseph has managed to free himself from mortal ignorance or temporarily did." She spoke with a hint of fear in her voice.

Shaking her head, confirming what she surmised, she added. "He has found where clarity lives. At least in the situation with his father he did. As Wei-Xing, found clarity during her time of intense human distress. That means Joseph's on his way. That makes our plight vulnerable."

Falene hoped both Victor and Anatoli understood how terrible this news really was.

Still no word from Victor who remained reticent in the lavatory.

Falene waited, listening for a response of any kind from him. She wondered how he could stand there this long, mute, with everything going on.

"So, we have to reevaluate things. He's different from most others. Remember, we have to consider that." Falene stressed, knowing she was being heard even though no one was answering her.

"Remember also, we know there are other ways to bare one's true character." She tried convincing everyone, including herself. "Ways in which one will exhibit their naked soul when they think no one is looking."

Frustrated, she looked around the room again. First, at an introspective Victor who appeared unconscious and paralyzed in the washroom. Then at Anatoli, who was currently useless. She wasn't sure they got it.

"How?" She marveled at the challenge before them. "How do we get Joseph to bare his naked soul?"

No one was acknowledging the gravity of the situation or offering any solutions. At least orally they weren't.

Falene put all the energy she had behind her lungs, shrieking.

"Now what!?!" She thrust her torso forward in her chair, bracing herself tightly between the armrests on either side.

Anatoli jumped, not expecting it. Victor was startled back into awareness as well.

"Now what?!!!" She bellowed again. "We can't just sit here and look at each other! We have to get to work! What do we do now?!!!"

Seething, both men glanced at each other. Neither was sure how to handle the situation.

Falene, Victor and Anatoli were failing to see that an unwanted condition was stealthily giving forth within them.

By focusing on Father Joseph and how he graciously and generously handled his final moments with his father, the detestable Joseph Maggiacomo, all three were subconsciously allowing his conscious and enlightened presence to invade their minds, bodies and souls.

That message subsequently repeated itself over and over in their heads, replicating the quiet and pervading light of purity and truth. That manifested more of the same, pushing Victor, Falene and Anatoli further toward their own darkness.

It was beginning to spread like a disease within them.

Victor, Falene and Anatoli also all knew they felt atypically weak, emotionally drained, short-tempered and a little sick to their stomachs, but didn't fully understand why.

They were manifesting physical and emotional symptoms, which reflected the brewing conflict deep inside of them.

Father Joseph was already beginning to shine a beacon of hope into the world through his actions. So much so, it was even starting to affect them.

Joseph's forgiveness of his father, his love, his compassion, his honesty and thus enlightenment were eating away at all three equally without them comprehending the universal process, which consumed them.

The more repulsed they were by Joseph's altruistic and unsullied behavior the more energy they put behind it and the stronger their self-created destruction grew. It chewed away at their core like a ravenous parasite.

As they'd set out to intentionally move into Joseph's subconscious to render him disabled, so was he now moving into theirs, only unintentionally.

Joseph wasn't even cognizant of this complex concept. Joseph now simply, just *was*. Just in *being*, Father Joseph was a formidable foe.

In this heightened state of agitation, Victor and Falene began to take swipes at one another.

"Well?!!! What do we do now?!!" Veins fully engorged with blood bulged from Falene's neck, as she demanded suggestions from Pope Victor.

"Say something!!!" She pounded her fists on the arms of the chair she was perched upon. "What should we do now?!!! Any God Damned ideas?!!!"

Reaching his limit with her, Victor flew out of the bathroom in a rage, shouting back. "Shut up! Shut up! Just shut up! Let's figure out what the hell is going on, first! Then we'll decide what to do!!!"

"I told you what was going on!! Weren't you listening?!!! I told you what happened! The question I'm putting to you is... What should the next step be?! We need a new idea, a new plan!!!" She fired back, sliding her ass forward to the very edge of her seat cushion, ready to lunge.

Anatoli waited for a break in the argument before deciding to pipe up.

"Why don't we just let it be." He recommended. "Forget about what happened between him and his father! It's over! Forget about it and let's move on."

Falene's voice reached a crescendo. "Whaaaaaaaaaat?!!!"

"So what, he had a *moment*! Doesn't mean anything." Anatoli reiterated. "Let's stay on course and keep focused. Don't worry about one fleeting moment of lucidity with his father! That's all it was! A fleeting moment!"

Anatoli felt they were getting bogged down on one insignificant event.

Falene snapped her head around with the deadly force of a mythical fire-breathing dragon.

"Oh my! What a glaringly obvious solution Anatoli! Righty O! That's right! No plan! Just go with the flow! No big deal! Nothing here to consider or worry about!!!" She gestured wildly with her hands.

Incensed Anatoli couldn't comprehend the relevance of Joseph's actions that day; Falene sliced him up. "Good idea Vankov! Got any other brilliant suggestions you inept imbecile?!!!"

Anatoli remained stoic despite her ridicule.

"So glad you're here! You're quite the help!" She started laughing dismissively to embarrass him in front of Victor.

"I've got an idea Anatoli. How about you jump off the roof right now?!!! How 'bout that? Head first!!!" She ordered.

Falene flicked her wrist in Victor's direction. "While this one over here and I watch. Sound good? Sounds good to me!"

Anatoli sat there and took it.

"We'll watch as you split your empty head open at the bottom." She described graphically.

"You might as well!!! You might as well serve as entertainment, if you're not able to serve in any other way!"

"Shut up! Shut up both of you!" Victor insisted, waving his arms at them to quit.

He took a seat in a comfortable royal purple suede chair in between them. The natural glow he'd carried in his cheeks earlier had dulled, replaced by a shade of pale gray.

"Maybe the P.R. guy is on to something." He said, nodding his head in Anatoli's direction.

"Correction." Anatoli interrupted. "Director of Communications for the Vatican."

"Oh… I just wish you'd shut up." Falene stated angrily.

Victor explained why he thought Anatoli was on to something.

"Maybe he's right. Maybe it was just a fluke. We have some time. We'll come up with something else. We have to. Bickering amongst ourselves is just wasting time." Victor seemed a little defeated, and uncharacteristically calm.

"Let's figure this thing out together. We all have something to offer. If we put our heads together, we'll come up with a sure fire plan." Victor implored, knowing it was imperative for everyone to unite.

"We have to think about who Joseph is, understand him, explore where he came from and how he achieved what he achieved in his life. Think." He told them. "That's where the answer to stopping him lies."

Falene and Anatoli listened.

Victor asked that they consider the following.

"Think hard. What's important to Father Joseph?" He asked.

"What was his childhood like?"

"How and why did he seek the experiences he did in adulthood?" Victor pressed.

"What's he afraid of?"

Falene and Anatoli tried to answer these questions independently in their heads.

"Do we know whom he loves and whom he hates?"

Pope Victor challenged them to answer all of these.

"How does he learn? What does he enjoy learning?"

"Where do his insecurities lie?"

Victor knew understanding who Father Joseph was, was key to taking him down. "What is Father Joseph's greatest dream? If we can answer these questions and much more, we've got a shot at him."

A light bulb went off in Falene's head. "Right!"

A renewed vigor charged her voice. "The only way to destroy something forever is to take it apart piece by piece and destroy each individual part."

That piqued Victor and Anatoli's curiosity.

Falene expanded on Victor's idea. "You must first learn what something is made of."

Her bluish-green eyes locked on pieces of furniture in the room as she thought it through.

"Before one may begin weakening the integrity of an entire structure, one must first ask themselves… What are the individual parts that once assembled create that structure? Once you discover what those parts are, one may begin to effectively disassemble the structure and destroy each piece individually until the structure is totally compromised and can be taken over completely."

She knew she was right.

"We are all… The sum of our parts."

For hours there in the Pope's private chamber, the three of them commiserated about the situation.

They dissected Joseph's life history layer by layer to get a full understanding of who he was.

Together, they thought up a plan of how to strip Joseph to his essence.

Once fully agreed upon by Falene, Victor and Anatoli, it was set into motion right there and then.

As outrageous and complicated as their conception was they knew they could pull it off. They would bring a flawless succession of events in which to snare Joseph.

One question remained.

How would Father Joseph react to what he was about to face? Therefore, who was mankind?

The answer couldn't be predicted by anyone, not even Joseph.

Who he was, was yet to be revealed.

CHAPTER 25 -- A MARKED WOMAN

After meticulously calculating each facet of their plan Victor, Anatoli and Falene were satisfied they had arrived at the perfect strategy to lure and entrap Father Joseph.

They were all bushed. It was time for a breather.

"Get a bite?" Victor asked Anatoli.

"I'm famished. Let's go." Anatoli couldn't get up from his chair fast enough to join him.

Falene was perturbed by the deliberate snub.

"Not that you asked *me*..." She emphasized, planting her hand flatly against her chest. "I'll stay behind. I just got off that stupid plane. I'm wiped out." Falene explained, lethargically looking around for something.

"Shit! I think I forgot my purse on that plane!" Falene realized that was the last time she had it with her. "Where the hell is it?!" The clutch was nowhere in sight.

"That's just great." She said, worn to a frazzle. "Just great."

"Anything important in it?" Victor asked, sweeping the room with his eyes to see if he saw it anywhere on the floor. "Someone will find it... Turn it in. The airline will probably send it back to you."

Falene released a deep, Machiavellian belly laugh. "Oh... Whoever finds MY purse is in for a big surprise. *That* person will never be the same. They'll be too afraid to try to find the person that it belongs to. That's for damned sure!"

All three snickered.

"O.K. then. I don't want to know. Good luck with that. We'll be back later." Victor informed her.

Starving, the two men left. They set out from the Vatican in search of dinner and good wine somewhere in Rome.

Falene, gladly left alone in the Pontiff's private chamber, decided she'd spend her time relaxing by taking a soothing bath in Victor's lavish bathroom.

After all her hard work in Rhode Island and long journey back to Rome, she felt she deserved a little rest and relaxation.

Slowly getting to her feet, Falene stretched her arms and legs to get the blood flowing again. Instantly, she felt the burning sensation of pins and needles gradually intensifying in both legs. From sitting so long, both lower extremities had fallen asleep.

"Oh!..." She whimpered. "Owwww!..."

Trying to walk it off, she limped over toward the bathroom, high heels and all. It didn't work.

"Ouch!" As nerve impulses carried sensation information from the nerve endings in her legs to her brain, she felt a tremendous amount of pain.

It impeded her ability to walk properly.

Falene bent down to rub her limbs, but the stinging continued to intensify.

"Ooooohhhhhhhh!" She moaned.

She caressed her calves until the soreness subsided enough for her to be able to hobble into the bathroom.

Once there, she looked around. It was deliciously pretentious.

"Very nice." Falene cooed, able to stand freely with much less pain now. "Very nice indeed!"

Ornate gold fixtures gleamed everywhere, surrounded mostly by marble veined with shades of brown, tan, gray and white.

Against the far wall, alabaster-colored sheers hung blowing in the breeze in front of a cheery, bright window.

Just below the window a blazing-white roll top claw-foot bathtub. Sloped at both ends, the stunning double slipper was a classic as far as tubs go, an elegant 1887 European design. The stout enamel-coated cast iron tub with chrome ball and claw feet was just what Falene was looking for.

"Mmmnnnhhhhhhhhh................" She already knew how good it would feel to lay in it.

Falene reached over turning both of the tub's shiny, silver faucet handles. She held one hand directly beneath the flow of water to feel as she adjusted the handles methodically. She let the water run until the temperature regulated to approximately one hundred four degrees Fahrenheit.

For her, the hotter the better.

Now that the water temperature was just right, she put the stopper in the drain and let the tub fill as she undressed.

She shut the window, so as not to let the heat out.

Wearing no bra or underwear, once she pulled her dress over her head she was completely disrobed.

Stripped, she walked over to the mirror Victor had been staring in like a zombie during most of their discussion.

As Falene stood there, looking at herself in the very same mirror, she didn't like what she saw in her own reflection. Looking back, a tired, weary version of herself. It wasn't pretty. Crows feet were beginning to appear around her eyes, hollowness settled under her eyes. Her face was drained of color.

"I look like a vampire. Not that there's anything wrong with vampires, but they're not that… Well… Alive and well-looking." She spoke to her mirror image like it was another person.

All the stress was taking a toll on her looks.

Seeing herself like this made her feel insecure. She hated that more than anything.

Falene twisted her hair up and knotted it, creating a makeshift bun to get it out of her face. "There we go. That's better. Let's get a look here."

Using the tips of her fingers, she delicately tugged at the skin around her eyes, stretching it outward to make the crinkles disappear.

She couldn't bear to see herself this way.

Pulling on the lower left hand corner of the mirror, a latch released causing the mirror's entire left border to swing forward at an angle and open toward her.

The mirror served as a decorative door, concealing a medicine cabinet behind it. There, she found a half-empty box of soap flakes. Written in Italian on the front of the box she read, *bagno schiuma.*

"Bubble Bath!" Tickled, Falene walked over to the tub.

"Here we go."

One tip of the box and all the white waxy soap shavings contained within the carton sprinkled into the tub, which was now filled three quarters of the way. The scalding water dissolved the flakes, reincarnating them as much more amusing and ever expanding soapy suds.

When the tub was full enough and the suds were luxurious enough, Falene shut the water off.

Over one leg went.

Submerging her nude body in the sultry, hot water felt so good.

"AAAaaaaaaaaaaahhhhhhhhhh……….. This is ecstasy."

With her derriere, Falene felt for just the right place on the bottom of the inside of the tub to plant her buttocks, so her toes could reach the far end of it. This put her at the perfect angle to rest her back against the other end.

Her bath was so soothing, she felt sleep calling her name.

"This is sweet. This is very sweet." Her eyes rolled back into her head. The sheer pleasure of this experience drove her ingrained nastiness into dormancy.

Soaking there, falling in and out of a doze for hours in Victor's tub, Falene thought about the plan they'd all come up with.

"Would it work?" She asked herself.

"Will Joseph take the bait?"

The temperature in the bathroom was sweltering.

Steam from Falene's bath lifted off the water, covering her hair, face, neck and shoulders in a light, wet mist. The walls were sweating as well and the mirror on the medicine cabinet had fogged up.

She thought again about the clever questions Pope Victor had asked them all to consider regarding Joseph.

"What's important to Father Joseph?"

"What was his childhood like?" Falene knew this answer already.

"How and why did he seek the experiences he did in adulthood?"

"What's he afraid of?"

"Whom does he love and whom does he hate?"

"How does he learn? What does he enjoy learning?"

And…

"Where do his insecurities lie?"

Falene thought about all of it again, carefully re-answering each question in her head.

She then prudently reviewed their plot for potential flaws, just in case.

So far, she couldn't see any.

As she thought about Father Joseph and all she knew about him, she felt she had a handle on things.

What she didn't know, nor did Victor and Anatoli, was that their prey had just arrived back in town.

Unbeknown to them he had already made his way past the entrance and inside the Vatican. At this very moment, his heavy footsteps briskly carried him to the Pope's private chamber where Falene was.

He was very close.

Nearby, Falene could hear a grandfather clock faintly chime once.

She cast a brief look at a lovely little hand painted antique clock sitting on the vanity and noticed the time.

"One o'clock. Wow. It's that late already?" She turned to look out the window.

Darkness.

"Oh yeah. It's later than I thought. I've been in here a *really* long time."

The bath had done its job, rejuvenating her sore muscles and joints and now it was time to go to bed.

Using her forearms to grip the slick sides of the tub, she sat up. Leaning forward and reaching down into the water between her legs, she yanked on the tarnished pull chain attached to the drain's rubber stopper, to allow the tub to empty.

As it did, she stood and stretched.

"That was soooooo marvelous."

Very dizzy but still standing in the partially filled tub, Falene leaned against the wall to steady herself as she opened the window to allow some of the steam to escape the bathroom to the outdoors.

It began to clear immediately.

The light cool breeze that gusted in from the window felt good against her overheated body.

Falene then looked around the room to locate a towel.

"There's got to be one around here." She said convinced, eyeballing every shelf.

"In this whole big bathroom... There's got to be at least..."

Not a single one in sight.

"Crap!"

With the window wide open, the sound of a dog yipping and yapping outside carried up to her.

Bending through and over the windowsill, peering down many stories, Falene saw a little black and white dog looking up at her through the darkness of night.

"Whhhhoooooooooffffffff! Whoooooffff!" The dog called up, wagging his tail a mile a minute.

His big-dog bark misrepresented his petite size.

"What are you so cheerful about, stupid?!" She yelled back.

The dog's tail immediately fell still and his body stiffened at the very sight of her, as if he'd expected someone else to appear in the window instead.

He let out a low, mean growl. "Grrrrrrrrrrrrrrrrrrr."

Falene leaned back inside, standing totally unclothed in the window.

"Dumb dog." She grumbled.

Little did she know Father Joseph was standing behind her in the doorway of the bathroom, quietly watching her.

What he saw made him shake involuntarily with fear.

Completely naked and dripping wet head to toe, Falene stood there with her back to Joseph. Her hair was still twisted up in a bun, with one rebellious lock dangling down. Her well-toned, shimmery backside was fully exposed. Joseph watched as long streaks of water raced down her back; pass over her firm, well-rounded rear end, and stream down her body all the way to her feet.

"Oh my...." Joseph lost his breath a little.

From the base of her neck all the way down to the backs of her ankles, Falene's entire backside was covered in dark squiggly lines, which formed horizontal rows down the entire length of her body. He wasn't sure if they were designs, symbols or what.

"What the..." The expression on Joseph's face revealed his incomprehension at what he was looking at.

To him, they looked like burn marks, which didn't make any sense at all.

"Can't be... They must be... Tattoos." He said quietly to himself.

At least he thought they were.

Leaving the safety of the threshold, Father Joseph took a step closer, hoping to better see.

It was more decipherable from here. "Oh gosh..." The harder he studied it, the more squeamish he became.

"Why?" He asked himself. "Why have that?"

Everything about Falene was so eccentric, unconventional, peculiar and downright scary.

A chill ran up Joseph's spine as he squinted to make out exactly what was all over her back.

"It says something. It's words." He could make that much out.

Falene, pretending not to know he was there, was still standing stark naked in the window, not caring if anyone saw and in no rush to sheathe herself.

Father Joseph so far could confirm that it was dark writing, which covered every inch of Falene's backside. Flesh barely visible between letters and words.

In tiny handwriting in what looked like black ink, one sentence followed the other in an endless trail but it wasn't written in English or Italian.

"What language is… this?" His eyes turned to slits.

Joseph bravely took another single step forward; almost forgetting Falene could turn around at any moment and catch him.

The closer Joseph got, he could see what he was looking at wasn't black ink at all, but what appeared to be blackened-over burns. Those burns forming words, which appeared to be branded into Falene's soft tissue. The edges of each word had swollen raised borders as if a searing hot iron had been pushed into her skin to scar those words into her body permanently.

"Labeled in some way with an identifiable mark." Joseph conjectured. "Perhaps a punishment?"

From where he stood he leaned in. The handwriting was so small it was almost impossible to read but he had to try. He focused his aging eyes as best as he could.

"Latin." He verified. "It's in Latin."

Father Joseph was so terrified his innards began to quiver.

Before he gave himself permission to read what was on the back of this wily Beast before him, Father Joseph blessed himself and traced the shape of the cross over his body with his right hand for protection.

Joseph's eyes then scanned line after line, beginning at Falene's mid-back.

Once he realized what it said, his eyes opened wide with intense internal alarm.

"Oh….." He gasped, taking a step backward away from Falene, a judicious decision.

"Oh my… Oh my… the *versio vulgata*."

Father Joseph recognized it immediately.

He took two more steps backward to distance himself.

"Why is that there?" For the first time in a long time Father Joseph felt truly susceptible to harm.

"*Versio Vulgata*." He repeated, disbelieving his own eyes. "The Vulgate Bible."

Joseph asked himself. "Why does she, who vows to destroy the creation of the Devil's former master, bear the sacred writings of the holy book upon her back?" It made no sense to him.

Joseph began to feel his throat close from the overwhelming anxiety he felt internally. He stroked the length of his neck to calm his nerves.

The Vulgate Bible was an early 5th Century common translation of the Bible in Latin. In 383 A.D. Pope Damascus I. commissioned Jerome to make a revision of the Old Latin translations. Jerome did as requested and his work became the definitive and officially promulgated Latin version of the Bible of the Roman Catholic Church.

Joseph once had the rare opportunity to read an original printing of the Clementine Vulgate from 1592 shortly after joining the seminary to become a priest. He remembered the great honor it was.

Her back still to Joseph, Falene turned her head to the side, holding him in her peripheral vision and smiled devilishly. Joseph could see her face only from her left profile and now knew she knew he was there the whole time.

Even though she remained shamelessly bare Joseph was compelled to speak to her.

There was no way to ease into the subject, so he just went for it.

"Why is the... the... The Bible... The Vulgate Bible, word for word, etched into your backside?" He asked her, deafened by the sound of his own beating heart thundering in his ears.

"He speaks." She said softly.

Turning immodestly to face him, Falene lifted one leg, then the other over the tub, stepping to the floor.

"You've been there a while... Haven't you, Joseph?
Watching me." Falene tried to embarrass him. "Did you like
what you were looking
at? Hmmnnnnnhhhh?"

Joseph refused to answer her but couldn't resist letting his eyes fall to her breasts.

"You did… I mean you do. Don't you?" Falene fixed her gaze at him as residual bath water trickled down her body, pooling on the hard marble floor beneath her feet.

"You do, but you won't admit it to yourself or to anyone else. Your Church tells you you're *wrong* for wanting a woman… The way you want me right now."

Joseph blinked nervously, trying to conceal the mortal war waging within himself, between man and priest. His eyes now fell lower to her tight, sexy stomach.

"Does it *feel* wrong, Joseph?" She asked him sarcastically, arching her back.

Father Joseph wouldn't allow himself to react in any way.

"That's what I thought."

Falene knew she was getting to him.

"A bit cruel… Don't you think? To put a man through that sort of thing… Deny him what he wants and *needs* most."

Father Joseph remained a man of iron in his compromised state.

Falene took one defiant step toward him, never taking her eyes off him.

"You can have me if you want me Joseph. No one has to know."

Falene reached for Joseph's arm, grabbing his bicep tightly. He could feel the heat from her hand penetrate his clothing.

Rising up on her toes, Falene whispered in Joseph's ear. "All you have to do is ask Joseph… Just ask and I'm yours in every way you'd ever want a woman. In any way you've ever dreamed of a woman. I *know* you've dreamed of women Joseph." Falene teased flaunting herself. "Wouldn't you love to be with me… Just once?"

Joseph didn't move an inch. He wasn't giving in despite feeling overwhelmingly weak and vulnerable.

She gave the frustrated priest one last long look at her naked body before backing off. She walked over to her dress in a heap on the floor and bent down reaching for it.

"O.K. have it your way. My way would have made you never want to put that collar back on." Falene bitterly relented.

Joseph closed his eyes tightly to try to erase the images he had in his head.

Partially dry now Falene easily slipped her outfit back over her head and began adjusting it around her middle.

"Now, what's the question again?" She asked totally blasé.

"Something about..."

"Why is that there?! On your back?!!!" Father Joseph redirected his energy into demanding an explanation from her. "Why do you have that on your back?!"

Falene wasn't ready to give Joseph his answer right away. She made him wait.

The two stood there facing each other, challenging each other's will.

As Falene worked at getting her hem straight across her knees Joseph reached up with his chubby hand to scratch his cheek. Still revved up, he accidentally dug his nails into his skin too hard and sliced his face open in a straight line down his jowl. Dark blood filling the laceration revealed the total length of the excruciating cut.

"Owwwww!" Joseph keeled over in agony holding the side of his face. "Oh! I can't believe I just did that!"

Pulling his hand away, he looked down at his burly mitt. He saw the blood he'd drawn jammed under his nails and smeared between his fingers. Using his thumb, he spread the crimson gore in a thin layer across his palm.

Pulling a clean handkerchief out of his pocket, Father Joseph applied pressure to his cheek hoping to clot the blood.

"This is never going to stop." Joseph complained. "Never." He said, dabbing his bleeding face as Falene watched.

Prompted to speak, Falene cleared her throat.

"It's there because it was singed into my backside." She said nonchalantly like it was nothing.

With his handkerchief pressed closely against the side of his face, Joseph briefly stopped tending to his wound to turn to her.

He knew it looked like burn marks on her back, yet he still couldn't believe it. Slack-jawed, his mouth managed to shape the word... "Singed?"

Falene only nodded, signifying it was true.

"What?" His voice lent itself this time. Father Joseph wanted to make certain he heard correctly.

Falene assured him he had. "You heard right. I said, it's there because it was singed into my backside…" She enunciated each word slowly and clearly for him.

Joseph detected truthfulness in her voice.

"Uh, Ohhhhh." He stammered.

With his imagination spinning wildly out of control, he starved for every word she had to say… Any clue to what happened to her. Only something extraordinary and inconceivable could explain this.

"Singed into your backside?" He repeated.

"That's right. Singed. Burned, Scarred. Whatever you want to call it."

This corroborated what he saw but the baffling details of who, how and why someone did this to her remained a secret.

"When?" He pushed for answers. "By whom?"

Much to Joseph's shock, Falene had no intention of keeping the how's and why's a secret. She was completely forthcoming.

"…When your God cast me into hell." She avowed.

The night air lifted the alabaster-colored sheers off the frame of the window causing them to flap gently at Falene and Joseph. It was the only ambient sound in the room.

Immobilized, Joseph stood there in the bathroom with only his lips having the courage to move.

"The All-Merciful…? Did this to you?!" He squealed.

Falene remained expressionless. "With pleasure… he did."

If this was true, Father Joseph feared whatever had transpired between her and the Creator, was between her and the Creator, and not intended for anyone else to ever know about. He wondered if his having this knowledge put him in peril in any way.

He was almost afraid to ask any more questions, not knowing what his place in this should be.

He HAD to know.

Questions flooded his mind one after the other and in no particular order of importance. “How was this possible? How could *she* have ever been before God? Wasn’t she simply born of pure evil?”

Then a thought popped into his head. “Had she once been a mortal here on Earth? One who faced judgment?”

Instinct kicked in and Joseph knew to gather all the information he could.

“You’ve really stood before the face of God?” He asked, his heart palpitating.

She shook her head up and down, with her bluish-green eyes now piercing his.

“That’s right.” She said. “A very, very long time ago.” Recalling the very day in her memory.

“How long ago?” Joseph wanted specifics.

“Long before you or anyone you have ever known were born.” Falene deliberately unclearly defined the timeline of her existence.

Exasperated, Joseph looked to the shiny marble floor.

Falene not wanting to waste anymore time, answered exactly what she knew he wanted to know.

“Yes, I was once before the face of God.” She reestablished.

Her confirmation of direct contact with the Deity made Joseph feel unprotected in her midst.

“That’s because a very long time ago Joseph, I was just like you… A living, breathing human being with hopes and dreams.”

To keep from fainting, Joseph concentrated on the flow of air in and out of his lungs to remind himself he was still alive as he listened. His guess was right; she had been a mortal here on Earth.

“When I was here as a little girl so long ago, I felt a calling.” Falene confided, with downcast eyes.

“A calling by a higher power to love and have respect for myself, others and the world around me. I did this by living my life with respect for all of God’s creation.” She related.

Joseph was engrossed in her story.

"To me. Life was sacred. All life, in any form." Falene spoke, anathematized with a steely, lifeless gaze.

"It just felt right and it made me happy." She shared earnestly. "I knew it was what I was supposed to be doing. I naturally *yearned* to stay true to my beliefs. In doing so I set an example for others. I understood with every fiber of my being that I was called to protect people and the planet by living my faith with respect for God's creation. I showed respect for the Creator through my stewardship of His creation."

Father Joseph was taken aback. What Falene was saying was precisely what the Catholic tradition insists upon from every human being.

He had to interrupt her. "Everything you're telling me is exactly how I've always believed *I* was meant to live my life. I was blessed with blind knowledge. From what you're telling me, I can see *you* were endowed from birth with the same inborn drive. If that's true, then I don't understand how you wound up…" Joseph didn't know how he wanted to finish his sentence.

Falene understood his confusion.

"Beeeeecaaaaause… Joseph. Holding true to my blood knowledge became increasingly difficult for me as I lived out my life."

Joseph had also felt the incessant nag of temptation tugging at him throughout his life, but managed to find ways to -- stay the course. He couldn't comprehend why she wasn't able to do the same. "Why?"

"My life was not easy, Joseph." Falene looked surprisingly sad recalling these memories.

"God set me up. To fail." She said indignantly.

Joseph couldn't believe the gall, even from her. "What are you talking about?! God set you up?!"

"He SET me up! That's what I mean! SET UP!!! He's setting you up now, without you even knowing it." Falene forewarned angrily.

"Why you blasphemous little… B… B…!" Incensed, Father Joseph almost allowed himself to say exactly what he thought of her but he had to hold back if he was going to get her to share more.

He regrouped and apologized.

"I'm, I'm… I'm sorry for that." He said, his hands shaking from nerves. "I just don't understand how that could be or why you would think such a thing. God doesn't set people up. Quite the opposite, God wants peace to live in the hearts of all people. Please continue. I'm sorry. Please." Joseph's hand slid across his brow as he wiped perspiration away.

"Go on." Father Joseph encouraged. "I want to hear the rest."

Falene didn't hold his outburst against him.

"There were life experiences God inflicted upon me, which took a great toll on my faith." She explained.

Joseph could understand this more than anyone. "O.K. Like what?" He asked calmly.

Falene took a page from her life to illustrate.

"Well, for one… When I was fourteen years old I watched helplessly from under a bed as my father beat my mother to death." She blurted out.

"Oh my goodness!" Father Joseph exclaimed, his mouth agape.

The details were still painfully vivid in Falene's memory. "My father, without provocation would regularly beat, humiliate, ridicule and torture all of us, including my mother, my three brothers, my two sisters and I. But one day he went too far. During an argument with my mother one evening after dinner, he began hitting her in their bedroom. He beat her so violently that she started to lose consciousness. Knowing she was going to be knocked out, she began calling out my name for help. She knew I was hiding under the bed playing before they'd come into the bedroom, and yelled for me to run to get someone to pull him off of her." Falene's eyes glazed over.

"But, I couldn't move. I was frozen in place, afraid to be next. So I did nothing. I stayed there, never moved. I watched as my father held my mother down on the bed. He kept beating her and beating her and… He pummeled her until she stopped fighting back. Her body went limp. Her eyes rolled up into the back of her head. She died right there before my eyes."

It brought Father Joseph back to a similar time in his own life experience. He solemnly uttered his little brother's name. "Peter."

As vile as Joseph found Falene, he couldn't help but feel bad for her as she told her story. It reminded him of his own upbringing and the devastating end to his own beloved's life. Joseph had the strangest sense that at around the same age he and Falene were kindred spirits.

As Joseph would soon become aware, although their lives had begun in much the same way, they would play out drastically differently.

Joseph stood there in the steamy washroom with her, coaxing her into revealing the rest of her tragic tale.

"So then what happened?" He pried.

"I was blamed for her death." Falene said inexpressively.

"What?! How!!!" Father Joseph howled. "You were just a child. An innocent."

Falene drew in a long, deep breath. It had been eons since she relived this nightmare.

"Well…" She exhaled. "Even though my brothers and sisters had often been in the same position I was that fateful day, as well as having been victims themselves of my father's abuse, they still blamed me for my mother's death."

"How in the world could they?!" Joseph cried out gutturally, unable to imagine the logical basis behind it.

The emotional scar of that blame still present in the way Falene uncomfortably held herself when she talked about it. "They said, I was there and could have done something to stop it. I thought to myself that maybe they were right. Maybe I *could* have done something. I replayed that day over and over in my mind, inserting different scenarios where I abandon all reason to fearlessly come to her aid."

"Oh Falene." Joseph whispered quietly with empathy.

"I never got over it." The words rolled off Falene's tongue robotically. "I hated myself for not having the courage to do anything to try to save my mother's life. I hated my family for not loving me enough to understand the anguish and despair I lived with as a result of what happened. I begged for their forgiveness, but they never forgave me. That's when I gave up and I abandoned my faith in God."

That's where Falene began chartering a course in a totally different direction than Joseph did. Their kindred spirits parted ways – here.

Falene's voice grew deeper with vindictiveness. "After that, I took my revenge out on the world. My mission, to punish God as he'd punished me. I hurt myself. I hurt others. I hurt anyone or anything I could because of how *I* was forced to suffer during my lifetime. If I had to suffer, so would everyone else. Anything I could destroy, I did, but not before I paid my father back just as violently."

"What do you mean?" A breathless Father Joseph grilled. "Not… What is strictly forbidden in the Decalogue?!"

Falene grew quiet and still, almost in a trancelike state, muttering in subdued grumbles. "You shall not murder. Exodus 19:23."

Joseph nodded. "Yes, The Ten Commandments Falene, authored by God. You shall not murder. You didn't! Did…?!"

He was sure she'd done the worst.

"Yeah, fuck those!" Falene erupted truculently, swaying back and forth in a half-psychotic state. "Bullshit on two stone tablets. You can shove them up your ass!"

Father Joseph knew what Falene must have done while blessed with the breath of life here on this Earth. She'd committed a grave mortal sin. She'd taken a life.

That would have set her feet upon an irreversible path toward damnation and it would explain a lot.

"Falene. Please tell me you didn't…"

"Joseph!" She cut in uncivilly. "At that point in my life The Ten Commandments were no longer the moral imperatives I chose to abide by. I put my faith elsewhere."

"So what did you do?" Joseph asked, afraid to hear.

Falene's eyes were ablaze with defiance. "I ambushed dear old dad in our family home, forcing my siblings to watch as I murdered him before their very eyes. An eye for an eye… I felt that most appropriate under the circumstances." Falene smiled in an affected manner. She'd exacted her pound of flesh.

Father Joseph shook his head. She'd made a decision one cannot come back from.

"You should have seen their faces!" Falene grinned. "My brothers and sisters didn't feel so superior to me then! While I slew our father before them, avenging our mother's death. They cried and wailed as I overcame him with all the ferocity of a hellhound. He never saw it coming. Neither did they. When I'd bloodied my hands thoroughly, I dragged and laid his lifeless corpse at their feet. Everyone went completely mad."

Joseph knew this denoted how and when Falene forever lost her humanity while she was alive.

"When I was done, I looked at each one of my siblings in the eye and I asked them in a childlike voice. "Why didn't you help daddy?"

Falene reached up with both hands to untwist her bun, letting her thick, long, layered hair fall to her shoulders.

Puckering her lips, she looked at Joseph without an ounce of regret. "Not one had an answer for me. No one could speak… because I'd just twisted their minds."

She bent to the side, letting her two-tone reddish-blonde mane hang free while she combed through it with her fingers to untangle any snarls.

"My intent… Just to clarify." She said sternly, holding up her index finger.

"To exonerate myself by reminding my coldhearted brothers and sisters what it feels like to be helpless in such a situation. To put them in my shoes, the day I watched our father end our mother. I wanted them to bear the burden of guilt for our father's death, as they decided I should for our mother's death. They were my emotional and spiritual executioners on this plane. So, I theirs. I imprisoned them as they'd unjustly imprisoned me."

Falene's searching fingers discovered a large mass of knotted hair. "I knew this would happen." She said, gently wrapping her bony digits around it to feel how big it was.

"What a mess." She roughly began yanking small hunks away from the massive tangled ball of hair to separate it into sections. Joseph could hear the stress she put on her tresses, as she stretched and broke it in any direction she could just to undo the snarl.

"That was just the beginning." She said. "After that, I wreaked havoc any chance I could. Anywhere I could. On anyone I could."

"I see." Father Joseph said pitifully. "I see why you did what you did."

Then he thought about his own family dynamics growing up and what he had to deal with. He shared a sliver of his then mindset with Falene. "I guess I didn't… I decided not to… I rejected that overwhelming desire for vengeance, no matter how strong it was and it was strong. It felt as though *my* father was my and my family's executioner." Father Joseph admitted.

"I knew I was being tested and I knew I had to be strong if I were to survive it in all the ways I needed to… spiritually, emotionally, physically or otherwise."

Joseph told her how he struggled to tame *his* beast. "I did my best to suppress my rage but it was hard, real hard. What I did was, I committed myself to good works only. Nothing else. I left room for nothing other than that in my life. Because, if I left space for anything else other than good in my heart… What *you* allowed to fill your void… Would have undoubtedly filled *mine*. There could be no other way for me."

Joseph was afraid to ask what happened next but he needed to know. "Then what happened?"

Falene was more than forthcoming. "Well, when I finished my work here on Earth, they way *I* wanted to and I died… It was my time to go before God like so many others before and after me." An accursed smile threatened. "But... I already knew he wouldn't let me stay."

Joseph hoped she was getting to the part he really wanted to hear. The part where she stood before God.

Falene went into greater detail.

"You have to understand Joseph. While I was alive, I felt if God sent such pain, such horror for me to experience during my lifetime, then he couldn't love me. That he had renounced me for some reason. I knew I didn't deserve what came into my life, so I couldn't come up with any reason he would pardon me."

Falene shook her head. "I was so good… So pure. I did everything according to his word. I couldn't understand why he would sentence me to such suffering." She still didn't understand it.

"Mmmmnnnh. Hmmnnnnnnnhhhhh." Joseph listened.

"I was *very* angry with him." Falene stressed. "Unforgivably angry!"

Father Joseph took a brave step closer. His fear of her began to melt away as he started seeing her as a real person.

"We've all been that enraged at our circumstances at some point in our lives Falene." Joseph owned up. "Even me."

He expounded. "It's our faith that carries us through. No matter what happens, having faith that God loves us and that it is His will, helps us all welcome our challenges and see that they are really *gifts* or *lessons* for us. Sent to us lovingly, to carry us to a higher consciousness. God's love also gives us the courage to stand up to our fears to grow as human beings. Falene, as we grow we need to accept that some experiences come to us *for a reason*, even the awful ones. We cannot always be privy to the plan God has for us. That's what faith is Falene. Faith in God. Faith in yourself." Father Joseph smiled in the spirit of friendship.

His words were ignored.

Falene rattled on; oblivious to the insight Joseph had gained during his life.

"So I decided to show God just how strong I really was." She boasted ignorantly. "I rose up against him… I became the ugliest, the meanest and the most vicious person he could ever imagine. I targeted the innocent, just to hurt him and the world he so loved. If he didn't love me, then I wasn't going to love others, His creation, or myself. I would do everything within my power to destroy all of it. What a job I did."

Joseph knew he could have just as easily followed the same path but something lived inside of him that wouldn't allow that.

"During my lifetime I was responsible for some impressive work, Joseph." Falene acknowledged her depraved acts. "I managed to take loads of people down with me. Others who were lost… Who allowed me to lead them down a darkened path, when they believed the light within them had failed them. They were the easiest prey. Together, we toiled under the Black Sun."

Joseph gasped.

"Knowing God was watching as I ruined other peoples lives felt like my greatest victory."

Hearing how Falene decided to live out the remainder of her years turned Joseph's stomach.

Father Joseph felt compelled to pipe up. He wondered if Falene ever considered the possibility that God was prepping her for a plan he had for her.

"I…" Falene began, before being interrupted mid-sentence by Joseph.

"Wait. Wait!" Joseph held up his hands, stopping her. "Did you ever think that those experiences, the ones you had with your father and your family, were brought to you… Because God *did in fact* know how very strong you were?" Joseph asked Falene.

"And because of your strength, had a big plan for you? That he was preparing you for a greater mission, a mission that would have brought joy into the world? And that – that was the way to prepare you somehow? Did you ever consider that?"

The expression on Falene's face didn't say one way or the other whether she comprehended what he was saying.

Joseph elaborated to try to get her to see his point. "I once read, and I believe this, that those who suffer the most in their lifetime often are destined to become the most enlightened among man, forced to seek true inner peace in the midst of unbearable emotional and physical pain and that these people go on to become this world's spiritual teachers, great healers and visionaries."

The idea was way over Falene's head.

"Falene, perhaps you were meant to be one of those people but the path to get you there needed to be brutal. Maybe… Just maybe, the experiences you had were meant to bring you to a new level of consciousness so you could grow into the magnificent creature you were meant to." Joseph posed to her. "Maybe you needed those experiences to take you to the next phase of your life."

It was all just words to Falene.

"Well, so anyway…" She waved him off. "I… I… Guess He felt my contributions to the world during my lifetime didn't earn me a place in His Kingdom and the reward of eternal life." Falene recounted, uncharacteristically bridled.

"Imagine that?!" She said facetiously, throwing her hands up.

"I couldn't help myself." Falene told Joseph honestly. "It's just who I became. When my human intelligence met animal diligence... Watch out! Boy, was I committed to my new calling when I set my mind to it. The Lord knew it."

Father Joseph just let her ramble. The more she rambled, the more useful information he got.

Falene's voice turned angry as she spat on the bathroom floor. "But eternal life he couldn't deny me. I found it, in spite of him."

It was obvious to Joseph where she'd sought refuge. She'd identified with the Fallen Angel, a tragic mistake. "I see…" He said cautiously, watching her temperament turn foul.

The well-educated priest knew much about the Devil and the traps he set for people here on earth.

Lucifer was once an archangel, the brightest amidst the host of Angels in Heaven but was banished from Heaven for rebelling against God. It was he who contrived to make his throne higher than the Lord's and therefore cast out of Heaven with the velocity of lightning. Regarded forever since as the author of all evil, the Old Serpent and his realm are regarded as an entire ubiquitousness in all events of daily life. The one who beguiled Eve and brought death itself into the world. Since his exile, the Great Dragon has been flying in the air continually above the abyss, in search of weak souls to corrupt to increase his legion.

Apparently, unfortunately for Falene, Satan crossed her path at a time in her life when she was without faith, confidence and conviction. Once a bright star herself, like he, she fell far and hard under his spell... And the gates of Heaven were forever closed to her because of it.

"So... The Devil promised you eternal life and you aligned yourself with him for the hope of it." Joseph gathered from her story. "A choice you made of your own free will."

"Yup. That's about it." She shook her head.

"What do you think of his promise to you now? It wasn't worth it, was it Falene?"

"I knew what I was getting into Joseph. I knew! I saw no other choice. The Prince of Darkness gave me a mission, one I could sink my teeth into. I was drawn to it like a moth to a flame. Fueled by my own anger and disappointment, I was drawn to others like me with the same negative energy and I made them the same promise he made me. That's how I persuaded multitudes to join our army. I marveled at how quickly my mission consumed me."

"So... What happened when you died and you were brought before God?" Joseph was trying to get to the bottom of things. "That's what I want to know."

Falene drew in a long, deep breath. If he didn't know better, Joseph would say she regretted her decision.

"God looked me in the eye..." She said.

Her one-man audience hanging on her every word. "Yes..."

"... In his eyes, like a motion picture, I watched my life play out before me. He saw everything I'd ever done. Everything. The good, the bad and the... Well, you know." Falene's eyes gazed out at a bare wall, rapidly scanning from left to right as though she were watching her life in instant replay again.

"As I stared into his eyes watching my life, reliving it from birth to death, he silently sat in judgment of me."

Joseph's intuition had been on the money his entire life. He'd always felt something like this happens when we die. Now he *knew* his gut instinct had been right.

"Then what?" Joseph asked, twitching from anticipation. "What did he say to you after reviewing your entire life?"

"Nothing." Falene disclosed surprisingly. "Nothing."

"What do you mean nothing?!" Joseph was dumbfounded. "He had to say something!"

"No." Falene said with a sighing sound.

"That's the weird thing. I thought there would be detailed explanations of what I should and shouldn't have done during certain circumstances in my life. Maybe even some scolding. But, there was nothing. He said absolutely nothing. I guess, he didn't have to." Falene wore a curious look as if she still couldn't believe it.

She tilted her head. "The Lord remained silent. Once we both watched, I knew what my fate was and so did he. He didn't need to say anything. There was no begging, no excuses. It just was. I just was who I was and that was that. No more chances. I did it to myself, knowing I was doing it to myself during my short existence on the earth." Falene took responsibility.

"There was nothing I could say, nothing I wanted to say. It was what it was. I braced for the impending consequences of my actions."

Falene adjusted her dress, making the material even all the way around her waist.

"Then what did he do?!" Joseph begged for the rest of the story.

"As punishment, God asked me to turn my back to him."

"Did you?!" Joseph's eyes bulged out of their sockets.

"I did, slowly." Falene said, her lip quivering. "He made me turn my back to him, just as I had during my life."

"Oh my..." Father Joseph had never thought of God in such a way. It scared him. But it made perfect sense. There could be no other treatment for such rogue souls.

"And then?..." Father Joseph leaned in toward her, balancing on his tippy toes.

"And then... He stripped me bare, and cruelly and painfully branded my backside with his Word so that I would never forget. That, before I was cast down out of Heaven into my rightful place, the abode of the devils where the wicked after death remain in a supreme state of punishment and misery." She said, her voice trailing off like she was losing her soul again.

Joseph was horrified.

"All that without saying a word to you?!" He had to ask again.

"Yes, and it sure hurt like hell, too." She reached around to her back, the tips of her fingers tracing over the words of the Bible, which were gouged into her skin from the scorching process.

"It's still bumpy. He sure never wanted me to forget it."

"Exactly how was it burned into your back like that?" Joseph pointed.

Extending her arm in Joseph's direction, Falene pointed her finger at him. "Like this."

She began pretend-writing in the air, using her own finger as an imaginary pen to demonstrate.

"A shaft of lightning bolted from God's fingertip, which he used as a writing instrument to carve into my backside."

As a reflex, Joseph straightened up.

"I know every word." She said. "Every word."

Then she looked at Joseph disdainfully. "Bet I know the Bible better than you do."

Joseph knew that memorizing the words of the Bible verbatim wasn't necessarily the key to understanding its profound messages.

"I guess we'll have to see about that." He answered, shrewdly.

Then Joseph couldn't help himself but to ask what he wanted to know most. "What was he like? What did he look like?"

He was desperate for Falene to paint the true image of the Lord in his mind and awaited her answer with bated breath.

With a cold stare, she snapped at him. "You'll never know Joseph! So, you don't have to worry about it! I have a hunch, the final decisions you'll be making here on earth, will earn you a life sentence in hell... So don't worry about being before the Lord. Even if you do make it to the place where God dwells, your stay will be very brief... Like mine was."

Joseph knew it served him right for even trying to ask Falene that.

"That's O.K. Falene. I'll see for myself."

With that, Father Joseph turned and exited the bathroom and the Pope's private chamber.

His time with Falene served him well. He'd learned all he needed to know and the ticking of the clock was growing louder by the second.

Father Joseph, the priest, the man, knew what he had to do.

CHAPTER 26

THE WILL OF GOD WILL NEVER TAKE YOU WHERE THE GRACE OF GOD WILL NOT PROTECT YOU

Joseph made his way down to the first floor of the Apostolic Palace via a secret stairway designated for the Pope's private use, so the Holy Father could covertly come and go from the Papal Apartments as he pleased.

Father Joseph used it smartly to keep him out of plain sight, so he would be harder to follow by anyone wishing to do him harm.

Using other hidden passageways and tunnels he knew about, Father Joseph navigated his way to the *Basilica Papale di San Pietro in Vaticano* to surface in a totally different location in Vatican City than he was last seen.

With a new appreciation for life, he exited through the main entrance of the Basilica using both ample arms to swing one of the five famous bronze doors open in one sweeping blow. He burst through the center one, made from melted down bronze from the old St. Peter's.

"Mmmmnnnhhhhhhh! Ahhhhhhhhh!"

Winded from the trek, Joseph stopped to rest right where he stood at the entrance. Needing to clear his head of the bizarre but informative encounter with Falene, he inhaled as much fresh air as possible for a quick recharge.

"Mmmmmnnnhhhhhhhhhhh! Ahhh! Yes, that's nice." He beamed, sucking in the air through his nostrils. It was exactly what he needed.

The natural smell of the outdoors was especially exhilarating. Fragrant and cool upon his face, Joseph delighted in how alive it made him feel. His senses heightened, the very molecules of life seemed to bombard each of his faculties.

He closed his eyes, surrendering to rapture.

Father Joseph had never felt so alive, so spiritually fulfilled by the Holy Spirit and the integral life force of this planet.

Not that he could remember, but he thought this is what we all must feel like at the very moment of our birth.

Joseph enjoyed this precious state of just… *being.*

He merged his consciousness with the world, seeing it as an extension of himself. The priest felt as one explores the world, one explores himself or herself. As a devout Catholic, he saw himself and the world as an extension of God.

Father Joseph walked off, away from the main entrance of St. Peter's Basilica, mulling over everything Falene shared with him about the realms of heaven and hell.

What he learned, gave him greater clarity.

As he continued along, he suddenly stopped, looking up.

From where he stood he caught a glimpse of the upper three floors of the Sacred Palace where he'd just left, the massive building looming in the distance. On the top floor, he pinpointed the exact bathroom window where he'd had his eerie encounter with Falene.

The light was still on.

The hair on his arms stood on end. He didn't have to see her to sense she was still up there.

"Hmmnhhh."

Father Joseph knew he couldn't focus on it, or the negative aspects of his experience with Falene would intensify within him and corrupt him, distracting him from his mission.

He intentionally took his eyes away.

The sounds of compact cars chugging along, birds chirping and the dialogue between people on the street were unusually loud, sharp and crisp.

Joseph's hearing was so acute, he swore he could discern the make, model and year of a car with a transmission problem, speeding past.

It took Joseph about twenty minutes on foot to make his way beyond the great and imposing fortress surrounding the Vatican and into the city of Rome.

At his usual pace, Father Joseph plodded along at a slow but steady rate, relishing every vivid sight and sound.

It was all he had to do to keep himself sane.

Dining at a nearby outdoor café under the cover of night, Victor and Anatoli sat conversing with each other about the details of the plan they'd come up with regarding Joseph. Both were confident and pleased with its potential.

Seated there, unrecognized by anyone, Victor tore apart a piece of hard, crusty Italian bread and stuffed a white fluffy hunk into his mouth. To wash it down, he reached for his wine glass, which was filled generously with an expensive, locally produced Merlot.

He held his nostrils over the rim of the glass and took a sniff. "Mmmnnnnnnnhhhhh. A supple nose of strawberries, sour cherries and green peppers." He educated Anatoli, who wasn't really that interested in listening to Victor speak with his mouth full, on the subtle aromas of his wine.

"It spent eight months in French oak before being bottled. And…" Victor added, swirling the vino around in his glass.

He took a sip and swished it around in his mouth. Most of it absorbed by the bread he was chewing.

"It's showing a woodsy flavor, rich in tangy fruits, cassis and has a lively acidity."

Anatoli could see everything inside Victor's mouth as he spoke. "Gross." The Director of Communications disgustedly whispered under his breath.

Anatoli waited patiently, tapping his fingers on the table as Victor analyzed his wine to death, spitting bits of his food here and there at him as he talked.

"You know Anatoli…" Victor swallowed.

"Finally." Anatoli whispered again.

"It's through the aromas of wine that wine is tasted."

Half of Anatoli's mouth dispassionately curled upward. "Ah hah."

As Victor tipped his goblet back, he took a generous mouthful of the red wine.

As he did, a passerby caught his eye.

It was Father Joseph.

Surprised by the sight of him, Pope Victor sucked in his drink accidentally, choking on it.

"Uggghhhhhh!" Victor threw himself forward, gagging. He waved his hand in front of his mouth, trying to keep his drink contained.

"Uuggggghhhhhhhh!" Trying desperately to regain his composure, the Pontiff hunched over the table so as not to cause a scene. "He's… Ba..ck! H…e'…s Ba…ck!" He painfully coughed the words out.

Coughing violently with his lips pressed tightly together, streams of pressurized Merlot sprayed in random directions across the table.

Victor pressed his hand tightly over his mouth.

"What the!!… What's wrong?!" Startled, Anatoli reached over across the table, patting Victor on the back, trying to help. "Who?! Who's back?!!"

At the same time, Anatoli did his best to protect himself by holding his napkin lengthwise across his nose and chest to keep from getting showered with wine.

"Are you all right?!"

Others started to look over from their tables.

As Victor choked and coughed, he did everything he could to clear his airway without calling any more attention to himself. The last thing he needed was to be recognized.

He pointed toward the street for Anatoli to see what had caught him off guard.

As Anatoli turned from Victor to see what he was referring to, he caught sight of Father Joseph nonchalantly walking by.

They saw him, but they knew Joseph didn't see them. That was good for them.

"Oh! I see…" Anatoli said, leaning back in his chair, craning his neck. "Where's *he* headed to?"

With Victor's coughing fit coming under control, he leaned back in his own chair, dabbing the corners of his mouth with a white linen napkin he'd taken from his lap. When he was finished, he began to wipe down the tabletop, which was completely covered with tiny red dots.

"Khhhmmmnnnhhhh." Victor lightly tapped his chest with his fist and cleared his throat one last time, while he and Anatoli trained their eyes on Joseph.

Sight of their rival forced them to adjust their concentration.

All was serious now.

"It's time." Victor spoke in a low, hoarse voice to his dinner companion.

"It's time."

Anatoli nodded his head in agreement.

Joseph, who had no idea they were watching him, steadily moved along. One clunky foot in front of the other, and soon he was out of their sight.

Victor and Anatoli let him go. Now that they knew where he was, they could take things from here.

On his way he went, the priest who for decades had ministered to the multitude of devout and faithful Catholics he was blessed to meet. Not to mention, anyone else who would listen. The man who'd finally found it within his heart to forgive his father for his ungodly transgressions against him and his family. The man who currently had the weight of the world on his shoulders.

Joseph.

About a quarter mile down the road from where Victor and Anatoli last saw him, Father Joseph walked past an alleyway where something moved oddly, catching his eye. So he stopped, trying to see what it was.

He squinted, with his eyes half shut.

There, way down the narrow back street, sticking out from behind a dumpster he saw a black stumpy tail wagging.

He smiled.

Dogs always made Joseph smile and a dog it was.

Joseph took it as a *good* sign and made his way down the dark passageway toward the pup one step at a time.

Once he got there, his instincts were correct.

"Hey Lucky!" He said, happy to see him again. "How's it going?"

Lucky spun around, looking up at him and wagged his tail even quicker. The dog's back end swinging left to right.

Joseph laughed out loud, bending down to greet the dog.

"Watch out there mister. You're going to need a realignment." He joked, holding Lucky's butt still as he scratched him along his backside.

"Oh, that's good. Isn't it?" Joseph spoke sweetly.

Panting, Lucky's mouth hung wide-open, displaying a mouthful of razor-sharp, pointy teeth. Father Joseph was sure this is how Lucky smiled.

The priest returned the bright smile and straightened back up.

Taking the liberty, Lucky jumped up on his hind legs, stretching his body up on Joseph's chubby limbs for more affection.

A die hard animal lover, Joseph bent back down, massaging Lucky all around his neck with his thick fingers. Lucky loved it, twisting his head all around with pleasure and contentment.

Joseph then began to knead the muscles in Lucky's back as well.

"Oh, you're a little lovable thing, aren't 'ya?" Joseph asked him, grabbing him by his front paws to pull him closer and kiss him on his furry cheek several times.

Joseph stood up.

Satisfied, Lucky jumped down and walked over toward where he was by the dumpster before Joseph arrived.

Father Joseph took another step forward to see just beyond the very large trash container, where he could sense someone standing.

And sure enough, there he was. Lucky's permanent companion.

"Glenn." Saying his name made Joseph smile.

Glenn returned the warm greeting.

"Hello my friend." Glenn said affably. He was glad Father Joseph listened to his instincts and came down the alleyway.

"It's our buddy Joseph, Lucky." Glenn said.

Lucky looked up at Glenn with that generous smile. His rear-end back in full swing.

Both men laughed.

Glenn pointed to a nearby spot he wanted Lucky to come.

The good-natured, Boston Terrier pinned his ears back and walked over, sitting on the ground near Glenn without a fuss.

Joseph knew Glenn must have been there for a reason and that their time together could possibly be only moments long. So, he remained quiet so that Glenn could tell him everything he needed to before he had to leave.

"I know we don't have much time… So, I'm listening." Father Joseph told Glenn.

Glenn looked Joseph directly in the eye. "Remember Joseph." He said seriously.

"The will of God will never take you where the grace of God will not protect you." Glenn was determined Joseph understand this.

Joseph tilted his head sideways, thinking about those words. He repeated them out loud to Glenn.

"The will of God will never take you where the grace of God will not protect you."

Glenn stared into Joseph's eyes for confirmation he grasped the true meaning of the message. This was critical.

"Do you understand, Joseph?" He asked urgently. "I mean *really* understand what that means and how to apply it to your life?"

Glenn waited as Joseph considered it.

"Yes, I do." He answered, massaging his chin as the words sank in.

"The *will* of God will never take you where the *grace* of God will not protect you." With two fingers, Joseph tapped the words out in the air as he said them, digesting each word as well as its overall profound meaning.

The sage priest let it absorb into his mind.

"I *do.* I *do* get that." Joseph professed to Glenn. "And somehow, I've known it all along, as though that innate knowledge has been there within me from the very moment of conception."

Glenn was so glad to hear that.

In unison, both Joseph and Glenn repeated it one more time.

"The will of God will never take you where the grace of God will not protect you."

They rested their voices.

This would be Glenn's final meeting with Joseph before… the inevitable. He felt more at ease knowing Joseph heard him. Truly heard him. It was important this be foremost in Joseph's mind, so he could draw from it when he would need it most and he *would* be needing it.

Glenn had done his job. He'd given Father Joseph all the tools he would need to be successful in the future. Now it was up to Joseph.

The sound of men's voices grew louder as Glenn, Father Joseph and Lucky stood there meeting in secret in the alley.

Two men, sounding irritated, were advancing toward them.

"Down here, I think." One said to the other.

Father Joseph recognized their voices. "It's Victor and Anatoli." Alarmed, he turned to Glenn.

The heavy footsteps of their enemies thundered in their direction.

Glenn leaned forward to peer beyond the dumpster. "They're getting close." He knew it best to take off before anyone saw them together.

"Time to go."

Lucky's tail grew stiff and still, his smile fading from his snout as his black and white whiskers turned downward. Joseph had never seen Lucky like this before and knew there must be a reason for him to grow so apprehensive.

Glenn grabbed Father Joseph by the arm firmly.

"Good-bye Joseph and good luck." He said sincerely. "Remember what I told you. Never forget those words. Hold on to them when you feel you can't hold on to *yourself* any longer." Glenn reminded Joseph.

"Trust me on this."

"Always." Joseph promised.

With those final words, Glenn scooped up Lucky in his arms and headed down the dark, lonely passageway, disappearing into the night.

Joseph remained there blending into the shadows.

CHAPTER 27 -- A PRIEST, A MAN

Pope Victor and Anatoli never spotted Father Joseph concealed within the shades of partial darkness as they raced past and down the narrow lane. Joseph knew to remain still and quiet until they had made their way far enough away, for him to safely steal off.

Joseph hugged the side of the dimly lit path, carved tightly between homes and buildings, as he jogged up to the dumpster. He snuck around the side of the massive refuse receptacle and tiptoed all the way to the mouth of the alley and took off.

He kept a quick pace, thinking about what he and Glenn had discussed. Joseph stared at his feet, one foot passing in front of the other as the words repeated in his head. "The will of God will never take you where the grace of God will not protect you."

Somewhere deep in his subconscious he'd known this all along to be true. However, having Glenn reaffirm it made it more poignant.

With passion, he said it one more time. It was the last time he would feel the need to. "The *will* of God will never take you where the *grace* of God will not protect you." He smiled humbly knowing Glenn's appearance was by special permission from the Almighty and God's final gift to him before he was to stand as representative for the entirety of humankind.

"Thank you my Lord." Father Joseph said modestly, bowing his head.

There was a very specific reason Glenn must have wanted him to remember those words. Father Joseph didn't know what it was but knew that that answer would undoubtedly reveal itself in the future. So he held on to it, mentally.

Joseph was more confident than ever he was equipped to handle any situation, which came his way.

His soul was awakening with awe faster than the speed of light. He was evolving as a human being by unprecedented leaps and bounds. He was evolving *so* rapidly it was similar to what is known in physics and the fundamental laws of nature. That is, if one can travel greater than the speed of light, one can travel to the future.

Since Father Joseph's soul, not body, was evolving with such velocity, it was as if his intellect was visiting the future and transforming him and his mind *today* into the man of *tomorrow.* The enlightened state of mankind the world would eventually see, centuries or millenniums from now, if given the time and opportunity to further mature and develop on this earth.

In other words, Joseph's brain could now effortlessly comprehend deeply profound thoughts and ideas well beyond his years, well beyond his *time.*

Father Joseph was no time traveler, but had through personal exploration and awareness discovered the key to living in a perfectly enlightened state of consciousness as a totally connected part of the greater whole. A *state of being* every person on the planet was capable of but didn't necessarily know it, let alone know how to achieve it.

Father Joseph felt his consciousness as a *being of pure energy* merging with the energy of the world and the universe. He felt connected to the *whole* of the world, everything in it, and the universe. Rather than an isolated, individual life force which was separate and apart of the whole.

Joseph's instincts told him his soul was no longer housed and confined strictly within his body. But emitted outward from within him, reaching beyond the constraints of his physical body.

As though he could see with precise clarity, without human or earthly limitations.

He knew with certainty that his spirit had always been and therefore would always be. That it could never be recreated or destroyed and that it constantly moved into form, out of form and through form. In essence, he would always be a part of the universe no matter what. He existed, therefore he would exist *always.*

No matter what happened, Father Joseph knew his mark on the universe could never be erased.

Any mortal fears he had… were now gone. There was nothing to ever fear, nothing to ever lose. Who he was and what he had evolved into would forever remain a constant in the universe.

A calmness… A knowing… came over Father Joseph as he continued his journey on foot.

It was like being in a total state of love and understanding, and closer to God than he'd ever felt.

After all he'd lived through, the experiences he chose to learn from, and the way he purposefully lived his life, his soul matured beyond what is considered *normal*.

He was special in this way… Why he was the chosen one. Mind, body and soul, Joseph was ready for anything now.

Father Joseph kept walking until a sign hanging on the front door of a tiny gem of a church captured his attention.

He stopped and read it. *"St. Hector's."*

It was a Roman Catholic Church.

"Hmmmnnnnhhhh. St. Hector's? One of ours?" He asked himself, baffled.

"Guess it is." Father Joseph confirmed, reading the sign again, but he had never heard of it. "St. Hector's... Why haven't I...?"

The word saint, denoting this person was believed by the Church to have been called to holiness or had fulfilled the necessary criteria set for sainthood by the Church.

The name Hector, *the person* sainted by the Catholic Church.

"Hmmmmnnnnnhhh. St. Hector's. St. Hector's."

The priest searched and searched his memory. "Hector. Hector. Who is…?"

Father Joseph shook his head. He couldn't remember who Hector was.

Just then he heard footsteps stop behind him and sloppily shuffle off to a nearby building, where the person hastily opened and shut a door behind them.

Joseph turned but no one was there. He wondered if he was being followed.

The well-studied priest *thought* he knew all the churches in the area and their history but this one... He never remembered seeing it. "Why can't I remem...?"

It *was* along an out of the way street, barely visible from the main thoroughfare. But still, he felt he should remember who this person *Hector* was in history, more easily. Joseph was stumped for the time being.

Whomever Hector was, he was greatly revered by the Catholic Church. So much so, it named one of its churches after his namesake to reward and honor him.

"But reward him and honor him for what?" Joseph asked himself. It bugged him he didn't know or couldn't remember anything about this person or this church. He fancied himself a scholarly theologian and historian. But this... for some reason, got by him somehow.

"It'll come to me. It'll come to me." He said, sure of it.

Then a ridiculous idea passed through his mind. "Is it possible the Church *doesn't* want anyone to know who this Hector is? Or, why this Catholic Church was named after him?"

As quickly as it entered his mind, he shrugged it off as paranoid and speculative. "Ridiculous. Ridiculous. Now I'm reaching..."

Joseph decided to forget about it for now to concentrate on more pressing matters.

Before he knew it, his feet had carried him to where he apparently was meant to be.

The airport.

"Rome International Airport. Here we are. Again." He declared, exhaustion dripping from every word. The trek on foot had taken its toll.

He went inside to see what new adventure lay waiting there for him.

Sauntering mid-way into the airport, he stopped to look around and absorb the energy here.

"Well..." Joseph took a quick moment to let his gut instincts speak to him. This is how he would determine whether to stay.

"Hmmmnnnnhhhhh. Well... It *feels* right here. So... This is where I *must* be." Joseph accepted, without questioning it.

"For some reason, I think this will lead me to my next calling." He felt confident.

Father Joseph walked further into the airport.

The last time Joseph was here, he was flanked by Pope Victor and Anatoli who took him on a flight bound for Boston, Massachusetts.

Although Victor, Anatoli and Falene had their own ideas of what would happen to Father Joseph once they arrived on the Eastern seaboard of the United States and he was transported to Rhode Island. Things turned out, not quite as they had planned.

That trip ended with Father Joseph seeing his father after what seemed like a lifetime and forgiving him, which was long overdue for he *and* his father. Leaving both healed and able to move on to the next level of their earthly experience.

His father moving on peacefully to death. *He* moving on positively in his life.

It turned out to be a life-altering experience for Father Joseph. In a good way.

That's *not* what his enemies had anticipated.

Joseph knew this trip would be just as powerful.

What the reason was for *this* trip or what would happen once he got there he was eager to learn.

Cautiously, he would take it one step at a time.

With no formal agenda, Father Joseph decided it was time to select his destination.

Tongue in cheek, he did this very "scientifically".

Joseph walked over to an assemblage of monitors suspended overhead for travelers to view. Several read, Arrivals. Others, Departures.

Father Joseph focused on one particular screen labeled Departures and closed his eyes tightly.

"One... Two... Three..." He blindly counted slowly, popping his eyes back open on *three*.

"And the winner is…"

His eyes fell to the eighth line.

He gulped.

"Italian Airlines flight #1020 bound for the United States." Joseph's eyes moved over one column to the right.

"Kismet, Nebraska?!" He shouted as if he were the only person there.

"Wha...! Well...! I... I... I...! What the heck is there...?!" His speech stuttered and stammered.

"All the way back to the United States?! Uhhhhhhhhh....." Joseph sighed. The thought of it exhausted him further. "Another long plane ride."

Oddly, something about it felt right even though Joseph didn't know why. He looked back up at the monitor. "I guess something must be there."

Father Joseph knew nothing of the grassy land of Nebraska and couldn't begin to venture a guess to what could be there for him.

"Kismet, Nebraska. Hmmnnhhhh. Nebraska." In his head he tried to picture where it was on the map.

Second guessing his intuition was no longer something he did.

"Nebraska it is then." He said, sure as sure could be. "Let's go."

Up to the ticket window he marched to buy a ticket to, of all places, Nebraska.

"One ticket for Kismet, Nebraska please." Joseph politely requested from the slender, female ticket agent.

"Yup. Back to the United States it is." Father Joseph whispered under his breath as he rummaged through his pockets for his money. "For *some* reason."

A few quick strokes of the congenial ticket agents computer keyboard and the priest was now an official passenger of Italian Airlines.

"Certainly father. Here are your tickets... and your boarding passes." She placed the documents on the elevated shelf between she and Father Joseph. "You'll just need to take your passport with you to check-in."

Father Joseph paid the airline employee and slid his tickets and boarding passes across the counter toward him.

"Have a lovely trip father and thank you for flying with Italian Airlines. Enjoy your flight." The cheerful airline professional winked.

"Grazie. God Bless."

"Prego. Prego." She answered, checking her watch.

"Oh Padre, you must hurry! That plane is leaving like... Now!" The ticket agent urgently warned him.

"Terminal G! Go! Go!" She shouted, pointing in the direction. "You only have moments! Maybe!"

"Grazie! Grazie!" Joseph hollered to her as he took off in a sprint across the airport.

As Joseph jolted toward the terminal, he heard... "Italian Airlines flight #1020 bound for Kismet, Nebraska now boarding." ...come over the airport's public address system.

"Oh no..!" He quickened his pace. "I'm going to miss it!"

Tired and weary and many pounds heavier than he knew he should be, it took him a couple of extra minutes to get to Terminal G.

Again, the announcement. "Last call... For Italian Airlines flight #1020 to Kismet, Nebraska... Now boarding."

"Oh my gosh! I'm never going to catch this flight!" Running and wheezing, Joseph rounded the corner of Terminal G, expecting a lengthy wait behind everyone else already there.

However, there was no line. Because no one was there.

"Everyone must be aboard the aircraft already!" Joseph dashed to the check-in counter for an airline employee to take his passport and boarding passes and allow him to get on the plane.

"Am I too late?! Do I still have time to get on?" He begged desperately, holding on to the counter for support.

"Just in time father. The plane is about to leave." The check-in clerk reached for his paperwork. "You're the last person confirmed for this flight. After you, we're shutting the doors and..." The airline attendant made her hand act as an airplane lifting off into the sky.

"Thank you. Thank you." Father Joseph huffed and puffed, turning over his documents along with his passport. "Good. I made it."

She looked down at his information.

"So, what takes you to Nebraska father?" She asked, checking his paperwork.

"Not sure." He said honestly.

"Not sure?" She repeated, looking him in the eye, wearing a confused expression on her face.

"That's right. Not sure. Just know I have important business there. What it is, I'll have to wait to see." Joseph grinned, while laboring to catch his breath.

The check-in clerk made sure not to grill the priest too severely. After all, he was a priest.

"Ah ha. I see then." She said, matching him up against his passport photo. "It's you all right." The woman confirmed, placing it back down on the countertop.

Father Joseph looked down at the photo. He still wasn't fond of it.

"Well, good luck with whatever it turns out to be once you get there." She said. "I'm positive whatever work awaits you... It will help you make the world a better place for *all of us*." She spoke wearing a bright gleaming smile. "I just know it. I can see it in you."

Her personality was as warm as the sun.

That stopped Joseph right in his tracks. "Interesting choice of words my dear." He shared, half-laughing. "You have no idea. No idea."

Her smile widened.

Beneath that brilliant smile, a glimmer of light caught Joseph's eye. There, hanging from around the porcelain-faced check-in clerk's neck, a gold necklace bearing the Star of David.

The symbol of Jewish identity and Judaism. As she moved, it caught the light which reflected in Father Joseph's eyes.

He stared at it, zoned out.

"Have a nice flight Padre." She waved her hand in front of his face to get his attention.

"Everything O.K.?" She asked, concerned.

"Yes, oh yes, I'm fine. Just a little tired." He explained. "You're right, you know, hopefully, I can make the world a better place for *all of us. All of us.*" He emphasized.

She handed him back his paperwork and passport and welcomed him aboard. "Welcome to Italian Airlines father. You can board the plane right over there." She pointed to where.

"Once inside, please take your seat and put your safety belt on. We're about to take off very soon."

"Grazie." Joseph thanked. "Grazie. I will." He briefly looked back down at her necklace and smiled, reminding himself that we were *all* God's children.

Joseph left the counter and walked through the telescopic gangway, extending over the plane's wing, connecting the airport building to the airplane door. He could hear the wind from outside whistling through.

"Oh gosh." He groaned. "Everyone's going to be seated already and they'll have to wait for me." Father Joseph felt embarrassed to be the one to be holding up the flight. "They're all going to stare at me with contempt." He worried.

Once he made his way inside the jet, far enough to see down the aisle, he was shocked.

"What the.... Where is everyone?"

There was only *one* other passenger on the aircraft. A man, sitting about halfway down the aisle on the right, in the window seat.

From where he stood, Joseph made a nervous half-smile at him. But the man had no reaction and slumped down in his seat.

Father Joseph located his seat assignment on his boarding passes.

"18E. That's me."

He looked up to the right, where the overhead compartments were to store carry on luggage. Affixed to the bottom of each compartment, a row bearing numbers and letters denoting the corresponding seats beneath them.

"4 D-E-F."

Joseph took a step forward down the aisle.

"5 D-E-F."

"6..." He saw to his right in his peripheral vision.

"9 D-E-F." Went by him.

He was halfway there.

His brain told his feet it wasn't long now before they could rest.

"16..."

Father Joseph continued down the aisle until he came to his section.

"And, finally... 18."

"Here we are." Joseph was so busy concentrating on the seat numbers, he just realized where he was standing.

Looking at his seat, he was more dumbfounded now than when he first boarded the plane.

That *only other* passenger on the plane was sitting smack dab in seat 18F. Right next to *his* seat.

"Wow. How 'bout that!" Joseph joked to the man who sat there totally still.

With his head bowed and wearing a hat pulled down low over his face, the passenger said nothing.

"This whole big plane empty, and *we're* the only two aboard. And we're sitting together? How strange is that?" Joseph tried to get the man, whom he now realized looked dirty and unkempt, to look at him.

He wouldn't.

Father Joseph stared harder at the man who kept his head lowered to conceal his identity. Joseph leaned over to get a peek at him. "Everything O.K. sir?"

The shy, scruffy man turned toward the window.

The priest got just enough of a look at him to make out who it was.

Like he'd seen a ghost, Joseph stumbled backward, caught himself just as quickly and then steadied himself, getting himself back up on his feet.

"Holy..." Joseph put his hands up to his face to cover his mouth which was hanging wide open.

"Oh my! It... It can't be! Is it? Is it really you?!" He shouted. "What happened to... y... y...?"

Joseph stretched his neck to get a better look at the man's face from the front to make sure it was who he thought it was.

"D... D... DA....! It IS you!"

Only then did the cowering, beaten-up looking man with bloodshot eyes turn back around to face Joseph. Barely raising his head to look Joseph in the eye, he smiled gently with the last bit of energy he had left. He looked like he'd been through a war. Banged up, bruised, cut and emaciated... He kept a low profile to conserve his strength.

Joseph, still standing in the aisle, reached out with both arms. "Brother David! Oh my... David! I thought you were! How...? Where did you?! I... I... Can't believe...! This!" Joseph looked all around for someone to tell the good news to, but... There was no one.

Telling anyone he was alive was the last thing Brother David wanted Joseph to do.

"Shhhhhhhhh! Shhhhhhhhh!" Brother David, hushed him.

Figuratively back from the dead, the monk pressed his index finger vertically up to his lips to silence his friend.

"Shhhhhhhhh! Don't make a fuss! Just sit down! Please!" Brother David directed, frightened who might hear Joseph.

"Someone might... find us tog...!" David stopped to listen to a rustling sound up ahead toward the nose of the plane.

"Just sit, please!" David pleaded.

The monk peered over the seat tops to see if anyone was paying any attention to them. Absolutely no one was around other than a flight attendant in first class, where no one was sitting. She must have been making the sound he was hearing.

"... Quick, sit down!" David pointed to the seat next to him.

Father Joseph flung his backpack on a vacant seat across the aisle and took his assigned seat immediately.

"Brother David..." Joseph said in a whisper. "I thought you died in that car accident in Newport, Rhode Island." A look of total confusion came over Joseph's face. "How did you...? I was sick! Sick!"

"I know. I know. I almost did." David calmed his friend. "But... Well... Guess it wasn't my time. There was more work for me to do here."

"I'm so glad you're all right, David." Father Joseph couldn't believe this was happening. Thankful beyond belief, but still couldn't believe it. His friend being alive was a miracle.

"So, what happened after the crash? What happened to you? Where were you? How did you get back to Rome? And what are you doing on this plane?" The priest begged for answers quicker than David could answer and he had more.

"Well... I'll tell you about the car accident later. I arrived back in Rome several days ago." Brother David admitted.

"Then why didn't you....!" Out of pure frustration, Father Joseph's voice steadily rose out of a whisper and into a yell.

"Shhhhhhhh!" David reminded him to keep his voice down.

"Sorry. Sorry. Then why didn't you come to find me sooner?" Joseph, using a much lower voice, pleaded to know why he waited.

"I did. I did find you Joseph." He revealed to the priest.

"You did? Wha... Wha... What do you mean you did? This is the first time I've laid eyes on you since..." Father Joseph's brain was on overload. "... Since that fiery crash on Ocean Drive."

David explained. "I did find you Joseph but *they* were too close to you. *They've* had their eyes on you ever since you arrived back in Rome yourself, after seeing your father. It was too dangerous to approach you with *those three* hovering over you, watching your every move."

"You know about that? About my father? But how?" Father Joseph was shocked to learn David knew so much.

"Yes I do. Let me finish..." Brother David insisted.

Joseph backed down. "Sorry. Sorry. I have so many questions for you. Like, what about the scrolls? Why did you turn them over to *them*? Why? I don't understand."

"Joseph, I'll get to that. Just let me finish. I promise. I'll tell you everything." David assured his friend.

At that moment, both men heard the plane's intercom system come on. "Ladies and Gentlemen, this is Italian Airlines flight #1020. I am your pilot, Stephan Ricci. I will be flying with you during this Transatlantic flight. Please fasten your seat belts as we await takeoff."

Brother David made sure his seat belt was secure. Father Joseph did the same.

"I've been following you for days, waiting for just the right moment to approach you." David said. "When I could get you alone. Without anyone watching."

Father Joseph listened respectfully, trying not to interrupt again.

"I followed you here today, through the streets of Rome and I watched as you walked by St. Hector's." Brother David shared.

Joseph's eyes grew wide. "You were following me?" Then he remembered hearing the footsteps behind him, stop and shuffle off into a nearby building. "That must have been David," he thought to himself.

"I saw you stop to examine the Roman Catholic Church named for someone you thought you couldn't remember. I knew you couldn't figure out who Hector was. Or, why a Roman Catholic Church was named after him. Could you?"

"You're right, David." Joseph confirmed David's intuition. "I turned my mind inside out, trying to figure it out. But, for the life of me, I couldn't remember who this *Hector* was. Or, why the Church believed he'd been called to holiness or had fulfilled the necessary criteria set for sainthood by the Church? Who is he? I... I... I just can't remember."

Brother David drew in a deep breath.

"You wouldn't remember him Joseph, because the Roman Catholic Church doesn't *want* anyone to know about him."

"Huh." Father Joseph was speechless. "Why? What do you mean?"

"You see Joseph. Hector *was* a man in history, greatly revered by the Catholic Church but not for a good reason."

"O.K. I'm listening. Who was he then?" Father Joseph's curiosity was killing him. This wasn't the first time the devout priest was hearing the Church kept secrets from its followers. So, he was open to anything.

"Well... You know the scroll? Our scroll?"

"Yes." Father Joseph answered, feeling a sense of dread in the pit of his stomach.

Brother David clarified. "Well, the author of the scroll, Yashmiel... and you know how most of this story goes... placed it inside a box which Christ made for him with his own two hands, and then buried it deep beneath the earth before his death for safekeeping."

A lightbulb went off in Joseph's memory.

"Remember that secret room we found at the Vatican?" David continued. "Where we found the scroll translated to English, framed and up on the wall? There was a timeworn, beaten-up, old broken-down wooden box that you found there. Do you remember smelling it and saying it was old?"

Father Joseph did remember. "Yes, I do."

Out of a knapsack sitting on the floor between his feet, David pulled out the same box.

"Oh my... That's it! That's it!" Joseph exclaimed in short breaths, catching himself.

"While we were ripping that copy of the scroll out of its frame for us to read and use, I slipped this under my clothing." David confided.

Joseph stared at the hand-crafted wooden relic, knowing Christ once held it in his own hands. He felt afraid to touch it again, now that he knew for sure what it was.

"This IS that box, Joseph. Over a thousand years after it was buried by Yashmiel for time to reveal it again to mankind, it was eventually found by a little blind girl in the area of Galilee but she couldn't open it. It was locked."

"So what did she do with it?" Father Joseph hung on every word David had to say.

"Well... It was taken off her hands by her neighbor. A man by the name of *Hector*."

Father Joseph inhaled frantically. "Oh... I see."

He knew this is where the story takes a horrible turn for the worst.

Brother David elaborated further. "Hector, had heard rumors of such a sacred box, which carried with it great fame and wealth. He knew its great historical and monetary value. When he saw the child with it.... With his own selfish interests in mind, he took the box. Kept it. Never opened it and sold it to the highest bidder."

It didn't take Father Joseph but a split second to figure out who that highest bidder was. "The Roman Catholic Church."

"Precisely." Brother David answered. "Where it remained shrouded in secrecy for centuries. That is, until its contents, the scroll, was revealed and two crude copies of it were made and stolen from the Church and... Well... Thankfully through fate... Found their way to us. As I believe, it was always meant to be. But you know most all of this already."

The priest finished Hector's story for Brother David.

"*Part* of the agreement, was... In exchange for the sacred box, along with its concealed contents... That the Roman Catholic Church immortalize Hector as a saint by naming a Church after his namesake. So whomever sees the Church bearing his name will forever know that he was a Holy person, one who has won a high place in heaven and is worthy of veneration. To say that he, Hector, is one of the souls of the dead in paradise. Guaranteeing 'til the end of days, that whomever lay their eyes upon St. Hector's Church, regard him with deep respect and honor him as hallowed."

David nodded. "The Church gave Hector everything he wanted."

"Oh, I'm going to be sick." Joseph pushed into his middle. His insides always acted up when he became upset like this.

Brother David bent over, cupping his hand over his mouth. He had more, very important information to share.

"Yashmiel, I have since learned, was born and originates from the Western area of what is *now* known as Turkey. About where Istanbul is today."

"O.K. That I didn't know." Joseph wondered how David could have possibly learned more about the author of the ancient document in such a short span of time.

"But what does Yashmiel's place of origin have to do with anything?" He asked.

Again, more rustling from the front of the plane by the flight attendant.

Brother David watched her suspiciously, clearing his throat. "Ahem."

Suddenly, both men felt the plane's wheels begin to turn beneath them. Outside, the airport began to pass by their window.

"Looks like we're headed for takeoff." David said.

"Any idea why Nebraska?" The monk asked his friend, switching gears for a second.

"No, just felt right to me, but no, I don't know why. Why? Do you know something I don't?" Joseph was beginning to really get stressed.

Again, the pilot addressed passengers. All two of them... As another flight attendant emerged from the back, rushing by to take her seat up front and strap in.

"Ladies and Gentlemen, please remain seated, as we've received clearance for takeoff. In just about two minutes we'll be in the air bound for Kismet, Nebraska. Again, thank you for flying Italian Airlines."

Both men felt the plane taxi down the runway.

Father Joseph turned his attention back to David.

"So why?... Why am I being drawn to this place, Nebraska, out in the middle of nowhere in the Central part of the United States?"

Brother David looked at Joseph with a serious look upon his face.

"Not sure exactly *what* is there Joseph but know *something* is there for us. I do have some idea what."

David held out the palm of his hand and imaginarily drew on it with his finger. "Here is the United States." He traced along the entire perimeter of his inner hand. "Right about here." He pinpointed to the geographic center, as if on a map. "Is where Nebraska is."

Joseph did his best to follow.

"So..." Father Joseph remembered to keep his voice below normal speaking levels. "... How do you know something is there for us?"

"The latitudes and the longitudes say so..."

Father Joseph was lost. "Oh please. More stuff to figure out. My brain is at capacity now." The priest gripped the front of his head. "I can't hold anymore up here."

The Tibetan monk gave Joseph a moment to catch up.

"What do you mean the latitudes and longitudes say so?" Joseph kept firing off questions in spite of being overwhelmed by the information he already had.

As exhausted as he was, he needed to know what David knew. "Tell me everything you know."

Brother David knew this man, this priest, was ready to hear. He drew in another long, deep breath to prepare himself to share the following legend with his friend.

"In Tibet where I am from, ancient seers have for centuries been predicting the coming of a newborn into this world. A newborn child conceived of both Heaven *and* Hell." David squinted as though he could see it himself.

He orally illustrated the vision the seers had and shared with only a few. "They have foreseen a child or children, it's unclear, born of the Breast of Heaven and the Groin of Hell."

Father Joseph looked paralyzed with fear. "Sounds like a creature born out of the imagination of Greek mythology. A being that's half-good, half-evil. How could that even be? I mean... in real life. Come on!"

Joseph shook his head, disturbed by the very thought of it. "Preposterous." He criticized with disdain.

David knew at first, it would sound too far-fetched for Father Joseph to consider it probable at all.

He waited.

"How could that be possible?" Joseph ordered David to give him a sound explanation for what he thought was impossible.

The fact that Joseph was asking questions told David his friend's mind was open.

"Not sure yet." David answered truthfully. "That child... Or children..." David affirmed. "According to the ancient seers... Would originate from a place that is the precise latitude on earth as the origin of the creator of a scroll that is the direct word of the Messiah. The precise latitude of the birthplace of a *chosen one,* selected by a member of the highest order of angels in Heaven and the precise latitude where a child cradles the entire world in his hands."

It was too mysterious for Father Joseph to try to wrap his mind around. "Another riddle." He said in a defeated tone. "I don't know anything about latitudes and longitudes. I learned that stuff in grade school. I... I... What does that all mean? Do you know?" Father Joseph wiped perspiration from his brow.

David smiled a knowing smile.

"I do have some idea." He said.

"Well, tell me." Joseph said frustrated, tired of trying to dissect all these mystical matters. "Just tell me, please."

The monk pulled an old, crinkly, folded-up map of the world out of his pocket. A perfectly straight horizontal line, drawn in pencil, virtually cut the world in half, into two hemispheres, exactly along the 41 degree North latitude line. Three big red dots were marked along that line.

Brother David made sure Joseph noticed the red dots. They were significant to understanding the prophecy.

"Joseph. That child or children... That the ancient seers said will be either conceived or born of Heaven and Hell, will arise from a place that is the same latitude as the origin of the creator of a scroll that is the direct word of the Messiah."

"Who is that?" David quizzed his fellow passenger.

"Yashmiel." Joseph stated matter-of-factly.

"Where did I say Yashmiel originates from?"

"Western... What is *now* known as Turkey." Joseph answered correctly from memory.

David pointed to the red dot, farthest right, along the horizontal pencil-drawn line. "41 degrees - 10 minutes North of the equator."

"I see that there. Yes. O.K." Joseph looked hard at the map. He could see David was definitely on to something.

"Secondly, the child or children would originate from the same latitude as the birthplace of a *chosen one* selected by a member of the highest order of angels in Heaven. We know who that is." David gazed at Joseph.

"Where were you born, Joseph?" David forced him to answer, even though he knew Joseph was a humble soul and wouldn't want to say it aloud.

"You know where I was born. You said you know about me seeing my father."

"Just tell me please." Brother David pressed.

"Providence, Rhode Island." Joseph reluctantly responded.

David pointed to the next dot, in the middle of the other two.

"Providence, Rhode Island. 41 degrees - 44 minutes..."

"... North of the equator." Joseph finished David's sentence for him and then leaned over, examining the map closer. He was starting to get nervous now.

Lastly, the next indicator they were on the right track.

"O.K. Father, when I came to the airport today... Just ahead of you... I looked at the Departure monitors to find a destination along the same latitude as *those* two locations, 41 degrees North. For a clue as to where I needed to go. Something along the 41 degree North latitude. Guess how I picked Kismet, Nebraska?"

"It fell along your line here." Joseph said flatly, running his finger along the smudgy pencil-drawn line on David's map.

"It was the ONLY destination with a latitude of 41 degrees North!" David erupted, louder than he planned to. "This has to be where we're supposed to be heading." He established logically, his voice falling back into a whisper.

Brother David, on a roll, revealed it's geographic coordinates, which are measured in degrees and represent angular distances calculated from the center of the Earth. "Kismet, Nebraska is approximately 41 degrees - 18 minutes North."

Joseph referenced David's map and saw a red dot farthest to the left. "I see it is." He accepted, his lip quivering as he contemplated all three red dots in a row.

David huffed. "This is the third clue Joseph. This must be where the child is. The child, who cradles the entire world in his hands."

A look of reluctant acceptance came over Joseph's face.

David finished. "Therefore Kismet, Nebraska must also be the place where another child or children, born of the Breast of Heaven and the Groin of Hell, will either be conceived or be born into the world... Don't know which. Just know the newborn or multiple-birth will originate there."

This was a lot of new information for Father Joseph to factor in.

David had yet another bombshell for Joseph. "There's more..."

Stone-faced, Father Joseph turned to him. "As if it weren't already complicated enough. Let's hear it." He nervously adjusted himself in his cramped airline seat, which was undoubtedly built for a more slender man.

Brother David spoke slowly so his friend could absorb it all.

"The seers also always believed Joseph, that the date of conception or the date of birth of this half-good, half-evil child or children is signified somehow within that exact latitude in degrees and minutes."

David added. "I suspect, there is a clue in these geographic coordinates of Kismet, Nebraska. 41 degrees - 18 minutes North. I'm just not sure how though."

Joseph looked back down at David's crumpled map.

Now completely sucked into this prediction by the Tibetan ancient seers, Joseph tried to crack the code. "If we break up the coordinates to signify a date of conception or a birthday..." Joseph did a little math in his head. "We're looking at a month and day here. The first number... 41... There is no 41st month."

Joseph scratched his head. "But there is an 18th day."

Brother David paid close attention.

"Let's take the 4 for the month. The fourth month... April. And the 18th day. That would be April 18th." Joseph decided.

"I see that." David agreed.

"But..." Joseph pointed out. "There would be a 1 left over. That's got to mean something, but what?"

"A 1 left over. A 1 left over." David couldn't figure it out either.

"Unless it's the 1 we're supposed to focus on. That would be January. January 18th. In that case, a 4 would be left over." Joseph figured it the other way around.

Father Joseph looked to David to see if he had any better ideas. Or, could figure this out by using a different formula.

"What about that? A 4 or a 1 is going to be left over... For the month part of it... If *that's* the equation we're using." Joseph said.

"Not sure." Brother David answered. "Not sure. But what I am sure of, is that all the numbers account for something. I'm also sure, that we will definitely be meeting a child in Nebraska. A child who cradles the entire world in his hands. And that somehow, some way, a new life *will* come into the world there."

Both men then felt the plane vibrate violently beneath their feet as it picked up speed down the runway.

Father Joseph braced himself. "We'll be in the air in just..." He squeezed his eyes shut.

He had another question for David... Something to take his mind off going air-born and the danger associated with it.

"So... Who's the mother and the father of this... Half Heaven, half Hell child? Excuse me. Or children supposed to be?"

David thought about how to best answer that.

"I suppose... One could conclude... The Redeemer of mankind and the Tempter of mankind?"

"Ah hah." Joseph paused. "Who do you think it'll look like?" He said in jest.

David rolled his head to the side to look out his passenger seat window as their plane launched into the sky.

Joseph could see David's reflection in the window cracking a slight smile.

Both men settled in for a long flight over the Atlantic Ocean, as they headed for Eastern Nebraska, a state located on the Great Plains of the Midwestern United States.

CHAPTER 28

GEOGRAPHIC COORDINATES 41 DEGREES, 18 MINUTES NORTH OF THE EQUATOR

In the distance a huge lone tree stood in the middle of acres and acres of corn fields. Tall and imposing its branches bloomed with healthy green leaves which spread themselves wildly over the dry corn stalks below. Its decades-old, gnarled armlike limbs reaching up into the air to swipe angrily at the crystal-blue sky above.

With heavy sacks in hand a determined Father Joseph and Brother David walked down a long dusty dirt road heading toward a diner they could see in the distance.

After deplaning, both shared a taxi to this small farming town in the Missouri River Valley, just outside Omaha, about 25 miles north of the mouth of the Platte River. A few miles out, they asked the taxi cab driver to drop them off. They'd decided to walk the rest of the way to take in the scenery in the hopes of finding any clue that might help lead them to what it is they were meant to do here.

"It's beautiful here, this Kismet." Brother David couldn't help but notice. He'd never been anywhere like it. "Heartland of the United States."

Surrounding them on both sides of the road, as far as their eyes could see, miles and miles of cornfields consisting of single cornstalk rows. Tight, narrow lanes between each.

"God's country." Father Joseph thought out loud. "It's quiet here. You can hear yourself think. I like it."

David too, noticed the undeniable level of peace here.

"Listen..." David called his friends attention to a beautiful Western Meadowlark singing her little heart out on a nearby rickety old fence, which was half falling down on the side of the road.

There she sat proud as can be. An adult, medium-sized female with yellow underparts, and a long, pointed bill. Her head was striped with light brown and black streaks. On her breast, a black "V".

Her flute-like song with a gentle trilling note was a pleasure to their ears.

"That's two notes she's singing..." Joseph perceived by listening closely. "Just a tone... Or a semitone apart. She's quickly singing them alternately."

Both men smiled at the petite, little bird showing off to them.

"Kind of place Glenn would like." Joseph said, as if he could feel his presence here.

"Mmmmnnn." David agreed. "I could picture him here. Yes. He would like it. Something about this place reminds me of him." He didn't know how or why. Just knew it did.

"Do you hear that?!" Joseph cut in.

David stopped to listen. "What?"

The sound of rustling in the cornstalks was louder than normal and getting louder. Like something or someone was in the thick, dense field.

Visibility was limited in the cornrows. They couldn't see what it was.

"That there! Hear it?!" Panicked, Joseph pointed to the field to the left of them.

David heard it. "I do! That there... Yes! What do you think it is?!"

Neither was sure what was coming their way or what to do about it. Whatever it was, was closing in and fast.

Then, before they could worry about it another second, an enormous whitetail deer with an impressive rack of antlers, each side bearing ten points, emerged from the cornfield and leapt onto the dirt road with them.

Joseph and David jumped back to give him room.

The mature male buck stood there as regal as could be looking at them, but breathing heavy like he was being chased.

Joseph and David weren't sure what to do.

The deer's lungs were painfully expanding and contracting quickly and hard. A sign he had been running for miles.

Staring at the men, the nervous deer waved his big bushy white tail side to side, indicating he was just as startled as they were.

The buck had to be about three-hundred pounds and ninety inches long. His reddish-brown summer coat giving way to a duller grayish-brown winter coat underneath. He was a beautiful old boy, strong and healthy.

Joseph and David, standing there still and quietly, allowed the deer to rest. He was obviously in distress. They didn't want to frighten him more than he already was.

The only noise Father Joseph and Brother David could hear right now, other than the pounding of their own heartbeats, was the heavy breathing and wheezing of this magnificent creature meshed with the sound of the dry cornstalks brushing up against each other in the field.

"It's O.K. boy. Just rest. You're O.K. with us here. Don't worry about anything. We've got you." Joseph reassured the animal in a loving tone.

The deer blinked it's big brown eyes at Joseph and then turned his head to the West. His acute hearing caught something approaching, on the horizon. He kept his eyes trained on the dirt road, curving up and over a hill.

Joseph and David watched him curiously, making sure not to make any sudden moves.

The buck's nostrils flared, sucking in the air.

"He's picking something up upwind." Joseph saw, turning his head also toward the horizon. "We're downwind of something. Or *someone*."

A scent molecule the buck detected on the wind's current, alerted him there was danger coming this way.

He looked back at the men, blinked a couple of times and nodded his head up once.

"He *definitely* knows something." Joseph murmured to David.

Then as fast as the reserved, intuitive whitetail buck appeared, his big, strong, muscular body sprung back into the cornfield from where he came.

The only part of the ruminant swift-footed animal Joseph and David could see as he bolted back into seclusion, was the beautiful white, fluffy underside of his tail which he held conspicuously erect like a flag.

He was definitely alarmed. Joseph and David could see that.

They knew if he was, then they should be.

Disappearing like a phantom into the dense cornfield within seconds, the deer's coloring and markings served as perfect camouflage to keep him hidden from any predator.

"I hope he'll be O.K." Joseph worried.

"He'll be all right, Joseph." David assured him. "He's smart and quick and he probably knows this cornfield better than the farmer that owns it."

They listened to the dulled rustling of the corn stalks as their friend made his way deeper into the cornfield and into hiding.

"Hey, where's our beautiful little bird?" Father Joseph wondered, hearing nothing now.

In fact, there were no ambient sounds around them whatsoever. All sound other than the wind ceased as if all the animals, even the birds were driven from here.

"I don't hear anything." David noticed. "That's odd." He said, peeking back at the rickety old fence. "Guess she flew off."

That's when their attention was called to the roar of a mean-sounding engine behind them.

They turned to look at the horizon.

Closing in on them from behind, a faded red 1957 Thunderbird convertible tore its way up over the hill and down Route 137. The car's tires kicking up dust and dirt, creating a dark, swirling tornado cloud behind the classic two-seater. It trailed the car like a gigantic flapping cape.

They couldn't see who was driving yet, but whomever it was drove like they were trying to win a race.

The faster the car drove, the louder the radio became. Its Volumatic Radio System, automatically increasing the volume as the car's speed increased.

"Look! That car! It's coming this way! Fast!" Father Joseph extended his arm out to corral David to safety.

Barreling down the road toward them, the T-Bird shook violently as though the gas pedal was depressed all the way and the tires were about to blow.

A woman, they could now see, was behind the wheel.

"She's going to lose control!" Joseph hollered. "Watch out!" He warned Brother David. "Get into the corn! Get into the corn!"

Both men ran to the side of the road and dove into one of the cornrows.

Before they knew it, the classic car was upon them, radio blaring as loud as it would go.

The cornstalks at the edge of the road bent to the will of the wind as the angry driver whizzed by, sending dirt and tiny pebbles into the air, creating a filthy dirt cloud which descended upon and assaulted them in the field.

Father Joseph listened closely to make out what song was playing on the woman's car radio.

"I... I... I... Think that song... If I remember correctly." Joseph scratched his head, remembering back to the seventies. "Paul Anka. Times of Your Life. 1975. Big hit. I used to *love* that song. I'd forgotten about it. Until... Until just hearing it now."

Brother David, of course, being a Tibetan monk was lost. He had absolutely no knowledge of or understanding of American music. Therefore no reference point in his life, unlike Joseph had.

Father Joseph reminisced back to a time when he was a younger man. During the seventies, his favorite musical era, this was one of his favorite songs. Written by one of the most prolific, successful songwriters in history.

Forgetting where he was for a second, Joseph gave himself permission to slip back in time. Still able to hear it faintly as the convertible T-Bird hauled its way up Route 137, Joseph sang along.

"Reach back for the joy and the sorrow.

Put them away in your mind.
The memories are time that you borrow.
To spend when you get to tomorrow."

Joseph sang from his diaphragm, belting out the lyrics along with the Canadian-born 60's teen idol.

"Here comes the setting sun...
The seasons are passing one by one.
So gather moments while you may.
Collect the dreams you dream today.
Remember.
Will you remember the times of your life.... Dah, dah, dah."

David allowed Joseph his trip, in song, down memory lane. He could see this song made his friend happy.

"Gather moments while you may.
Collect the dreams you dream today.
Remember.
Will you remember the times of your life.
Of your life......... Of your life...." Joseph sang, stretching out the final note with Paul Anka, before the song faded.

As Father Joseph sang, something inside him kept telling him those lyrics had something to do with him and his journey here to Nebraska. Each note, each beautiful word in the song nagged him but he wasn't sure how or what they had to do with him.

"Who was that driving?" Brother David asked, knowing there was no way Joseph could know.

"I just caught a glimpse of her as she sped past." Joseph said. "She was wearing sunglasses. So it was hard to... Her hair was neatly tucked beneath a scarf she wore over her head and tied under her chin. Her face was hard to make out. Petite female, fair skin. That's it... I couldn't get a good look at her."

Then it dawned on him.

It was Falene.

He didn't share that with David. He didn't want to scare him, David had already been through so much.

As Father Joseph thought about it, he realized she was wearing the same scarf she wore in Newport the day they transported him from Jan Reichmann's mansion along the water to Providence, Rhode Island. That day, as Falene sashayed across the driveway to her car, he'd noticed her wearing that very same scarf. A long, thin couture scarf which looked very expensive and made of silk charmeuse. It was mostly all white like this one and also had a pattern of giant red flowers on it, outlined in black dotting the length of the scarf.

It was too coincidental. It was the same scarf. It was her.

The one who dwells where Satan's throne is.

Joseph knew it with certainty.

"She's headed toward the diner." David noticed, turning his attention down the road as he stepped out of the corn. "Do you think that woman is headed there?"

Joseph followed closely behind.

They watched as Falene's car sped in the direction of the diner.

"It doesn't matter where that woman is headed. We need to worry about ourselves. Let's go." Joseph instructed. "Forget about that car. Her. This way. This is where we're headed anyway."

Joseph redirected David successfully and both of them got back onto the main road and continued walking.

Soon their ears were blessed again by birds returning with song, including their little friend the Western Meadowlark.

"There we go. See David. There she is. Her and all her friends."

It was music to their ears.

Quicker than they thought it would take, the priest and the monk were at the entrance of the diner they'd seen in the distance.

"Harry's Lunch Spot." Father Joseph read the sign to Brother David. "Let's see what's inside. Get a bite, and figure out what our next move should be."

David was on board with that.

From the outside, both men noticed clean circular spots in the grime-caked window glass. By the number of cars and trucks surrounding the eatery, this was a gathering spot for area farmers. So it had to be fairly decent inside.

Joseph and David stepped up to the front door and looked at each other. With one huge heave Joseph swung the door wide open. One step forward and both he and David were inside.

Here, time had stood still.

Looking around, they saw silver metal stools with round, red leather seats, all in a row, lining the dining counter. Old-fashioned coffee pots behind the counter and a black and white checkered pattern beneath their feet on the floor.

Everywhere they turned, inquisitive eyes stared back at them. It was quite obvious to the regulars, they weren't from around here.

"I feel like I've gone back to the fifties." Joseph said quietly to David.

Harry's Lunch Spot was dated and a bit rundown. But that was just fine by the locals.

An overworked waitress with an eighties hairdo greeted them. "Welcome fellas." She said, failing her best efforts to look cheerful.

"Take a seat anywhere. Any clean table. I'll be right with you."

Along her forearms she balanced plates of hot food. Each hand clutching the edges of two dishes. Bright red welts marked the length of her arms. Proof of a full day's worth of work, delivering orders by hand.

"There's one." With her nose, she pointed to a booth in the window as she dashed off to a table to serve their orders before they burned her arms any further.

No smile for the newcomers. Just a long face with dark circles under her eyes and an overall depressed demeanor.

Everyone in the diner was curious about the two. It looked more like a punchline, a priest and a monk walking into a diner in Nebraska, than real life. Yet, here they were.

One farmer spoke to another at a nearby table.

"Reminds me of that guy that came here some time ago. That guy... Glenn, I think was his name."

Joseph overheard the man but didn't acknowledge it. He knew he had to be talking about *his* Glenn.

Joseph and David took a seat at the vacant booth in the window the waitress suggested and got comfortable. Grease-stained menus were sitting on their wobbly table before them.

Immediately, they were greeted by one of the friendly customers sitting at the next booth over.

"Chuck Jones at your service gentlemen." He welcomed, extending his arm over the booth's backrest, to shake Joseph's hand.

"Welcome to Kismet, Nebraska. You two look like you're from out of town. What brings you to these parts?" He asked, glancing at Father Joseph's collar.

"Joseph." Joseph answered, kindly shaking his hand. "Father Joseph."

"David." David piped up, peeking over the top of his menu, trying to hide his battered face.

"Well... Uh... We're... Uh... Here to..." Joseph glanced at David, trying to figure out in that instant what to say about why they were there."

"We're here on business." David answered coldly, never taking his eyes from his menu.

Mr. Jones wasn't sure how to take it.

Neither did Joseph.

"I see." A bewildered Jones responded. "Well... Uh..."

Mr. Jones' wife Darlene leaned to the side to see beyond her husband. She wanted to get a good look at whomever it was that spoke to her husband that way.

Diner patrons at other tables who heard the exchange turned around as well.

Chuck Jones, not sure what to do, slowly turned back around to his wife. "Well, enjoy yourselves gentlemen. And welcome to Kismet." He said sincerely over his shoulder, leaving the two strangers to their business.

"If you need anything during your stay... I'm right up the road there." He pointed east, up Route 137. "Jones Farm. My wife Darlene and I have a soybean farm... 'bout nine miles that way. Just stop by. Door's always open. You're welcome there anytime. Both of you."

Now Joseph really felt badly about how rudely David spoke to this man.

"Thank you Mr. Jones. You're a fine man. That's a very generous offer. God Bless you. If we need anything... We'll definitely stop by." Father Joseph thanked the affable farmer profusely for the offer.

Darlene Jones felt more at ease now and relaxed back in her seat.

Irritated by his terse remark, Joseph turned back around to David. "Why did you say that like that?!" He whispered sharply.

"No one needs to know what we're doing here. We don't even know ourselves Joseph." Brother David snapped, disrespectfully reviewing his lunch and dinner options while he spoke. "The less people who know about us being here. The better."

Joseph was taken aback.

David seemed to have an edge to him he didn't have before.

Joseph noticed it on the plane shortly after seeing David for the first time since the accident in Newport and discovering that he was still alive. Joseph had no reasonable explanation for David's attitude other than to chalk it up to stress. David had been through so much recently, the accident, whatever else followed that and then hiding out, which he apparently was still doing.

So, Joseph decided to cut him a little slack. After all, the man sitting across the table from him looked like he'd been through hell and back. Maybe he had. Joseph didn't know because David still hadn't shared all the details with him.

Father Joseph, who could now hear everyone in the diner whispering under their breath in the background, everyone including Mr. and Mrs. Chuck Jones, picked up his own menu to try to figure out quickly what he wanted to eat before the waitress came over.

"Anything look good to you?" Joseph asked David, trying to change the subject.

David paused.

"Venison." He said, pointing to it on the menu under the heading Meats. Not because he wanted it, because of what they'd just experienced out in the fields.

Father Joseph searched his own menu and sure enough he saw it. He felt sick, also thinking about the big buck out in the cornfields.

"I think I'm going to become a vegetarian... Like, now." The disturbed priest announced. "Instead of deer's flesh for food." He joked halfheartedly. "How 'bout the... the..." He searched and searched the menu. "The vegan faux-meat pie with soy protein and mushrooms."

Joseph showed David where he could find it on his own menu.

"Me too." David settled on that as well.

Both put their menus down on the table and waited for their waitress to come over.

"Be right with you fellas!" The frazzled waitress called over, rushing by with another full-arm of piping hot plates.

Joseph caught the name on her name tag as she whirled by. It read Terri.

"No problem. Take your time Terri." Joseph graciously gestured with his hand. "We're in no rush."

By the looks of things, Terri was the only waitress in the place. The diner was full.

David spoke pensively. "So.... Joseph."

Father Joseph's large brown eyes lifted to look at Brother David.

"We finally have a moment to catch up...."

Joseph first looked around the diner, on high alert for any sign of Falene, before engaging in any meaningful conversation. She had been traveling in this direction and could have stopped here at the diner, although David still wasn't aware of that.

Joseph didn't see her anywhere inside the diner and he definitely didn't remember seeing her sporty red car parked outside among the dirty farm vehicles when they came in.

As far as he could see, she wasn't there. Not now anyway. So they were safe.

Joseph relaxed. "Yes.... finally. You're right. We have a moment to catch up. What's on your mind?"

Terri was back in a flash and looking even more exhausted than when they'd come in.

"O.K. fellas. What can I get you?" The tip of her yellow, number two lead pencil poised to her pink order pad.

She tapped her foot impatiently like she couldn't wait to take off again. "Let's start with drinks."

Then she noticed Joseph's white Roman collar, attached with a collarino, identifying him as a member of the clergy. She stopped tapping her foot out of respect.

Before she let her new customers answer, Terri had to let them know about their famous house special. "Oh... Goodness... I almost forgot. Just to let you know, we make great omelets here at Harry's... Even at lunch or dinner time. Our cook prides himself on the dish." A weak smile barely noticeable on her face.

"Thanks Terri." Father Joseph thanked her almost apologetically.

"That sounds great. I'm sure it's really delicious but I think we've both settled on the vegan faux-meat pie."

Stunned, she stood there with a vacant expression. The tip of her pencil suspended directly over her order pad. She couldn't bring the tip to paper to write.

"Oh... O.K... Wow... No one ever orders that around here." She stared at her pad like she didn't even know how to begin to write the words.

"Well, it is on the menu so..."

Terri turned around, eyeing the restaurant. The cook blessed with a strong, heavy and hairy body was behind the counter pouring himself a cup of steaming hot black coffee from one of the large, old coffee pots.

"Hey Charlie! These folks here want the vegan faux-meat pie! Any left?!" She had to ask, even though she already knew the answer.

Charlie looked just as shocked as she did to hear someone ordered it.

"What?! Who the...!" Hastily shoving the coffee pot back on the burner, he spun around on his heels to see Terri standing before the booth by the window with two newcomers looking back. One a priest.

"Uh... No. None left today but I can whip one right up, right now. Take about thirty-minutes though, if that's O.K." He estimated in a gravely voice, taking a swig of his coffee.

Terri turned to her customers to see if it *was* O.K.

Joseph did the talking. "Sure. Sure. No problem. We can wait. How about two coffees while the cook is making our meals?" He suggested politely.

Terri mustered the best smile she could. "Sure. Be right over with that." Off she went to get their drinks.

Charlie hit the kitchen. Pronto.

"Boy she looks distracted and upset about something." Father Joseph detected a great sadness behind Terri's forced smile.

Then Joseph remembered David was trying to tell him something before all this.

"So... David... As you were saying. We finally have a moment to catch up."

In his seat, David twisted to the left and twisted to the right to see if anyone was listening.

They weren't. Everyone had resumed what they were doing before the two strangers came into the diner.

Thankfully for them, the novelty of their visit had worn off.

Before David had a chance to begin, Terri was back with their coffees.

"Here you go. Two coffees." Terri placed a full cup before each of the men.

"Enjoy. That vegan faux-meat pie will be out before you know it." She said, the sound of her depressed voice decreasing as she sprinted to another table with a bottle of ketchup.

"She's definitely sad about something." Joseph followed Terri's every move for a few seconds. "Definitely. Something is bothering that woman. It's in her voice. In the way she holds herself. Everything. I wonder what it is?"

Then he caught himself.

"David. Oh... I'm sorry. Please. Please go on. I forgot myself for a second. You were trying to say something."

David sat erect in his seat.

He paused, gathering his thoughts.

"It's O.K. Joseph. Don't worry about it."

Another uneasy pause.

David rubbed his hands together roughly, examining the fine lines in his palms. A nervous habit.

Father Joseph patiently waited for Brother David to compose himself enough to say what he needed to say.

"Joseph, remember I told you I'd been in Rome for several days but couldn't approach you because *they* were too close to you?"

Joseph nodded. He knew David was going to reveal something important to him.

"Well... After you arrived back in Rome from Providence, Rhode Island, I followed you to the Vatican. Then, straight to the Pope's Private Quarters because I needed to see you. To talk with you."

"Mmmnnnnnnnhhhhh. Hmmmnnnnnhhhhh." Elbow up on the table, Father Joseph rested his chin on the back of his hand. He was feeling apprehensive about what David might have seen and heard.

David added. "I saw you in the bathroom with Falene. So I couldn't get to you."

He confirmed it.

Joseph didn't know what to do. What to say. He grew tense with embarrassment.

"You saw... How much of that?!" Joseph insisted on knowing. Secretly he feared what Brother David might think of him if he only spied on them momentarily. Out of context, Joseph's meeting with Falene could have appeared to be something it wasn't.

"All of it Joseph. I saw all of it. I saw what she was trying to do to you."

Joseph grew less defensive, hearing David might have understood Falene's true intentions.

"What do *you* think she was trying to do to me David?"

With certainty David answered. "Bait you."

Joseph's muscles stiffened.

"You can say that again." Joseph began to perspire. The whole situation made him uncomfortable then and even now by just thinking and talking about it.

David leaned in. He lowered his voice.

"In the beginning Joseph... As you well know... Satan appealed to the woman through her senses."

"Genesis." Joseph could quote chapter and verse in his sleep. "In the Garden of Eden."

"Correct..." David nodded. "But in your case, it was the opposite. With you... It was Satan *through his helper*, trying to appeal to man through *his* senses. Same principle."

"I know." Joseph offered, his face flushed. "I thought of that. I knew what was going on."

Brother David described in more specific detail. "Satan's desire... In this case, substitute Falene for Satan... Satan's desire for worshippers leads him to offer them the strongest sensual inducements disguised under the sacred sanction of what is considered *right* and *holy*."

"That is correct David." Joseph was impressed with David's religious knowledge and understanding of it.

Brother David, pushing his coffee cup to the side, leaned in even further over the table. "He tempts the unspiritual person, who gains information only by the five senses of sight, sound, taste, touch and smell."

Joseph, no slouch when it comes to theology finished David's idea. "Satan's depths are found in consecrating the most debased passions to religion. Every appeal to the senses, whether to the eye, in magnificent architecture and ritual, or to the ear by the mesmeric influence of music, or to the taste in suppers and banquets, or to the lower sensual appetites, is a descent into the depths of Satan and hell. These *wonders* eventually degenerate into despicable sexual activities that will be defined as *divine*. But they are anything but! And that's what Falene was doing to me. She was trying to tempt me with sex."

Father Joseph began to go numb thinking about what happened between him and Falene in the bathroom in the Pope's Private Quarters.

"My friend... She was trying to bring you down and bring you down hard. I saw how cunning she was... Trying to seduce you."

Father Joseph ran his fingers through his messy hair on the top of his head. "By the way. Where were you? In the Pope's Private Quarters?! Where?... That I couldn't hear or see you, David?!"

The priests own feelings of guilt made him want to tear his skin off.

"I'd snuck in through the main door and then I made my way toward the bathroom when I heard the two of you. I saw what Falene was trying to do to you. I hid and I listened."

"Oh." Joseph felt queasy.

"You were tempted Joseph. I saw it. You were."

"Well... I... I.... She took me by sur..." The words were like lead in his mouth. The were heavy, unwilling to lift off his tongue. Joseph didn't know how to explain himself.

"Uhhhhh... Well..... I.... She..." Father Joseph's eyes rolled around, as he searched for just the right words. He felt pressured to clear up what happened.

"Listen... I... I know it was difficult for you." David spoke understandingly. "I could see that."

"I... I... She is so... I didn't..." Guilt took Joseph's entire mind and body prisoner.

"I can't..." He trembled. "Oh, it was awful. She is a most wretched conniver. I pray to the Lord that he find it in his heart to forgive me."

Joseph began to perspire all over his body. It made him itch beneath his clothing. Even the arches at the bottoms of his feet itched.

"Joseph. Joseph. Stop. You don't have to explain yourself. Forget it. Nothing happened. You resisted. Like I said. I saw the whole thing."

Joseph interjected.

"I just feel like I was... Compromised in a way... Like I had little to no self-control. I... I hated it. I hated the way she made me feel about myself. The way she made me question myself, my faith, my beliefs, my commitment."

Then Joseph thought about being back in that bathroom with Falene and the feelings he felt. He felt ashamed she got to him the way she did.

"I was able to resist. She got to me, to my mind. She really got to me. I'm... I'm ashamed to say. When I left that bathroom I felt pitiable, poor, blind and naked."

Joseph shook, thinking about how close he came to surrendering to his carnal desires.

"Don't think for a second David, that's not what she was striving for." Joseph said, anger swelling in his throat.

He concentrated on a breathing exercise to calm himself down.

Joseph took in a long, deep breath, focusing on his lungs as he inhaled through his nose. He thought about the clean Nebraskan air traveling down into his trachea, then into his bronchi, and eventually ending up in his lungs where it was absorbed by the blood, sending fresh oxygen around his body. He counted to five as he did this.

Joseph held the air there for a moment.

Then he counted back from five as he exhaled the stale air as carbon dioxide.

He did this a couple of times with his eyes closed, in silence, as David watched.

Brother David waited until Joseph was done before speaking to him. "I'm just pointing it out Joseph. Keep that in mind. Remember how vulnerable you are. You, after all, are just a man... Subject to the same temptations as every man." David compassionately reminded.

Father Joseph's stress level came down half a notch. "I know... I know... I've always been strong, in the face of temptation.

But, for some reason, I was really weak for *her*. She beguiled me." Joseph admitted.

"She won my attention with flattery and coaxed me mentally and physically to a place I didn't want to go." The priest shook his head.

"Let's say a prayer David. Pray with me?" Joseph begged, feeling exposed.

He reached for David's hand across the table.

Brother David's body became rigid. He pulled his hands off the table and away, resting both on his lap. "I... I... I don't feel like praying right now." He stated firmly, turning to stare out the window.

Father Joseph found David's response, his refusal to pray with him, odd and out of character. His friend seemed different. Something was wrong. Joseph could sense it.

"David, what is it? Something's not right."

"Nothing Joseph. Nothing. You pray. I don't want to." David looked down, back at his menu. He wasn't interested in participating. This was clear.

Father Joseph, not sure what to think, made the sign of the cross over his body, bowed his head anyway and began quietly praying by himself to St. Jude for help.

"*Most holy Apostle St. Jude, faithful servant and friend of Jesus, the name of the traitor who delivered the beloved Master into the hands of His enemies has caused you to be forgotten by many, but the Church honors and invokes you universally as the patron of hopeless cases, of things despaired of. Pray for me who am so miserable; make use, I implore you, of this particular privilege accorded to you, to bring visible and speedy help, where help is almost despaired of. Come to my assistance in this great need, that I may receive the consolations and succor of Heaven in all my necessities, tribulations and sufferings, particularly with respect to my near failure to resist being tempted by the Devil's Mistress, may I never fall victim in any way to her and her wily ways ever again, and that I may bless God with you and all the elect forever.*

I promise you, O blessed St. Jude, to be ever mindful of this great favor, and I will never cease to honor you as my special and powerful patron and to do all in my power to encourage devotion to you. Amen."

When he was through, the devout and faithful priest rose his head.

David was still reading his menu for absolutely no reason at all.

The sound of small feet made their way to their booth.

"Here 'ya go fellas. Vegan faux-meat pie with soy protein and mushrooms. Two of 'em. Hot and fresh, made to order. Charlie back there, sends his regards. Says he hopes you didn't have to wait too long."

Terri placed both dishes down on the table before the men.

"I see you're still working on your coffees. Anything else I can get you two?" The words came with little to no feeling as if the waitress felt like she was dead inside.

"Yes." Joseph said sympathetically, tears beginning to well up in his eyes.

Terri turned to him with no life behind her eyes.

Joseph got a chill.

"You can tell me what's wrong with you? Why are you so sad?" He asked her sincerely. "I can see it. I really want to know."

Joseph reached up to grab Terri's wrist gently. He looked deeply into her eyes.

David interfered, waving Joseph's hand away from Terri's wrist. "Joseph, let her alone. It's none of our business. We have our own business to take care of."

David seemed adamant Joseph not get into anything personal with Terri.

"I'm sorry Miss." The monk apologized for his friend. "We don't want to bother you."

Joseph wouldn't hear of it. "No. No. I want to know. I mean... Don't feel obligated because I'm a priest. But... I want to know. You seem so sad. And I... I just have a yearning to know why." Joseph told her kindly. "Maybe I... or weeee." Joseph shot a disapproving look to David. "... Can help."

Terri looked around the diner to see if anyone was trying to hail her down for an extra fork, grated cheese or another drink. But everyone seemed fairly satisfied at their tables.

"Well..." Terri slumped down into the booth alongside Joseph and exhaled. "I haven't had a rest all day. This place has been jammed since I got in. It does feel good to sit for a second."

The bright sunshine from the window washed her face of what little color she had.

David wore a pained expression as he watched the two together. Joseph noticed but couldn't for the life of him, understand why this would bother him.

"Tell me Terri. Tell me what's wrong." Joseph delicately tried to get her to open up.

"Well..." She began. "It's my son. Tommy." Terri's voice cracked with great emotion.

Joseph put his arm around Terri, who looked like she was going to fall apart right there and then and break into tears.

"He's sick. Very, very, very sick." Her face crinkled up.

Sure enough her eyes flooded with tears, which began streaming down her face.

Charlie, who'd come out of the kitchen to pour himself another cup of coffee saw. Right back into the kitchen he went, minus the coffee.

Some of the customers began to look over. No one dared call to her for service. They knew her well, knew her story and felt sorry for her, but there was nothing they or anyone else could do to help her.

"Tell me Terri. Tell me what's wrong." Joseph encouraged lovingly.

David interrupted again.

"Joseph. Really. I don't think we should...." David tried persuading Joseph to stop. "... Pry like this."

"David! Let it alone." Joseph warned. "What's wrong with you lately anyway?! This woman needs us. Can't you see that?!"

Brother David backed off.

"Go ahead Terri. I'm listening." Joseph squeezed her skinny shoulders like a dad. "What's wrong with your son Tommy? He's sick? Really quite ill, isn't he?"

Choked up, Terri nodded yes.

"He's going to die the doctors tell me." The poor woman squeaked out the words in syllables. "H.. Hee... He has can...cer. He's been in treatment for a while, but recently he took a turn for the worse." She started to hyperventilate as she thought about the gravity of the situation. "He's all I've got!"

Terri sobbed uncontrollably in full voice.

It was horrible for all the customers in Harry's Lunch Spot to listen to, especially Joseph and David.

"Where's your car dear?" Joseph asked her softly in her ear.

Unable to speak, she pointed out the window.

"O.K. O.K.... It's one of those out there. We're going to go with you Terri to go see your son. Perhaps... Perhaps I can say a prayer for him. Maybe there's something else I or *weeeee...*" Joseph glared at David, like he better go with the program. "... Can do. Who knows. Let's go. Take me to him. To Tommy."

Joseph scooted Terri out of the booth and held her by her arm so she could stand.

Charlie, who appeared more rough and tumble than he was, waved through the cook's window. "I'll take care of things here Terri. Don't worry about it." The cook reassured her.

"Take her wherever she wants to go guys." He motioned with his hand for Joseph and David to guide her out of the diner.

Everyone in the diner looked relieved someone was taking care of her for once.

"See 'ya tomorrow Terri!" In his own way, Charlie let her know he was feeling for her too.

"Tell Tommy Uncle Charlie was askn' for him! And... That I don't know how those Boston Red Sox are gonna do this season against a *real* team... Like my New York Yankees! Them's fightn' words to that kid! He'll get some spunk behind him when he..." Charlie's voice cracked. "When... He hears..." He stopped, unable to finish.

Charlie looked down at his grill behind the cook's window and just waved. He couldn't even look at Terri.

Terri barely cracked a smile.

Joseph and David walked Terri out the front door of the eatery and followed her to her car.

Joseph took the driver's seat, behind the steering wheel of the old Chevy. Terri took the passenger seat aside of him. David got in the back. Everyone putting on their seat belts at the same time.

"St. Joseph's Hospital." Terri said despondently. "Up the road, that way. East, up Route 137."

Joseph pulled out of the parking lot, which really was just a big section of earth where the grass had died because so many cars constantly parked on it.

Up Route 137 they drove. Eastward bound.

Ten minutes into the ride, Terri pointed out the window on Joseph's side.

"That's Jones Farm right there. Chuck and Darlene live in that small white farmhouse set back there."

"Oh. I see." Joseph squinted, studiously inspecting it from the road.

"Those two there... That's Siris and Georgie Girl romping around on the front lawn. They're Basengi's, one of the world's most ancient dog breeds. We don't have those kind of dogs around here. They're a special kind of dog, originally from Africa, because Darlene only wanted a dog that's smart, quiet and doesn't smell. They bought them from an out-of-state breeder."

"Wow. Nice looking dogs. Elegant. Kind of like a miniature deer." Joseph thought.

"Oh yeah, those are their kids." Terri half-laughed. "And they're quiet too... They produce a yodel-like sound, not loud barking. I guess that's what Darlene likes about them. Pretty, huh?"

"They are. I like dogs."

Father Joseph couldn't help but think about Lucky. He wondered where he and Glenn were at this very moment.

Joseph admired the farm as it slowly slid sideways in his driver's side window and eventually moved out of sight.

"Great guy. Mr. Jones. He and his wife Darlene. What a lovely set up they have here."

"Yup. Been here their whole lives. They're in the diner every day around this time, socializing with the regulars. They grow soybean. That's what was in your dish today... Soy protein. From their farm."

Joseph smiled. "Oh.. O.K. How convenient. They supply your diner with local produce." The priest found the lifestyle here in this part of the country quaint, simple and wonderful.

David, still sitting in the backseat, offered nothing to the conversation.

For twenty-minutes they drove. All three mostly strangers to each other, heading for a local hospital where an innocent child lie in critical condition, fighting for his life as cancer ravaged his body.

CHAPTER 29

THE SOUL OF MANKIND FEELS ITS WORTH

"Right here." Terri pointed to the Visitor Parking entrance for Joseph to pull her car into.

They'd finally arrived at St. Joseph's Hospital.

"He's in here." A grief-stricken Terri said. "In this big, cold, building... My son's life hangs in the balance between life and death." She described, staring up at the many floors of the hospital through the windshield.

"Just park anywhere and I'll take you up." Terri instructed in a deadened voice.

"O.K." Father Joseph kept his eyes open for a spot.

As Terri opened her handbag to search for a tissue, Joseph got a peek inside. Nestled among a wallet, hairbrush, papers, hand lotion and numerous other personal effects was a small black Bible with a gold cross on its cover. A pink, silk bookmark marked a place for her.

Joseph wondered if there was a specific reason that very place was marked in her reading. Perhaps a favorite passage or prayer.

Terri, rummaging through her large sack of a purse, pushed her Bible to the side along with her other belongings to reach for a pocket size packet of white facial tissues before heading into the hospital.

"Here we go." She said, shoving the plastic covered packet into her pocket. "These days... Never *don't* need these."

Father Joseph had now learned something new about Terri, she was a religious woman. He liked that.

The priest smiled warmly at his new friend as he continued surveying the parking lot for a free space.

"Ready?" She asked.

David, speaking for the first time the whole car ride, made an unfeeling statement from the backseat. "I'm going to wait in the car for a minute. I'll be right up."

Frustrated, Joseph peered at David in the rearview mirror.

"Why David?"

Brother David, avoiding Joseph's glare in the mirror, turned his head to look out his backseat window. "I have something to do first. I'll be up in a minute. What floor Terri?" David asked, redirecting the conversation.

"He's on the fourth floor." She said, drained.

She temporarily paused.

"But... But... I..." Her nose wrinkled. "... Wish it were me there instead." Terri buried her face in her hands, whispering the words with a great deal of anguish. "I would give anything to take his place. He doesn't deserve this!" She wailed in the car.

The truth of how sick her son truly was, reduced her to tears once again.

She pulled the packet of tissues back out of her pocket and pulled a single one from the bunch, wiping her eyes.

"See... Told you. Never *don't* need these."

Joseph and David sat in silence as she collected herself.

Terri leaned forward in her seat to look up at the tall, imposing hospital as Joseph drove her car around the lot. This was where her son's life might end. She loathed the sight of it.

"David, when you walk in through the main entrance you'll notice the Information Desk straight ahead of you. Walk past... Beyond that, you'll see the elevators. Take any one up to the fourth floor. That's where the Pediatric Oncology Wing is and all the pediatric cancer patients, like my son are." Terri explained.

"When you come off the elevator, walk toward the Survivor Clinic. There's a big sign. You can't miss it. Go past that to the Nurse's Station. When you're there, just ask for Tommy. He's on a first name basis with everyone." She smiled, proud of how easily her son made friends with his bright, cheery personality. "They'll know who you're talking about."

David was clear on the directions to Tommy's room. "Thanks. See you in a few minutes."

Joseph pulled Terri's Chevy into a parking spot right in the front row and quite close to the main entrance of St. Joseph's.

"See that Terri. We're lucky today. Look at this... Right in." There was just enough room to squeeze Terri's vehicle in between two trucks.

"One of the last times we were here..." Terri reflected. "We were here for Tommy to have his chemotherapy... Afterward, he tried to race me to the car... We were headed out to get ice cream after his treatment."

Joseph listened with a sympathetic ear.

"He wanted strawberry." She sobbed, pressing her tissue to her nose.

"I know. I know dear." Joseph consoled, reaching over to rub her shoulder. "It must be so hard. I too lost someone recently. Let's go inside. I'd like to meet Tommy."

Joseph put the car in park and shut it off.

Terri nodded that was a good idea and unbuckled her seat belt.

"David, we'll see you inside later. Fourth floor. Remember?" Terri repeated to David from the front seat.

Brother David acknowledged it in the rear view mirror first so Joseph could see him. "Yes Terri. I'll be up shortly."

Joseph and Terri could hear David unbuckle his seat belt as well.

As Father Joseph and Terri exited the car, they walked toward the main entrance.

Looking back to see David still sitting in the backseat of Terri's car, another car in the parking lot caught Joseph's attention in the corner of his eye.

A red car.

The priest took a good look at it as Terri continued walking ahead of him.

Sure enough, it *was* a red car. A red car he'd seen just hours before.

A faded red 1957 Thunderbird convertible sat parked all by itself in the very back row of the hospital parking lot, far in the corner. No other car near it.

"She's here. Falene's here." Father Joseph said under his breath in a despising tone. "Not only do I know she was driving that car today... I can *feel* her here."

Father Joseph could just about make out the plate from the distance he was at. The car had authentic Nebraskan state license plates. The vehicle registration plate reading APR 532.

There had to be symbolism in the letters and numbers on the plate of Falene's car, but he didn't know what. He'd seen that number before, 532.

"532, 532. Where have I seen...?" He thought out loud.

"The Italian Airlines flight number!" Joseph realized. "It was 5-3-2-1! That's it. That's where I've seen that number before. It has something to do with me... This place. Something."

This number kept popping up for him. The number 532 was significant to him for some reason. It was undeniable.

He wondered if David knew all along that that was Falene driving past the cornfield in that very same car earlier, as they hid in the cornrow. Did he see her car here now? The reason he opted to stay behind?

Joseph had no way of knowing but he surmised.

This made perfect sense. She'd been driving East along Route 137 when he and David saw her race by.

She obviously didn't stop at the diner, so she must have continued straight up the road here, to St. Joseph's Hospital.

The pious and ostentatiously virtuous man of God knew more about Falene now, after their meeting in the Pope's Private Quarters.

Joseph knew for fact that Falene had willingly sold her soul to Satan and his Rebellion. That she had been one of the many cherry-picked by the Devil and with great deliberation, to come into his service to help him reach his impious goal... To destroy all of mankind and the Earth.

If she was here, then this must be where Father Joseph was meant to be. Something must be here that Falene wanted to interfere with.

Then Joseph had a flashback to something Brother David told him.

He remembered about what the ancient Tibetan seers saw.

On the plane, David informed him that a child or children born of the Breast of Heaven and the Groin of Hell would either be conceived or born into the world and would... " ...Originate from a place that is the precise latitude on earth as the origin of the creator of a scroll that is the direct word of the Messiah. The precise latitude of the birthplace of a *chosen one*, selected by a member of the highest order of angels in Heaven. The precise latitude where a child cradles the entire world in his hands."

He also remembered what David revealed about the forty-one degree north latitude.

Kismet, Nebraska fit the bill.

Then it became evident to him.

This must be where... "... A child cradles the entire world in his hands... Therefore is the location where a child or children born of the Breast of Heaven and the Groin of Hell would originate from."

Everything else had come true. He felt positive that the rest would as well, although the details of how weren't clear to him yet.

They were here along the forty-one degree north latitude. A child, whom he was drawn to for some unexplainable reason, was inside the hospital.

This was part of his destiny. He knew he was where he was meant to be. Where he was *always* destined to wind up.

Something lead him here because he had a job to do.

Now Joseph just had to figure out the rest of the puzzle.

How did the child who lie dying in a hospital bed here at St. Joseph's hospital cradle the entire world in his hands? How would *another* child or children, with Heaven *and* Hell as his or her or their parents, possibly come into this world?

Father Joseph's mission here, his fate, was beginning to show itself.

"Oh my goodness." Joseph uttered a sigh to himself.

He placed his fingertips to his chin.

"I've come here to learn the reason I live."

Hearing himself, he sharply drew in breath in astonishment.

Every nerve in his body caught fire as though the myelin sheath insulating the nerves in his body had disintegrated, leaving them exposed and able to feel intense sensations.

All up and down Joseph's body felt hot and tingly.

The priest could feel everything his body was capable of feeling... Of thinking. All at once it seemed.

"There is a *reason* I live." He said, fully aware. "I live for a reason. There is something inside of me... I've always known it was there... It's the reason I have always felt invincible. It's because I always knew I was."

His mouth became dry.

"There is a *reason* I live."

He turned around.

Standing there in the parking lot before the multi-story hospital, Joseph craned his neck back to look up. In contrast to the gorgeous bright blue sky, he saw white puffy clouds passing over the top of the building.

He pondered what unearthly event would happen inside the sterile-looking structure serving as temporary home to the sick, infirm and dying.

God had called him here. So be here he would.

The soul of mankind was feeling its worth as Joseph allowed himself to feel the worth and weight of *his* soul.

But he had a strange feeling. Something inside him told him he might face his own mortality within the walls of this building.

This man of the cloth who'd come so far in his life, who'd learned so much asked himself a single question.

"Do I know who I am?" He asked out loud, his eyes darting all over the place.

Joseph shut his eyes and concentrated.

In darkness he took in the sound of the wind wrestling the tree tops, shaking their branches bare of leaves, as autumn closed in.

"Do I *know* who I am?"

He thought about that profound question carefully, meditating on it.

"Come on Joseph!" Terri called. "Over here!"

Startled, Father Joseph opened his eyes to look at her.

She was waving to him from the front entrance.

"He'll be in! Don't worry about David! He knows where to come, I told him!" Terri hollered across the parking lot. She thought that's why Joseph stopped, to see if David was coming yet.

Little did she know.

"Come on!"

Father Joseph swallowed hard.

"Here I come!" He trotted his big thickset body toward her and to her side.

Both Terri and her new friend the clergyman walked in through the hospital's main entrance and hustled their way through the lobby, heading for the elevators.

One was free.

Once inside, Terri pressed the number four on the rectangular metal panel inside the elevator.

Up it went, never stopping until it hit the fourth floor.

"Ding." It chimed pleasantly.

As the doors slid open and they exited onto the Pediatric Oncology Wing, Joseph immediately noticed a striking painting through a glass window in a segregated area.

It took his breath away.

A life-size portrait of an angel.

Portrayed in a manner he'd never seen or considered before.

Yet the painting, the image of the angel in it, felt like it had been a part of him his whole life. In fact, he felt like he *was* the celestial being in the painting.

He couldn't take his eyes off the bold work. He was hypnotized as they walked toward it.

"Oh, that's the Survivor Clinic. Tommy's not in there. This way." Terri tugged at Joseph's sleeve.

Joseph looked up seeing the sign, Survivor Clinic, over the door exactly as she'd described to Brother David.

"Wait.... I... That picture there. I want to see that." Joseph pulled back, stopping in the aisle.

"Isn't that gorgeous?" Terri admired through the glass. "Tommy said it's the most beautiful painting he's ever seen. He says the artist drew the angel in *his* image and represents who he is inside. He came up with that all by himself! What an imagination. Little does he know it was painted long before his great-grandmother was born, or even thought of."

Blowing her nose, she barely had enough strength to chuckle.

Although Joseph didn't say it... The painting reminded him of *himself*. It was odd she said Tommy felt it depicted an image of him as well.

"Want to hear something bizarre?" Terri asked Joseph.

He turned his head to her.

"I feel like I've met that guy. I met someone recently, that looks just like him... This angel here. It reminds me of *him*. I swear it." She pointed. "Isn't that weird? Never seen him around here before. Strange person, but very pleasant to be around. Gave me something to hold on to."

"I want to see it close up. Can we stop in there?" Joseph asked Terri, walking to it regardless.

"I know I sound like I'm loony. Heck, maybe I am by now. Forget I said that. I think my mind is... I don't know. Sure. We can go in there."

An emotionally bankrupt Terri opened the door to the Survivor Clinic and welcomed Joseph inside.

"This is where Tommy comes... or used to come... when he felt better, to talk about his illness. Tommy has Neuroblastoma, the most common extracranial solid cancer in childhood and the most common cancer for infants."

The overworked, underpaid waitress with a son on his deathbed broke down again. A regular, daily occurrence for her.

"Terri I'm sorry."

"Tommy's high-risk." She shared. "Meaning it's difficult to cure even with the most intensive therapies available in this country."

Joseph could feel her pain.

"When he was up for it, he came here to the Survivor Clinic to talk with other kids about what it's like to be sick. What they miss out on because they're too ill to participate in anything. Basically, how it stinks in every way possible. There's a lot of doctors and nurses here that provide the patients and survivors with specialized medical care and psychosocial support. They are wonderful people. Couldn't have gotten this far without them."

Terri's voice trailed off as depression strangled her spirit.

"But... anyway. This painting. It's captivating, isn't it? Tommy certainly thinks so. My little boy used to come in here even when he didn't have to be in here, to sit on that chair right there..." She pointed to which one.

"... And stare at it."

Joseph walked right up to the painting.

A brass plate affixed to the bottom of the frame read *Warrior Angel*. The name of the artist beneath that, *C. Caparrelli*.

What a sight to behold. Warrior Angel.

Joseph's eyes traced every line, every curve and every expressive and vivid color that the artist passionately created.

He was in love with it.

Terri gave Joseph a bit of history behind the six-foot tall oil painting, an ornate gold frame bordering the picture.

Joseph stared at it awestruck, immersed in it.

"This picture is apparently very old. 1800's I think. It was donated by the wife of a deceased local state Senator. The estate had a great deal of wealth after he died. Cash, jewelry, cars and lots of artwork. The late Senate President collected millions of dollars worth of art, most of it housed in a warehouse in Lincoln. All of it went to his wife, Mary Ann."

Joseph, very much interested in the story behind the painting, listened to her.

"Well... I guess when the wife passed away, she donated this piece to St. Joseph's Hospital, to be hung specifically on the Pediatric Oncology floor. She and her husband lost a child early on in their marriage. Cancer." Terri's lip stiffened.

"This was her gift to the Pediatric Oncology Wing."

"Know anything about the painter? Caparrelli?" Joseph asked.

"No. Nothing."

"She is a virtuoso of fine art. A master storyteller." He could see.

Joseph observed Caparrelli's work closer, hoping to see what she saw in her mind when she put her brush to canvas.

Caparrelli strived to paint with a bold color scheme, using complex shading and tinting techniques. She developed contrasts in her oil painting with warm and cool colors.

Joseph had never been so moved by any painting in his life. Not even by Leonardo daVinci's famous masterpiece, the Mona Lisa at the Musee du Louvre in Paris. That was perhaps the most famous painting in the world.

He'd never beheld such a staggering but fascinating image of an angel in ancient or even modern day artwork.

It was triumphant and inspiring and heart-wrenching and sorrowful all at the same time.

The Warrior Angel, behind brittle varnish weighing on the painting's surface, stood tanned on a yellowing hill of tall withering grass. An ominous overcast sky taunting him over his shoulders. He was tall and muscular with a medium build, blessed with a handsome, delicately painted facial complexion and a head of thick wavy hair. Wide brown leather straps criss crossed his chest. A small piece of fine, sheer, white fabric wrapped around his waist, to cover his groin. Worn sandals adorned his feet. At his ankles, thin golden leather ties snaked up his calves, crossing his shins in intersecting lines, leaving a deep impression in his skin. Most impressive of all... Out of the middle of his back sprouted enormous and magnificent white feathered wings.

But unlike how people usually think of angels and see them glorified in expensive artwork, the Warrior Angel was all dirty, beaten, burned, battered, scratched and bruised. The wild lion-heart staring down, brave and courageous from his place on the wall. Ready for battle.

The reserved seraph with confident defiance in his face and brazen determination in his eyes had bleeding cuts marring his beautiful face and body. His perfect skin was blemished with dark blue and black bruises, which dotted his strong physique. Too many to count.

Somehow during a brutal conflict, his right wing had been viciously severed to the bone. The site of the wound spilling his blood down his backside, coloring the ground below red. Cut almost totally off, his wing hung down low to his feet... Broken and permanently unusable.

He looked like he'd crusaded to the lake of fire and back again.

There was something unseen in the painting that Joseph could sense. The Warrior Angel was surrounded by someone or something evil, he was poised to challenge. Whomever or whatever it was remained out of frame. Caparrelli never included it in the portrait.

Only she could see his hardship and knew the dreadful opposition which lie before him. She and those who understood the important role this angel was serving. That which remained out of frame was evil itself. In any form.

The Warrior Angel had been called by God to defend Him and slay His enemies... Those who'd gone over to the side of the Beast. This was his eternal plight.

He was the defender of humanity.

His job would never end until evil itself was eradicated from the world.

Willing to fight to his death against what he saw as wicked and wrong.

Joseph wanted to walk away from it. Every muscle and joint in his body ached to be taken from the image of the angel who committed himself to such a heavy burden.

Joseph couldn't move. He identified with the angel, and his affinity for him held him there.

Caparrelli communicated the true message of the painting in the expression on the face of her subject.

Unrelenting perseverance.

The Warrior Angel rose to challenges a hero would beg to be spared.

As badly as he'd suffered, this valiant messenger of God persisted. As continually tested as he was, he wouldn't give up and as daunting as his mission was, he never lost his nerve to fight the good fight.

All in the name of God.

There was a look of unquestionable faith in his face. Faith in himself. Faith in his beliefs. Faith in God.

The portrait of the angel, Joseph could see, was not about angels. Nor was it about war.

It was about perseverance in the face of the impossible.

It was about *knowing* who you are and holding true to it, no matter the personal cost.

It was the most inspiring piece of art Joseph had ever laid eyes upon.

The Warrior Angel.

Depending on who viewed the painting, the impression it left varied. For those who align themselves with the Lord, feeling they bare the same mission in life as the angel, the painting was exhilarating, uplifting and inspiring.

For those devoid of spirituality, those unwilling or too weak to rebuke God's chief enemy and his followers and those who were out of touch with their human soul; *they* felt guilt and shame and intimidation when looking into the penetrating eyes of The Warrior Angel.

For they who mentally and spiritually fornicate with God's nemesis... *They* felt impassioned with rage when they viewed the portrait.

Joseph then thought about the artist.

Who was she? What inspired her to come up with such a vision of an angel? Was her painting strictly a visionary work?

"Has to be... visionary... made up from her imagination."

"What's that?" Terri asked still standing there, thinking Joseph had asked her something.

"Uh... nothing. Nothing. I'm just trying to get into the mind of this C. Caparrelli, the woman who painted this."

The priests eyes lifted to the Warrior Angel's face once again.

He made an astounding discovery as he studied the angel's face.

"Well... I'll be... Can't be." Joseph couldn't believe he'd missed it, even when Terri said she'd met someone who looked just like the angel in the painting.

"I can't believe I didn't notice this before." He said.

"Terri. You said you met a man around here who looked just like him?" Joseph asked her.

"Yeah. Nice guy. Never saw him around here before. What was his name?" She searched her memory.

"Recently?" He quizzed.

"Yeah. Yeah. Once at the diner. Then again one day, not too long ago, when I was leaving the hospital with Tommy."

As Father Joseph stared at the angel's face he knew who C. Caparrelli had painted.

The portrait wasn't a creation from her imagination.

C. Caparrelli had a live subject.

Glenn.

The Warrior Angel was Glenn. Depicted as who he really is... Not as how he presents himself to mere mortals here on earth.

There was more to Glenn and more to the artist C. Caparrelli than met the eye.

CHAPTER 30

ENDURING THAT WHICH A HERO WOULD BEG TO BE SPARED

"Come on Joseph. Let's go see Tommy. This way." Terri had to pry Joseph from the painting in the Survivor Clinic.

"Come on. I'm sure David will be up shortly. He'll find his way." She reassured him, just in case that's what was keeping Joseph.

She didn't realize it was the message the Warrior Angel communicated to him that had a dominating influence over him.

"I want you to meet Tommy with me, alone first." She tugged at his sleeve again.

"Sure. Sure." Joseph tore himself away from the portrait for her sake. "Which way?"

Exiting, Terri led Joseph down the long hospital corridor, past the nurse's station and to Tommy's room.

"Here we are." Terri said, moving over to the right side of the hall. "This is his room, right at the end."

She gently pushed his patient room door open.

"Tommy has a private room." She whispered. "But he might be asleep right now. Shhhhhhh... Let's see."

Terri peeked her head in. Sure enough. Tommy was out like a light.

A nurse with her back to the door, hovered over him. Terri had never seen her before. She was doing something to her son, Terri wasn't sure what.

Still holding the door slightly ajar, she informed Joseph as she watched. "He's with a nurse. Let's wait 'til she's done."

She backed away quietly, allowing the door to close for privacy.

But it was just enough time for a terrible odor from inside Tommy's room to leak out into the hallway.

"OOoohhhhhhhffffffff!" Terri drew her head back. "That smell! What is that smell?!" She waved her hand in front of her nose.

Terri looked back at Tommy's closed door, not able to identify what would cause the room to reek like that.

"Did you smell that?" She asked Joseph. "It's... It's a foul, stale smell! What the heck is she doing in there?!"

Holding his nose closed, Father Joseph concurred. "Dreadful."

Joseph's radar went up. He certainly had an idea of who was in the room with Tommy, but he didn't want to scare Terri.

So he kept his mouth shut.

"Sure. We can wait 'til she's done Terri. How about right here. A chair for you and a chair for me." Joseph tapped the top of one of two seats just outside Tommy's room.

"What the heck is she doing in there?" She said again. "That stench is just awful!" Terri couldn't get the smell out of her nose.

It lingered in the hallway. Joseph tried to get her to focus on something else.

Terri and Father Joseph took a seat against the wall just outside Tommy's door to wait until the nurse was through.

Directly across the hall from where they sat was a waiting area.

"Want to go sit over there? Where it's more comfortable?" Terri suggested. "Couches, magazines and plants..."

Father Joseph wanted nothing to do with it.

"No. Here's fine. This way we can hear if anything goes on in Tommy's room." He stated flatly.

Terri thought it an odd response.

"O.K. sure. Here is fine. We can still see the T.V. from here anyway. So that's good."

From where they sat they could easily see and hear the television set in the waiting area, suspended high in the corner with black brackets.

The news was on.

"Hey look!" Terri called Joseph to the segment that was on. "There's more on that story!"

She seemed overly enthusiastic about it.

Joseph looked perplexed. "What...? What story...?"

Terri gave him an abbreviated version.

"Oh... You might not have seen it. It seems there was this tribe of... Of... I guess they were villagers that lived in a far-removed settlement in the jungle. They say, the news reporters say, they all went missing or were killed... Or evacuated for some unknown reason. Basically, disappeared right off the face of the earth. No one knows where they went."

"Hmmnnhhh. Do you know where this is? Where they're showing right now?" Joseph's interest in the story grew.

"Somewhere in Asia, I think." She replied, half-sure.

The priest took a harder look at the television, hoping to learn more. They had nothing else to do but wait anyway.

Just then, Tommy's mother reached down for her big sack of a purse.

She scrambled the contents of her bag until she found what it was she was looking for.

Out came the small black Bible with the gold cross on it's cover. The pink, silk bookmark still marking her place. She placed it on her lap, stroking its cover with her hand, as she watched.

Joseph was still dying to know which page was marked.

Bold text appeared at the lower left-hand corner of the television screen. It read, Asia.

"Oh. I was right. Asia. I wonder if they ever found out where those people went? Or, what happened to them? Oh, you should see where they live... The close ups of that place. It's unbelievably gorgeous. Almost like a Garden of Eden. A heaven on earth. I hope they show it. So you can see..." She smiled, breathing a heavy sigh. "Experts call them *uncontacted,* a *lost* tribe, and it's the last group of it's kind in the world."

With one ear to Terri, another to the broadcast, and his sixth sense trained on Tommy's room, Joseph listened.

"Tommy and I watched a news story about this together. He loved it too. Said he wanted to go there. Swing on the trees with the monkeys. Can you believe that?" Terri sniffled. "As sick as he was, he wanted to explore that place, investigate everything there and... According to him, swing on the trees with the monkeys. That's just the type of kid he is."

Her nose began to run.

Terri pulled her personal-size packet of tissues back out of her pocket to peel off a fresh one from the bunch.

"I told him we had to concentrate on getting him better first." She cried quietly. "But that I wished I could. I'd already told him we couldn't go to Disney World because of his cancer. So *he* thought... Maybe I'd take him there instead. I don't think Tommy ever fully understood how sick he is."

She put her head down, looking to her Bible for comfort, passing her hand over it again.

In a guilt-ridden voice she condemned herself. "He was frustrated with me, because I said I couldn't take him right now. I should have told him I *would*. Just a little white lie... What would it have hurt?"

More long, wet tears streamed down her face.

There was nothing Joseph could say or do to comfort her. Her son was dying and chances were... Things weren't turning around.

"There! There it is! See. Just like I said."

Archive video of the village came up on the screen.

Father Joseph now saw what had Terri so enamored with the crude village he saw on the television.

The remote settlement, tucked away within the most isolated part of the wild impenetrable land, sat upon a ring-shaped clearing. Shabby teepee style tents dotted the dirt floor of the modest colony and what appeared to be four-hundred-year old trees surrounded the village, forming an imposing border. The towering trees and vegetation of a prehistoric-age era dwarfed everything else in comparison. The primitive people there, peacefully going about their business.

"Peace. Peace and harmony lives there." Joseph stated.

An older hispanic male broadcaster who was greying at the temples introduced an update for viewers.

"We have a special report for you now. Coming to us live via satellite is Avis Gallagher, The Indigenous Peoples Foundation Spokesperson. She's on the scene and has more for us about what may have happened to this *lost* tribe which were fully aware of the outside world, but chose isolation for as long as they've been in existence. Also, what eyewitnesses say they saw. Avis."

"Thanks Norberto. We have no concrete evidence to say where these people went for sure, but based on reports from witnesses, their disappearance may have been divine in nature."

Avis fiddled with her lapel mic. on her collar and continued.

"Now I know this sounds a bit far-fetched, and I must agree it is, but witnesses who live on the other side of the jungle say they were passing through a portion of the jungle about twenty miles Northeast of the missing tribe's village, and that's where we are right now, when they came across something they've never seen before. If you look over my shoulder right now, you'll see what I'm talking about as my photographer zooms in."

The cameraman pulled away from her and got a tight shot of something behind her in the distance.

On the screen Terri and Joseph saw a big, blindingly bright beam of sunlight breaking through the clouds from the sky and touching down upon earth.

"This beam of light you're seeing... believe it or not ladies and gentlemen... May have something to do with it." Avis explained.

Terri froze.

She reached for her bag again, pulling another piece of literature out. Her Bible still firmly planted in her lap.

"Those witnesses, through translators, tell us a group of people, described to look exactly like the tribe of villagers that went missing from this location, that you at home have seen in our archive video, came here to this site and sat and waited for days."

Terri gulped.

"... And..." Avis looking like she wasn't sure she believed what she was reporting.

"... And... Well... eventually disappeared from this very spot." She reported with a question in her voice. "Without ever moving."

Gallagher gathered her thoughts.

"They say, now again I can't confirm this to be true, but *they,* the witnesses say... They saw the villagers sitting in a circle together in this very patch of land where the large ray of sunlight is still coming down, before the ray of sunlight ever appeared. Once it did, they simply vanished."

The anchor had a question everyone at home wanted to know.

"Avis, did they say if the villagers were saying anything at the time? Doing anything? Because this sounds very supernatural. Critics will speculate this is a hoax of some kind. Isn't it possible they got up from the area and relocated?"

"No Norberto. The witnesses insist the villagers sat there quietly as if they knew something unearthly and miraculous was going to happen. Like they were called to the spot, and waited there for something to happen. It seemed they knew what it was that was going to happen. No talking, no eating, no drinking, no moving. Just sitting. The witnesses, who by the way are afraid and have asked not to be identified, say they knew it looked odd so they kept an eye on the tribe for days until the giant beam of light appeared and then, they report, the tribe slowly disappeared into thin air within the brilliance of the giant ray. They are positive it has something to do with God and Heaven. They are terrified."

Terri reached over to Joseph. She grabbed his knee.

Both took their attention away from the television set for a moment.

She opened the other piece of literature she'd retrieved from her purse and quickly found a place in it.

"I read many books Father. The Bible, novels and a whole bunch of other stuff. I'm fascinated with religion and the world and people. In my spare time I'm always reading, always trying to learn."

Terri looked down into her book.

"I keep this book with me because I am fascinated by many of the ideas within." The waitress tapped a page with her fingernail. "There is a legacy of end-of-days prophecies, many of which are biblical in origin."

She looked at him frightened.

Terri caught her breath. So much was happening.

She read. "It is believed that the time before the end of days... Will be marked by a special light which will shine down to earth from the Heavens. It will come at a time when many natural and other catastrophic events will take place on the earth."

Fear ignited in her eyes.

"Like we see on T.V. Joseph, every time we turn on the news. Bad news. It's literally in our faces. This is... That time. We *are* at the end of days."

Father Joseph patted Terri's hand on his knee and embraced it within his.

"Terri... I." He began.

"Wait. There's more." She interrupted, turning the pages to another part in her book.

She pointed to a picture for Joseph to look at.

"Saint Malachy, right here. See him?"

"Yes." Joseph answered, inspecting the person in the picture.

He already knew of him, but remained tight lipped.

"He was the first Irish Saint canonized by a Pope, Pope Clement III. He was said to have been blessed with many powers bestowed upon him by the Almighty. One of those powers, the power of prophecy. Well, in the 12th Century, Saint Malachy had one well-documented vision. In that vision he said he saw the entire line of popes from his day until the end of time."

Joseph looked at her with great sadness in his eyes.

"The last pope he saw..." Terri dragged out her sentence, afraid to finish.

"... Was Satan in the form, of man." Joseph finished her sentence for her.

"You know?" She gasped.

He shook his head yes.

"It is this "person" who is the long-anticipated Antichrist." He confirmed. "Or... *working* for the Antichrist. Either way, that last Pope... is the one doing Satan's work, to help bring an end to mankind and the world itself."

Joseph saw Victor and Falene in his mind.

Terri added. "Yes and when *He* comes in glory it is the Final Judgement, the end of this world."

Terri's voice grew hoarse.

"The years before such a manifestation there will be a special light from Heaven. Like we see there." She pointed to the television.

Both looked to the T.V., still broadcasting images of the giant beam of light coming down from the Heavens.

Terri's mouth slowly opened to speak as thoughts raced through her mind. "To purify and prepare for this time on earth, there will be many natural and other disasters which will take place."

One simple statement said it all.

"They knew." She said.

"They already knew and they were waiting. They've been taken. That's where they went." She smiled. "For some reason, because they were so good. Maybe better than the rest of us... One with the earth... One with the Lord. Living the way man was always meant to live. Simple. Pure. With love always in their hearts. They were called there to be taken home."

A single tear rolled down Terri's cheek.

Father Joseph who was so sad to see Terri bear more pain, took her tissue from her to wipe her cheek clean of the teardrop.

There was something else Terri wanted to show Joseph.

The modest waitress with more intellect than one might guess, grabbed her Bible still sitting on her lap and opened it to the place marked by the pink, silk ribbon.

Joseph glanced over.

"By the way... Where are you at in your reading? That place... marked there." He finally had the courage to pry.

Terri looked to her page.

"About the apostasy." She said hesitantly. "This also seems to be fitting in to what's going on in our world today."

"The apostasy." Joseph's curiosity peaked. "Interesting."

With Joseph being a religious man, obviously. Terri felt obligated to explain what she'd learned so far and run it by him for his opinion.

"Yes... The apostasy, which is prophesied by the Bible to occur before the rapture, the tribulation and the rise of the Antichrist. You know... You know all this far better than I do. I would only hope to understand the Bible's passages as well as you." She smiled through her pain.

"If you'd be so kind. Read me a passage." He winked.

"O.K. Let's see... Here, 1 Timothy 4:1-2." She pointed to a place on the page, reading a quote... *"Now the Spirit speaketh expressly, that in the latter times some shall depart from the faith, giving heed to seducing spirits, and doctrines of devils; Speaking lies in hypocrisy; having their conscience seared with a hot iron."*

Joseph paused.

"Your understanding of apostasy is what?" Joseph wanted to hear her put it into her own words.

"Well... It's supposed to involve a departing from the faith by those who call themselves Christians, but who are not really true Christians. Regarding the second coming of Christ."

Terri furiously flipped to another page in her Bible. That place was marked by a folded page corner.

"Here. Paul said in 2 Thessalonians 2:3... *Let no man deceive you by any means: for that day shall not come, except there come a falling away first, and that man of sin be revealed, the son of perdition."*

Terri looked at Joseph to see what he was thinking.

"Apostasy is defined here in the Bible as, I would say... a defection from the truth. A renunciation of one's religion and principles. Am I right?"

The impressed priest nodded she was correct in her understanding.

More confident in herself now, Terri elaborated. “I think we see in our world today, just watch the news, that human nature is enticed by teachings or desires that deny the true gospel. It’s all coming together. All of this... In my reading. It’s all coming together. This is all happening in the now.”

Joseph agreed with a heavy heart. “Sadly Terri. I think you’re right. It seems evident that we are *this very day* in a time of apostasy as well as at the end of days. The collective human spirit has pushed aside sound biblical teaching for heretical doctrines based on social gospel rather than the gospel of the Lord.”

He’d given her all he could without revealing *all* that he knew.

Little did his friend know her own son played a role in what would happen next.

The waitress who’d always felt like a second-class citizen due to her lack of education and low-skill job, felt smart and accepted around the priest. He was easy to be with. Like someone she could talk to anytime, about anything.

“The good news...” Terri perked up a tad as if she had an instinct about something.

“... It is said that prophets are sent, especially during times of apostasy.”

Joseph said nothing. He let her finish her thought.

“Perhaps one is here now. A divinely inspired teacher, an interpreter of God’s will. Here to speak for all of us. Maybe even to represent us. To show the Lord who we *really* are, who mankind *really* is.”

Joseph looked upon her warmly.

“Maybe Terri. You never know.” Joseph playfully leaned against her shoulder. “We may very well be in the time of apostasy, one which will be the climax of all previous apostate tendencies throughout history.”

“That smell... It’s still around, just hanging in the air.” She noticed suddenly. “Gosh it’s bad and it’s not going away.”

"The source of the odor is still here. That's why." Father Joseph blurted out.

Terri just looked at him. How could he possibly know what the source of the smell was? She didn't know.

The fidgety clergyman adjusted himself in his chair. The plastic seat so hard, his bottom was beginning to get sore.

Father Joseph turned his head and leaned back in his chair, so he could better hear what was going on inside Tommy's room.

Joseph knew he couldn't make any sudden moves or say anything to Terri, or she would just fall apart. She was ever so fragile. Right now he didn't need to anyway.

So he waited, just listening and observing. He knew that he'd know when he needed to act.

Just beyond the door, Joseph could hear the nurse saying something to little Tommy in his hospital room.

He concentrated on the female voice as Terri remained engrossed in the news program.

In a very kind, pleasant tone the nurse was reading a poem over Tommy as he lie critically ill in his hospital bed.

God sees you getting tired Tommy
A cure is not to be
So he's wrapping His arms around you
And whispering 'Come with Me.'
With tearful eyes
We watch you suffer
And see you fading away
Although your mom loves you dearly
She cannot make you stay.

Your golden heart will stop beating
Hard playing hands need to rest
God is breaking our hearts to prove to us
He only takes the best.

"Why you..." He grumbled, restraining himself.

He recognized the voice.

It *was* Falene. As usual, his instincts were right on from the moment Terri said a nurse was in with Tommy.

She was reciting a popular poem used to honor and remember the dead, but guilefully changing the words.

Joseph squirmed in his seat. He didn't want Terri to hear this. Thankfully, she was still focused on the news program.

He listened attentively to what else Falene was saying.

"God is spitting you out of his mouth, Tommy."

Father Joseph's eyes grew wide, his jaw in mid-drop.

"Why I'll..." He gritted his teeth with contempt. Falene was trying to get Tommy's subconscious to pick up her melodic voice and the meaning of her words, hoping his organs and then his body would systematically shut down upon command.

Father Joseph could hear a faint wheezing coming from the room. Tommy was having difficulty breathing. "The cancer must have spread to his chest," Joseph thought.

He clenched his fists, as Falene continued.

"I ask you to buy from me... Gold refined in the fire of my Master. Become rich Tommy. I stand at your door and knock. Hear my voice Tommy. Let me come into your house to eat with you, and you with me. Sit near my Master on his throne, just as I sit down near him. Hear what I say. Hear what I say."

Joseph knew he had to act and act immediately. Tommy was struggling to get air into his lungs. He was beginning to labor.

Falene's subliminal messages were reaching Tommy's subconscious. His health worsening every second longer she stayed with him.

Falene was trying to get Tommy to give up on life and die.

"But was her real goal to then steal his soul?" The idea passed through Father Joseph's mind.

The intuitive priest had the overwhelming sense that his time had come.

"Die Tommy. Die." He could hear Falene whisper into Tommy's ear as he lie helpless and innocent in his hospital bed.

Falene's voice grew louder and more sinister as she tried to force Tommy to relinquish his life. "You're a burden to your mother Tommy. Release her. Allow her to live her life. Unburden her of you and your sickness. *Die*, so she may *live*. Come with me to a place where you will live eternally. Where you will do the hurting instead of others or diseases hurting you. Be the King of your own Kingdom. I promise this to you."

That was it.

Joseph got up from his chair.

Stone faced, he spoke to Terri sternly but compassionately. "Wait here Terri."

Tommy's mother looked baffled.

"No matter what you hear inside. Don't come in there." He said, aiming his index finger at Tommy's door.

Terri blinked nervously not sure if she should agree to something she didn't fully understand. She was Tommy's protector since the day he was born. He was her number one priority in life. "Uhhhh...."

Joseph was adamant. "Do you hear me Terri?! No matter what you hear in there. Do not come into your son's room!" Joseph wasn't asking her, he was telling her.

He leaned over to grab her shoulder for reassurance. "Please trust me. I can't tell you why but I beg you to just trust me. Your son's life is just as important to me as it is to you. I know that may be hard for you to believe or to comprehend right now, but it's true. I can't tell you what it is I'm about to do in there but there is something I need to do... That might be able to help him... Maybe even save his life... God willing."

The waitress looked him in the eye and then down at his Roman collar and then back again in the eye. She trusted Joseph, really trusted him. Not so much because he was a priest, but because of the man he was beneath the collar.

So she nodded she was O.K. with that, even though she hadn't a clue why he wanted to go into Tommy's room so badly, or what it was he was going to do once he got in there. Somehow she knew whatever did happen, her son would be safe as long as Father Joseph was by his side.

Terri leaned back in her chair facing the waiting area and spoke with tears running down her cheeks. “Please help my son. Whatever you need to do. Do it.”

Joseph had her blessing. That’s all he wanted. All he needed.

“I will Terri. Don’t you worry about a thing. You and your son will have all that I have to give.”

Terri looked back at Joseph, so grateful he’d come into her life. “Meeting you was not a coincidence you know.” She said. “It was an appointment.”

He smiled, knowing exactly what she meant by that.

With that, Joseph turned from her and to Tommy’s door.

He pushed it open, slowly walking into the room.

The stench nearly drove him back out. He put his hand up to cover his nose and mouth. “Ooooofffffffffff.”

There she was with her back to the priest. Falene. Her and the stink of the devil himself. Standing there like a vulture over Tommy’s body.

“Well, well, well, Joseph.” Falene said turning around to face him. She was wearing a nurse’s uniform, similar to the one she wore at the Vatican when she told him the Pope was dead.

Joseph, still standing at the entrance, leaned to the side so he could see behind Falene. He saw Tommy with his eyes closed, lying near lifeless in his hospital bed. Tubes coming out of him from every orifice. Falene moved over a step to try to block his view.

The sight of Tommy in such a critical state made Joseph feel deeply distressed.

“What do you want anyway?! I’m busy here. Get out!” She yelled.

Falene knew whatever the priest did here would counter her hard work with Tommy. The boy was almost where she wanted him. Dead.

She stared him down.

"I said!!! Get out!! Get out of here!!!" She screamed, lunging forward.

Joseph stared hard at her, never flinching.

Falene didn't frighten him. Her ability to reach Tommy's subconscious, convincing him of untruths, did.

"I'm here to save Tommy's life." He said simply, walking toward the child's bed.

Falene stretched her neck with disgust on her face.

"Save his life?!" She threw her head back, cackling like a jackal. Figuratively, that's all she was anyway, a wild flesh-eating animal.

"He doesn't *want* to live anymore, Joseph! Can't you see that?! Look at him! Look at him!"

Standing at Tommy's bedrail, looking down, Joseph could see how the cancer had ravaged the boy's body and taken from him his zest for living. The sheer agony of the disease eating away at his very essence. His chest barely rising and falling as he breathed, making an audible hoarse whistling sound.

"He doesn't want to burden his mother anymore! He doesn't want to be in this pain anymore! Life is a waste anyway! Was for me! And certainly is for him!"

Her voice softened as she leaned down and over Tommy, so he could better hear her insidious words. "Look what your God did to him Father... Gave him cancer before he's even had a chance to live. Guess he doesn't love him either." She said, hoping her words would further chip away at Tommy's will to live.

Terri's son lie with his eyes still closed, either asleep, unconscious or heavily sedated because of the pain from his cancer.

Joseph brushed the boy's hair from his forehead.

Falene watched him like a hawk.

There Joseph and Falene stood, each on the opposite side of Tommy's bed, staring each other down as Tommy lie near death in his bed between them.

Falene grew quite anxious as the priest inspected her prey.

Joseph could see, Tommy was pale with dark circles around his eyes. Still wheezing and laboring to breathe. He was weak, very, very weak. If he didn't know better, he'd say the boy was ready to cross over.

"God saw to it he suffered with chronic fatigue, diarrhea and bone pain for months." Falene snickered cruelly. "Nice way to go out."

Underneath his eyelids, Joseph could see Tommy had some uncontrolled eye movements, mimicking REM sleep. He was also sweating profusely.

He felt so badly for the boy.

"The tumors are now widespread." Falene gladly informed Joseph. "Usually, surgery alone is enough for something like this... The *early* stages of Neuroblastoma. But, in Tommy's case...." She held her finger in the air. "Chemotherapy was recommended... Because he's in the *advanced stages*."

Joseph was growing angrier and angrier. Tommy, he knew, was hearing all of this.

Falene wouldn't let up. "It began in his abdomen. A mass. The doctor found it in here." Falene pushed into herself with her fingers, below her chest and diaphragm, where her digestive organs are.

The more Falene spoke about his cancer, the worse Tommy looked.

"Tommy also has high blood pressure and a fast heart rate because of the other additional tumors in his adrenal glands. You know... Those ductless glands on top of the kidneys... Secretes adrenaline, the hormone that stimulates the nervous system. Love the adrenal glands! Without adrenaline... One can't get up the gumption to say... Get out of harms way... Save themselves... Get that Ooommmfffff for life, to live!" She described over-dramatically.

"Hiiiis ain't wor-kin' noooooooo mawhhhhh!" Falene purposely exaggerated and mispronounced her words like an ignorant hillbilly, toying with Joseph.

Father Joseph didn't need Falene to tell him the condition this child was in. He could see it with his own eyes.

Tommy was on his death bed. Falene was wooing him and his soul for the Devil.

"It's so bad... He's barely able to move his hips, legs and feet." She said, checking a drip-bag next to Tommy's bed, like she was a real nurse.

He watched her, seeing the hateful, vindictive, mean-spirited person she was, bent on hurting others. Blind to the fact it was her own pain that caused her to engage in outrageous acts of torment.

He'd seen enough.

Just then, Father Joseph bowed his head and closed his eyes.

Praying.

"What?! What are you?! Joseph!!! What are you doing there?!!!!!" Falene shouted angrily.

"Joseph!!!"

"Joseph!!!!!!!!" She stamped her feet, kicking one of the bed legs.

"Joseph!!!!" Falene kicked it again, hard.

Tommy's body shook in his bed as Falene continued striking the bed with her foot.

"Hey!!!! Joseph!!! Hey!!!! Stop that!!!" She ordered, waving her arms in the air.

Falene didn't want any priest praying in the room with Tommy, especially this priest.

Father Joseph wouldn't lift his head. But he opened his eyes to speak to Falene as he remained looking at the floor. He didn't want to make eye contact with her.

"Remember that wager you placed with Glenn?" He reminded her.

"Yes. Of course I do." Venom lacing every word of her answer.

"You told him to select any person on earth, man or woman, that he felt possessed mankind's best qualities and had the purest of heart among man."

Falene seethed. "Mmnnnnn Hmmmnnnnhhhhhhh."

"I *am* that person Falene. As you well know." Joseph spoke slowly and deliberately. "There *is* one soul left on earth that is still pure and that's me. That's why Glenn selected me among billions. He knew I could handle whatever you threw at me. You know this and is why you're frightened by me. You know I possess the power to defeat you Falene. I will show you what truly lies within my heart, within the soul of mankind. I know my test has come. So let it be done."

An animal-like growl came from the deepest part of Falene's throat.

"Unlike the many souls I'm sure you've snatched from this earth, *my* soul cannot be weakened and coveted and thrown into the flames. Never will I turn against God to worship His sworn enemy. No matter what you do. No test will I fail. No test can take me from my mission in this world."

Father Joseph heard a death rattle. He wasn't sure if it was coming from Tommy or out of Falene's neck. He wouldn't look either.

"I am here before you to fulfill my destiny. To show you and all of mankind that the human soul is worth preserving on this earth. I am here to prove it to God. To prove it to you and to prove it to all of God's children around the world."

The priest planted his feet firmly on the ground, shoulder width apart, for perfect balance.

"Let me show you the power of the human soul, that which you cannot imagine and rid you of this earth forever Falene. Let this world be cleansed of those wearing the crown of deceit and hate... Of Satan and his minions. Your work here is done. When I reveal the true nature of man's spirit, you and yours will be hurled back into hell to the punishment of the Searing Blaze where you belong. This planet will be scraped clean of evil in the face of man's inherent goodness. Man will again live and prosper in peace."

Falene's tongue slashed at him. "The true spirit of evil has succeeded in bringing man's demise, Joseph! For years and years throughout time, many... Young and old, male and female, heads of state and beggars have succumbed to the wiles of the Beast, their soulless carcasses joining us in Hell! Now even God sees it fit to consider what should be done about your unwell kind... Created in

His image! He sent Glenn, because He himself has seen from his arrogant perch in Heaven that man is not worthy of the gifts He has blessed him with. And is this day... Considering abandoning man as man has abandoned Him. I'm just here to collect what belongs rightfully to my Master. The soul of every human being. That's all."

Joseph drew in a deep breath. His belly expanding fully.

"Many have allowed themselves to be seduced to the dark side. This is true, but this does not define man's collective heart."

Falene listened with fire in her eyes.

Joseph spoke with a controlled, even tone. "God the Father has reserved to himself the power to destroy beings as well as humans who violate his principles, precepts, and laws. This is also true Falene. Only God has absolute control over life and death as said in the Book of Matthew... *And fear not them which kill the body, but are not able to kill the soul: but rather fear him which is able to destroy both soul and body in hell...* Mankind has come to a crossroads. A fact. I'm here to say which direction we're taking." Joseph said defiantly confident.

Falene looked like she was going to go mad.

"Watch what happens next Falene and see for yourself who man really is, within the best of ME."

With that, Father Joseph head still bowed, closed his eyes again and began praying.

The truth was, he wasn't sure at that point what he was going to do. He just knew it would come to him. The will of the Almighty always led him down the proper path. He was open to it. Therefore, the will of God worked through him. Always did. Always will.

"Joseph!" Falene screamed at him again to prevent him from trying to derail her war on humanity.

"Joseph!!!!"

She had an idea what he might try to do.

Falene began again violently kicking the legs to Tommy's bed. His little body shaking back and forth from the force. Yet he never awoke.

Joseph didn't let it break his deep thought.

Silently, with God ever present in his consciousness, as well as that of the Warrior Angel with whom he identified with, Joseph prayed to the Lord begging for Tommy's life.

Falene did everything she could to annoy and disrupt Joseph's concentration.

She reached for the metal IV drip-bag pole beside Tommy's bed. The IV was administering fluids directly into Tommy's veins through a syringe taped to his arm. She got a good grip on it and smashed it to the floor. The clear plastic intravenous bag bursting open upon impact, spilling a clear liquid all over the floor. It splashed on Joseph's black shoes.

Then, as he'd expected. It came to him as though the words were breathed into him. He knew what he had to do, as if the thought had been there all along, just waiting to be discovered at just the right time. It was Divine Inspiration. As God gave the men who penned the Bible, the very words to write. So did He give this thought to Father Joseph but it was still up to him to do it.

"Thank you." He said appreciatively and meekly.

Joseph then asked to endure that which a hero would beg to be spared... He asked God to trade his life for Tommy's.

Through prayer he implored God to hear and grant his request.

"Dear God, help me take this disease from this innocent child and bring it instead, into me. Let this be your will and let it be done. Let this cancer Tommy has feast off my tissues and muscles instead of his. Let it eat away at my organs, destroying my body and not his. Grant Tommy life. My life. Give him my life so that he may live another minute, another day, another year, another decade. I have lived a long, satisfying life. Let *him* live as *I* have lived. Oh Lord, I pray you. Take this curse from Tommy and Terri so that they may enjoy a long life together as mother and son; so that he may continue to age with his friends and grow up to be a man. A good, strong man of God. Let him be well. Let him find a spouse and marry and multiply with your blessing. Let me bear his burden for him. I exchange my life for his. Take my life, so that he may have one. I give it freely, willingly, with love, to him. Lord hear my prayer.

Lord hear my prayer." Father Joseph's words were as sincere as he'd ever spoken.

"Noooooo!!!! God Damned You!!!! No!!!!!" Falene was shouting at the top of her lungs. "Nooooooooooooo Joseph!!!!!!!!!!!! You can't do thaaaaaattttttt!!!!!!" Spittle was flying out of Falene's mouth. Her face and neck turning beat red, she was getting so burnt up. She knew what Joseph was praying for and she was trying to stop it.

He paid no mind to the ranting lunatic.

Joseph combined prayer along with everything he had within his power as a mortal to help make his wish come true.

The priest looked at Tommy. He concentrated on him. Observing every inch of his body from his head to his toes, studying him, so he knew his body so well he could see it even if it weren't there.

Joseph imagined his eyes were electron microscopes, looking at Tommy's cancer cells magnified hundreds of thousands of times, watching them divide beyond normal limits, forming tumors within Tommy's little frame. He looked at those tumors three-dimensionally, inspecting every bulge and bump in them. He looked closely, still as if under a microscope, at the abnormalities in the genetic material of the transformed cells.

Joseph needed to see the enemy, to feel the enemy, to know the enemy, to understand the enemy, to intellectualize the enemy, to taste the enemy, to smell it, to attach an emotion to it, before he could ever even begin to lure it from Tommy's body and serve as a replacement host.

The priest believed with his whole heart that if you can see something in the mind, you can go there in the body.

That's where he began.

He fixated on the little boy and his cancer. He became one with Tommy. One with his cancer.

In his mind, Joseph saw each individual nasty, little, killing cancer cell within Tommy's tiny tumor-riddled body.

Then, the clergyman commanded each one of those cells to ignite. He compelled the disease to spontaneously burn within Tommy's body. All at once. Right at that moment.

Joseph said it was so in his mind. He believed it to be.

He waited.

Father Joseph imagined seeing the cancer set afire beneath Tommy's skin and feeling its heat against his face from where he stood.

He waited still.

Until it was so.

And it was.

The cancer within Tommy's body did begin to spontaneously smolder and then burn. A sizzling sound confirming the cancer was breaking down to its molecular components and becoming combustible.

The explosive and painful chemical change raging within Tommy's body caused a sad, involuntary physical reaction. Tommy convulsed violently in his bed as his eyes rolled back into his head. The whole clunky hospital bed was shaking under the pressure, causing one of the bed rails to collapse to its lowest position.

Joseph was in a trance-like state. He knew what he had to do. No matter how badly Tommy was suffering, he had to continue.

He concentrated... Hard.

As the infected cancerous tissues burned within Tommy's body, gases and steam were building up beneath his colorless, pasty white skin, making Tommy bloat.

Still convulsing and going into a seizure, Tommy's body traveled to the edge of the bed where his head half hung off the mattress. Another inch and he'd be on the floor.

Falene watched Tommy endure the misery with delight. She was sure this would kill him sooner than the cancer would and that Joseph would be to blame. It couldn't be more perfect.

Father Joseph focused even harder on Tommy and his cancer. He couldn't stop now.

The burning lethal material beneath Tommy's skin eventually found its exit. Through the pores in Tommy's skin.

A fine dry gray smoke, the color of ashes, hissed out of the tiny holes in Tommy's skin as visible vapor.

The cancer had changed form, but it was still alive. It was still cancer.

As it slowly escaped his body through pinhole-sized pores, the toxic material suspended directly over his body like a foreboding cloud.

The whole scene was like something out of a science-fiction novel but this was real life.

Joseph looked at the foggy mass hanging over Tommy's body.

If it didn't find a new organism on which to attack healthy cells and change them to cancer cells soon, it would return to Tommy's body to finish its charge.

Father Joseph knew this and had to act quickly. He had a short window of opportunity here.

He thought about the vapor and what he should do.

Then he had an idea.

He closed his eyes.

Knowing what he was about to do, Joseph recited Psalm twenty-three to himself privately.

"The Lord is my shepherd, I shall not want. He maketh me to lie down in green pastures: He leadeth me beside the still waters. He restoreth my soul: He leadeth me in the paths of righteousness for His name's sake. Yeah, though I walk through the valley of the shadow of death, I will fear no evil; for thou art with me; thy rod and thy staff, they comfort me. Thou preparest a table before me in the presence of mine enemies; thou anointest my head with oil; my cup runneth over. Surely goodness and mercy shall follow me all the days of my life; and I will dwell in the house of the Lord forever. Amen."

Ready, he opened his eyes and took one last breath of fresh air for himself, remembering who he was and why he was there. He thanked God for the long, beautiful life he had.

He exhaled, knowing the very next breath he took could be his last.

He did it anyway, without reservation.

The priest drew in the deepest, longest breath he possibly could, filling his lungs, to create a draw.

"MMmmmmnnnnnnnnnhhhhhhhhhhhhhhhhh!!!!"

A wisp of the gray, smokey vapor broke from the cloud, streaking through the air toward Joseph.

When it came close enough to his face, he sucked in as quickly and as hard as he could through his nostrils and his mouth to take the material into his body, making it his.

It smelled just like what it was... Evil in its purest form. The malodorous scent of cancer, of dying and rotting flesh. Of death itself, slowing claiming life.

Joseph looked harder at Tommy. His little body pathetically hung off the edge of the bed as it shook uncontrollably. The boy was in severe pain and wouldn't be able to take much more of this.

Father Joseph sucked in hard again. "Mmmmmmnnnnnnnnnhhhhhhhhhhhhhh!!!!" His eyes bulging as he did. The smell of it was nauseating. He could taste it in his mouth. He gagged, trying not to vomit.

He held his breath for as long as he could to get the poisonous substance to stay, settle in, spread throughout and infect its new home. *His* body.

As he did this, Father Joseph's eyes glanced over at Tommy's nightstand, which Falene was standing in front of. She shifted over to prevent him from seeing what was there.

On it sat a stone. A dark stone with yellow squiggly lines all over it. Joseph couldn't figure out exactly what it was or why it was there, but his eyes kept going to it. It was Tommy's. He must have brought it to the hospital with him and placed it there for a reason. It meant something to him.

The stone intrigued Father Joseph.

Then suddenly, in the hall, he heard someone. Frenzied, the man spoke quite loudly.

Joseph was still holding his breath at this point.

"Terri! Is *he* in there?! Father Joseph?!" He overheard a familiar male voice impatiently ask.

It was David. He'd finally left the car in the parking lot and made his way up to the fourth floor. He was pacing back and forth out in the hallway.

Terri didn't vocalize her answer, but must have nodded yes, because he heard the sound of exasperation come from David as he let out an agitated sigh.

Something was very wrong.

Father Joseph knew right then what was so different about Brother David. He'd felt the difference all along, since the flight.

It was the fact that Brother David wasn't *really* Brother David anymore. He just looked like him on the outside. On the inside, he'd been gutted and reborn a mutation of his former self.

Somehow, David had survived the car accident in Newport, Rhode Island. After that, was captured by and succumbed to the will of Falene, Victor and Anatoli. During that time, he'd given himself permission to embrace the dark side of his personality, with the intention of beating them at their own game, but that wasn't what was needed to defeat them... They were too powerful... David lost himself in the process. Forever. He was one of *them* now.

Father Joseph knew to just forget about him. He was gone. Another damned soul lost forever to the dangerous underworld ruled by demons. Brother David, after death, was condemned to walk a steep, thorny road... Destined for punishment in the afterlife.

It was all coming together for Joseph. He could see it all so clearly now.

Joseph couldn't help but feel sad. Sad that he lost his dear friend, the ambitious and dedicated monk whose friendship he thoroughly enjoyed and appreciated.

He felt sorry for Brother David as well. That in a noble quest to help humanity... He lost his own soul, through a lack of faith. Faith in himself and faith in God. David failed to see that he already had within him, the power to defeat evil. Never, did he have to alter who he was... To become *like* his enemy in order, to be victorious. That was his downfall.

Joseph also felt sorry that Brother David, in the end, didn't rely on his faith in God to pull him through his darkest hour. Faith that He would illuminate a path for him, when he was in desperate need... To show him how to slay his foe.

It didn't matter now. Father Joseph had to carry on, himself. Alone.

There was a critical mission at hand.

Not able to hold his breath a second longer, Joseph exhaled the stale carcinogenic air, going into a coughing fit as he did.

He sucked in yet another deep breath immediately as he stared at Tommy.

The priest mentally commanded the cancer to continue to burn within Tommy's body, using itself as its own fuel, and rid itself from each cell, organ and tissues and exit his body.

As it did as he'd ordered... Joseph repeatedly breathed in and exhaled the noxious gases over, and over, willfully giving the cancer rights over his entire body.

As the deadly, diffused vapor was introduced into Joseph's body through his nostrils, mouth, throat and lungs, it was absorbed into his bloodstream almost instantly. This was the cancer's path to diseasing Joseph's blood, organs and tissues. His big, healthy body, serving as the perfect breeding ground where it could spread with destructive consequences.

Father Joseph could feel his effort succeeding. The cancer was effectively leaving Tommy and laying claim to him instead.

Joseph's temperature was steadily rising and he was starting to break a fever. His face felt totally flushed and he was suddenly really, really sick to his stomach and very tired. He was also starting to lose his ability to breathe with ease.

The priest stumbled one step forward.

He could see the exact opposite happening to Tommy. Still convulsing, the little boy started to gain some color in his face. A sign good health was starting to return.

Falene could see it too and screeched as though she were being drawn and quartered. The harsh, high-pitched sound causing the large hospital windows to tremor.

"NNNNOOOOOOOOOOOOOOOOOOOOOOOOO!!!!!!"

She arched her back as far as it would go and tilted her head all the way back, letting out the most awful shriek.

"NNNNOOOOOOOOOOOOO!!!!!!!!" She insisted in a shrill cry. "JOOOOOOOSEPHHHH!!!!!!!!!! NNNNNNNOOOOOOOOOOO!!!!!!!!!!"

Father Joseph was being overcome by his symptoms. He felt dizzy and his movements were pitifully uncoordinated.

He did his best to focus as his vision blurred.

Then.

A flash.

A blinding white flash.

Followed by the sound of a deafening explosion. "BBBOOOOOOOOOOOOOOOOOMMMMMMMMMM!"

Father Joseph collapsed to the floor, now convulsing himself, and writhing in unimaginable pain. He looked like he was being electrocuted.

Falene rushed toward him as he lay there, helplessly thrashing about in the hospital room. Without hesitation, she dropped to her knees and began ripping his full collar shirt and cassock off. She stripped him bare of his priestly clothing while he remain shaking, unable to control his body's jerking movements. He couldn't understand why she was doing this and he unfortunately lacked the ability and strength to defend himself.

Falene had him exactly where she wanted him.

Her victim.

She studied his heavy, nude, hairy body up and down.

Then, without warning him, she clumsily grabbed his flaccid penis in her hand. Joseph could feel her thin, bony fingers wrapped around it, gripping its girth. She was measuring it in her hand.

Inspecting it from all angles.

Although he desperately wanted to, he wasn't even able to lift his head to see what she was doing as his arms and legs flailed unpredictably. He didn't have to, he just knew she was up to no good.

From the pocket of her tidy white nurses uniform, Falene pulled out a syringe, filled with a clear liquid. Some kind of medicine in the vial.

She held it up high over her head for Joseph to see. "Lookey here friend! I've got something for you!" She teased, waving it to and fro.

The priest caught a glimpse of it as his body spasmed on the floor, causing his head to uncontrollably turn left and right. Enough of a glimpse to know what it was. A needle.

Upon sight of it, he thought he was going to pass out.

In the hypodermic syringe... "Twenty micrograms of Caverject!" Falene announced. She gingerly depressed the plunger, spritzing droplets of the vial's contents into the air, forcing out any air bubbles.

Straddling his legs, she indignantly yelled into his face. "YOU AND ME... WE'RE GONNA HAVE A LITTLE PARTY, JOSEPH!!!!!!! A LITTLE PARTY FOR JOSEPH AND FALENE!!!! HOW'D 'YA LIKE THAT BABY??!!! HAH???!!! LITTLE PARTY???!!!... YOU AND ME?????!!!!" Still waving the needle in the air to provoke him.

Falene suddenly swung her arm downward, pointing the syringe directly at Joseph's penis. She held the tip right to the shaft.

Joseph flinched, his whole body tensing up.

"This will just hurt... A LOT!!!" She hollered at him, wearing an ignoble smile.

"Guess *I'm* the one in control now Joseph! You think you're so smart?!! So well-intended?!! So good?!!! You think you can beat me?!! Think again!!!!" She warned, resentfully.

Avoiding visible veins, Falene insensitively plunged the sharp, hollow end of the hypodermic syringe, hard into Father Joseph's organ. It only took four-seconds for Falene to inject him with the full dosage of the male impotence drug, generically known to patients as Alprostadil.

"Since you're too stubborn to allow yourself the pleasure of getting hard over me... *THIS* is going to give you permission... Whether *you* like it or not... and help things along!"

Falene yanked out the needle at a different angle than she'd stuck it in, just to make sure it hurt really badly coming out.

It did.

The injection site began bleeding immediately. Falene deliberately failed to apply pressure to it to stop it from discharging blood. She wanted him to suffer.

Father Joseph's face started turning red as he lie there on the floor... A frothy saliva produced from his mouth.

He held his breath to try to lessen the feeling of intense burning in his penis and ride it out but he couldn't. There was nothing he could do, he had to just take it.

The pain was excruciating, but Joseph was too debilitated to cry out for help.

Falene threw the used syringe across the dirty hospital floor and grabbed the sides of Joseph's face, staring into his eyes. Beneath her uniform, her heart beating so wildly he could hear it thumping against the inside of her chest cavity.

She shoved her throbbing eager tongue down his throat. His head and body flat against the tile floor, he was unable to pull away from her sexual advances.

Falene continued forcibly kissing him and roughly biting his neck against his will...

In five minutes, the drug produced the desired effect.

Father Joseph had a pharmaceutically induced erection.

"Excellent! Excellent!" Falene looked totally entranced by the sight of it. "Good job Joseph! Good job!"

Grinding her pelvis down on him, she humiliated him.

"You wasted *this* for God?! What a shame!!! It'd be a shame to waste such an impressive part of you, the *best* part... for an undeserving God! What'd he ever give you?! Fuck Him!!! If I were you, I'd have used this cock to screw everything in sight, Joseph!!!"

Then she bent down, whispering in his ear. "Or *did* you waste it, Joseph?!"

Joseph closed his eyes shut. He didn't want to hear her ugly words.

"Maybe you've stuck this..." She took it in her hand again, strangling it. "... Up the ass of another priest? Hah? Did 'ya? You gay?!" Falene tormented.

"Or... Or... Maybe... Little boys? Hah? Maybe you defiled a little boy? That your game, Joseph?! Like little boys?!"

She squeezed him hard and then twisted.

Joseph's eyes rolled up into his head.

Everything started to go fuzzy for Joseph. The room started spinning.

Then, Falene started hurriedly undressing herself. She couldn't get her clothes off fast enough.

Joseph started to lose consciousness as he watched her.

Now *she* was stark naked too.

Falene was physically stronger than she looked. She grabbed Joseph by his sides and easily slid his husky body, on his back, across the hard, cold floor with the strength of a man twice her size. His body was now positioned directly beneath her, between her opened legs.

She held him down. He had no capacity to fight her off.

Father Joseph suddenly felt a very sharp pain in his groin.

And then... The priest's world fell dark.

He saw nothing but blackness.

He heard nothing but silence.

He felt nothing but numbness.

He smelled and tasted nothing other than the cancer, which overpowered all other senses.

It seemed to stay that way for a very long time.

Father Joseph accepted that he was dead.

Until...

A sensation.

Wetness.

Water everywhere.

All over his naked body, tiny air bubbles tickled his skin as they passed over every inch of him and floated up over his head.

Joseph was underwater. Totally submerged.

He wasn't holding his breath, but breathing... He was able to breathe the cool, clean, fresh water.

"I can think. I can feel." He said to himself, trying to get his bearings in this new world.

Then he became aware of another sensation.

Arms.

Strength.

Divine power... Encompassing him.

Father Joseph could feel himself being carried in someone's arms deep beneath the water, but he didn't know by whom. He felt a man's powerful, muscular, strong arms around his back and behind his knees, carrying him like a small child.

Joseph felt safe, yet afraid.

He was disoriented and didn't know what was happening.

That's when the crown of his head broke through the surface of the water and he began to breathe air.

Fresh air.

He could breathe easily.

He wasn't in pain anymore.

"Is this what happens when you die?" He thought. As his body, held and carried by another, slowly emerged from the water.

The priest knew he was nude but felt no shame or embarrassment.

He knew he was being delivered somewhere by someone but was too weak and timorous to look upon their face.

This was all he knew before passing out cold again.

He was right. His weight was being supported by another and moved out of the water's depths by someone he knew of.

The Warrior Angel.

He was *as* imperial and elegant as C. Caparrelli had portrayed him in her painting and more so. *No* painting could truly do him justice.

God's bravest messenger was walking out of the deepest part of a freshwater pond, with Father Joseph's lifeless body in his arms. With each step, the Warrior Angel brought the priest's body straight out of the water and closer toward the shore. Water pouring down both their bodies.

The tranquil body of still water secluded, surrounded by a dense green forest, tall mountains and curious wildlife bounding everywhere.

Joseph was now totally unconscious, his head hanging all the way back, his mouth gaping open.

The perfectly dignified and honorable defender of humanity gently placed Joseph's unclothed body on the sand, within the path of a golden, glittering beam of sunlight, which bathed his entire form. Dozens of people, appearing as three-dimensional holograms, stood there watching as the Warrior Angel handed him over and stepped away.

They surrounded Joseph.

In attendance, looking down upon Father Joseph was his father Joseph Maggiacomo, his mother, his brother Peter and Mr. Buonopane, who'd passed away right after Joseph's last visit with him. Standing behind them, in half-moon rows, all the slain Cardinals who were murdered at the Vatican.

They were all there.

All, bowed their heads and began praying.

Father Joseph had unselfishly given his life for another, regardless the cost. He paid the ultimate price.

Now he was here. Wherever *here* was.

The Warrior Angel stood there, looking down upon Joseph as well, smiling. He was proud of him. So very proud. They all were.

Then, the Warrior Angel looked at everyone else standing there with his penetrating, knowing eyes and smiled at them and they at he.

There was a knowing, an understanding among the group.

The Warrior Angel then stepped forward, bent down on one knee and laid his hands upon Joseph's cherub face. Then, he took them away and waited for something to happen.

Every member of the select group took one step closer toward Joseph and leaned in over him to see better.

From out of nowhere scenes from Joseph's life, like a motion picture, played out over his face like a projector projecting a film onto a big screen.

Everything. From birth until this day.

Everyone there saw, heard and even felt the same emotions Joseph felt during these specific highlights from his life, playing like a documentary in chronological order.

Washing over his face transparently, images of...

The playful, rough-and-tumble times Joseph had with his brother Peter when they were children and how happy it made them both. Inside, all there could feel the deep sense of family and well-being it brought Joseph.

Peter's face lit up. Tickled pink he was chosen by God to be Joseph's little brother.

The assemblage also saw images from the horrifically destructive experiences Joseph had with his father growing up and how psychologically punishing and damaging those encounters were, during this time of his life. The emotional suffering Joseph sustained as a boy and later as a young man, making everyone there recoil with pity and empathy.

His father grimaced with regret.

They saw Joseph with his affectionate, devoted mother. She doted over him with the tender love and kindness only a mother has for her children. These times were rare for Joseph, but cherished. When schizophrenia set in those good times ceased permanently and she died... at her own hands. Although it had a devastating affect upon Joseph for the rest of his life, he never blamed her. Never resented her. His love for her never waned, even after she was gone.

Joseph's mother smiled, knowing she was blessed to have given birth to such an amazing son.

The group continued watching as Joseph and his siblings found refuge at Mr. Buonopane's house when things became so unbearable at theirs, they fled, seeking shelter and protection. They saw the compassion the tender hearted, old man bestowed upon their lives. The group felt how safe Joseph felt in his neighbor's care when he and his brothers and sisters had nowhere else to go.

Mr. Buonopane teared up. In life, he never truly knew how his support affected Joseph. Now able to feel firsthand Joseph's mental state at the time, Mr. Buonopane fully comprehended the very important role he played in Joseph's life. He thanked the good Lord for giving him the wherewithal to aid Joseph when he needed him most.

They, the group, their three-dimensional, transparent figures still standing on the pond's shore, then saw Joseph leaving home... Searching for answers about life, developing friendships, making his own mistakes, finding himself, making better decisions, growing up, discovering the world, becoming a man...

Eventually... Making a life and taking his place within the Catholic Church.

Every member of the group continued watching highly attentively as Joseph finished seminary school, took his sacred vows and entered the priesthood. Within their own bodies, they all felt Joseph's heart swell with God's love. During his life-altering personal journey within the Catholic Church, Joseph discovered a newfound understanding of himself, others and the world around him and is where he ultimately found the peace and contentment he so craved and *truly* found his calling, redefining himself as who he *really* is, *Father* Joseph.

Then...

Joseph's father, his mother, his brother Peter and Mr. Buonopane spaced themselves apart.

Allowing the slain Cardinals to step forth between them and come an additional pace closer, tightening the circle around Joseph's body.

The violent sights and sounds of their vicious murders blended over Joseph's facial features. The horrid scenes of the sitting Pope, self-appointed Pope Victor in a deranged fit, slashing their throats and their wrists as they attempted to restrain him, filled the length and width of Joseph's face. Victor's fury was mightier than their best efforts to subdue him. He managed to extinguish every one of their lives that fateful day.

It was grisly. Every member of the group winced.

Each of their faces wrinkled with compassion, seeing poor Father Joseph burst into the room, discover the gruesome carnage and try desperately to save Cardinal Shanley's life.

The Cardinals were all grateful. Especially Cardinal Shanley who listened to the final words he uttered to Joseph, "... Hell... hath... nooooo..." before he exhaled his final breath in Joseph's arms.

The group also watched with great pride as Father Joseph sat in a hospital room with his dying father at the end of his father's life and forgive him.

All, feeling their spirits soar free, as Joseph's did, when he was finally able to forgive his father. Graciously setting his father's spirit free as well; since his father lacked the courage to seek a path to do it for himself.

Joseph Maggiacomo, Sr., now felt worthy to smile with the others. His son was merciful and had taken pity on him... When he didn't deserve it. When it wasn't owed to him. This he knew. *This* is who his son was. All of it.

They saw all of it.

The good, the bad, the difficult and challenging as well as the enlightening and inspirational times. They saw the laughter, the tears, the times of fear and the times of personal triumph...

They saw Joseph relentlessly searching, growing, developing into a man, into a priest.

Finally... They witnessed the single-most defining moment of Father Joseph's life; his moment of truth.

When he begged God to trade his life for Tommy's and did all that he could within his mortal authority to take the child's suffering from him and bring it to himself. Unselfishly, turning his life over for another in the spirit of love.

All of it, every experience, made Joseph the man he was.

The Warrior Angel with tears streaming down his face and still kneeling, placed his hands back on Joseph's face and softly whispered into his ear.

Everyone waited quietly.

And then... Father Joseph awoke. His eyes opened, stinging from the sun's abnormally powerful, sweltering rays.

The blazing sunlight blinded him. Blinking and with his eyes watering, he held up his hand to block the sparkling light from his face.

He looked all around, although he still wasn't sure exactly *where* he was.

Still bare, lying on his back on the sand and confused about his whereabouts, Joseph was not sure what to do.

That's when he recognized the Warrior Angel, standing directly over him. Father Joseph gasped.

"Oh... Oh.... It's... It's... I can't believe it. You're... You're here...." He stared in awe at the glorious angel.

God's attendant was even more regal and intimidating in real life but Joseph knew there was no need for him to fear him. To Joseph, he was friend not foe.

Joseph was humbled to be in his presence, visiting with him in the flesh like this was an honor of the highest order.

He was just as he'd appeared in Caparrelli's artwork.

The Warrior Angel was tall and handsome with a muscular build, like that of a gladiator. On top of his head... Thick, wavy dark hair.

Dressed for battle, wide, brown leather straps criss crossed his chest. On his feet, those worn sandals with golden leather ties snaking up his shins in intersecting lines, which the skillful artist drew with such detail.

The length of his body dirty. Marred by bruises, burns and scars from doing God's work. Upon his face... bleeding cuts and scrapes.

Joseph looked deeply into his eyes... As did the Warrior Angel into his.

There it was. The confident defiance and brazen determination that made the Warrior Angel who he was. Joseph saw it. He felt his energy.

There was one more thing Joseph wanted to see for himself. The saddest thing of all... The Warrior Angel's enormous white feathered wing. The right one.

It crushed Joseph to look at it. But he had to.

Hanging down, dragging along the ground behind him... His broken, permanently unusable wing. In a wicked, unjust act it had been severed to the bone, cut almost totally off, during a conflict the likes of which no mortal man could fathom. The site of the wound still bled.

"Ohhhhhhh. I'm so sorry." Joseph expressed his sincere regret for what the Warrior Angel must have endured to have received such a crippling injury.

In spite of it, the Warrior Angel had persevered.

Here they were. Together. The two of them.

There had to be a reason for it. Joseph knew this.

"What are you doing here...? Where am...?" Joseph asked shyly.

Then... Joseph slowly began noticing and recognizing everyone else who was there at the edge of the pond with him, surrounding him.

His mother, his father, Peter... and Mr. Buonopane. And all the Cardinals from the Vatican who'd been systematically executed by Victor. They were all there... Smiling warmly.

He was so thankful to be able to lay his eyes on each one of them again. "But they are all dead." Joseph then thought to himself.

"If I'm able to see them... Then that must mean I'm dead too."

Adrenaline surged through his body.

Starting to regain some of his memory, he looked back at the Warrior Angel.

"Tommy! Tommy! What happened?! Is... Is he...?!" He lifted his head off the ground. "I... I... Have to know if...?"

The Warrior Angel gazed down at him.

Joseph nervously looked around at everyone else for an answer... "Do you know...?! Or you...?!!!" He pointed. "Or you?!" He pointed to yet another. "Tommy?! What happened...?! Is he alive?! Did he die?!!! Tell me! You *must* tell me! PLEASE!!!" He pleaded. "PLEASE!!!!!"

Not their place... Was the expression they all wore on their faces.

Then the priest turned back to the Warrior Angel, his eyes praying he'd answer him. Anything he could tell him.

The Warrior Angel smiled reassuringly at the priest, suggesting the boy was all right.

"Oh... Thank heavens." Joseph became emotional, his voice cracking. "Thank heavens." He began to sob, allowing his head to rest back on the sand. "As long as that child is O.K. That's all I need to know. Now he and his mother can have a long life to... t... tog..." Joseph couldn't finish.

The Warrior Angel's eyes continued welling with tears as did everyone else's.

Then, he bent down again to whisper into Joseph's ear.

This would be the first time Joseph heard the voice of the archangel. Before now, he'd only known him as how he represented himself on earth, a man named Glenn; and how C. Caparrelli masterfully depicted him within her painting. Two versions of the same holy entity.

Joseph considered this, possibly the very first time *anyone* ever heard the voice of this celestial being, who sat among the highest rank of angels in Heaven.

He couldn't begin to imagine what he was about to say to him.

With a strong, commanding, masculine tone. Yet beneficent voice. The Warrior Angel spoke to him.

"God emanates from you, Joseph." He said. "You are the true light. You transcend all others. Doing God's will, you are the epitome of love, compassion, forgiveness and generosity and have a repentant heart. By faithfully committing your life to God, you embody how mankind is supposed to live... How God always meant it to be. Through you... God sees that purity of heart still does exist within the human soul and that it is capable of rising up against and defeating the Evil One. And... Has every desire to do so. Therefore, you and yours shall live."

Father Joseph listened with reverence.

"See everyone here Joseph." The Warrior Angel whispered.

Joseph's lip quivered, his eyes darting around.

He saw them. "Yes."

"They were *all* introduced into your life for a reason, Joseph. To help you become the man you were always meant to become. They were there... To shape you. To encourage you. To challenge you. To make you reach into the deepest part of your soul for answers. To make you stronger, wiser. To help you grow. To help you develop and mature. So that you might realize and fulfill your destiny. It was God's wish for you. As it is God's wish for everyone. It was always up to *you* to do the hard work and you did. You are a shining beacon of hope for the entire human race."

That's when Father Joseph understood his entire life and everything he'd been through. There was a plan all along. He knew it.

"That's why *you and you alone* were selected to be put to a test like no man has ever known, Joseph. As you were told you would be and you accepted." The Warrior Angel refreshed his memory. "Not knowing the perverse fate soon to befall you.... Dictated by the Devil himself. You accepted without question and without hesitation."

"I didn't *need* to know. Because I *knew myself*." Joseph shared respectfully.

"The day you met Terri. The moment you knew about Tommy... You were being watched, Joseph. Watched by all of us. Not only by all of us in Heaven but by all the damned in Hell. To see what you would do."

The Warrior Angel and Joseph looked seriously at each other.

"As we in Heaven hoped and anticipated, you remained true to your heart, true to your calling... True to your faith. You did everything within your power to save a boy's life, Joseph. A boy you never met. You willingly sacrificed your life for another. For you, no price too high. You paid, regardless the cost to you. In doing so, you have inherited the earth and purchased liberty for all of humankind. Man has been cleansed of his sins through you and your pure, unconquerable heart and has been reborn again; redeemed from the bondage of sin and guilt and evil itself has been wiped off the face of the earth. This day, good not evil has taken root within the heart of mankind. The sun will continue to shine upon man and upon the earth for many days... From this day forward."

Father Joseph's heart filled with joy. He'd accomplished what it was he felt inside he *must* do, what he was *compelled* to do. By doing so, he answered his calling.

Joseph was right with God.

The Warrior Angel had one more thing to say to Joseph.

This was personal.

He knelt closer and confided in Joseph.

"Because of you... Joseph... I may rest. I may lay my sword down upon a grassy hillside and retreat from the battlefield. God has set a place in Heaven for me where I may eat my supper and rest my weary body. A rest... Upon a fine bed made of soft feathers, warm and dry. A rest... I have longed for, for a very, very long time. I can hear the seven angels sounding their trumpets, calling me home. Finally. My work is done. For now... The Beast has been driven back and I thank you, Joseph." The Warrior Angel clenched his right fist and held it to his heart as he continued looking at Joseph. "I call you... Brother."

This was the defender of humanity. God's warrior.

Thanking *him*. Calling him *brother.*

He was speechless.

Touched beyond words.

Joseph prayed the Warrior Angel would never again be summoned to battle. That he would enjoy that long, well-deserved rest he so longed for.

"I will remember you all the days of my life..." Joseph pledged. "...Brother."

Then it occurred to him. He still didn't know where he was.

Was he dead? Or alive?

As fast as that thought came into his mind.

A flash.

A blinding white flash.

Followed by the sound of a deafening explosion. “BBBOOOOOOOOOOOOOOOOOOOMMMMMM!!!!!!”

CHAPTER 31

THE SEED OF GOOD AND EVIL

And then...

The priests world fell dark once again.

He saw nothing but blackness.

He heard nothing but silence.

He felt nothing but numbness.

Until...

Sound.

The sound of music.

Nature's music, reaching his ears.

It was the most exhilarating noise he'd ever heard. Albeit loud, harsh and confused.

When Father Joseph was finally able to open his eyes...

He awoke to the birds' Dawn Chorus as the day's first ray of sunshine gently graced the earth.

He heard different bird species perched higher in the trees and those with larger eyes piping up to do their dawn singing first. As it is they, who initially perceive the first glimpses of light on the horizon.

Every songbird in the area was chirping full-voice at the same time, in non-harmony.

The sound... Deafening and chaotic, but beautiful as they heralded the start of a very new day.

Morning broke.

A new beginning.

A new beginning of a day.

A new beginning for man.

A new beginning for the earth.

The world surrounding him reborn.

Peace befell the earth.

"Springtime." Joseph vocalized weakly, listening to it.

He came to.

"Yes, Springtime."

Then...

A sensation.

Pain.

Acute pain. That which human beings don't ever know possible until they experience it themselves.

Joseph's entire body was in absolute total distress.

"OOOOHHHHHHH! OHHHHHHHHHHH!!!!" The priest yelled, squeezing his eyes shut again.

His body stiffening in defense.

"SHHHHEEEEEEEEEEEESHHHHH!!!!!! OOOHHHHHHHH!!!!!!" Father Joseph had no idea how to make it stop.

It ran throughout his body. All at the same time... Indescribable, incomparable pain.

"OOHHHHH NNNNOOOOOO!!!!! I CAN'T TAKE THIS!!!!!!!!" He bawled at earsplitting levels.

"HELLP MEEEEEE!!! PLEEEEEEEAASE!!!!!" He called out to anyone who might hear.

His pain, the direct result of a physiological series of electrical and chemical events occurring within his body.

Joseph turned on his side, burying his face in a pillow that was cradling his head. It was too much for him.

He got into the fetal position.

"I don't think I can... This is far too..." He rocked.

The priest had no where to turn. No one to turn to.

He was no longer at the place he was... No longer with the Warrior Angel or the others.

He was here now. Wherever *here* was.

Then, with all his will he lifted his head, looking around at his surroundings, trying to get his bearings again.

Hospital. The first word that popped into his head.

"What...? Why...? Where am I? What am I doing here?" He questioned, totally confused.

Then he took a closer look, surveying everything around him.

"Oh my goodness..."

Father Joseph was beginning to understand what was happening to him.

His internal compass told him he was back where he started. St. Joseph's Hospital in Nebraska.

"How can this be?"

Not only was he in the hospital. He was in Tommy's hospital room... In Tommy's hospital bed. "Well... I'll be..."

The boy and his mother, nowhere to be found.

"He's gone. Tommy's gone. The Warrior Angel. He... He told me he was O.K. So, I guess...." Joseph felt a tremendous sense of relief. "He must have left... With... With Terri... They're both O.K."

Joseph then looked down at his body, feeling the deep, aching, bone pain that only Neuroblastoma patients understand.

"But... I'm... I'm not... O.K... The cancer... It's in *me*." He said, realizing the cancer had successfully transferred to him as he'd commanded and was now consuming his body. "It's in *me*. I did it. I did it!"

Much to his surprise, he was also still alive. That, he didn't expect.

"Oh my... I'm... I'm... Still here. How can that...? Why? I... I... I thought... I was..." He didn't know what to make of it.

Totally dumbfounded, Father Joseph reassessed the situation, just to make sure.

He looked around at the antiseptic hospital room one more time.

Then he examined his arms, his legs, his middle. He slapped his face with his hands.

"Yes, I'm alive. I'm really alive. God graciously let me keep my life." He gulped.

"But why? I thought I was..." He thought about what had just happened, trying to put the pieces together.

Joseph's prayers had indeed been answered. He'd traded places with Tommy. It was a blessing, even though he was on death's doorstep. Still, a blessing to Joseph.

The fact that he was alive forced him to consider the possibility that God had more plans for him and could explain why'd he'd been allowed to hold on to his life, even if for just a short while longer.

Joseph began to feel a disabling burning pain now. Probably from a tumor pressing on a nerve. The priest could barely contain himself. He just wanted to scream out in the most horrible, bloodcurdling way.

The level of agony he was in... Inhuman. He couldn't believe the human body was capable of enduring such severe chronic pain, all over the body, all at once like this.

It was as if he could feel the tissue damage happening at a morbidly decelerated rate, magnified by one thousand.

"Uuuhhhhhhhhhh!" He groaned. "This is way too torturous for any living thing to suffer through.... That poor child, having to feel this... So unfair." He twisted around like a pretzel, trying to dull the pain. Nothing alleviated his misery.

Joseph was sweating through his bed clothes, the sheets and the mattress. His temperature well over one hundred degrees, he was drenched.

Delirious and struggling to sit up a bit in his bed, Joseph managed to raise his head high enough to peek out the window.

He saw new life outside. Trees budding. He counted in his head.

Many months had passed since he blacked out during that very physical tussle with Falene on the floor, while Tommy lay dying in his hospital bed. The last thing Joseph remembered was Falene, with the strength of ten men, sliding him across the tile floor beneath her. After that... nothing.

Joseph wondered where the Devil's whore went after that. Was she still here?

Joseph figured, after Tommy's cancer had chemically broken down, left the boy's body and transitioned into *him,* that he must have passed out cold. That's probably when medical staff found him, laying on the floor where they assessed, treated and then heavily sedated him.

There was another possibility. He fell into a coma, from which he was now awaking.

The events between... Anyone's guess.

Here he was. Those were the only viable explanations he could imagine.

The priest turned from the window, looking at the other side of the sterile, white room.

That's when he noticed Tommy's rock. Still sitting there on the nightstand beside the bed.

"Look at this. He forgot his thing here."

Joseph remembered seeing it when he came to confront Falene in Tommy's hospital room. But, the rock didn't look the same. The first time he saw it, it was very dark, black, with some yellow squiggly lines, forming the shapes of puzzle pieces all over it.

It didn't look that way anymore. It had changed.

Father Joseph reached over, picked it up and took a closer look at it. That's when he found the note that Tommy had left him.

"What's this?" He read his name at the top.

Joseph picked up the note written on yellow lined paper and began to read the child's grade-school, chicken scratch.

Tommy wrote.

"to our new freind father joseph. i'm feeling much better now. and I think this luckey rock had something to do with it. it got pretty when I got better. but now you are sick. i hope you feel better soon. my moter and me are leeving this for you as a good luck rock. i hope it helps you as it did me. Keep it with you allways and think of us when you look at it! p.s. -- Whenever you feel sick and sad. go to the Servivor Clinick and spend time with the warrior angel.

that's what I us to do when I was sick. he answewers preyers. he is my freind. and he will be yours to. i love him. and I love you to! Momma says you are the best freind she ever had. and mine two! p.s.s. -- don't eat the vechtabls from the kafateria. they stink!!!! i hid mind under the matras. (Shhhhhhhh!!!!! Don't not tell.) love, Tommy."

His misspellings and grammar were adorable. The intent, priceless.

Joseph sniffed.

He could smell it. Rotting vegetables.

"Asparagus." He sniffed again to make sure. "Yup. That little bugger." He chuckled, reaching down beneath the mattress, his fingers searching for the decomposing soft pulp, left behind by the child. Nothing. Tommy must have shoved his greens way in, so no one would find his stash.

Joseph rolled the thoughtful gift around in the palm of his hand.

The stone was small, circular and smooth. Now colored deep, dark-blue with green and white trails running through it. No more puzzle piece shapes dividing it up. Its coloring and markings consistent. It was cool to the touch.

It reminded him of the map at the center of Yashmiel's ancient scroll. "Like a perfect little replica of the world; unblemished, clean, pure, new and whole and the squiggly lines are gone. It doesn't look like a puzzle anymore." Joseph said to himself.

He scrutinized the precious object.

"That's because the puzzle has been solved." He suddenly realized. "The squiggly, puzzle-piece shaped lines have disappeared... because it's no longer a puzzle... but a representation of the solidarity among all of mankind, and the newly restored unity within the world."

Modestly, he knew he had a little something to do with that.

Turning it over, Joseph noticed some writing on the bottom.

A word.

He squinted. The letters were small.

Joseph brought it closer to his eyes.

"Ara." He said out loud.

"Ara. Hmmmnnnhhh. Ara."

Father Joseph had come across the name once before, somewhere in his reading.

He couldn't remember where he read it, but could recall its definition.

"It faintly comes to mind..." Joseph pondered. "King. I think." Once he said it out loud, he was certain. "Yes... Yes... The... A *name*... Ara... meaning King. That's precisely the meaning of the word."

It was such an unusual stone, yet exquisite. Even hypnotic. He'd never seen anything like it before.

He held it between his thumb and index finger, so that the bottom was fully exposed.

"Aramaic... Possibly. If memory serves me..." He ruminated, trying to figure out where Tommy may have found it. It was special in some way, like it wasn't from around here. "Where did this come from? How did it find it's way into Tommy's hands?"

Then mysteriously the name Ara on the bottom of the stone began to glow sending out an intense, brilliant, golden light, illuminating each letter... *Ara.*

"Look at this..." Joseph said in awe, more curious than afraid.

He held it closer.

Blindingly bright, sparkling rays as powerful as the sun's, bathed Joseph's face in the shimmering brilliance. Yet, the stone remained cool to the touch.

Narrow beams of light gently reached out, touching Joseph's face, tracing and scanning each facial feature.

It recognized him.

The degree of the light radiating from the rock suddenly grew more intense.

"It feels so good... So good." Father Joseph was in a state of nirvana.

As the light passed over and caressed Joseph's face, a feeling of perfect bliss came over him, as though his soul had been freed from all suffering and he was absorbed into the supreme spirit.

"Such a warm, loving feeling, such peace." Joseph let it soak into his face. "Mmmmnnnnn."

Streaks of the twinkling rays began penetrating his skin.

As they did, something started happening...

They shared with him, absolute knowledge.

Joseph was given omnipotent knowledge of the universe. The mysteries of the universe had been unlocked for him and him alone. Father Joseph knew the answer to every question he or anyone else in existence had ever asked. He saw and understood all of it, including the origin and development of the universe... And, the *true reason* why human beings were put on earth by God.

"Oh... This is fascinating. I know. I know. I understand it all now. Absolutely everything one could know, I know. There is no answer I long for. It all makes perfect sense now. I see... I see... Anything I've ever wondered about. Anything that *anyone* has ever wondered about. I now know." He spoke with extravagant enthusiasm and emotion.

Father Joseph became one with the universe. His spirit soaring with God's love. "I see now. I see. Thank you. Thank you."

Joseph was grateful indeed for the gift Tommy left for him. But it was more than that.

This stone was meant for him all along.

He inspected it over and over, turning it every which way. "Here it is, in my possession where it always belonged."

Once the stone fully communicated its message to Joseph, the light shining from it began to slowly dim. It was finally home.

"I will keep you with me all the days of my life... Until the angels close my eyes." Joseph clenched it within his fist, holding on to it as tightly as he could as he reclined back in his bed.

"My eyes have been opened. My heart is full. I thank you God. I thank you for this most sacred gift of enlightenment and intelligence you have blessed me with." He prayed.

As the light from the rock gradually faded out, a corresponding event started happening. Joseph steadily slipped back into reality.

Father Joseph grimaced. A brief flare-up of severe pain reminded him of the gravity of his situation. He had cancer.

The priest closed his eyes, absorbing his mind in thinking about all that he now knew, to escape the bleak reality of his personal sentence.

It wasn't long before he drifted off to sleep where his sickness thankfully could not follow.

Father Joseph enjoyed his restful state of sleep for as long as he could, grateful for the reprieve. He dreamed wonderful dreams, where he again visited with the Warrior Angel, his parents and brother, by the freshwater pond.

Hours passed.

Then...

As he lay there peacefully, undisturbed, a patch of shade in the shape of a body cast a shadow upon Joseph, blocking the sun's rays coming in through the large hospital windows.

It cut the warmth from Joseph's face, triggering the automatic response to awaken.

Feeling the increasing, burning pain of the cancer return as he woke up, the priest made a startling discovery.

Someone was standing over him.

A female. A nurse he expected. "Oh... You scared me. I didn't realize anyone was standing there." He said, adjusting his pillow beneath his head.

Drowsily, he focused his eyes, getting a better look.

A female it was.

A nurse. It was not.

It was...

Falene.

She was heavier than he remembered her, by about thirty pounds. Very unlike her.

"Well... hello there." She greeted sarcastically. Her voice a bit deeper from the weight gain.

Father Joseph was shocked. This made absolutely no sense.

Joseph tripped over his tongue, trying to get the words out as he looked up at her. "How…? How…? I thought…? Where did you? This can't be right."

Knowing how confused he must be, she slyly stared at him with a knowing and mischievous smile. She had a secret, which she was dying to share with him. He could see it on her face.

Joseph, alert as a watchdog now, sat himself up in his bed.

"Why are you here? *How* can *you* possibly be here? I thought... You... Were... Supposed to be gone... The earth was... I... I... Glenn won the wager you placed with him..."

There was a hitch. He knew it, but he couldn't figure it out right this minute.

"Things don't always turn out as planned, Joseph." Falene said with a firm tone, holding her head up high. "I *am* still here. Live and in the flesh."

The priest didn't understand.

"Where did you…? I thought…?" The words just wouldn't come out. "This is impossible! How can this be?!!!" He wasn't even sure what he wanted to say, what the next question should be.

"You're *not* supposed to be here, Falene! You're NOT supposed to be here! Why *are* you here?! *How can* you be here?!"

Joseph pounded his fist by his side on his bed.

He ordered her to answer him. "How?!!!"

This didn't make any sense. "What is it I'm missing here?" He thought quietly to himself, trying to figure it out.

"Sometimes Joseph, the devil's... In the details." Falene quipped, rubbing her stomach.

Joseph's eyes fell immediately there.

To her stomach.

He froze, unable to utter a single syllable. His eyes feeling hot and teary. His heart started racing, like he was going to have a heart attack.

"What's the matter Joseph?! Cat got your tongue?!" Falene asked, jeering him.

"Oh my... No... Please... Oh no... Oh no... No... No... No..." He begged, looking up at her.

There Falene stood, with a swollen belly, as proud as she could be of herself.

She was pregnant.

Father Joseph buried his head in his hands. "Oh no, no, no, no...."

The memory suddenly came flooding back to him.

He remembered vividly, what had happened between him and Falene just before he passed out on the hospital floor.

What he was afraid was going to happen... Apparently *did* happen. She raped him.

Carrying the result of that rape like a badge of honor.

"You're..." He said, uneasily. "Why... You're..."

Joseph was sickened. He felt all the nerves running throughout his body surge with electricity.

Falene wore a wicked smile.

" ...Pregnant." He barely could say the word, knowing it was *his*.

The priest lowered his head in disgust. "You're pregnant."

Falene rubbed both of her bloated hands along the expanse of her full midsection.

"Yep! Pregnant!" She confirmed. "And... Unmarried. The Catholic Church is against that, right?" She snapped her fingers, pretending to try to recall.

She looked to be early in her third trimester but ready to give birth any day.

"Oh! There! I feel a kick!" She announced gleefully, pressing her puffy fingers into the right side of her gigantic tummy.

She shot a look at him.

"Want to feel?" She asked Joseph. "Right there... I'm getting kicked in the side... here." She pointed, reaching for his hand.

Joseph leaned away.

"Daddy!" Falene insisted. "Give me your hand now. Don't be afraid."

Joseph locked eyes with Falene. "Don't say that!" He shouted.

"Daddy." She whispered again cruelly, looking him directly in the eye.

"Stop it!" He screamed at her.

"Daaaaaddddddddddyyyyyyyyyyy." Falene tormented him. "Explain *this* to your maker, when you die. How you impregnated a woman. Not just any woman. ME!" She laughed wildly.

Joseph stared her down.

"Because... You really wanted it... Didn't you, PRIEST?!" Falene leaned in over him. "You really, really wanted me. Just like in the bathroom. Pretended not to. Told yourself you didn't. But you did. You could have fought me off if you tried harder. But you didn't want to. You gave in."

"Stop saying that!" Joseph yelled. "Stop it!!! It wasn't like that! You know it!"

"Daddy." Falene held her belly as she laughed. "Daddy! Daddy! Daddy!" She sang, refusing to stop.

"What's the matter Joseph? That's what you are... The father. Only a different *type* of father than you're used to being."

"Oh! I can't believe this is what's happening!" Joseph hollered in frustration.

"Hey! I think your little one is stretching out its tiny hand to you, Joseph. Touch through my stomach." Falene taunted. "Come here. Touch. Right here."

She reached out to grasp Joseph's hand again. "Don't fight me Joseph. After all, I am the mother of your child."

"No. No." He pulled away, farther out of her reach. "I don't think I…" Pains gripped his intestines so fiercely he tucked his knees up to his chest.

Between the cancer and her, he didn't know how he was still alive.

Falene put her hands back down. She was losing her patience.

"So you've got the cancer now. Hah Joseph?" Falene asked, rhythmically tapping her foot on the floor.

"Thought that selfless act would save your kind from joining *us*... Those whose souls are stripped naked and burn eternally in Hell*?* You took cancer away from that pathetic little boy so he can be with his white trash, waitress mother. Quite a remarkable feat. I'll give you that but you should have known that would only temporarily hold off the onslaught."

Joseph just looked at her, wondering what ever did happen to Tommy and Terri and where they were right now. He hoped they were somewhere safe, far away from here.

With conviction, Joseph addressed her comments. "I did not take Satan on with his own power to defeat him Falene, I took him on with the power of God. One cannot go head to head with Satan, playing by his rules, for they will be crushed. Only when man is cloaked within the glorious power of God can man be victorious against evil. *This* is how I defeated the Devil and defeat him, I did. Causing He and His like to be relegated permanently not *temporarily* to the bottomless pit. So, I don't understand how you could be here? Unless..."

Falene coldly interrupted.

"Unless... The Foul Fiend was invited to stay, somehow, someway..." She paused, coyly.

"Guess who figured out how that somehow, someway was?" Falene teased, rubbing her stomach in front of his face.

"The earth *was* cleansed of evil because of your pure heart... That's true Joseph but don't think I came here unprepared... I had a little trick up my sleeve all along, just in case I underestimated you. You're looking at it...." She said, glancing down at her pregnant belly.

He looked at it as well.

"I knew that if you accomplished what Glenn felt you were capable of accomplishing, humanity would be granted another chance... So I made my own plans, in case that happened."

With a fixed gaze, Joseph awaited the details of her carefully calculated scheme.

"I carry within my womb Father, new life. The sacred seed of the redeemer of humankind. A seed you planted firmly and deeply inside of me. A new life God had no choice but to allow the opportunity to live. Even though it *is* half... Me. What clings to life in my uterus, has your blood flowing through its veins. Therefore, is holy. Until the day your offspring draws their first breath... I possess immunity. I stay on this earth. The Almighty has said it and it is so."

Falene smiled. She'd succeeded at her mission.

"Threw a little snag into the works, for 'ya! Didn't I?!!!"

Father Joseph let out a sorrowful sigh. Falene had indeed found a way to again root evil within the soul of mankind, making it a natural, permanent force within man and within the world, where it would intend harm and spread corruption everywhere it goes.

"Through this birth Joseph, I will deliver the seed of evil back into the heart of man and woman... You see my friend the priest, Satan has an ingenious way of finding His way into anything He wants to. *Evil will* again walk this earth and destroy. Because this new life is half me, it will continue my work where I leave off. As you live out the rest of the days of your life... You will watch helplessly as your own flesh and blood aligns themselves with their inner enemy and answers the call of their true Master. From where I am seated, I will watch as it splits your soul in half."

Father Joseph listened closely to every word.

"And *that...* Is what will finally kill you." Falene stated.

Chills ran up Joseph's spine at the thought of that, but he knew better. He needed to remind her of a minor detail she failed to consider.

"Falene... Seems to me you didn't think this quite through enough. You're overlooking something here." He challenged her theory.

Falene stood there, saying nothing. Not sure where he was going with this.

"Whether you're aware of it or not... The process of ensouling *any* new life, is left to God. God *will* ensoul our child. So, it could take after either one of us. Like me, for example." He corrected her.

"... Continuing *my* work." He added.

Falene shifted her weight where she stood. She couldn't debate him on this fact.

He suddenly felt differently about the child she carried.

Going completely on instinct, Joseph reached up to Falene's stomach on his own. With love in his heart, he massaged her impressive midsection. She let him.

This was *his* child. Even though it grew inside of *her*.

He loved it.

Joseph never saw this twist of fate a possibility. He... A father.

He wanted this child. It didn't matter who the mother was. It was still his. He was willing and ready to take full responsibility for his son or daughter and wanted to. He'd already begun loving him or her.

Before he knew it, tears snuck through his tear ducts, lining the ridge of his lower eyelid. Joseph started imagining what he or she might look like.

"Do you know if...?" He started to ask, but then stopped.

Falene smirked.

"... If it's a boy or a girl?" Falene asked.

"Yes, I do." She offered, sidestepping the answer he was really looking for.

Joseph took a deep breath.

"I'd like to know, Falene." He said honestly.

Falene continued tapping her foot on the floor, this time out of rhythm and then just blurted it out.

"Both."

Father Joseph's mind raced. Was this another game she was playing?

"What do you mean, both?" Joseph didn't understand. "Can't you just answer a question?! What do you mean both?! That's impossible!"

Falene cleared her throat and stopped tapping.

"Twins." She said softly.

Father Joseph's face fell.

Falene nodded. "Two heartbeats, Joseph."

He didn't expect to hear that.

Joseph thought he felt his heart stop. Now he was sure he was going into cardiac arrest.

"Twins...?! You're carrying twins?! TWINS!!!!" He kept repeating himself.

"So... So... So... When you say *both*... You meant twins... You mean a boy and a girl?! Is that what you mean?!!!"

"That's exactly what I mean, Daddy-O." Falene sneered.

"So... You're telling me... You're having a boy *and* a girl?" He asked her again just to make sure."

"That's about it. Boy and a girl. Due April 18th."

"April 18th?" The date meant something to Joseph. "That's any day now." He guessed.

Joseph felt there had to be some symbolism in the date of the birth.

Then it occurred to him. *That* was the geographic coordinates of where he was. Kismet, Nebraska, 41 degrees - 18 minutes North. That was the 4 and the 18 or April 18th. He remembered about there being a 1 left over in the equation when he went over it with Brother David on the plane. The extra child... That was the *1* that was left over. One extra child was to be born. Twins. That's what it meant all along. April 18th coincided with the precise location he was on earth. The very date his children were to be born. He was meant to come here... This was where his test was.

"O.K. so that's it then!" He declared to Falene.

"The child or children, born of the Breast of Heaven and the Groin of Hell, in other words me and you, would originate from a place that is the precise latitude on earth as the origin of the creator of a scroll that is the direct word of the Messiah. The precise

latitude of the birthplace of a *chosen one,* selected by a member of the highest order of angles in Heaven. The precise latitude where a child cradles the entire world in his hands. They all fall along the *41 degrees North latitude.* Here, where we are right now, is 41 degrees, 18 minutes North of the equator! The ancient Tibetan seers predicted this. They said, the date of conception or the date of birth of this half-good, half-evil child or children is signified somehow within that exact latitude in degrees and minutes, April 18th. That's it!"

Something else dawned on him.

"Let me guess Falene... They'll be born at 5:32 either a.m. or p.m. Am I right? The number on your license plate. APR 532."

A treacherous smile snuck across Falene's face. "With my children Joseph, comes a new era of man's internal struggle between good and evil. Through these births, it will again be an integral part of the human condition. As fast as evil was eradicated from this world... It found it's way back in... Because mankind is so very fallible."

Her words were poison.

Falene walked closer to Joseph's hospital bed, pressing her swollen stomach against his bed rail.

"I've named them Joseph." Falene whispered.

Father Joseph's eyes met hers.

"Put your hand here Joseph." Falene grabbed his hand again and forcibly placed it on her belly. "Feel that?"

Within her, Joseph could feel movement.

"I want you to meet... Fallon and Roarke." She said.

Those were their names. Fallon and Roarke.

"They're going to be beautiful children, Joseph. Gorgeous. Smart. Overachievers. Everyone will love them. Admire them. Worship them." Falene explained. "*That* will be their way in to people's hearts."

Father Joseph wouldn't say a word. Nothing that could upset the children, whom he knew were already aware of the world around them.

"Aren't you just dying to see who they take after?" Falene asked.

ABOUT THE AUTHOR

Author Raina C. Smith is a native Rhode Islander. Growing up an only child Smith was a natural storyteller who delighted in using her imagination to entertain herself, her family and friends. A Communications major and proud graduate of Rhode Island College Smith spent most of her professional career working in broadcasting as a television news reporter and radio talk show co-host and executive producer. This is where Smith honed her research, writing and storytelling skills and is what helped her bring such dramatic characters and scenes to The 13th Apostle. Smith considers The 13th Apostle her proudest personal and professional accomplishment. To learn more about The 13th Apostle or Author Raina C. Smith please visit www.rainasmith.com